Matchmaki

Kiley Dunbar is Scottish and lives in England with her husband, two kids and Amos the Bedlington Terrier. She writes around her work at a University in the North of England where she lectures in English Literature and creative writing. She is proud to be a member of the Romantic Novelists' Association and a graduate of their New Writers' Scheme.

Also by Kiley Dunbar

Christmas at Frozen Falls
The Borrow a Bookshop Holiday

Kelsey Anderson

One Summer's Night
One Winter's Night

Port Willow Bay

Summer at the Highland Coral Beach
Matchmaking at Port Willow

KILEY DUNBAR

Matchmaking *at* Port Willow

hera

First published in the United Kingdom in 2021 by Hera

This edition published in the United Kingdom in 2022 by

Hera Books
Unit 9 (Canelo), 5th Floor
Cargo Works, 1-2 Hatfields
London, SE1 9PG
United Kingdom

A CIP catalogue record for this book is available from the British Library.

Print ISBN 978 1 80032 997 3
Ebook ISBN 978 1 912973 79 8

Look for more great books at www.herabooks.com

Printed and bound in Great Britain by Clays Ltd, Elcograf S.p.A.

1

This book is for Debbie, Stephanie and Leanie, with lots and lots of love. x

Highland Crafting Holidays at the Princess and the Pea Inn, Port Willow

Retreat, refresh, make. That's our mantra here at the Princess and the Pea Inn, your Scottish Highland destination for unique crafting holidays.

Check in to our characterful nineteenth-century inn on the shores of beautiful Port Willow Bay with its growing reputation as a hub for crafters and makers, and let us look after you.

Brothers Atholl and Eugene Fergusson have recently expanded the family business with the assistance of new co-managers Beatrice and Kitty, ensuring a warm welcome, wonderful food and a host of craft activities for you to choose from.

Try your hand at painting with a local watercolourist, or spinning and dyeing at the tartan mill nearby. There are cookery lessons with Eugene, willow-weaving with Atholl, Gaelic lessons with Kitty, as well as painting, glass-making, silversmithing, knitting and crochet. Let us help you plan your bespoke crafting getaway.

Singles discounts available.

A choice of rooms and suites are available including the historic 'Princess Room' with its towering fairy-tale-inspired bed. Originally installed by the Fergusson brothers' parents in the nineteen-fifties, the Princess

Room has recently undergone extensive renovations making it an ideal destination for honeymooners and romantics looking for a cosy coastal getaway.

You'll find us in our remote, Gulf Stream location amidst wild, open countryside – a must for hikers and sightseers – and close to one of the white coral beaches with exotic blue waters that are unique to the Scottish Highlands.

Don't forget the inn's varied entertainment programme, new for this season, including singles and dating events. The inn prides itself on welcoming lone travellers looking for a home from home.

Limited spaces available, book today and start dreaming.

Chapter One

Setting off

Beatrice and Atholl waved off the minibus-load of knitters into the crisp wintry morning from the steps of the Princess and the Pea Inn. One of the knitters, sad to be leaving after their week-long crafting holiday, mournfully waved their scarf from one of the windows, its tasselled ends flapping against the group's logo on the side of the bus. *Knit Fast, Die Warm.*

'I'm going to miss that lot,' Beatrice smiled, still waving.

'Aye, they were certainly lively,' agreed Atholl, placing an arm around the shivering Beatrice. Even after five months living in the Highlands, the frosty December mornings took her breath away with their sharpness. 'Their bar tabs were almost as long as the scarves they knitted.'

Beatrice leaned into the warmth of Atholl's body. 'Did you notice that little spark between the two younger ones? Alex and Selma?'

Atholl only narrowed his eyes. He hadn't noticed.

'There was definitely something there, I reckon,' she said. Beatrice lowered her arm as the bus turned up the hill and out of sight. 'Given another week and a bit of

Christmas romance, I think those two would have got together. I'd have made sure of it.'

Atholl held the door open and let Beatrice pass through into the warmth of the inn's reception. The silver tinsel draped over the wall-mounted deer antlers shimmered in the chilly, salty breeze coming in off the bay.

Atholl shook his head and smiled indulgently. 'I'm sure they'll find their way to each other once they're back home at their knitting club.'

'That's just it. They might, but I'll never know.' Beatrice followed Atholl under the arched opening into the bar room, which at this time of day was pleasingly tidy and empty.

'Well, rest assured your hospitality and our braw holidays will have set them on the road to being something more than they were afore they arrived.' Atholl flicked the switch on the Christmas tree's lights.

Beatrice stopped just for a second to enjoy how his blue eyes picked up their golden gleam. Feeling herself drawn towards him by the bar, she slipped her arms around his middle, her favourite place to be. 'I think it might be time, Atholl.'

Intrigued, he tipped his head. 'Oh aye?' The low, drawling notes in his voice betrayed what he *hoped* she was talking about, and he brought his mouth down to hers to confirm it. She welcomed his kiss.

Quiet mornings at the inn, before most of the guests were awake, and before Gene started up the stoves in the kitchen, were always a precious time for Atholl and Beatrice: slow, dark mornings when they could luxuriate in each other before their busy days began, taking Atholl off to the willow-weaving school above the coral beach way across the rocky headland, and Beatrice taking up her place behind the reception computer where she ran the crafting holidays and co-managed the inn.

Normally, Beatrice would be glad to let Atholl lead her back to bed, but today she had something else in mind. She pulled out of his warm grasp and made her way behind the bar. Atholl watched her go, his eyes alight from their kiss.

'It's time to put this up, remember?' Beatrice told him, catching his dismayed look. 'My dating board?'

'You're going ahead with it, then? The matchmaking?'

'Well, *we* found love at the inn, didn't we? And your brother and Kitty. I did a good job of getting them together.'

'*We* did a good job of getting them together,' he replied, reaching over the bar to take the wood-framed pinboard from her hands. He'd made it himself according to her exact specifications.

'Right, *we* did,' she said.

'And now that wee bit of success has you itching to introduce more couples?'

Beatrice lifted Atholl's tool box from behind the bar onto the counter. 'That's right. I got my happy ever after, what's wrong with encouraging a few more?'

'And you're no' worried about the competition?' Atholl grabbed his hammer.

'What competition?' Beatrice drew her neck back, genuinely bemused.

'Online dating apps?'

'*Pfft!* We met in the flesh and knew there was something between us right away; no screen can tell you that.'

'You didn't like me one bit when we met,' Atholl said with a gruff laugh.

Beatrice laughed too. 'Well, just because I didn't like you *immediately* doesn't mean I didn't know for sure that I fancied you. Anyway, we've made up for the bickering since then.'

Atholl rummaged for the nails and placed two between his full lips. 'Good point, well made,' he conceded, the nails still in his mouth.

A matter of days had transformed Atholl Fergusson in Beatrice's opinion from the grumpy, standoffish inn manager she'd first formed unfavourable ideas about to the gentle, caring bear of a man she now adored. Five months of growing steadily closer had sealed her resolve to stay here with him forever.

Beatrice couldn't stop the little flip in her stomach at the sight of him working now. She'd have had no problem putting the board up by herself but she'd miss the view of him rolling up his plaid sleeves, the cinch of his waist, and the breadth of his shoulders opening out as he hefted the frame into place. Plus, she wasn't feeling all that great for a second day running. Or was it the third? Having a busy inn full of guests arriving and departing was great apart from the coughs and colds they brought with them.

'You'd better tell me where you want this then,' Atholl was saying.

'And then we'll head back to bed?'

Over his shoulder Atholl fixed his gaze upon her. 'Aye, and then we'll head back to bed.'

As the alarm clocks buzzed and holidaymakers blinked and stretched their bodies all through the inn, Atholl drove the nails into the wall by the fireplace and securely mounted Beatrice's low-tech lonely hearts board for all to see.

Beatrice watched on, pressing her palms together and bouncing on her heels at the thought of all of the possibilities for finding love that the board represented. Who knows, she thought, which of the singles looking for love around the village or amongst the inn's holidaymakers and workers would benefit from just a little bit of encouragement and become the next pair to find love in Port Willow?

She revelled in the sense of promise. The inn managers never knew what kind of guest was about to arrive in the village, but what Beatrice did know from her own experience was that nothing could prepare newcomers for the magic they'd encounter in their little corner of the Highlands. Somewhere out there, entirely unsuspecting, is somebody missing something – or someone – that they don't yet know is waiting for them here in Port Willow.

The thought of it sent her nerves fizzing with anticipation, making her forget the initial troubles she and Atholl had to overcome at the start of their relationship. Beatrice told herself that love had come so easily to them, surely the inn's next love story would be just as sweet.

Chapter Two

New York, 20th December

Nina Miller had almost made it. Two more hours and the Christmas break would be here. Sure, there'd be brand engagement figures to keep an eye on over the holiday and her cranky expat boss, the company president, Seamus Ryan, would still expect her to pick up the phone as usual when he got his PA, Mitch, to call her at any hour of the day or night, but in one hundred and twenty minutes she'd be walking out of the Microtrends Brand Development and Lifestyle Forecasting offices and heading back to the apartment where, if things were going according to plan, the holiday staging coordinator would be trimming the ten-foot-tall Christmas tree Nina had ordered and making everything perfectly festive and cosy ahead of Luke's return from business in Tokyo tonight.

'Can't you come home, just for one Christmas? We're dying to meet Luke,' her mother had lamented when she'd broken the news she wouldn't be flying across the pond to her family's home in Hove for the family festivities.

'We're taking a social detox,' she'd retorted, making her mother tut, but Nina wouldn't be put off. She'd planned this Christmas break down to the last Lanvin bauble and Tiffany & Co. silver bell. It was going to be perfect. A whole week with no work commitments for the first time ever, just her and Luke.

She had wrangled with her high-flying boyfriend to get his PA to clear his calendar, which he'd reluctantly agreed to, and she'd declined every invitation that had arrived for them at his West End Avenue art deco apartment which she shared with him.

He'd protested, 'It isn't smart to turn down the hospitality of my friends and clients, Nina, especially during the holiday season when everyone's out to impress.'

She knew that, of course. It was risky and not at all usual, but after the last two relentless holiday seasons spent hopping with Luke from festive launch event to client cocktail party to corporate dinner, she was sure they had earned one perfect, romantic Christmas alone together. Evenings, weekends, birthdays; she'd surrendered them all to work and hadn't really minded, but Christmas still felt like it should be special somehow.

'They'll still be around come New Year's,' she'd reassured him, dreaming of the luxury catered Christmas she had in store for the two of them.

Luke's social circle was like no other, and falling for Luke had meant she'd inadvertently been handed an access-all-areas pass to a new world of billion-dollar brand management, lifestyle gurus, creative geniuses and their many, many painfully cool collaborators. These people were the visionaries. These weren't the ones following trends; they were setting them.

Luke was a glamorous insider, born into riches, travelling the globe and bringing brands to life with his golden touch. His networks consisted of people who prized rarity, exclusivity and, above all else, money.

Being within their reach meant Nina had skyrocketed from her position as entry-level employee almost three years ago straight into Mr Ryan's good books at work.

She found, as Luke had increasingly let her take the reins with the smaller accounts, she was able to discreetly namedrop exactly the right celebrity endorser at sessions in the glass room reserved for spitballing (that's what Mr Ryan called it, and she never failed to feel queasy at the term) and she'd say that she might be able to 'put in a call' or 'pull in a favour' and, lo and behold, she'd help secure Microtrends Brand Development and Lifestyle Forecasting another priceless connection, making Mr Ryan a lot of money and helping her climb to the next rung on her career ladder.

It helped that she was smart and efficient, tireless and always available. She'd earned this Christmas break, she told herself as she hit 'send' and submitted her final brand engagement report of the year to her boss.

It was her job to help foster relationships with the company's newest or smallest brands. She was years away from reaching Luke's level – overseeing the luxe brand accounts, directing their development into new product lines and bigger markets – but that's where she had her sights firmly set.

The view from the (third from the) top floor of the glittering high-rise office block with the wintry Hudson below was especially beautiful today, but she had no time to admire the scenery. It was already growing dark outside. Luke's flight would be circling JFK right about now and the holidays were so nearly within reach she could practically taste the Pierre Hermé gingerbread cookies and Louis Roederer champagne.

The clack of smart shoes across marble and the sound of Mitch's voice reached her before he'd even swung his head around her office doorframe. 'Nina? Nina. Mr Ryan wants to see you.'

Her boss's PA didn't wait for her to reply before turning on his heel, expecting her to follow, which she did. He took her back through the lounge that led to the elevator doors which led to the modern-art-lined corridor which then led to Seamus Ryan's penthouse office – all glass and air, leather and sunlight – a room that never failed to make Nina want to gawp in wonder and barely concealed hungry ambition.

As she reached the lift, she was surprised to see Fournival, Luke's PA, stepping out and coming to an awkward stop by the potted giant monstera plants.

For a second her heart swelled. 'Is Luke with you?'

'No, ma'am, he, *uh*, asked me to retrieve your keys... please.'

Nina couldn't stop. Being invited to Mr Ryan's office was a rare occurrence and she couldn't leave him waiting. 'My keys? Has he lost the apartment keys in Tokyo? Couldn't the doorman let him in?'

'No, ma'am.'

Nina was already hurriedly reaching into her Kate Spade and tossing him the keys. 'Fournival, can you make sure the apartment dresser gets paid, and tell Luke I'll be home on time tonight.'

She didn't wait for a reply and had stepped inside the waiting elevator before she could catch Fournival's sheepish, guilty look as he clutched her keys in his hand.

–

'Ah, Nina! Sit, sit.' Seamus Ryan smiled, beckoning her towards the vast coffee table on the far side of the room where he had been lounging, reading from a leather folder.

Looking around to see Mitch closing the door, leaving them alone, Nina did as she was told, crossing the room to perch on one of the Fritz Hansen chairs, a design classic.

She knew from office lore that mid-level employees were only ever invited to the coffee table when there was bad news. Mitch had told her once, 'They call it the last-chance saloon. So long as there's no *pastries* to soften the blow, you might stand a fighting chance of keeping your job.'

Nina looked at the platter of cinnamon buns on the table and felt her adrenalin spike.

'So, good news!' said Seamus, making a gregarious show of pouring Nina a black coffee from a gold pot, something she'd never seen him do for staff before.

'OK?' She waited expectantly. She'd spoken with Seamus a handful of times in meetings, but she definitely couldn't say they were on friendly terms. Maybe Seamus was giving her the VIP treatment because she was Luke's girlfriend? Even if Seamus had seniority over Luke in the company hierarchy, the men were still golfing buddies and colleagues right at the top of the organisation. It was only right he'd be kind to her. Was she being singled out for a special Christmas bonus, perhaps?

His voice was surprisingly flat compared to his pleasant smile. 'We're taking you off your accounts.'

'You are? But why? I helped secure those accounts' celebrity and influencer buy-ins, I led all the early discussions...'

'That's right, and I want to thank you personally for your stellar work, but Mr Casson has head-hunted a colleague in Kyoto and is flying her in to take over your role. She's very well connected in the markets we want to tap into going forward.'

'Luke's scouted someone to replace me? *Luke* has?'

Seamus was still smiling over his coffee cup, legs crossed, casually flaunting his shiny Gucci slipper shoes. He only nodded. Of course he knew about Nina and Luke; the company's 'it' couple. They hadn't made a big deal of their relationship at work, but it was common knowledge that Nina had moved in with Luke only a few months after starting her internship at Microtrends three years ago, her first job in the States.

Nina's mind raced, trying to understand why Luke would bring in someone new to oust her, and her heart thumped hard under her silk Prada blouse.

'Am I being promoted?'

'I wouldn't say it was an *upward* promotion. Think of it as a… parallel move, with a moderate deceleration in salary and benefits.'

'You said it was good news.' Nina tried to keep the wobble out of her voice.

'Oh it is. I have a new assignment for you. You're going home.'

'To England?'

'Close enough. Scotland.'

'*Scotland?*' At the back of her mind she was still processing the news that Luke had replaced her without having so much as mentioned the fact he was looking for a new Trend Forecaster and Client Brand Relations Facilitator. She'd thought the fact she was dating one of the top execs would mean she'd be involved in these restructuring discussions before they happened, especially when it meant she was for the chop.

Seamus was spreading a folder open in front of her. 'The Scottish Highlands, to be precise. Someone in Creative picked up a lead about a new movement of craft collectives, real grass roots stuff. We want to scope it out before anyone else does. Let's see what's going on over there that might align with our upcoming luxury heritage brand launches. I want you to assess the scene, find new product, scout some talent. At the very least treat it like a recce of backdrops for editorials and brand shoots, okay? Scottish heritage and nostalgia is still selling and we want the consumer buy-in that real Scottish authenticity brings. You should be looking for real deal craftsmanship steeped in tradition. I'm thinking new designer whiskies, I'm thinking crystal, I'm thinking new trends in tweed...'

Nina knew she should be taking notes, but she was frozen in her chair at the news that she was, essentially, being demoted to a product scout when, minutes ago, she'd been a rising star in line for promotion in the New Year and ready to lead a brand relaunch of her own. Luke had promised her.

Seamus talked on. 'Mitch has arranged your flights and hotel. It's all there in the documents.'

'But, I don't under—'

This time his voice was firm. 'You've been relieved of your accounts, Nina. This is your new assignment. I advise you to make good connections *of your own* over there and come back with a strong portfolio of client offerings for our buyers and brand developers stateside, OK?'

She nodded. It's not like she had any choice. 'Why me?'

'You're the only British junior in the office,' he shrugged. 'And the rest of us have family and client commitments for the holidays. Besides, you're single.'

Nina stared. 'I'm not a junior, and I'm definitely not single,' she said flatly. Why the hell would he say that? Had Luke mentioned the arguments they'd been having recently over her dreams of a quiet Christmas together? Had they talked about it at the golf range before Luke flew out to Japan last month? That's all they were, arguments. Things were still very much OK between them, even if Luke had struggled to call her much lately, what with the time difference and being so busy working with his Japanese colleagues.

Seamus ignored the fact she was on the verge of tears and furiously embarrassed about it.

'To be frank, Nina, we *could* have let you go. You've been relieved of your old accounts, but you've worked hard and I recognise that, and Mr Casson was adamant we reassign you. Think of it like this: you've been hand-picked to act as an ambassador for our company overseas. This is your chance to prove your worth…'

'My worth? Mr Ryan, it sounds as though you're saying if I don't find a way of making us some money on this trip I may as well not come back?'

Seamus nodded and pulled a face that told her she wasn't far from the truth. 'You've made it this far in the company through your excellent networking, but now that… seems to have dried up, you must show us what you can do, on your own merit. This is the only such posting we have for you. If you mess this up, there's no point coming back.'

Nina pressed her fingertips to her throbbing temples. How could Seamus know that for the last month the calls from the brands she'd been courting, hoping to work with them one day soon, had suddenly dried up? Even the start-ups she'd been getting to know hadn't responded to her lately. She hadn't told anyone, hoping it was just the holiday season keeping everyone busy and that they'd return her calls come January. Come to think of it, why had Luke delayed coming home from Japan for over a week now? Why had Fournival taken her only key to Luke's apartment, her home? What on earth was going on?

She reached for the folder, trying hard to right herself in front of Seamus even though she felt her life capsizing.

The words on the pages before her swam a little under her blurry gaze, but she caught something about 'wild, open countryside', 'remote location', 'extensive renovations', 'growing reputation' and 'Highland destination for unique crafting holidays' and there was a photograph from an online magazine article headed 'Scottish crafts heritage travel' with a red-haired, rustic-looking man doing something arty with sticks outside a little white cottage in what looked like a sleet shower.

'You'll be going home. You'll enjoy it,' Seamus said, clapping his hands to his thighs, signalling the meeting was over. She hadn't even been offered a pastry.

Nina thought of what she knew of Britain: the pebbly beaches and mellow sunsets of Brighton and Hove, the views over the gentle South Downs, and the homely feel of being beside the seaside and looking out across the Channel towards Dieppe and the sunny continent.

Back home, she'd never once ventured up North. She'd had everything she needed in Sussex; her mother, her younger brother; a gaggle of school friends, all the colour and busyness of Brighton nearby with its bars, spas and boutiques, and London only an hour away at weekends for some serious retail therapy.

The Scottish Highlands, she suspected, were nothing like that. They were rain-soaked and midge-infested. Or did the winter storms kill off the midges? She had no idea, but she knew for sure she wasn't a wellingtons and waterproofs kind of woman.

'Come on,' cajoled Seamus, as he stood and walked back to his desk, offhandedly drawling to her over his shoulder. 'Buck up. It's the Highlands, not Mars. How different can it be? Oh, and I've asked HR to furnish you with a cubicle down on four with your new colleagues in Creative. I'm sure you'll appreciate the opportunity to work more closely with them.'

When Nina returned to her office there was no sign of Fournival, but there was a cardboard crate with the meagre contents of her desk inside, along with her complete set of Louis Vuitton luggage from her dressing room at home, now lined up by the door with a thin-looking envelope tucked through one of the handles with her name inscribed on it in Luke's rushed, sharp handwriting.

The tears brimmed in her eyes as she grabbed for the door handle of her office, desperately needing its sanctuary, a place where she could cry unseen, but the door was locked. So she wheeled her luggage to the bathrooms and, once alone inside, opened Luke's cowardly farewell letter with her hand clamped over her mouth to stifle the sound of her sobs.

Chapter Three

A Scots' Wassail

Beatrice watched as Atholl raised the bowl, steaming and brimming with wine, to the dark winter sky. His pale Celtic skin shone like pearl in the moonlight, warming to rich cream and amber in the shifting glow from the villagers' flaming torches.

'Wassail!' he called out, and the crowd burst into whooping applause – all of them shivering and in varying degrees of inebriation, huddled together in the grassy backyard between Atholl's little craft school above the coral beach and his willow fields.

Atholl passed the bowl to Kitty Wake, the beautiful Gaelic teacher, Beatrice's new best friend, and now a permanent fixture in Port Willow since falling in love with Atholl's brother, Gene.

Kitty, dressed in a long white gown with a green paper crown on her head that the children from the local primary school had made for their 'Wassail Queen', took a sip of the wine before shouting out a loud 'drinkhail', sending the crowd into an even louder frenzy.

All the while, the tall, slightly stooped, wide-eyed Gene Fergusson stood to one side, a tartan blanket bundled in his arms, half fretting that his beloved Kitty would catch a cold and half frozen in staring amazement that this red-haired, dazzling light of a woman actually loved him back.

Beatrice was responsible for that little bit of summer matchmaking and it gave her no end of pleasure to see her two friends now so in love. She surveyed the whole scene, smiling to herself as the villagers, who had fully embraced her as one of their own in the last few months, brought out their own bowls and vessels, filling them from bottles with wine and whisky and even, Beatrice noted delightedly, Irn Bru.

Kitty led them all in a Gaelic Christmas carol that Beatrice neither recognised nor understood, while the crowd dipped slices of toast and slabs of shortbread into their drinks and then lobbed them gleefully in amongst the willows, making Atholl run for cover towards Beatrice on the steps of the old But and Ben, now his fully functioning willow workshop and craft school.

Some of the older members of the wassailing party, including Seth McVie, the long-since-retired originator of the seal-spotting tourist boats down in Port Willow Bay, were reverently dipping white bread into alcohol and spearing the sopping slices onto the sturdiest willows, and meanwhile the singing swelled into a wild chant.

Beatrice was struck by the notion – as she often had been since she'd run away from her old life to this strange, beautiful, remote place in the West Highlands – that this scene could have played out at any time in the last ten centuries, even if old Seth's bicycle clips and every single teenager's phone were glowing and flashing in the dark. The whole effect was breath-taking, and Atholl made it even more so by reaching for her in the dark of the cottage doorway and pressing a kiss to her lips.

'Well, do you think this is enough?' she asked him, keeping her face close to his.

'To appease Mother Nature and ensure a good crop next year? Who can say? I saw some of my cousin's bairns from Skye in amongst the willows, scattering Jaffa Cakes as an offering. I'm no' sure what Mother Nature will make o' that.' Atholl smiled, distracted by the look of his girlfriend, calm and quiet on the workshop step, dark hair splaying over her shoulders, her red bobble hat making her chilly pink cheeks look all the sweeter.

Her colour had come back to her over the autumn now that she was far away from her old, disjointed, buried life in England. She'd found a carefree peace that showed in the way she held her body and in the way she met her lover's eyes.

The wassail had been her idea, and all she'd had to do was mention it to Atholl and he'd enthusiastically helped her organise the whole thing, steered by her organisational zeal and talent for seizing upon new opportunities to expand the inn's offering. She was forever list-writing, researching and making things happen. It was one of the many things he loved about her.

He'd wanted tonight to make her happy and to brighten the depths of winter for her, and he wanted to thank her for pushing him to buy the old But and Ben and willow fields that he'd been renting for years, never fully committing to turning it into the international willow craft school he'd always dreamed of running. At least, not until Beatrice arrived and showed him all the ways it was possible to heal, share and grow.

Beatrice had first heard of wassailing as a child, being from Warwickshire, close to Shakespeare's Stratford where old customs fed the tourist and theatre industries. She had lived most of her life just down the motorway from leafy Evesham too, with its many orchards where wassailing customs persisted and were reported on the local news each December, but she'd never seen it with her own eyes until tonight.

Up here under the black, starry skies of the Highlands, the custom seemed to have taken on a wilder, more elemental importance. That is if the local young farmers and fishermen were anything to go by. Some of them had really got on board with the whole idea of a winter's wassail to bless Atholl's willow fields and christen his expanded workshopping business. Most wore a sprig of holly on their coats or hats and two had come dressed as some sort of nightmarish horse figure, the significance of which nobody was entirely sure of, but had been part of ancient local custom long ago. Seth had thought he could remember his grandfather telling him about it so everyone agreed they'd better give it a go and not risk displeasing whichever impish natural spirits presided over the growing of healthy willows in these parts.

If there *had* once been an ancient tradition of winter wassailing in Port Willow, somewhere along the way the custom had been all but forgotten. The event certainly felt archaic and magical to Beatrice, and she could tell from the look in Kitty's eyes that her friend felt it too. Beatrice supposed that's what wine and moonlight, music and dancing can do to pretty much anything; transform it into something ritualistic, something elemental.

The crowd were singing loudly now, having decided they'd offered quite enough booze to the frozen earth and fallow field margins. Between verses they swigged from their cups and bottles, staving off the bitter midwinter's night chill.

Wassail, wassail, all over the town,
My bread it is white, and my ale it is brown,
And my bowl it is made o' the sweet willow tree,
With a wassailing bowl I'll drink to thee.

Under Kitty and Gene's instruction, the whole village had over many recent evenings crowded into the bar room at the Princess and the Pea Inn to learn the ancient wassailing songs. Gene had assumed more of a supervisory position, humming along in his deep, bassy way, pouring the pints and working the till while Kitty took on the role of folk customs tutor – somehow it felt in keeping with her being the village's only fluent Gaelic speaker. Yet tonight there were many more carousers up on the hill above the coral beach than just the villagers.

The sounds of their accents and languages mingled in the air now. Beatrice could hear German and something Scandinavian, Icelandic, maybe? It sounded very much like Kitty's Gaelic to Beatrice's ears. Some were visiting family for Christmas, some were tourists filling the rental cottages along the Port Willow waterfront for the holidays, and some were crafters drawn to the inn by the opportunity to learn a new skill and meet new friends. There were quiet, respectfully observant Minnesotans, and loud Texans, and many, many Scots from all across the parish – and their voices were all combining now into a heady cacophony.

Just when it was getting too much and some of the fiery torches were puttering out and the youngest of the children were nodding off on their parents' shoulders, one of the farm lads shouted out that they were leading the party back across the dark meadow and down the hill to the inn for a nightcap.

Beatrice and Atholl watched the crowd slowly departing – the glimmer from phone screens dancing with the flashlights and the candles lighting their way. Kitty's voice rang out the loudest as they left, wassailing all the way back to Port Willow Bay.

'Go on, lad,' Atholl instructed the adoring collie dog by his side. 'Go'an get some supper at the inn.' Echo accepted a scratch on the ear before darting off to catch up with the crowd, leaving Atholl alone with Beatrice in the growing silence.

'We're not leaving?' Beatrice asked, not in the least wanting to follow the noisy rabble, content to be anchored to the spot by Atholl's hands around her waist.

'I lit the fire in the But 'n' Ben earlier. Shame to let it go to waste.' Atholl pushed the door open behind her, letting Beatrice glance in at the cosy scene. He'd cleared the work benches where earlier that day eager students had crafted ambitious willow sculptures under Atholl's expert tutelage. There was a spruce in its pot in the corner, strung with gold fairy-lights with dainty willow spheres hanging from its branches. He'd laid rugs and cushions on the flagstone floor before the fire, and Beatrice caught a glimpse of a picnic basket by the blazing hearth.

'Another of Gene's famous picnics?' she said, smiling, as Atholl led her into the room, closing out the cold and dark behind them.

'Aye, just a spot of breakfast.'

'Breakfast? We're staying out? Isn't it a bit chilly for camping?'

'It's this or trying to clear the bar at closing time? It'll no' be an easy job the night. Besides it's warm by the hearth.'

Atholl had already bolted the door behind them and walked Beatrice over to the broad stone mantle, gently lifting her coat from her shoulders before taking the opportunity to brush his lips against her temple, then her cheek, making her instantly drowsy.

Dim shushing sounds from the waves on the coral-strewn shore down below the cottage made their way to the couple. The smoke from the fire combined with the mellow smell of the peat burning and the heady, clean natural scent of the willow bundles piled up by the door. She'd come to recognise this as Atholl's scent too. It was in his very skin.

'Midwinter's night at the cottage school is probably a tiny bit nicer than chucking out time at the inn,' she agreed, reaching up to run her hands over Atholl's shoulders. As always, the feel of his broad frame left her reeling and Atholl took the hitch in her breathing as his cue to kiss her lips. The pair sank down onto the rugs and coats in the firelight.

'Longest night of the year, the twenty-first, and probably the coldest,' Atholl murmured, rolling Beatrice onto her back and pressing his long body against hers, making them both shudder and gasp between kisses.

'Good, I want a long night with you,' she said, pulling off Atholl's top layers, knowing the heat from the flames and from Atholl's touch would warm her through until morning.

Chapter Four

Up in the Air

Despite the midnight departure time or the Percocet and the Ambien that she'd washed down with a hard seltzer in the airport bar, there was no chance of Nina getting much sleep tonight.

The thing about a seven-and-a-half-hour flight, squeezed into Economy when you've long since grown used to the comforts of First Class, surrounded by twelve hungover and chattering Glaswegian bachelorettes in 'I heart NYC' t-shirts is, it gives a girl plenty of time to mull things over.

First of all, shortly after take-off, she'd re-read Luke's letter.

> *Nina,*
>
> *By now Fournival will have returned your belongings and retrieved your keys. I hate to end things like this but I know you like efficiency and there's no point dragging out a break-up. I'm sure you'll agree.*
>
> *Seamus Ryan said his PA would help orient you in your new role. I hope you thanked Seamus for me. I'd have got you set up myself but things got kind of busy in Tokyo and, well, you know.*

Scotland sounds fun! I wish I could take off on a scouting spree to the Highlands.

I hope you can see that this is for the best – you'll thank me one day – and I hope you find someone who makes you as happy as Himari makes me. She really is something else.

Thanks for the Christmas tree. The apartment looks swell.

Happy Holidays, L

She'd ordered a second gin and tonic from the trolley, making the hen party in the seats nearby cheer for the sad, pretty young woman who hadn't stopped crying since she'd boarded at JFK, and they'd all ordered one too in sympathy. Nina wasn't in the mood for talking, but the women tried to engage her nonetheless.

'What do you reckon, Jo?' probed a yellow-blonde woman in a snowman jumper, nodding her head in Nina's direction. 'Dumped, I'd say.'

'Think you're right there, 'manda,' slurred the drunkest one of the lot, who was jammed into her seat surrounded by Macy's bags full of Christmas shopping that had probably cleared out her entire December pay packet. 'Here, have a tissue,' Amanda said, passing them along the aisles and over multiple disgruntled travellers towards Nina. 'Bloke trouble, is it?'

Nina sniffed and reluctantly took the tissues. 'You could say that.'

'Go on then, spill it, nobody here but us girls,' urged another of the women, the bride judging by the pink plastic tiara squint upon her head.

Nina weighed her options and chose the temporary humiliation of telling her sad tale against keeping it inside and sobbing all the way to Edinburgh airport. She'd never see these women again anyway and she was in need of exactly the kind of protective solace a coven of boozed-up, shopped-out women could offer a broken-hearted stranger. Nina didn't really have close girlfriends in New York, and the ones back home she'd all but lost touch with over her three-year stint in the States, apart from the occasional message.

Luke had obviously given their joint friends advance notice of the break-up (at least, *now* that was obvious) and not one of their circle had reached out to her in the last few days since Luke's direct hit bombshell.

Here goes nothing, Nina thought, *just my pride*. 'He chucked me out of his flat and he moved his new girlfriend in, just like that,' Nina snapped her fingers, 'no warning.'

These words, along with Nina's mascara-soaked tissues and empty gin miniatures on her little folding table had the power of a summoning circle for the hens, who were by now craning round chair backs and leaning across the aisles saying, 'And at Christmas too!', every one of them cursing this evil ex-boyfriend and calling him all manner of entirely appropriate names.

'I had to sleep at the Ramada for three nights by myself while they were at home eating the holiday food I ordered, drinking our champagne, sitting in front of my tree… sleeping in our bed.' Nina, more than a little tipsy, couldn't help sobbing again, encouraging another chorus of sympathy and fresh curses from the women and a lot of angry shushing from fellow passengers trying to get some shut eye. One of the women handed over her miniature bottle of red wine, which Nina immediately swigged from.

'He's obviously a right idiot, chuckin' a knockout lassie like you!' slurred one of the party's mothers, resplendent in a foam Lady Liberty pointed coronet.

There followed a long discussion amongst the hens about how Nina could be a supermodel, and doesn't she look like that one from the telly, the *Big Brother* presenter, you know, the one that's married to that pop star? One of them pronounced her 'a true English rose' and everyone clucked in agreement and Nina boozily waved away their kindness, all the while wanting to ugly cry and have the women sweep her up into their arms, if only there wasn't an aisle and a snoring businessman wearing earplugs between them.

By the time they were halfway across the Atlantic and the women had forgotten their ire at Luke and were being lulled to sleep by the engine noises and the two a.m. round of Bloody Marys that had seemed like a good idea at the time, Nina had turned her face to the window and let herself get lost in her memories once more.

An English rose. Luke had called her that too on that first fateful day when he'd swept into the building to see Seamus and stopped dead by the elevators just to talk to her, the new intern. Back then she wasn't yet used to the forthright New York way of speaking and his directness in asking her out to dinner that night had shocked and thrilled her. He was so unlike the English men she'd known back home.

She'd told herself it didn't matter that he was technically her big boss. Some women would have seen that as a challenge, or even a perk of dating him, but Nina wasn't so superficial. She'd liked him with all his confidence and charisma. He'd been exciting and seemed so free compared to her boyfriends back home at school and college. He'd drawn her to him like a magnet and not one bit of her had wanted to resist him.

They'd met back when she was still learning to temper her South Downs accent and hadn't yet acquired the upwards inflection her sentences were punctuated with nowadays, back when her hair was glossy brown and wavy and not the platinum-blonde, blown-back and quiffed crop it cost her a fortune to maintain today.

Luke had swept her off her feet, immediately taking her under his beautifully tailored Armani wing. Cocktail dresses and evening gowns started turning up at her place and she'd never paid a penny for them, and there had been lavish flowers and corporate goodie bags and freebies of all kinds. It was a glamorous, and swift, courtship. She'd seen nothing wrong in accepting his gifts – they were in love, after all, not that he'd actually used the L word, not even once, she realised now, but she'd felt looked after and desired – and she'd moved out of the shared interns' apartment and into his place after only four months in the city.

He'd started taking her to events pretty soon after that, introducing her to his friends; a complex web of glamorous, influential people. They'd been loud and impressive, waspishly thin, and always immaculately dressed. They'd thrown big house parties in the Hamptons and even bigger product launches and influencer gatherings in the city. They were all so charming and generous, cultured and cunning, just like Luke.

She'd only found them abrasive or braying for the first few weeks, and then she'd found she was one of them, even if she *could* spend a booze-fuelled afternoon at a luxurious pool party with them one weekend, where everyone behaved like they were family, spilling secrets and spilling drinks, and by the next they'd have forgotten her name, but that was OK.

'That's just how things are in this industry,' Luke had reassured her when she mentioned for the first – and only – time that maybe these people were a bit fickle and heartless.

'What? Even your best mate, Seamus?' she'd said, having seen how everyone, including Luke, gravitated around the richest man in their set. Seamus Ryan was, after all, the president of the luxest of lux companies. His employees talent-scouted designers and 'lifestyle practitioners' from across the globe, flying them to New York, developing their brands for consumption by the top two percent – brands the other ninety-eight were too gauche to even hear about.

'Especially Seamus,' Luke had told her. 'You don't have to *like* everyone you do business with, but it pays to get on with everyone.'

Nina scoffed now to think of it. It had been Seamus's private jet that had flown Luke and Himari, her replacement, into the city, into *her* Christmas. It turned out the men were as thick as thieves and now Nina was on the outside of the circle wondering at what point she'd been pickpocketed because she hadn't felt a thing at the time they were robbing her.

The worst thing was she wasn't even going to get to see her mum, not that she'd told her she was flying to the UK – or about Luke. Seamus's brief had made it quite clear she was to head straight to the Highlands and begin work immediately. Part of her was relieved, if she was being honest with herself. She'd been so absorbed in her New York lifestyle – and in herself – that the thought of going home to her mum with her tail between her legs would have smarted all the more, even if she really could do with a hug right about now.

She'd tell her soon, she reasoned, when she could face the truth herself, and maybe then there'd be no need to mention it at all. Her old life still hung in the balance. Everything depended on her success in Scotland. There was yet a chance she could snatch it all back and nobody need ever know about her sudden, dizzying fall from grace. She'd never get Luke back, of course. Not that she'd take him back, not after all this, at least that's what she tried to convince herself. He was always so bloody resolute. He saw what he wanted and he always got it. He'd wangled a better deal with this Himari. But there was still a slim chance she could win back her pride by winning over Seamus and the board. It meant starting all over again from scratch, this time without Luke and his buddies, or their lovely decadent home and everything they'd shared these last three years.

The captain announced a spot of turbulence ahead as the lights dimmed in the cabin. Nina didn't even hear it. She was crying again and, at last, on the verge of sleep, only vaguely, distantly brooding over how not only had Luke broken her heart but he'd staked his claim to all their friends too, and now here she was up in the air with no home to call her own, barely holding onto her job, and being sent into the back of beyond on a scouting mission she suspected was simply a way of getting her out of Luke and Seamus's hair while things settled down back in New York. It wouldn't do having her mooning around the offices or making a scene.

'I'll show them,' she mumbled as she drifted off. 'I'll find these Scottish "it" people. I'll sniff out *the* most crave-able products and beautiful brands… fly back to New York with my head held high, show them what I'm made of. I can play their game. I learned from the best, didn't I? Schmooze 'em and booze 'em, promise them the stars, sign on the dotted line…'

Nina was snoring and drooling, her hair flattened against the little window, by the time the pilot started their descent. She didn't even flinch as the plane buffeted and bumped in the stormy Scottish sky, conveying her down through the dark night to God knows where.

Chapter Five

A Big News Day

Beatrice gulped. She didn't often get nervous, but it had been a while since she'd done anything like this. The waves of queasiness she'd woken up to for the last few days and which she'd put down to a winter bug, combined with her nerves and made her gulp and flatten her palms over her stomach.

'Is my hair OK?' she asked, knowing it was blowing in wet whips in the snow storm that had descended on Port Willow overnight.

'You look great,' said Kirstie, the local news reporter, not looking up from reading through her notes on her phone.

Atholl was standing behind the woman and her camera operator. He whispered loudly enough for everyone to hear, 'You look braw, Beattie, especially with the Christmas lights along the jetty in the background. Pretty as a picture.'

'Going live in five minutes,' said the cameraman as he watched a screen showing scenes back in the Grampian TV news studio. It wasn't exactly the international attention Beatrice had been hoping for when she'd started working on the inn's refurbishment plans in the autumn, but it was a start.

'Highlands and islands telly today, tomorrow the world, yeah?' she quipped nervously to Atholl, who gave her an enthusiastic thumbs-up as the cameraman started his countdown and Beatrice felt a sudden panicked rush of adrenalin course through her body.

Kirstie faced the camera, straightened her spine and burst into life. 'That's right, thank you, Moira. Here I am in beautiful Port Willow Bay in Wester Ross where it looks like it's going to be a white Christmas for the first time in ten years, and I'm at a very special pub, the Princess and the Pea Inn. I'm joined by one of the inn's managers, Beatrice Halliday. Hello.'

The speed of the reporter's introduction in her clipped Morningside accent threw Beatrice off. She managed a garbled hello which the woman promptly spoke over.

'You're preparing for a busy Christmas season at the inn, can you tell us about that?'

The camera panned to Beatrice just as a gust of sleety wind swooshed her hair up around her face. She straightened the strands and swallowed. 'Yes, that's right, Kirstie. We're, *um*, we're booked out for the first Christmas in years here at the inn.' Suddenly unsure, she glanced at Atholl who was beaming with pride and nodding his encouragement.

The reporter looked less encouraging – as though she could think of nothing she'd rather do less on a freezing Christmas Eve morning than stand on the roadside by a pub interviewing some English landlady. Beatrice fixed her eyes on Atholl as she continued, addressing her words only to his blue eyes and broad grin and finding her nerves slowly giving way.

'Here at the inn we're welcoming visitors keen to try their hand at learning new crafting skills. We're using local experts to teach our guests the arts of knitting, weaving, spinning and dyeing, glass-working, willow-weaving, you name it. We've even got a Gaelic teacher.'

'And what do your visitors want to get from a crafting holiday in the Highlands?'

'Oh, *um*, well, they want to escape real life for a while and concentrate on learning a new skill. Some of them just want to slow down and take things easy. Making lovely things lets you do that.'

'And are you crafty, yourself, Beatrice?' Kirstie urged.

'*Um*, not really. I've tried my hand at willow-weaving with our resident willow tutor.' Beatrice couldn't help but smile at Atholl, who was doing the closed-lipped, curling smirk he saved for moments when he was amused and awed by the woman he loved. 'I, *um*, I wasn't a natural at it.' That was an understatement, she knew, and Beatrice was sure the freckled spots beneath Atholl's eyes were turning pink with good humour as he listened. He'd convinced Beatrice to try making a wreath back in the summer. That day she'd felt her attraction to him growing and he'd let down his grumpy armour, revealing the truth; that he was as soft as butter underneath the sternness.

The reporter, seeing Beatrice smiling at someone off camera, followed Beatrice's gaze and, hawk-like, turned on Atholl, motioning out of shot for the cameraman to turn his lens towards the big redhead leaning against the stone doorway of the inn.

Beatrice watched the reporter's eyes widen as the camera panned up Atholl's tall, broad frame. Atholl immediately uncrossed his arms and stood upright, clearing his throat, his face turning serious and brooding, the way it had when Beatrice first met him.

'Are you that willow tutor, by any chance?' the reporter asked.

'I am. *Uh…* I'm Atholl Fergusson, another of the inn's managers, and the willow tutor, right enough.' Atholl's voice was grave. 'But Beattie is better placed to tell you about the inn than I…'

'And how do your students respond to you, Atholl?'

Beatrice, now entirely forgotten, couldn't help drawing back her neck, affronted, as the interview carried on without her. The woman was asking Atholl to turn his hands, calloused from his craft, towards the camera and asking if his visitors always left satisfied. The reporter certainly had the look of a woman whose working day had taken a sudden turn for the better.

As he answered the next question, Atholl threw Beatrice a flash of wide eyes and quirked brow, showing his acceptance of the situation but letting her know he understood what was happening. Beatrice rolled her eyes with a smile.

She didn't mind this now-familiar reaction. She'd seen it all; the sudden giddy smiles and the shy or sometimes downright flirtatious introductions. Atholl Fergusson had that effect on people. Sometimes tourists stopped them in the street when they were on days out in Fort William or Inverness, wanting a selfie with a true redheaded Scotsman of the clan warrior type. She'd come to think of it as the *Outlander* effect.

Their reactions only served to remind her of the first time she'd seen Atholl's shocking blue eyes and his mass of dark-red waves down to his strong jaw. Weirdly, he still had no idea how handsome he was or how much, at over six foot and ruggedly fit from working on the willow fields since his late teens, he stood out in any crowd.

She couldn't help smiling at Atholl who was nodding and muttering, trying to be polite but wanting to keep his answers short and always trying to return the focus to Beatrice who was supposed to be the star of this interview. She was the one with all the media training from her old career running a big council arts organisation in the Midlands. She'd been the one dealing with the press releases and giving interviews and it had come easy to her, but watching Atholl with his laidback, unassuming confidence talking into the news camera now gave her a glow of pride and she was hit once more by the unwavering attraction that was always just there, drawing her to him in a way she'd never known before.

'And you've big plans here at the inn, I believe?' Kirstie pressed.

'That's right. Beattie – with some help from my cousin's eldest bairn, Mutt – has refurbished our famous Princess and the Pea room which has been welcomin' honeymooners and holidaymakers since my parents ran the place.'

'Ah, that's right, I've seen photographs of the inn's Princess and the Pea bed. How tall is it exactly?'

'Almost six foot of mattresses, enough to have you believing you're in your own fairy tale.'

Atholl flashed a quick smile at Beatrice once more, making her blush with the knowledge of what he was thinking in that moment. She too thought back to the summer weekend when they'd climbed the ladder of the inn's famous bed and lost hour upon hour beneath its four-poster canopy and chintzy drapes.

'Beatrice has, *uh*, also organised an exhibition of crafts this coming Easter,' Atholl continued, determined to highlight her part in the transformation of not only the inn but his fledgling craft holidays business too. 'We'll be taking over the village hall for the first weekend in April, displaying the things we make here in Port Willow. There'll be refreshments and baking and such like.' Atholl looked into the camera. 'And everyone's invited.'

'That ought to get the crowds rushing in,' the reporter said, smiling a little too widely.

Atholl had time to tell her about the wassailing evening of a few nights before and mentioned that the train would be arriving into Port Willow any second now with the new holidaymakers booked in for Christmas, and that was it, the interview seemed to be over within moments. Kirstie turned back to the camera.

'So there we are! If you're after crafting expertise and rugged scenery in a homely inn this winter, Port Willow is *the* destination for you. Why don't you come down and meet Atholl Fergusson and... *uh*, Bernice...'

'*Beatrice*,' Atholl put in, off camera, but the reporter was already signing off.

'Merry Christmas from a very snowy Princess and the Pea Inn. Back to the studio.'

'And we're clear,' said the cameraman.

Atholl was already wrapping Beatrice in his arms and telling her how well she'd done, guiding her back inside the inn to get her warmed through in front of the bar room fire, when Seth cycled up to the inn door wearing the green woollen beanie Beatrice thought must be stuck to the man's head; she'd never seen him without it, even in the summer months.

'Aww, did I miss it? I thought you'd want to talk to me about my memories of Port Willow,' he said. Kirstie was already packing away her mic. 'Will you no' come inside for a dram. It is Christmas Eve, after all.'

'We need to get on the road for one last feature this afternoon, sorry,' she said, not at all sorry.

Seth wouldn't be put off. 'Well at least come in and see the dating board.'

This made the reporter pause.

'Dating board?'

'Aye, it's all young Beatrice's idea.'

Beatrice paused on the steps of the inn and waved this away, resisting the urge to declare herself fully forty years old and not all that young, but she held back in front of Kirstie. The reporter was already asking Seth to lead the way with a look in her eyes that said she had sniffed out a Christmas scoop.

-

'Aye, so here it is. The dating board,' Seth announced proudly.

'Oh!' said Kirstie, visibly disappointed.

Beatrice watched on helplessly as the woman inspected the big board hanging between the bar and the crackling open fire. She'd even put a garland of tinsel around its frame in the hopes she could drum up some enthusiasm for Christmas matchmaking, but sadly only one of the paper 'profiles' had been filled out, and that was by Seth himself.

'What is that?' Kirstie asked, pointing to the hand-written form pinned to the centre of the board.

'It's my lonely heart, of course,' Seth informed her, unpinning and handing over the paper.

Beatrice prayed Kirstie would be kind and not sneer as she read it out aloud.

NAME: Seth Magnus John McVie

AGE: 80 years and 2 months

OCCUPATION: Retired boat man

ADDRESS: Port Willow, the blue hoose

HOBBIES: Taking my bike round the village and off to Skye, visiting my son's place, bird watching, draining a dram at the Princess. I make a braw tablet as well.

HOW WOULD YOU DESCRIBE YOURSELF: Widower. Right handsome moustache. Maybe no' awbody's cup o' tea but a gentleman.

LOOKING FOR: A companion. A hand to hold.

Own bike an advantage.

Kirstie only nodded and handed it back as Seth informed her sadly he'd had no takers yet but he lived in hope. 'You see, we've always had the problem here in Port Willow of too many men and no' enough lassies.'

'How'd you mean?' Kirstie wanted to know, signalling to the cameraman to order some drinks at the bar after all.

'Our lassies are too bonny and too clever to stick around in the village. They're drawn to the cities for work or for studies. Some o' them end up married and living abroad like Mrs Mair's daughter; she's in Cape Town, I believe.'

'That she is,' called the white-haired housekeeper from behind the bar where she was pouring two half pints of shandy for the cameraman. 'There's no' much to keep the young ones here.'

'Except the farmin', the fishin'; things the lads stay for,' Seth added. 'So for every lassie there's at least two laddies and so few young folk. It doesnae make for many marriages, you see?'

'Tell me more about the local dating scene, Seth,' Kirstie said drawing him towards a bar stool before asking if he'd like a drink too.

Atholl and Beatrice watched on, bemused. 'What's goin' on?' Atholl asked, under his breath.

'I think it's called finding a better news angle,' Beatrice whispered back, not entirely sure if Seth was the best person to fill the reporter in on the village singles' scene, meagre though it was, in spite of her best efforts to encourage a little romance between the locals.

They could do nothing but watch on as Kirstie took notes on her phone underneath the bar's coloured foil paperchains and tinsel which, along with the squeaky clean, polished glasses and spirit bottles, were sparkling in the dancing lights from the Christmas tree.

'Young Beatrice hasnae had the success she'd hoped for wi' the board; no' yet anyway,' Seth was telling the woman. 'Our local laddies are shy, you see? I thought if I came forward first, they'd all follow suit, but it hasnae worked. That's why she's organised the, *eh*...what's it called again, Beatrice?' Seth turned to her on his barstool, stroking his whiskers, his eyes peering black and tiny through thick round specs.

'Speed dating,' Beatrice called over. 'This Hogmanay. I thought it would bring an interesting twist to the New Year festivities if we kicked it all off with a speed-dating event.'

'And you didn't mention that in the interview?' Kirstie looked between Atholl and Beatrice.

Atholl cut in. 'Well, no, that's more a thing for locals. We didnae think you'd be interested in…'

'How many tickets have you sold?' Kirstie interrupted, too excited by the story to wait. This was far more interesting than the opening of a new visitors' carpark at the lobster hatchery she was supposed to be covering this afternoon.

'Well, *uh*… seven,' Beatrice conceded. 'But there's still time. You're coming, aren't you, Seth?'

'Wouldnae miss it!' he smiled, reaching for the Glenfiddich that Mrs Mair had laid before him.

Kirstie's eyes sharpened. She turned to the cameraman. 'Davie, get your equipment. Let's film a segment before we leave. We can get this on tonight if we're quick. Our viewers will love it. A return to traditional face-to-face dating in the Highlands. A rejection of the online apps with all their liars and fakers and that one from Kirkintilloch that says he'll meet you by the steps of the library, but does he show up?' Kirstie paused, suddenly self-conscious. She smoothed her skirt over her knees and smiled once more, composing herself after getting heated. 'Anyway. Mr McVie, will you do a wee interview for me?'

'Where do you want me?' said Seth, all seriousness, smoothing his tweedy lapels.

'Oh God!' Beatrice cried, watching on helplessly, as Atholl turned away, stifling a laugh.

Chapter Six

Bumpy Landings

Everyone at the inn was so preoccupied watching Seth being interviewed in front of Beatrice's dating board that they didn't notice when the young blonde woman with big black sunglasses and the worst hangover of her life stumbled into the reception. Everyone except Gene Fergusson, that is, Atholl's lanky brother and the inn's resident chef.

'Morning, are ye checking in?' he asked, peering at the woman as though he might see through the black lenses. Had he been able to, he'd know her eyes were crusted and dry from the flight and smudged with yesterday's make-up, and maybe he'd pick up on the signs this was a woman in survival mode, drowned in stress hormones and Diptyque eau de parfum.

'Apparently,' Nina replied, looking around shakily and not at all impressed. 'This *is* the Princess and the Pea?' Gene confirmed it was while Nina checked the paperwork in her hand again. When Mitch had booked her in he'd assumed, like Nina had, that the inn's name spoke of a quirky boutique guesthouse.

She'd been expecting something along the lines of the smart Edinburgh Airbnbs and the spa hotels she'd passed in the cab on her way from the airport oh-so-many hours ago when in her naivety she'd thought she had only a short drive ahead of her to reach her Highland destination. Four-and-a-half exasperated, exhausted hours later, she'd been dropped off at the top of the village.

'It's doon that way,' the driver had told her, as she'd tried to blink herself awake. 'I cannae get the taxi doon the waterside, no' with all the snow and parked cars.'

She'd grown used to New York snow. The kind that got cleared by ploughs as soon as it fell, the kind that turned grey and slushy at the sidewalk edges but generally it was out of everyone's way and no impediment to the commuters and dogwalkers, hotdog sellers, and, most importantly, her designer heels. This stuff, on her trudge along the blustery Port Willow waterfront, had been left in drifts shin-deep and was next to impossible to drag her two-thousand-dollar Louis Vuitton through without it getting horribly wet.

Her ticket had limited her to only one piece of luggage and a carry-on – the rest of her belongings had been by necessity surrendered to baggage storage at JFK, around about the time she was trying to check her emotional baggage too and determining to do her very best with this Scottish assignment so Seamus couldn't fail to see her worth.

Nina stood before Gene, bedraggled and disorientated, only half understanding the accents she'd been bombarded with since landing.

'Name, please?' he enquired.

'Nina Miller, booking by Mitch at—'

'Coming through,' interrupted Davie the camera operator, and Beatrice, Atholl and Seth led Kirstie through the reception and up the wide, creaking stairs towards the Princess room.

Gene paid them no attention, scrolling for her name on his computer screen. 'Aye, there ye are. This says it's an open-ended reservation, two weeks in the first instance? Bed and breakfast, no craft sessions booked.'

'That's right, I don't know when I'll be leaving.'

Gene ignored the desperate note in her voice that said she'd do her level best to get out of here as soon as she could escape.

'Are they filming a TV show?' Nina asked, watching in the wake of the latest stars of Highland and islands broadcasting now at the top of the stairs.

'It's for the news. About the refurbishments. At least that's what I thought it was about. It seems to have taken a turn towards the speed dating and Beatrice's lonely hearts board.'

'*Huh?*' Nina tried hard to hold on to her patience.

'On account of there being so many men in the village and so few lassies for the ones that want them. My co-manager, Beatrice, has a taste for matchmaking.'

'Does she? Well I'll be sure to avoid her.'

'Are ye no' wanting a ticket yourself, for the speed dating at Hogmanay, like?'

'That won't be necessary. I'm here to absorb the arts and crafts culture around here, not to meet lonely old Scottish men.'

Gene shrugged. 'You'll be wanting to look over the activities brochure in that case. These are all the crafting sessions available. You'll need to book in quick, mind, some are already full.'

'No, I'm not here to *do* crafts. I'm here to scout for them.'

'Well,' Gene stared blankly, 'you can scout them all ye like in the brochure. Every local maker is in there, just about.'

Nina only nodded. There was no point explaining to this BFG that she wasn't here for hobbyists and their amateur handicrafts. She was here for heritage creators and their internationally marketable, exclusive wares. This guy wouldn't understand.

He handed her a key from the board behind the desk. 'Room seven, top o' the hotel. Breakfast served eight 'til nine only tomorrow, what wi' it being Christmas.'

'Right, of course.' She took the key shakily. 'It's Christmas Eve.' Somehow, in all the mess, she'd forgotten. An ache struck her deep in her chest that felt like homesickness for her mother back in Hove, followed by bitterness at the reminder that some other woman was luxuriating in her perfectly premeditated Christmas back in New York.

'Have ye plans for Christmas day?' Gene asked.

Nina shook her head. 'I'll work through it. I've a lot to do.'

'Mind ye join us all for Christmas dinner at four just through there in the bar restaurant.' Gene's voice was gentle. He'd learned a thing or two about tearful-looking women arriving alone at the inn from the day he'd checked in Beatrice and got off on entirely the wrong foot with her. Little did he know then she was suffering from a pain and loss he couldn't comprehend. Gene resolved to be polite to this sullen woman standing before him now and gripping the handles of her case so fiercely tight that her knuckles were white. She was staring at her phone and getting paler by the second.

'There's no signal here?' she gulped.

'Signals come and go in Port Willow, you'll catch one soon enough. Maybe the snow's affectin' it?'

She threw him a dubious look. 'How can snow affect a phone signal?'

Gene only shrugged.

'Where's the media centre?' she asked impatiently, walking to the open door of the bar and peering in, seeing the place was empty save Mrs Mair in her curlers and white pinny wiping down tables and singing along to Elvis's 'Blue Christmas' on the radio.

'Media centre?' echoed Gene, desperately trying to remember what Beatrice had coached him to say in this situation.

Nina drew her sunglasses off and fixed him with a stare. She needed to check in with Mitch, right now. Only he could change her reservations and get her back to civilisation. This tiny backwater village was not in the least bit promising as a talent scouting location. From what she'd seen so far everyone was obsessed with fixing people up and solving the village's population problem. The whole washed-out tartan vibe of the inn told her everything she needed to know about whether there was a thriving arts culture here.

Where were the lifestyle practitioners, the poets, and the decadent, over-educated designers? Where was all the evidence of a thriving, vibrant underground scene? She glanced at the deer antlers hanging on the wall above Gene's head. They were festooned in silver decorations for Christmas. This place was eccentric, but in all the wrong ways. There must be a city nearby somewhere?

Gene pressed bravely on. 'Mutt, I mean Murray, is almost finished with the media centre. You can use it later today, I imagine. There's everything you'll need. A computer, a new printer, that sort of thing…' Gene tailed off, seeing how unimpressed Nina was with his answer.

She took a stoic breath and exhaled in a slow blow.

Gene quickly added, 'I'll bring some tea and shortbread up to your room in a wee minute.'

'Right, thanks,' she said with the thinnest of smiles. 'But hold the shortbread.' Turning for the elevators she found that, of course, there were none, so she started for the stairs. 'I'll take an iced bubble tea, with Boba pearls if you have them,' she threw back to Gene, who froze, wide-eyed and blinking.

'*Bubble* tea?'

'Yes. You know? Tea with tapioca pearls or…'

'*Uh*, I've breakfast tea? Or Earl Grey? I could try to get some bubbles into them, maybe, if I whisk the milk?'

Nina's face set like flint. She held it together. 'Breakfast tea is fine, thank you.'

She'd read in Mitch's paperwork that the Princess and the Pea was supposed to offer a destination dining experience, not that she had any appetite whatsoever, but some of her New York home comforts would be nice.

She thought of the creamery near the office where she'd grab her ten-dollar zero-fat Vietnamese iced coffee every morning and her matcha bubble tea every evening as she left work. She clamped her lips to stop herself sighing. So far there was nothing familiar about this place. There was no gloss, no buzz, no haste, and zero comfort.

Gene shuffled away through the bar to the kitchens, hoping to avoid the woman's glassy gaze and planning to ask Mrs Mair to get on her phone and Google 'bubble tea', while Nina began her climb to bed.

It would be seven o'clock in New York. The caterers would be arriving at Luke's place soon to set up the oysters and champagne surprise she'd shelled out for. She wondered if it was possible to sleep for twenty-four hours and skip Christmas entirely. 'Only one way to find out,' she told herself as she climbed the creaking stairs.

Chapter Seven

Kitty Knows Best

The noon train rumbled into Port Willow beneath a lowering grey sky, just as the snow turned heavy again.

'They're lucky,' said Kitty Wake, peering out the window of the Princess room and along the single row of cottages that made up the entirety of Port Willow Bay.

'Who?' replied Beatrice, shaking the cover onto the duvet and wondering why turning over the guests' rooms today had been such an effort. They were running late, what with the news crew staying far longer than they'd anticipated. Kirstie had wanted to know all about the competition winners who had bagged the highly sought-after month-long break in Beatrice's 'couple's retreat' giveaway. There had been thousands of entries from across the world, she'd been delighted to report. All the entrants had to do was tell Beatrice why they thought they should win, and out of all the entries, one in particular had shone out, instantly convincing Beatrice she'd picked a very special couple indeed. The winners, who would be celebrating their silver wedding anniversary later in the year, would be arriving on Hogmanay, she'd told Kirstie excitedly. She was determined to transform the inn into a place for lovers and romantics, no matter how long they had been together.

Kirstie had, admittedly, been less interested in this than in hearing Seth spilling the tea on the local dating scene. Seth had enjoyed every second of his interview. He was at this moment stopping to knock on every door along the waterfront, letting the locals know to tune in at six to watch him on telly.

Kitty was still looking out at the view along the street to her right towards the station. 'This lot, arrivin' intae the village. They won't believe their luck. Scotland in the snow, and tomorrow Christmas Day.'

Beatrice uncapped her water bottle and drank, coming to join Kitty by the window, taking a moment to get her breath back. She could do with a nap. It must be all the Christmas preparations to blame, and helping Gene re-set the breakfast room after waving off this morning's departing guests, then all the excitement of the news crew. It had taken it out of her.

Looking out at the wintery view across the bay to the far shore with its grey-walled castle, Beatrice remarked, as she often had recently, how it was even prettier than the summer views – and they took some beating.

Kitty was right; the new intake of crafting customers heading towards the inn for the holidays were very lucky indeed.

'This is my first white Christmas since I was a kid,' Beatrice said, awed by the sight and taking another swig of water.

There had been a gleaming blanket of snow over the higher hills for weeks now, and atop the dizziest peaks only a few miles inland – as well as over the water on Skye – there lay a permanent cap of white, even in the height of summer, but seeing it falling here by the water's edge since late yesterday evening had felt somehow miraculous.

'Here they come,' Kitty said, leaning closer to the glass and making it fog with her breath, obscuring the group traipsing with suitcases towards the inn. 'And not one of them a Gaelic student. Hardly surprising. Who wants to take language classes over the holidays?'

'These ones are all painters and willow-weavers,' Beatrice confirmed. 'And there's two potters, I think.'

'I'll have plenty of time to help out at the inn.' Kitty shrugged, not minding a break from teaching. She spent term time at her university campus in the north, coming home to Gene and the inn at weekends and on uni holidays. For Kitty and Gene each of these visits had the fervour of a reunion after years apart, Gene was so enthusiastically devoted to Kitty. 'You should get some rest, let me take the reins a bit this week,' Kitty said, turning her eyes away from the station road and the stream of tourists and locals with their last-minute Christmas shopping passing the jetty with its moored tourist boats. 'You're looking fair tired.'

'Thanks very much!' But Beatrice couldn't really disagree. She knew her eyes were sunken, even after eight hours' sleep. 'I'm fine. I'll have an early night.' Kitty frowned. 'But if you don't mind clambering up there with the fresh bedding?' Beatrice pointed to the bed beneath its newly refurbished gauzy white canopy, perfect for stylish young honeymooners now that she'd replaced the heavy green nineteen-fifties chintz that she'd slept under on her summer holiday. 'I'll hold the ladder steady for you.'

Kitty sprang up to help.

The bed was the invention of Atholl's mother and not something either of the Fergusson men would ever see dismantled. The whole room – from its towering, canopied four-poster piled high with mattresses, the half-panelled walls, and the claw foot bath in the corner – had been a tribute to their oldest sibling; a baby girl who never lived to admire the pretty views of the Highland village.

Sentimentality ruled the Fergussons and they all adhered to their mother's wishes that the room would delight generations of wee lassies and holidaymakers from all over the world, intent upon living out their very own fairy tale.

The Princess and the Pea Inn had been famous for its eccentric-themed room in the middle of the last century and was now having something of a renaissance, thanks to Beatrice's attempts at modernisation and the weekend supplement spreads and crafting magazine ads she'd bagged in exchange for free B&B in the Princess room – one of which, unbeknown to the women, had found its way over to New York and into the hands of one of Nina's colleagues, sparking the whole scouting trip idea. Port Willow was establishing a reputation as a much-sought-after destination on the radar of craft enthusiasts and those in search of wild nature and romance, even if it was happening slower than Beatrice would like.

'Oh, Kitty, I hope you don't mind me saying...' Beatrice said awkwardly from the foot of the ladder.

Halfway up and dragging the duvet, Kitty could only shout down, 'Go on.'

'Gene's new aftershave. *Um*, I hate to mention it, but... it's quite strong. Overpowering, in fact. I'd ask Atholl to mention it to him but you know what they're like, it might cause ructions.'

Kitty listened, wrestling the duvet into position at the top of the pile of soft new eco-mattresses that Beatrice had sourced at breath-taking expense from a company in Glasgow. Beatrice talked on, the atmosphere growing more awkward by the second. 'It's nice that Gene's making so much effort these days, only I'm noticing he's overdoing it a bit with the scent.'

Kitty made her way down to ground level again, her brow wrinkled in confusion. It was true the inn wasn't the only Port Willow resident enjoying a renaissance. Gene too had enjoyed – or more accurately endured – a makeover last August, thanks to Beatrice, and his new shaven-headed, smartly pressed look had kick-started his love affair with the younger Kitty.

'He doesnae have a new aftershave,' said Kitty. 'Just the one he's always worn and I'd be the first to tell him if it was pongy. Are you sure it's him?'

'Positive. At breakfast service all this week I've been holding my breath to avoid it. It's so strong it makes me queasy.'

Kitty narrowed her eyes and cast a furtive glance down her friend's body. 'Is anything else making you queasy?'

'Not really. I mean, Mrs Mair's homemade soup was definitely a bit off yesterday.'

'The Scotch broth?' Kitty replied. 'I had it for lunch, it was braw, nothin' the matter wi' it.' Kitty watched her friend as if weighing up what to say next.

Beatrice threw the laundry into its basket, dragging it towards the door, telling her to forget she said anything.

'Bea?'

'*Hmm?*'

'You're not late, are you?'

'The guests aren't at the reception desk yet,' Beatrice called over her shoulder as she opened the door. 'I'll head down in a sec, get them checked in.'

Kitty shook her head. 'No, Bea,' she said levelly. 'I mean are you *late* late.'

The words made Bea freeze as she stepped into the corridor and turned her head to meet her friend's stare. The whole world froze around her.

Blinking and calculating, trying to remember, Beatrice's emotions circulated. Perplexity, realisation, denial, and back to perplexed again.

'*Oh!*' said Beatrice, letting the laundry basket drop to the floor.

Chapter Eight

A Taste of Scotland

Nina hadn't slept well. The low radiators along the wall by her bed were clanking and kicking out an incredible heat. Checking her phone with a groan, she realised she'd only been out for an hour and her nap hadn't done her a bit of good.

Dry mouthed, she looked around for the bottled water that any hotel worth *anything* at all should provide. Nobody had told Nina about the fluoride-free tap water everyone in Scotland boasted about.

Beside her single bed lay the empty teacup. She'd been so bone-tired she couldn't really remember draining it after Gene had left the tray at her room door. She'd found he'd ignored her instructions to nix the shortbread which still lay on its dish on the tray now. It looked buttery and golden and smelled homemade in a way that made her think of her late grandmother and Hove and what her mum and brother might be doing now that it was early afternoon on Christmas Eve.

She hadn't eaten since New York and her stomach growled in spite of its training over the past few years to expect very little, and certainly nothing in the way of carbs. She and Luke were clean eaters. If it wasn't raw or organic or at the very least, exquisitely presented, it didn't make it onto their plates.

She climbed out of bed and opened the window, taking deep gasps of the fresh, icy air. It was growing dark along the waterfront and the tide was coming in. Had she even noticed the beach immediately across the road and beyond the low sea wall as she'd dragged her case along the snowy pavement this morning?

The waves were shushing quietly now in the two o'clock twilight and the whole waterfront was coming to life with strands of white lightbulbs swagged between lampposts all the way past the jetty and on towards the train station. The warm smell of coal and logs burning in countless Port Willow hearths and the sea salt on the air mingled on the chilly breeze with something crisp and clean like lavender – or could it be heather? Somehow it made her hungrier. Feeling her willpower snap, she turned upon the shortbread and took a furious, deep bite.

'Oh my God!' she couldn't help exclaiming over and over as she rolled her eyes back, sinking onto the rug by the window and devouring the sweet crumbly slabs of biscuit, licking her lips and fingers to catch every granule of white refined sugar from its golden crust. Luke's set often dismissed certain foods as 'not worth the calories' and she'd said it herself many times lately, but this? This tasted of comfort and sweetness. It was light, not cloying, and very, very moreish.

She found herself wishing for another cup of tea, and not the tea of her New York daily rituals either, but another cup of Gene Fergusson's real caffeinated black tea with – she couldn't quite believe she'd drunk it – real cows' milk which, no doubt, came from a massive plastic bottle.

She wanted to curse the deliciousness that had thrown her off the waspish New York diet that had simply become a way of life for her, and at exactly the same time she knew she wanted more.

The shortbread had done nothing for her hunger, but it had given her something she hadn't felt in a long time: the curious pangs of an enthusiastic appetite.

Just what were they cooking downstairs in that kitchen, anyway? It smelled of Christmases long forgotten, tapping into memories from her childhood, and from school dinners too, of tasty things served with gravy, and thick custard for dessert, memories from a time before green wheatgrass shots downed before early morning workouts in Luke's building's gym complex and spotting him as he lifted weights while she'd grown thinner and thinner and gained more and more approval.

Well, all the clothes in her case were sample sizes, she told herself, so there'd be no more shortbread for her, and to stave off her hunger and distract herself she ran the bath.

The little copper tub had, she had to admit, a kitschy appeal, and she'd photographed it as the bubbles reached the rim and her phone's camera lens had fogged with the steam.

Even if she did have a signal she wasn't sure who she'd have sent it to. She still hadn't told her mother she was in the UK yet, out of pride, maybe, at having blown her Christmas plans and lost her boyfriend and her important job, all in the course of days, *dammit*, and when she'd been so confident and secure too. Nobody in England was expecting a call anyway, except maybe tomorrow to wish them a happy Christmas, so she was off the hook for now.

Undressing, she let the airport-crumpled suit she'd napped in fall in a heap on the polished floorboards, and she stepped into the tiny tub under the inn's sloping eaves, her knees practically around her ears. Closing her eyes once more, she tried to acclimatise to her strange new surroundings and figure out how on earth she was supposed to succeed in Seamus's mission in a backwater like this, asking herself, in her newfound paranoia, Luke's final gift to her, whether she'd actually been set up to fail by her clever bosses.

Her dismissal would be unfair if it looked like they were trying to get rid of an unwanted girlfriend – something like that could draw Luke into a scandal and a lawsuit – but if she was, say, sent on a fool's errand to Scotland and she failed to bring back the goods she could be fired without any comeback whatsoever. She *had* to succeed, but how to do it, she had no idea.

Chapter Nine

Unpacking

Check-in wasn't going as smoothly as it usually did. Even with Kitty there to help, Beatrice was struggling to find the guests' names on the new booking system she'd insisted upon installing in her first month in her new job.

By the time they'd made it downstairs there had been eight new guests and their luggage squeezed into the little reception, standing on the threadbare tartan carpet that even with all of Beatrice's improvements she had conceded the inn couldn't afford to replace just yet.

The last person to come inside had closed the heavy oak door that led straight onto the roadside, shutting out the snow and wind and the view of the low sea wall and the wild, wet bay beyond it.

In spite of Beatrice's stumbling and confusion, the potters were quickly checked in and sent off immediately to their first lesson down at the village hall with old Mrs McPhail, the retired headmistress of the Port Willow primary school. Kitty had seen to them, but now the words on the monitor were swimming around before Beatrice's vision. She gulped and stared, narrowing her eyes, trying to pick out the surnames on the system.

'Ms Batsford and Ms Klein… Batsford, Batsford… *umm*, sorry, your reservation *is* here somewhere.'

Kitty leaned over Beatrice's shoulder behind the old oak reception desk, taking a key from the brass hooks on the board. 'Batsford and Klein. Room three, bed and breakfast, watercolour lessons with Mr Garstang along the front at his home-gallery. First lesson is this afternoon at four and then picking up again after Christmas, on the twenty-seventh, I believe.'

Kitty efficiently handed the smiling women their keys and directed them to their room. 'First on the left, top o' the stairs. I'll bring shortbread and tea to your room in a wee while.'

'Sorry,' Beatrice whispered to Kitty, as the artists resumed their excited chatter and went off in search of warm baths and hot drinks, and the next guests shuffled forward.

'Bea, why don't you go and make yourself a drink *and tell Atholl,*' Kitty hissed under her breath before greeting the next holidaymakers.

Beatrice whispered back, 'I can't tell Atholl. Not yet.'

Kitty's eyes rounded. '*Um*, Okay? But will he no' mind that I know before him?'

'I don't want to tell anyone,' Beatrice's voice quaked.

Their snatched conversation was cut short by the chatter of the willow-weavers: two middle-aged women and two girls in their mid-teens, obviously seasoned crafting holiday enthusiasts with backpacks and tote bags stuffed with all sorts of arty materials. Kitty proceeded to check them in. That's when Beatrice spotted Atholl, by the inn door, stopped on his way from the bar, a crate of the Christmas day champagne in his arms, his sleeves rolled up, simply watching his girlfriend, a quirk of a smile on his lips.

'You a'right?' he mouthed over the heads of the crafters.

Kitty caught the exchange too, before also looking at Beatrice inquisitively.

'I'm fine,' Beatrice mouthed back before giving Kitty a cautionary glance, warning her not to do or say anything.

Beatrice wanted to be the matchmaker around the village, but Kitty Wake had been known to interfere when she thought Beatrice and Atholl needed a shove in the right direction, which, in the early days back in August, they definitely had.

The pair's scrutiny was too much for her and Beatrice hurried round the desk, saying to the weavers, 'Right, let me help you with your cases, Ms... *um?*' She was sure they'd said their names as they approached the desk, but had forgotten already.

As the women reintroduced themselves, Beatrice rolled away two of their cases to the foot of the stairs. Kitty stopped her with a hand on her arm.

'You can't be carrying those up the stairs,' she whispered, horrified.

The colleagues froze, staring at one another. Beatrice hurriedly checked Atholl had left, which he had, thank goodness.

'I'll be fine, and not a word to Atholl, OK?' she hissed and bumped the cases up the steps, calling the women after her, only too glad to get away from Kitty's fussing.

As soon as the crafty mums and daughters were at the door of room four, the only family four bed in the place, she retreated to her little sun room, using the back stairs to avoid the inn's residents. Only Echo, Atholl's wandering dog, followed her from his favourite napping spot on the back landing.

'Come on, little guy. Let's light a fire and take a nap,' she told the obedient collie, making her way inside the room, being sure to turn the key and sighing with relief that she was alone at last.

-

Yet Beatrice didn't sleep. She'd given up after fifteen minutes of fretting and turning under the tartan blanket on the sun room sofa. The window faced south and the inn's back gardens, where, in the summertime, crocosmia bobbed their heads and blackbirds made their nests in amongst the bramble briars and teasel stems, but everything now looked tangled, damp and black and topped with snow.

Echo lifted his head lazily from his spot on the hearth rug as Beatrice got up and drew the curtains before coming to a stop in the middle of the room, fixing her eyes on the cardboard box that had for weeks now been shoved into a corner. After a moment's hesitation, she dragged it into the middle of the room.

The tape was still intact over its seals. She hadn't been able to bring herself to open it when it arrived; when she'd been too happy, too busy, too swept up in her exciting new life at the inn to want to face its contents.

The box was addressed to her in familiar handwriting. She ran her hand over the ink.

> *Sender: Richard Halliday, Apartment 21A, Castle View Wind, Warwick*

Reading the words stilled the voices in her head that had been chiming like alarm bells since Kitty had coaxed her into realising she might indeed be pregnant; voices that had been asking how she could have been so unobservant, so out of touch with herself not to figure it out. These were mixed in with other, less-persuasive, voices saying she couldn't be sure she really was pregnant until she took a test, and, anyway, hadn't she had a few, admittedly unusually light, periods in the last few months, so how could she somehow be carrying a baby?

Beatrice was very aware of her breathing as she tore the tape from the box, simultaneously wincing at the thought of what she'd find inside but also wanting to be occupied with anything that would take her mind off the clamorous baby thoughts.

Rich's new address on the box was the same one that had been on the lawyer's letter and the divorce papers.

Since the separation had been, in the end, amicable in its own way, she hadn't suffered too much when signing the documents and returning them. She'd done all her suffering and crying when he walked out, back in the spring.

The money from the sale of their Warwick two-bed had been split equally between them and Rich had packaged up her few belongings and sent them on to her at Port Willow. She'd opened the case of clothes when they arrived, but this box she couldn't bear to open at the time.

Taking a deep breath she plunged her hands through the scrunched newspaper, immediately finding a framed photo of her mum, her sister Angela and herself on the ramparts of Warwick castle on a bright spring day long ago. Angela was still only a teenager then.

Beatrice smiled. That was the summer they both got undercuts and Beatrice had instantly regretted hers while Angela looked and felt gorgeous. At that point the three women still lived together and the cancer diagnosis that would steal their lovely mum's retirement and the chance to meet her grandbaby, Clara, lurked seven thousand days away in their futures, just waiting to scupper all their plans.

Her mum was pictured carrying the picnic bag and with her coat over her arm. She looked quiet and content, the way she always had then – the midnight dash to the women's refuge, with Angela still a baby in her arms, escaping the girls' volatile, controlling father and the many months of rebuilding their lives that had followed was by then a series of distant unhappy memories for her. Beatrice could barely recall her father, and Angela had no memories of him at all.

Her mum had never remarried, even though Beatrice had dreamed of having a lovely step-dad like she'd seen in her favourite teen movies and for a long while in year eleven she'd conjured up an entire secret romance scenario between her kindly art teacher, Mr Greig, and her mum, after she'd seen him make her mum laugh at a parents' open day. Her mum had laughed again when Beatrice eventually confessed this to her and she'd told her she didn't want or need a man, not when she had everything she needed right there in her girls.

Beatrice couldn't help sighing, running her thumbs over the happy faces in the picture before laying it down gently by her side. Echo watched on, blinking by the fire, half asleep but keeping an eye on his boss.

Beatrice's old diaries came next, a few books, her watch, and various bits of jewellery, some precious (her mother's locket with the word 'mum' on the front), the rest mostly high street stuff and nothing special. Out next came her wedding band and engagement ring together in a little box she didn't open, putting them down in the growing pile by her side. An almost-empty bottle of perfume came next and the stale, sickly smell of her old life made her aware again of the queasiness in her stomach.

She wrapped the bottle in some of the scrunched newspaper. She'd bin it later. The scent had taken her straight back to the bedroom she'd shared with Rich, with his ties draped over the wardrobe door, and all his early starts for the station on dark winter mornings, and her own commute to her beloved Arts Hub, and all their late homecomings with M&S carrier bags and something easy to heat up for dinner; all the daily, dry rhythms of her old life.

Beatrice had the urge to get up and throw open the sun-room window for some sea air but remembered it was snowing outside, so she shook away the thoughts, making Echo side-eye her with concern before flopping his sleepy head back down onto his paws.

Reaching into the bottom of the box, her fingertips touched the bundle. This was it. The part she'd been dreading had arrived. She tentatively held up the tissue paper package she'd wrapped so carefully back in the summer, only days before she'd drunk all the white wine in her empty house and boozily booked a lone holiday to Port Willow. It seemed so long ago now, but the package reminded her that it wasn't even half a year ago. She slowly ripped the Sellotape free, letting the parcel spread open across her lap.

There it was. The pregnancy test stick she'd held up for Richard to look at. The expensive kind that had once read 'pregnant, 2+ weeks', but now the battery had drained and the little screen was blank. Beside it lay the first scan picture of a tiny little shadow and all her hopes and dreams for the future. Beneath those were folded the unworn maternity jeans with the label still attached that she couldn't face returning to the shop, and finally, grimly, there was the booklet on baby loss the nurse had handed her when she left the hospital heartbroken after what should have been a routine second trimester scan turned into shattering news resulting in a grim procedure under anaesthetic and a horrible, empty awakening.

She'd been unlucky, the doctor had said, but that word wasn't big enough to contain what had happened to Beatrice. She'd been crushed, despondent, utterly lost and untethered from her old life. She'd been angry too, and soon after she'd become desperate.

Weeks of tearfully trying to conceive again had followed, and arguments too, and the growing sense of failure and of time running out. Eventually Richard had gone out to work one day and never come back, letting her know from a hotel room phone that he couldn't cope with her anymore, that she needed help; his words had sent her spiralling further into deep and unrelenting grief.

Other women go through miscarriage all the time, Beatrice knew. Her frantic online research had told her as much, and every one of them responds differently to the shock and the grief, but mostly they adjust and carry on, at least that's what *seems* to happen on the surface, but not Beatrice. The loneliness of feeling she couldn't talk to anyone about her baby and the shame of forcing Richard out of their marriage because of her erratic behaviour and desperation to be pregnant again threw her headlong into a summer of bitterness and dejection which had eventually carried her here to Port Willow. A runaway who Atholl had found and fallen for, even though she was a wreck.

They'd been so happy these last five months as she'd come to terms with being childless, finding life with Atholl was beautiful and fulfilling in all kinds of new ways she'd never known before, but now the thought of going through all of that pain again and the very idea of seeing Atholl's great heart breaking… No. She couldn't bear to think about it at all.

If it really was all down to luck whether they ever got to meet their baby or not, Beatrice knew she didn't have it within her power to *make* that luck happen, to force things to come right for them. She'd have to be patient and brave and not make herself ill again with the worry and the feeling of helplessness and of urgently wanting a baby of her own to take home.

She didn't know where she was going to find the strength to do it.

The first sob made Echo jump up from the rug and stalk tentatively towards her. He pressed his whiskery muzzle to Beatrice's bowed forehead and sniffed sympathetically, and she wept there in front of the fire with her arms around the loyal collie until there was an even thicker blanket of Christmas Eve snow over Port Willow.

Chapter Ten

Meeting Mutt

It's amazing what a Shu Uemura hair mask and a DIY La Mer detox facial can do for a woman.

Nina was feeling a lot more like her old self in her favourite Balenciaga fuchsia-pink heels, oversized Maison Margiela distressed denim pants and the black Saint Laurent sweatshirt she'd bought for Luke and that he'd only worn once or twice as winter running gear. It had somehow got mixed up with her own things as, presumably, Fournival packed up every last remnant of her existence, preparing to return them in Luke's cowardly sneak-attack eviction she hadn't seen coming.

Luke's top still smelled of whatever delicious mystery elixir the housekeeper (Nina had literally never laid eyes on the woman and didn't so much as know her name) used to launder their clothes and she'd paused a moment before slipping it on, inhaling deeply and feeling her heart hurt a little, but telling herself it was one of the warmest garments in her suitcase and it would be less conspicuous than the designer knits she'd packed for the trip long before she'd realised there likely wasn't a specialist dry cleaner for miles in these parts, so how the hell was she supposed to look after them?

Her hair was blow dried and swept back into the sleek, bouncing quiff that was her signature look, though she was already worrying about how she'd get her regrowth done in the New Year. Nothing on earth compared to Warren Tricomi Salon and the magic her colourist could work upon her roots. She wouldn't think about it now. It was all the more motivation to complete her tasks and get out of here.

Imagine if she could be back in the Microtrends building before her booking was up, and with a portfolio fabulous enough to make Seamus reinstate her there and then, and, with any luck, send the imposter Himari packing.

She stumbled a little on the stairs, coming face to face with a faded movie poster of Gene Kelly in *Singin' in the Rain* framed on the wall. She pulled on the heel of her shoe with a finger, frowning at the inn's tacky art – obviously *they* hadn't been swept away in this supposed refurbishment that was going on. She held her head high once more and carried on her way.

Fournival had been meticulous, gathering up every last scrap of her make-up too, and so she'd been careful to curate a perfect travel beauty kit ahead of her flight in those lonely, wrathful nights at the Ramada when nobody in New York would take her calls. That morning she'd found herself wishing she'd spent that time researching her destination but in her shock and self-pity it had been all she could do to keep breathing.

Her make-up was immaculate now – anyone seeing her would never be able to tell what a cruel hand she'd been dealt this week – as she went in search of the media room, getting a little lost in the maze of back stairs and corridors that made up the Princess and the Pea Inn.

Eventually, she found the closed door at the very bottom of the building in what she guessed must be a recently converted basement. The corridor still smelled strongly of drying paint.

As she touched the door handle, she paused at the scratching, whimpering noises coming from the other side. 'What now? Is there nothing normal in this place?'

No sooner had she pushed the door ajar but the assault began. A grey and black fur ball escaped the room and bounced at her knees, yapping and drooling and turning in circles. The paint smell was even stronger now she was in the glare of the windowless room's downlights.

'Hey! Get off me, these were given to me by the designer, you know?' she said, trying to restrain the puppy and protect her pumps. The dog still danced and pounced, happy to have found a new playmate.

'*Bear!* Leave her alone.'

If the man's deep voice hadn't startled her, the sight of him emerging from around the door in his dark jeans, vest-T, and a shirt tied around his waist, certainly did. He grabbed the pup, scooping the wriggling bundle of fluff into a tattooed arm, and pushed his brown hair back as he straightened up, looking with concern at the scuffs and spots of doggy drool on Nina's shoes.

'Sorry about him. He's excited to see folk after being stuck in here with me most of the day.' His Scottish accent was thick, Nina observed, but he didn't use the same colloquialisms and shortenings that everyone else around here seemed to use. At least she understood this guy, which was handy as she now had a bone to pick with him.

'Are you kidding me? My shoes are wrecked.' She fixed her eyes on Bear.

'He's only little, he doesn't know. Look, I'll pay for them, how much do I owe you?' The man reached a hand to his back pocket and his wallet.

'They retail at five hundred dollars,' Nina replied dryly.

'Jesus! Five *hundred* dollars? For shoes?' His eyes scanned her face, disbelieving. 'That's crazy.'

She merely shrugged, tipping her head pointedly.

'You said they were free?' There was a note of challenge in his voice.

'I *said* they were a gift from the designer.'

'Right, well, that sounds...'

'Irreplaceable?'

'I was going to say stupidly over-priced, but no, I can't replace them. Sorry. But I could clean them up for you. Take them off.'

An exasperated laugh escaped her lips and she shook her head. 'What? I'm not giving you my shoes.'

'Go on, I'll be five minutes.' The man was stooping a little and indicating she should kick them off, flustering her and inciting her annoyance even more.

'Just forget about it. I'll get them fixed when I go home. And I'll send *you* the bill,' she added, narrowing her eyes at Bear under the man's arm. The dog's little pink tongue peeped out of his mouth as he happily swam stumpy legs through the air.

Bear's owner only watched Nina with his head tipped a little, amusement written across his face. He was smirking at her and she hated it, so she glanced into the room.

'You're using the computer?' she asked.

'I'm just finishing up in here. She's all yours.' He swept an arm, welcoming her inside, but she didn't move, looking askance at him now, telling herself to ignore that inadvertent flex of arm muscle as he restrained the squirming dog and diverting her attention from the way his brown eyes were framed with thick, dark spiked lashes – the likes of which Luke would have paid a fortune at Shibui Spa to emulate. Instead she glanced in at the computer and printer, shiny and new, beside a charging station on the table top.

'So this is where they keep the twenty-first century in Port Willow?'

'*Hmm?*' The man cocked his head.

'Nothing. There's no window in there,' said Nina, still on the threshold. 'This paint's probably toxic, you know?'

'Is that so?' He leaned back, relaxed against the frame.

'These cheap brands; they're all deadly. Haven't the owners heard of chalk paint?'

Nina knew a thing or two about decorating, having overseen the interior designer Luke had brought in to remodel his apartment last year, turning his walls from 'feather pillow' white to 'snow day' white and making everyone remark gushingly on the huge difference this carefully considered change had made.

He raised his brows, clearly entertained. 'I'm sure this stuff's fine. I've been working in here all day and I'm still breathing, and I know paint.'

Nina scanned the man's hands and arms where streaks and dots of black and white marked his skin and overlapped with the delicate Celtic knotwork of tattoo ink.

'You're a painter?' Her off-handedness turned to curiosity, then to charm. Finally, she thought. This must be one of the artists this place is supposedly crawling with. He certainly looked bohemian in a rugged sort of a way; Scottish, and stubbled, dark-haired and with something a little devilish behind his eyes. That must be the creative spark.

The man couldn't help but smile all the more. 'I am.'

'What sort of thing do you do?'

'Oh, ceilings, walls...'

'Frescoes? Murals?' She considered him for a long time. He didn't seem the fine art type. 'Street art?'

'Emulsion, skirtings, bit of coving.'

Her face fell.

'I'm a painter and decorator. Name's Mutt.'

He held his free hand out for her to shake before seeing her wince at it as though the dry paint might somehow spoil her immaculate clothing on top of his dog spoiling her shoes. He quickly whipped his hand back, wiping it on his hip.

'Your name's *Mutt*?'

'It's sort of short for Murray.'

'Right. Well if you're finished, Mutt...' She squeezed through the doorframe but not before the Newfoundland pup lunged its head to take a lick at her face.

Mutt pulled the dog away. 'Woah, no kisses.'

Nina didn't join in his laughter and the abrupt look she gave him made him stop.

'Sorry. Right, well... we'll leave you to it. I've just set the computer stuff up. Should all be working fine now. Mind, the walls are still drying.' Putting the dog down, he grabbed his tool belt from the floor and fixed it around his waist.

Nina didn't reply. She was already logging into her work's email server.

'Sorry again, about the shoes.' He hesitated, seeming to linger, watching her with his eyes sharpened, as though wondering if she'd answer. 'Merry Christmas?' Bear watched on too, panting happily.

Nina lifted her head but not her eyes, just as Mutt was giving up on the pleasantries and leaving. '*Hmm?* Yeah, yeah, sure, Merry Christmas. Can you prop the door open when you go,' she muttered, absorbed in her need to reach out to New York.

Mutt sniffed a wry laugh and left with Bear tumbling along behind him, but not before stopping to open the windows all along the outer corridor so the woman with the transatlantic accent, five-hundred-dollar shoes and an aversion to cute puppies could breathe easily.

Chapter Eleven

Sisters

'As long as you're sure?' Atholl said, eyeing Beatrice with concern as they stood on the inn steps that evening, waiting for the car to pull up. It was after eight and entirely dark and starlit along the Port Willow seafront, apart from the glow of the snow and swaying Christmas lights.

'I'm fine, honestly,' she insisted. 'Just excited, that's all.' Beatrice couldn't meet Atholl's eyes. All through dinner service she'd fought against the urge to march straight up to Atholl in the bar where he was pulling pints to tell him the news, but a stronger instinct had warned her off.

She'd done it before, told someone she was pregnant, and she'd watched their heart swell and all their loving, fatherly instincts kicking in. Then she'd watched Rich shatter when the sonographer told them their tiny boy was gone.

She needed to know for sure. A hunch wasn't enough. Even if all she had the appetite for at dinner time was sliced tomatoes on toast and even that she had almost thrown up straight afterwards, and, come to think of it, her waistband did feel kind of tight, but that could easily be from all the lovely inn food this winter. Luckily Gene had been too absorbed in cooking his cullen skink to notice how green she'd been as she helped serve his seafood specials to the crafters and locals getting festive in the busy bar restaurant, so he wouldn't be mentioning anything to his younger brother.

Atholl leaned closer. 'You know if there's anything worrying you, you're to tell me, don't you, Beattie? And I you. Even if it's just a sma' thing? Mind?'

Beatrice nodded, recalling the promise they'd made one another at the coral beach back in the summer. There was nothing the couple kept from each other now and their openness had enriched their relationship, making everything easier and more intimate, deliciously so.

'I promise I'll tell you whenever I have something to tell, OK?'

Atholl, looking not entirely convinced, turned to her and swept a gentle hand over her cheek. Beatrice could feel him surveying her eyes, dark-circled from crying earlier. She was relieved for the sudden flash of bright headlights that lit up the inn doorway.

'Here they are,' Beatrice cried, breaking away.

Atholl shifted the traffic cones from the best parking spot in town, right by the doorstep, and waved the car in.

'Angela!' Beatrice cried, seeing her sister stepping out, grinning and stiff from their ten-hour drive.

As the sisters hugged, Atholl walked round to the road-side and helped Vic, who was struggling with a nappy bag and some contraption she informed Atholl was a baby bumby, which didn't help the bemused Atholl at all, but he filled his arms and carried the women's luggage inside, coming back to lift the sleeping Clara into the inn in her car seat. Vic kissed Beatrice's cheek as she passed inside, following her tiny daughter.

'Did you get it?' Beatrice whispered to her sister.

'I did,' Angela replied, pulling the slim box from her coat pocket right there on the pavement.

'Oh my God, put it away!' Beatrice cried, before ushering her sister inside, glancing up and down the street in case they'd been spotted with the pregnancy test. Had Seth been nearby there'd be no hope of keeping their secret beyond the call for last orders.

–

Two pink lines. Bright pink.

Beatrice was still clutching her hand across her mouth, frozen to her spot, perched on the laundry basket. So far, no words had escaped her.

'It's OK, just take a minute,' Angela told her, letting the stick her sister had at first been too afraid to look at, fall to her side.

'Ninety-nine percent accurate?' Beatrice gasped at last.

Angela laughed. 'So the box says.'

'When did it even happen? I… I…' Beatrice shook her head, unable to fathom it.

'Come here.' Angela pulled her sister into a hug. Beatrice's legs wobbled beneath her as she stumbled into her arms.

'So?' Angela prompted.

'So, what?'

'Are we happy, or…?'

Beatrice bobbed her head, a lot. 'Course we're happy.'

Angela scanned her sister's expression. Beatrice was still nodding to herself with huge, wide eyes. 'OK, I believe you.' Angela couldn't help grinning. 'I didn't know you guys were trying.'

'We weren't. I mean, we were using condoms at first, then I went back on the pill and...' She shrugged. 'I don't know what to tell you.'

'Shall I go get him?'

'Who?'

'Atholl, of course.'

'No, no, no.' She stopped her sister leaving. 'Stay here.'

'You don't think he'll be happy?'

'I...' Beatrice couldn't finish the utterance. She was sure Atholl would be happy. Very happy in fact, and that's why she was afraid.

Angela pressed on. 'I'm so glad for you. Mum would be really happy too.'

Beatrice's smile bloomed then fell when the sadness of it all hit her. How she wished her mum was here. She'd have told her first, before anyone else.

Angela rubbed a hand up her sister's arm, letting the silence speak volumes about the great hole that had been left in their lives when she died. After a while she cleared her throat and wiped a tear. 'I can't believe you're pregnant again.'

Beatrice's stoic half smile faltered. 'Do you mean you can't believe I'm pregnant again, and to somebody else?'

'*What?* No! It sounds to me like that's what *you're* thinking.' Angela gave her sister a level look.

'*Shh*, somebody will hear!' Beatrice hissed. Damn Angela and her sisterly insight. She was right. If anybody in the world knew her best, it was her.

'Don't you think they'll be wondering why we're hiding in the toilet together?' Angela said, quietly this time, but Beatrice's mind was racing elsewhere.

She *was* thinking about what people might think – and what, deep down, Atholl might think after he'd had time to process the news. Here she was, pregnant again, when the baby she'd made with Richard would have been only a few months' old, had he lived. Beatrice took a deep breath. Pregnant so soon and with another man's baby? Something about it felt vaguely scandalous to her, or at least she was convincing herself that's how other people might see it.

'I know what you're thinking,' Angela warned. 'And you can stop.'

'What?'

'Who cares what the gossips are going to say. You're having a baby, and that's wonderful. Do you think me and Vic let the tattle-tales steal our happiness? *Hmm?* Besides, who here knows about you and Rich's baby anyway?'

Beatrice ran through the people she'd told when she'd realised it was the taboo nature of her grief that was making her ill, giving her panic attacks, and making her bitter. She'd started talking about her baby in the summer and found it helped her so much. She'd told Mrs Fergusson, Atholl's little sister, Sheila, Gene, and Kitty. Even Mrs Mair the housekeeper knew. She tried to imagine their reactions now. *What? Again?* they might say. *Already? Except this time it's not with your husband, it's with Atholl.*

Beatrice overcame her panic to find her voice. 'Even if other people don't think it's weird to be pregnant with another man's baby, they'll definitely think it's too soon. What if Atholl thinks it too? He'd be too nice to say it out loud, but still…' Beatrice said, her eyes darting around the room, seeing nothing clearly in her anxious state.

Angela was shaking her head, trying to calm her sister. She had met Atholl once before at her and Vic's Warwickshire wedding back in November, and if she'd had any reservations about him before that day they were definitely put to rest by the sight of him in his kilt holding Beatrice's hand all through the ceremony, offering her a tissue when she was sobbing happy tears, and bringing her *two* slices of wedding cake and a cup of tea from the buffet because he knew her well enough to understand one wasn't enough.

Beatrice rambled on. 'They'll think I'm mad, tempting fate. Maybe it'll happen again!'

'It might,' Angela said, very gently, and taking Beatrice's hands in her own. 'Statistically, it's more likely it *won't* happen again and you'll get a take-home baby this time. Three in every four pregnancies work out.'

This definitely helped. Beatrice liked figures and facts, things there was real-world evidence for, things she could research further to reassure herself.

'This time, things might be perfect, OK?' Angela said again.

'OK,' Beatrice echoed, realising she was shaking. The sisters leaned their foreheads together and Angela raised the test stick between them once more so they could both gaze at it, and through the strange dizziness and shock, Beatrice replayed her sister's words. Things might be perfect this time.

–

In the end, telling Atholl hadn't been as difficult as Beatrice feared. The words had just tumbled out. He'd watched her all through supper in the little private sun room that Beatrice had turned from a dusty and cluttered storeroom into their cosy, comfortable den. She'd been playing with Clara and asking questions of Vic and Angela but with a faraway look that had worried him. He'd seen

Beatrice ill before, back in the summer, sick from secrecy and heartbreak. He couldn't bear to see her suddenly so sad and had said so.

'I'm sorry to spoil your reunion, but do you no' agree Beattie's sickening for something?'

'I think you might be right,' Angela had replied, pointedly, and the little family had hurried through dessert and said their goodnights, leaving the couple alone.

Atholl had guided Beatrice into their bedroom next door.

'Sit yourself here,' he told her, watching her settle on the bed and pressing a palm to her forehead. 'You're no' hot, that's good. You might be coming down with something though. Patrick the fishmonger had the flu last week, laid him out for three days, his father told me.'

'I don't have flu,' Beatrice said, but Atholl was out the room again, stopping only to switch on the lights on their little Christmas tree.

Alone, Beatrice looked around at what had once been Atholl's bedroom and filled with willow projects and his designs lying around everywhere on paper. She'd worked hard making it a relaxing place for the two of them.

When he returned from the kitchens, Atholl was carrying a tray and laughing to himself.

'What is it?' she asked, glad he was happy, letting it lighten her mood too.

'I stopped Gene in the kitchens and told him wee Clara would be needing some dry oats, a nip o' whisky and a carrot, and maybe a mince pie. You should o' seen his face. He says to me, "Would she no' prefer some Weetabix?" I had to tell him it was for Father Christmas and his reindeer!'

He was still laughing when he reached the bed and presented her with a tray laden with black tea, honey and lemon, two bannocks, and a present wrapped in holly leaf paper.

'What's this?' she'd smiled, opening his gift as Atholl joined her on the bed.

'In case I dinnae hae time tomorrow to give you your present.'

Inside was a hinged frame of antique silver; on one side was a photo behind glass of the two of them, a selfie taken at the Coral Beach back at the end of summer with their heads pressed together and Echo peering over Atholl's shoulder, making sure he wasn't missing any fun.

Beatrice had laughed. 'It's lovely, thank you, Atholl.' She touched the empty frame facing their picture. 'What's this one for?'

'Whatever you wish. Maybe we'll get a braw photo of us all tomorrow? Your first Christmas at the inn. Or put in one of you and Angela, Vic and Clara?'

Beatrice only hesitated a little. 'Or a scan picture?'

Atholl didn't say anything, thinking.

'Because pretty soon we'll be having a baby scan.' Beatrice looked into Atholl's face and watched his expression shifting. She had never seen anyone react with such unfettered, simple joy.

'Beattie? Are we… are we having a baby?' The tears were in his eyes and his arms around her body already. Pulling back, he checked again. 'Are we?' The laughter and hope in his eyes made Beatrice's heart leap. She nodded and they sank into each other's arms again. 'And you're both all right? That's why you've been so pale!' He spoke each thought as it came to him, holding nothing back. 'I cannae believe it! My heart might burst! Have you told Angela? She must be made up for you. Are *you* glad? You're glad, are ye' no?'

Beatrice let her happy tears fall, listening to him, nodding all the while, telling him that of course she was glad, very glad. And so, Beatrice and Atholl got under the covers and talked away what was left of Christmas Eve, making plans to call the doctor when the surgery re-opened after Christmas, Atholl throwing out ideas to shift the wardrobes to make room for a cot, and a hundred other lovely things, all while Beatrice rested her head on Atholl's broad chest where his heart beat a wild ceilidh for happiness.

Chapter Twelve

A Christmas Gift

All along the waterfront at Port Willow Bay, the street is silent. Low tide and a hard frost have left slushy rock pools dotting the shoreline and all unexplored by the usual bands of dog walkers and happy children with crabbing nets and wellies, because today is Christmas day.

The sun has barely risen over the horizon, it seems, as the day holds onto its deep winter gloom and the snow still falls in flurries from a grey sky.

The morning church bells of St Magnus' have long since rung out, drawing a few early risers to the morning service where they'd sat shivering amongst the pews, singing about a baby's birth long ago and beneath a hot sun.

In the hills and meadows above the village every bird and wild creature now huddles for warmth somewhere unseen, and every farmer and fisherman takes their ease, enjoying their families and firesides. Yet for some, Christmas morning has brought not one ounce of solace and warmth.

–

Up in room seven, Nina sat on the floor at the foot of the bed, her knees drawn to her chest, preparing to make the call she'd been dreading.

'Mum?'

'Leave a message after the beep.'

Nina glared at the phone, which she held below her mouth with the speaker setting on.

'Oh, *um*, it's me. Maybe you're all still in bed? Or you're at Auntie Lynn's? And Toby's spending Christmas with Dad?'

Dammit, she thought. She should have asked if they had changed their plans for a cosy Christmas at home once they'd discovered that, once again, she wasn't coming back. Maybe they hadn't wanted to be alone today, just the two of them, and so they'd split up to spend the day in happier, busier households than their own. Christmas at Dad and Tina's would probably be more fun for Toby, her little brother, what with the three younger boys there too, her dad's other kids.

She looked down at her phone as she spoke into it. The clock told her it was eight a.m. In any normal year Toby would have been awake and ripping into gifts in front of the tree at least two hours ago, but now that he was sixteen and all he wanted was the latest iPhone, perhaps the excitement had faded for him? She wasn't there to find out, and she still had her news to break. Maybe an answering service declaration of guilt was preferable to trying to reach her mum on her mobile anyway? She could get it out of the way and avoid all the questions doing it like this.

'So, *um*, I'm not in New York. I was given an assignment over the holidays in... in Scotland, actually.' It sounded worse now she was saying it out loud. This information was likely to hurt her mum far more than thinking she was staying in the States for Christmas.

Here they were in the same time zone, albeit at opposite ends of the land, but still, her mum probably wouldn't be able to stop herself wondering why her daughter hadn't come home for a night or two.

'It was all a bit last minute. My boss said he was relying on me to represent the company over here in the UK. It's quite exciting really.' She winced at the truth-stretching but had no intention of admitting what had really happened; that she'd been dumped and sent away on some half-baked buying assignment.

'I'm here meeting with potential brand collaborators, lots of meetings lined up, you can imagine the sort of thing. Busy, busy, busy.'

She closed her eyes and pressed the phone to her forehead. *Ugh!* What had she become?

'Anyway, I'm having a great time. My contacts here are treating me to Christmas dinner later on.' She thought of that tall guy's invitation to eat with everyone in the bar restaurant at four o'clock today. There was nothing she'd rather do less, but her mother didn't need to know she intended to spend the day alone, researching the Highland arts scene.

'I hope my presents arrived from New York. You can always use the gift receipt and return them if you don't like them.'

Nina thought she'd done well this year, playing it safe by sending Jo Malone gift baskets. Who doesn't like candles and perfume? She knew, however, her mum had very different ideas about gifting, so maybe she wouldn't care for them after all.

She looked around the room, emptiness in the pit of her stomach like she'd never felt before. This wasn't just hunger, or homesickness; this was something else. This was waking up alone on Christmas day in a strange room in a strange country without a single present to open. This was wanting a hug from her mum and knowing she was miles away – they may as well have been separated by the Atlantic she was so distant and unreachable right now.

'Sorry I won't have time to come and see you,' she said weakly.

She'd searched last night on the inn's computer. How many miles between Port Willow and Hove? Six hundred and forty-one miles, or a twelve-hour drive.

She'd asked Mitch if he could book her a flight just so she could spend the day there and he'd told her not on company expenses he wouldn't, and she'd found there were no seats to be had on any of the cross-country flights anyway, not at this time of year and not at the very last minute. She'd tried not to cry in the media room in case that annoying guy with the laughter in his eyes was still hanging around to make her feel ridiculous just by the way he looked at her, as though she were only here to provide him with fun at her expense.

Anyway, there was no time for a journey down south, she had work to do. She had to keep her eye on the prize. She'd asked Mitch to firm up her return flight to JFK last night.

'January seventh, six-forty a.m., Edinburgh International,' he'd messaged back.

She was going home soon, and triumphantly too, she hoped.

'Maybe I can come and see you in the spring?' she told her mum's voicemail. 'I could try to get some time off.'

She knew this wouldn't be any comfort to her mother; she'd said it so many times before and had never once used her annual leave entitlement; she just couldn't escape her work commitments. In all her time in New York she hadn't even taken one whole weekend off. That's why this Christmas had been so important to her. She'd been pinning so many of her hopes upon it.

She shook away her most secret hope as it popped into her head again, thinking now how preposterous it seemed in the cold winter light – how naive and girlish.

She'd hoped that with a little encouragement to focus only on her and not on work, just for a few days, and what with it being the most wonderful time of the year and everything, that Luke would have had enough time to think about what mattered to him most and he'd conclude that it was her. And if she planned the perfect, cosy Christmas, just the two of them, he'd realise they really were a winning team, a dynamic duo, and maybe he'd produce a neat little box and get down on one knee in front of their ten-foot tree in his one-and-a-half-thousand-square-foot apartment and he'd ask her the question while a Cartier Destineé cushion-cut solitaire with its pave studded white gold band glinted and glistened and the Rat Pack crooned Christmas songs over the apartment's invisible sound system.

She tried not to sigh. 'Better go, Mum. Lots to do… Happy Christmas.'

She let the phone slide to the floor as she dropped her shoulders and hung her head, thinking she might just sit there all morning, feeling sorry for herself. A knock at her door made her pull herself together again.

On blowing her nose and trying to fix her face, she found that whoever had knocked had now gone but they'd left the breakfast tray she'd requested last night (egg whites, breakfast tea, no milk this time). Gene had taken the liberty of adding little dishes of grilled tomato and some buttery field mushrooms and granary toast. Beside all this on the tray was a little red tartan gift bag with greenery sticking out the open top.

Taking it inside, she found it was a tiny plant with a handwritten tag.

> *For you, Nina, a Salix bebbiana, better known as a North American or 'diamond' willow. It needs plenty of fresh air, water and light, as do we all at this time of year. If you plant it in the spring you'll find it can grow to twenty feet or more.*
>
> *We're so glad you chose to celebrate the holidays with us this year, and we hope you'll have a very Merry Christmas.*
>
> *From Beatrice, Atholl, Eugene and Kitty and everyone at the Princess and the Pea Inn.*

Nina looked at the sapling in the white light from the window, smiling quizzically. She'd never had to look after a living thing before.

She set the pot on yesterday's empty shortbread dish and let the plant drink a few drops of cold water from the sink. Closing the window so it wouldn't be in a draught she set the whole thing down on the sill before taking her breakfast tray to the bed where all her papers and notes lay. She was ready to work, but not before she made a start on her food. The buttered mushrooms on toast disappeared first and made her shake her head at their delicious, salty simplicity. She resolved to order the exact same thing tomorrow morning.

As the morning passed by and her eyes grew weary from reading, she'd check her phone waiting for replies to her texts – she'd caved and messaged old work friends in New York, hoping her Christmas greetings were enough to remind them of all the good times they'd shared – but not a single reply arrived, and so the day dragged on.

As four o'clock approached and the smell of festive food drifted upstairs, she prayed someone would remember to bring her tray so she didn't have to slope downstairs in her pyjamas to ask for something to eat. Glancing up at the delicate willow stems and little bit of leaf in its pot on the windowsill she found that, although her heart was heavy, she wanted to smile at it.

Chapter Thirteen

Mrs Fergusson's Secret

When Christmas comes to Port Willow it is a quiet affair; that is the Highland way. Good food and fellowship are all that matter today and nowhere along the snowy coast is that more evident than in the fairy-lit glow of the Princess and the Pea bar restaurant where Gene Fergusson served up his seafood special starters and champagne bubbles danced in every glass.

The room was bustling with Christmas Day diners when Beatrice made her way to the staff table, set beautifully with gold crackers. The guests were already on their turkey and trimmings course and Mrs Mair was hovering with the cranberry sauce and a gravy boat, making sure everyone had all they needed.

Paul McCartney was singing over the speakers about simply having a wonderful Christmas time and beneath the great ball of mistletoe in the middle of the room stood Atholl with Clara in his arms dancing to the music.

Clara was rosy-cheeked from teething and her wet eyes sparkled as she laughed with her uncle who, Beatrice thought, might be more than a little besotted with her. Beatrice could only stare at them, her heart expanding at the sight.

The glance Vic failed to hide from Beatrice let her know that Angela hadn't managed to keep her promise to tell no one about nipping into the motorway services in search of a pregnancy test for her big sister. Beatrice widened her eyes at Vic and the couple smiled knowingly at one another.

Mutt made to move from the head of the table to let Atholl and Clara take the top seat.

'No need for that. Sit, sit,' Atholl assured him, insisting that the next chair down suited him fine. With Atholl still bouncing the little girl to the music, the men chatted about what stage the renovations had reached now that Mutt had downed tools for Christmas.

'There's only the corridors to strip and paint, the breakfast room to re-paper and the outside masonry to freshen up once the weather improves,' Mutt told him.

'Reckon you'll need a few more weeks to fit all that in,' said Atholl.

'Mid-February, I reckon.'

'You'll no' want to leave us by then,' Atholl smiled, unusually bright and buoyant today.

'*We* won't want you to leave,' added Beatrice, sitting down. 'It's been nice having our very own handyman around, but, most of all, it's been nice getting to know you.'

'You're not from the village?' Vic asked, turning to Mutt. 'I thought you were related to Atholl?'

'He's my mum's cousin,' Mutt replied, 'but my family are from Pennan in Aberdeenshire. When Atholl heard I wanted to get away for a while, he took us in.'

'Us?' said Angela.

Mutt leaned back in his chair to reveal the sleeping ball of fluff that was Bear under the table.

Gene and Kitty appeared at once. Gene bringing the starters and Kitty with a big jug of iced water.

The plan was that Clara, Vic and Angela, Mrs Fergusson, Atholl and Beatrice would eat while Gene and Kitty snatched stolen moments from the Christmas kitchen to sit down between courses, have a quick bite and celebrate the day.

Mrs Fergusson was in her prettiest heather twinset and her rope of antique Scottish pearls for the occasion. She'd been unusually quiet since Atholl had driven her over from Skye that morning.

'Your Uncle Atholl's a braw dancer, is he no', wee Clara?' Kitty remarked, filling the water glasses before perching on a chair and taking a hunk of bread from the basket.

Laughing, Atholl delivered Clara into her highchair but, defeated, left the unfathomable straps and clasps to Angela.

Gene set down some scallop starters and bustled off again to fetch more. Mrs Fergusson inhaled their aroma approvingly and reached for her cutlery. The entire scallop shell was baked inside a case of golden pastry, Gene's recent speciality, since he'd embraced his role as head chef with renewed gusto – now that Kitty was around to inspire him.

'It's no' often I get to cradle a wee bairn,' Atholl said. 'My nephew Archie's no' so wee anymore either.'

'That he is not. Such a bonny laddie,' Mrs Fergusson put in, and everyone seemed to look pointedly between Beatrice and Atholl, all except the utterly unaware Gene, now back from the kitchen (he couldn't be trusted with secrets for fear he blurted them out) and Mrs Fergusson (who Atholl and Beatrice decided to tell only after a scan confirmed all their hopes).

Atholl glanced at his mum, clearing his throat, a little panicked she'd pick up on the strange atmosphere. 'Where's that sad-looking lassie in the fancy gear? Room seven?' he said, changing the subject.

'Nina?' Gene said, standing over Kitty's chair, accepting a hunk of bread from her and talking through buttery bites. 'She just asked to have her Christmas dinner in the computer room.'

'Media centre,' Beatrice corrected.

'Aye, well either way, she's alone on Christmas Day. Says she's got work to do.'

'Poor thing,' said Beatrice. 'Tell her I've put a ticket behind the bar for her for the Hogmanay speed-dating event. She can spectate and have a few drinks. She can't work all the time.'

Gene was shaking his head. 'I dinnae understand her, coming in here wearing sunglasses at noon in the depths of December and looking for lumpy tea.'

'Bubble tea,' Kitty corrected him.

Gene pressed on. 'Here, she gave me her card when she checked in.' Rummaging in his apron pocket, he handed the glossy grey card to Mrs Fergusson who, instead of looking at it, passed it directly to Beatrice.

'Nina Miller. Trend Forecaster and Client Brand Relations Facilitator,' she read aloud.

'Whit exactly is that when it's at home?' Gene carried on, bemused.

'Well, take your starter, for instance,' Kitty said, breaking the pastry casing and pulling open the shell, releasing the steamy fragrance of scallop and white wine sauce. 'You heard about a similar dish being served in that fancy place in Edinburgh, you tried the recipe and then you adapted it, giving it your own wee twist, and now it's taken off here. Folk come in asking if it's on the specials menu, don't they?'

Gene shrugged. 'They do.'

'Well then, you spotted a trend, picked up on it, and now it's getting bigger.'

'There you are, you see, Gene? You're a trend forecaster,' Atholl's eyes sparkled wickedly even as he reached a hand over the table top to take Beatrice's, having noticed how pale she'd turned at the sight of the scallops.

'You're no' hungry, Beatrice?' Mrs Fergusson asked as she polished off the creamy sauce inside her own shell with a hunk of bread.

'I had a big breakfast,' Beatrice lied. 'Nina's our guest, so we need to look after her. It's not easy arriving here all alone and feeling like a fish out of water,' she added, hoping to deflect attention away from her untouched food.

The room was growing livelier by the minute. Locals and guests were enjoying family meals, making toasts with Mrs Mair's mulled wine, and every one of them excited for more snowfall overnight. The two women potters had already joined forces with the watercolourists and were sharing a table with Mr Garstang, the painting teacher, who didn't often venture out to the pub. The teenage willow-weavers were at another table with their mums. Both girls had finished eating and were sipping Cokes and setting up the new iPhones they'd opened that morning.

'How do!'

Everyone turned to face Seth, who had just come in, brushing snow from his tweed jacket.

'Are you joining us, Seth?' Atholl asked.

'I wouldn't like to intrude, it's Christmas Day and a family time,' said Seth, already pulling up a chair in spite of his protestations and calling to Mrs Mair for a bowl of her Scotch broth.

'Merry Christmas, Eilidh,' he said to Mrs Fergusson.

'Seth.' The old woman nodded. 'Are you alone for Christmas?'

'I had a bit of lunch at my laddie's place at twelve. He's meeting his pals now for a drink.'

Beatrice set about introducing Vic and Angela, and Seth twinkled his moley eyes at the mothers.

'How old's the wee one now?' he asked, as Mrs Mair set a steaming bowl of soup in front of him.

'She turned one in October,' Vic informed him.

'They grow so fast,' Seth told her. 'That's my wee laddie over by the bar there.' Seth indicated the six-foot-tall sandy-haired man in a red Christmas jumper who waved back at his dad from where he was chatting with the other lads from the seal-spotting tourist boats.

'They do, I can hardly keep up,' Vic told him. 'One minute she was a helpless newborn, the next she's... well...'

Everyone at the table cast their eyes towards Clara, delightedly feeding herself great fistfuls of breadsticks and squashed banana, which was oozing out between her fingers. Echo had positioned himself by her feet, hoping for dropped scraps. The more discerning Bear slept on under the table.

'And you work, Vic?' Seth asked.

'We both do,' Angela replied. 'Clara's at nursery during the day.'

'Aye, well, you ken what they say. It takes a village to raise a bairn,' Seth said sagely.

'We'd have been lost back at the start without Bea babysitting and taking Clara for walks so we could catch up with work or get some sleep,' Vic replied. Angela smiled brightly at her big sister. 'And thank God her nursery's only down the road from our place in Warwick, and she likes it there. We miss Bea now she's left us, though. It's definitely harder on our own. My parents are in Gloucester, so…' Vic shrugged and let the words fall away.

Angela and Beatrice didn't have to look at one another to know what was going on in the other's head. They were thinking of their own mum who hadn't lived to see Clara born, and how bitterly she'd longed to stay to help with the baby and to see Clara growing up. Beatrice wrinkled her eyes at her sister, telling her she felt it too.

'Aye, it takes a village,' Seth said again, a solemn note in his voice. 'We had Mary's mother and her sisters nearby when Johnny was wee, they did a lot to help. I was away on the boat most days. Looking back, I missed a lot of things I should a' been there for.'

Vic was nodding and carrying on the conversation between bites of pastry. 'After Clara was born, Angela was exhausted from the caesarean. Nobody seems to remember someone's just had major surgery; they just expected her to get on with looking after a baby while she was just trying to master getting up and walking again.'

'You were there to help though, Vic, so we managed,' Angela said as though that were the end of the discussion.

'She needed all the help she could get after the surgery.' Vic was talking across the table directly at Beatrice now. 'And that's without the rib-flare, the SPD, the sleeplessness, varicose veins…'

'Well, that was delicious,' interrupted Angela pointedly, crossing her cutlery on her plate and throwing a warning look at Vic before glancing towards Beatrice who was visibly wilting.

'Oh, of course, that's all forgotten about when your baby smiles for the first time, or when she says Mama,' Vic threw in hurriedly.

'Except Clara's first word was frog.' Angela laughed, hoping the subject of pregnancy woes could be forgotten.

'Why don't we do presents?' Atholl asked, clapping his hands.

'Good idea,' Beatrice agreed, reaching beneath the table and drawing out a card. 'This is for you,' she said, handing it to Mrs Fergusson, who spilled a little of the champagne she was sipping in surprise.

'Oh! Thank you, dear, I'll open it later.'

'Go on, Ma, open it now. It's from all of us,' Atholl urged.

Mrs Fergusson looked panicked as she turned the envelope in her hands, all eyes upon her. Once she'd opened it and glanced inside, she laid it down on the table and smiled. 'Very nice.'

'Oh, you're not keen?' Beatrice asked, confused.

'No' keen?' she echoed, before looking down at her plate, a little guiltily.

'On the mani-pedicurist?' Beatrice urged. 'We thought you'd like her visiting you at home. She only travels through Skye once a month. She does facials too, if you'd rather.'

'Oh!' Mrs Fergusson opened the card again, nodding. 'I see. It says you've booked me in?'

'Of course, Ma.' Gene said, still hovering over Kitty's shoulder where he'd been stealing bites of her food and was now looking narrow-eyed at Atholl then back to his mother.

'Could you… could you no' read that just now?' Atholl asked gently, and Mrs Fergusson tightened her lips. By this time the whole table was in alarm and all thoughts of Christmas dinner abandoned.

'Mum, what's the matter?' Atholl asked, unsteady, and Mrs Fergusson steeled herself to say out loud the secret she'd been keeping for months.

–

'Macular degeneration?'

Kitty Wake repeated Mrs Fergusson's words after she'd finished explaining what the doctor had told her during the trip to the eye hospital and everyone had fallen silent making Mrs Fergusson scold them about fussing, but with the troubled look of a woman who lived alone on Skye, a road bridge and a twisting drive away from her adult sons, from whom she had kept her secret for weeks now, not wanting to worry them when they were finally settling down after so long adrift.

'Sheila's helping me around the house and with reading important letters and such. Dinnae fash yerselves about me. I'll be fine, and it doesnae hurt at all, that's a mercy, is it no'?' she insisted, though everyone knew that Sheila, the eldest of the Fergusson sisters, was kept busy with her own young family, especially baby Archibald, now a wriggling, rolling, chunky thing well on his way to his first birthday, and her husband always away in Edinburgh on business.

Sheila hadn't accepted the invitation to the inn for Christmas dinner, saying she'd rather have a quiet day at home since her husband was there so rarely. Everyone had understood.

Young Kelly Fergusson, Atholl's little sister, had taken a job teaching horticulturalists at a college in Wales, having at last flown the family nest back in the autumn, so she wouldn't be around to help her mum as the darkness drew in.

Mrs Fergusson tried to comfort her family. 'I can see the telly no' bad, when I sit close enough, and there's the wireless, and the audiobooks Sheila downloads onto the e-pod for me.' Nobody corrected the elderly matriarch. 'Only thing I'll mind missing is seeing wee Archibald growing; he's bigger every time he visits. And my films, of course, I'll miss my films.'

After that, Christmas day rather lost its lustre and the family had drawn their chairs closer together, talking more quietly, as Atholl held his mother's hand and Gene pulled up the chair by her side.

Beatrice, however, was already letting her thoughts run riot. She prized nothing better than a problem to solve, solutions to find, and plans to put in place. She wasn't going to glumly accept this new turn of events. Mrs Fergusson was alive and well and Beatrice was going to make her life the very best it could be for as long as can be. She longed to get back to her little sun room to start her scheming. She revelled in the familiar buzz of being needed and, yet again, she was finding she had exactly the right brand of organisational zeal the Fergusson family needed.

The fervour was enough to lighten her anxiety about her own recent discovery. If she helped Mrs Fergusson, she could put off thinking about her own predicament.

Yes, she was going to be as useful and as busy as possible helping Mrs Fergusson, and maybe by the time she'd exhausted her usefulness she'd feel a little more assured about the life growing inside of her. Until then she had every reasonable excuse to hold the tiny dream at arm's length.

Chapter Fourteen

Inviting Glenda

'Oh no,' said Atholl the next evening, coming to a stop inside the door of the sun room, having found Beatrice by the crackling fire, eyes narrowed with concentration, pencil in hand, hunched over the little yellow Formica table she'd picked up at the General Stores' thrift furniture section and now called her 'command centre'. 'You've got that look in your eyes.'

'The just-struck-upon-a-genius-idea kind of look?' Beatrice smiled back, watching Atholl stripping out of his waxed winter coat and dark scarf, enjoying the lovely buzz of seeing him again after seven hours apart while she had run the inn and he'd talked his – slightly hungover and overfed – crafting holidaymakers through Boxing Day's willow demonstration – making little woven birdfeeders.

'It's more of an up-to-no-good look,' Atholl said, coming to sit beside her at the table, pulling up one of the vinyl chairs Beatrice had rescued at the same time as the retro table.

Clara was fast asleep in a baby sleeping bag on the sofa, bundled beside a rolled blanket to stop her falling. Her mums were on a snowy, starlit walk along the seafront after dinner; their last chance for any time alone before heading home to Warwick in the morning.

Beatrice had talked them into it, waving them off from the door and watching them holding hands awkwardly as they strolled off remarking to each other how it had been months since they'd actually held hands; someone usually had pram handles to push or a baby to carry.

Atholl kissed his girlfriend and she lifted her eyes once more to smile for him. Since they were babysitting Clara, and Beatrice obviously had a bee in her bonnet about something, there was no chance of the pair of them sneaking off to their shared inn room, tumbling into bed and letting the evening slip away, as they often had as the dark nights drew in.

Beatrice waggled her eyebrows impishly and laughed. 'I might have outdone myself with this one.'

'Oh aye?' Atholl leaned close again for another kiss which she willingly gave. 'Better than the redesigned layout of the But 'n' Ben? Better than the willow products website you insisted the business needed? Or the turning of the inn's junk room into this cosy wee sun room, just for us?' Each question was punctuated with a slow, smiling kiss.

'Better than all of that.'

The moment Christmas dinner was over yesterday and the guests were all happily sleeping off the champagne or taking their Christmas day constitutional along the jetty and Mrs Fergusson had been safely shuttled back to her cottage in the shadow of the Black Cuillin on Skye, now permanently sitting under the damp grey haze of winter, Beatrice had done what she did best. She'd spent Christmas night searching every medical journal and text book she had access to online, paid a small fortune in fees to read scholarly articles behind paywalls, taken pages of notes and finally, sadly, broken it to Atholl that there was very little to be done to help. There was no remedy to be found. Mrs Fergusson was likely to lose her central vision completely.

Of course, then, seeing Atholl's breaking heart, she'd done what she always did next in these situations. She'd swung into action. A list of local nursing agencies had been found and she'd already emailed every one of them hoping to arrange weekly visits to Mrs Fergusson. Then she'd emailed the local paper with an advert for a daily housekeeper.

Hoping those would prove fruitful in the New Year, she had drawn up a rota to bring inn-cooked meals to her, lifting the weight of responsibility from overwrought but uncomplaining Sheila, spreading the load between the many, many people who loved Mrs Fergusson.

No one was surprised when Seth McVie volunteered himself and his bicycle for the job of helping ferry the food from the mainland to Skye, in spite of being over eighty himself and always busy with something or other. He wanted to help the woman he'd known since they were both bairns.

Yet Beatrice hadn't been able to stop there. She was no ordinary planner. Her brain had ticked away until the early hours, wishing she could do more.

'I've struck upon it, at last,' she announced to Atholl now as he tried to get a peek at her notebook, the glow of the fire making his hair shine like copper coils. 'I'm going to get Glenda to visit the village.'

'Naw, none the wiser,' Atholl said, tipping his head, seemingly to better take in her sparkling eyes, bright with enthusiasm.

'Well, you remember Richard?'

Atholl sniffed a wry laugh at this. Beatrice was in no doubt he remembered her ex-husband gate-crashing the Harvest Home ceilidh on the last night of Beatrice's summer holiday, trying to convince her to leave with him, even though he'd been the one jumping ship on their – admittedly sinking – marriage months before, leaving her to grieve the loss of their baby alone.

Seeing Atholl's cynical expression, Beatrice quickly carried on. 'Well, when I first met him, he owned a vintage cinema mobile, Glenda. She was *gorgeous*. Enough seats for a couple of families to squeeze inside, and I'm sure I remember a popcorn machine, and she only showed lovely old Hollywood classics.'

At this Atholl couldn't help smiling.

'Do you think your mum would like to see Gene Kelly on the big screen again?' Beatrice asked.

Atholl raised a what-do-you-think? eyebrow and Beatrice recalled the first time she'd seen the framed posters of the movie star lining the upstairs landing at the inn, a relic from the old days when Mrs Fergusson and Atholl's late father ran the inn by themselves, and their children – two of them named after the Hollywood legend – played on the beach across the road from breakfast 'til tea time.

Beatrice had found the obsession eccentric at the time but since she'd spent a run of lazy Sunday mornings in bed with Atholl binge-watching the star's biggest hits, she'd come to see the appeal too.

'Will Richard want to bring the van, though? It's a long way to come. And how would we afford to pay him?' Atholl addressed all this to the fire, getting lost in the logistics of it all.

The inn was certainly busier than it had been in years, what with Atholl's crafting holidaymakers coming for a fortnight at a time to try their hand at new activities with all the local experts Beatrice had rounded up and pressed into (well-paid) service during her few short months in the village. Yet, even with the upturn in guests, there wasn't money to burn bringing a travelling cinema all the way from England.

'That's the beauty of it!' Beatrice beamed. 'Rich sold the van years ago. It still does the rounds at festivals and game fairs, weddings and fetes all over the country. If we can convince them to bring Glenda to our Easter craft festival we wouldn't have to pay for the van. We could just book it and have it turn up. The van's new owner would keep any profits and your mum could see her films while she still can.' Beatrice was clearly enjoying the buzz of organising once more.

Atholl knew how much she missed her old job at the Arts Hub in Warwickshire; the job she'd lost due to council cuts after nineteen years spent bringing communities together – something Beatrice excelled at.

'A festival, eh? I thought it was a small crafting exhibition for the locals, a coffee morning kind of thing?'

'It wouldn't be a festival as such, but there'd be no harm in expanding upon an already good idea, making it a little bit bigger? It'll still be a fun community day, and your mum can watch her favourite movies along with the other villagers and visitors. Easy!'

'You've already asked the cinema van's owner, haven't you?'

Beatrice grinned, casting a quick glance at her phone where this morning's text conversation with Helena, Glenda's new owner, was.

Atholl nodded, knowing this was likely a done deal and nothing would dissuade her now, not even the fact that there was plenty to do running the inn, especially now Beatrice had revived the village's social calendar and singles' scene with all manner of events planned for the winter ahead.

'Easter it is then,' Atholl conceded. 'What are we calling it, then? Surely it needs a name? The Port Willow Bay Arts Festival?'

'Oh no, it'll be a *much* smaller affair than that, just a little something to bring the village together. Just a bit of fun. There's no need for the idea to turn into an all-singing, all-dancing extravaganza.' Beatrice turned back to her list-making as Atholl smiled indulgently at her. 'Ooh!' she cried, raising her pencil as another idea struck her. 'I'll invite a few food vans in too, and maybe a Punch and Judy show. You do Punch and Judy in Scotland, right? If the weather's bad it could go in the village hall too. And maybe the inn could do a special seafood barbeque? I'm sure Gene could handle that, and—'

'I'll put the kettle on. I'm guessing you forgot to eat this afternoon?'

'I wasn't hungry after smelling whatever Gene was grilling in the kitchens today, it was like old shoe leather,' replied Beatrice absently, still half absorbed in her plans.

'Doesnae sound much like Gene's cooking to me. I wish this morning sickness wouldnae torment you so,' said Atholl, knowing he wouldn't get an answer now that she was writing fervently in her book. 'I'll away, make you some sandwiches. Beattie?'

He shrugged at the silence, watching her absorbed in her work while baby Clara dozed peacefully in the fire glow, before going to make her something to eat. Best to leave Beatrice to plot and plan. It was, after all, the thing that made her happiest.

Chapter Fifteen

Singles and Malts

In true Scottish style all the tables and chairs had been pushed to the edges of the room, clearing the floor, firstly to accommodate Beatrice's speed-dating event and, later, for Hogmanay dancing. Gene and Mrs Mair were busy in the kitchens preparing the haggis, neeps and tatties for the revellers at midnight, many of whom were crafters leaving tomorrow after a happy week creating treasured souvenirs and celebrating the season.

Atholl was following Beatrice around, making sure she wasn't doing too much, and Beatrice was pointedly ignoring his insistence that she needed to slow down and take it easy.

'Don't be daft, Atholl. I'm fine! It's such early days yet, I'm barely feeling it.'

She hadn't told him the reason she was wearing her slipper boots (and hoping nobody noticed) was because her feet were too swollen for shoes and she hadn't dressed up for Hogmanay because her party dresses were all a little tight around the middle. In the end, after a long time spent staring into the wardrobe, she'd opted to tear the tags off the maternity jeans with the big black elastic band that went all the way up over her ribs, even if they were still too big and slid down her hips every so often.

Even if she didn't think she looked pregnant yet, and the only concrete proof of that fact was the little test stick, she felt very pregnant indeed.

'I've got an event to manage.' She bustled on, gathering the name badges and pens for the participants.

Atholl was about to say more when something across the room caught Beatrice's eye and she cried out, 'Oh my God, look! The news programme worked! Somebody's actually filled in a lonely hearts slip.' Beatrice carefully made her way through the throng to her dating board, but her face soon fell as she reached it and read under her breath.

> NAME: Echo Fergusson
>
> AGE: 7 (or 49 in dog years)
>
> OCCUPATION: Wandering dug
>
> ADDRESS: The Princess and the Pea Inn/ Wherever there's trouble
>
> HOBBIES: Skulkin' aboot. Cadging scraps from Tam's chippy
>
> HOW WOULD YOU DESCRIBE YOURSELF: A Good Boy
>
> LOOKING FOR: Damsels in distress to rescue, scratches behind ma lugs, anybody's open front door or unwatched packed lunch.

The sniggering from the boat men at the bar – with Seth's son smiling over his pint at their centre – stopped promptly when she turned to confront them. He only winked as she raised her eyebrows at him, hand on her hip.

'Johnny McVie! Will you stop messing with the dating board or I'll have Gene present you with your bar tab for this last week.'

The young man grew suddenly interested in the bottom of his pint glass. Luckily for him, at that moment Seth found Beatrice in the crowd, excitedly holding up his son's iPhone for her to inspect.

'Johnny tells me I'm a me me. Would you credit it?' Seth said, earnestly, presenting Beatrice with his phone.

'A me me?' Beatrice stared at the phone. 'Oh God. You mean a meme, don't you?'

On the screen, wearing his green woollen beany, his moustache ends freshly twirled for the camera, stood Seth in front of the inn's dating board talking into Kirstie's mic. A thumping beat played over his voice as he repeated on a loop the words, 'A *date*? I havnae had so much as a sniff of a lassie this forty years.' Across the screen appeared the words 'Same dude. Same.' The clip auto-replayed over and over as Beatrice stared, aghast.

'Great! *Excellent*. Well done,' she said, a little too loudly, and made her way back to Atholl.

'So, apparently Seth's gone viral.'

'Aye, I've seen it. Half of Scotland has by now, I imagine.'

'Nobody's taking this seriously, you know. We've only sold eleven tickets for the speed dating in spite of the news coverage, and not one person's filled in a real dating profile yet. Well, nobody except Seth and, apparently, Echo.'

'They will. You've got to remember the Port Willow lads aren't used to having lassies all around them, let alone having to talk with them face to face in the pub. It's easier for them to scroll through women online and hardly ever actually meet any of them – at least, so they tell me at the bar.'

'Is that what it is? Not very romantic though, is it?' She thought for a moment. 'Did you ever do any scrolling?'

'Nope. I was lucky. I met the bonniest lassie ever to arrive in the village, and I was smart enough to ask her out before anybody else got the chance.'

'Before Seth could?'

'Exactly, just think, you could be living with him now had he caught your eye first.'

Beatrice inhaled through her teeth, shaking her head. 'I missed out there. Regret's a terrible thing, you know?'

'So you're stuck with me unfortunately.' Atholl pulled her closer and she smiled up into his eyes.

'What a pity.'

-

Mutt was at the bar by seven-thirty, attracting a lot of attention from the other patrons due to his helplessness in preventing Bear from stumbling over his own furry little legs and bounding from person to person, snuffling under chairs, looking for dropped bar snacks and enjoying being petted and fussed by everyone.

'Your usual?' Kitty asked from behind the bar, beautiful in a jumpsuit and obi belt that had made Gene's eyes round with love when she'd presented herself for work earlier in the evening.

'Please.' Mutt smiled, and Kitty poured him a pint of Highland honey pale ale.

'You've brushed up braw,' she told him, nodding approvingly at his cabled, fitted fisherman's jumper in navy yarn, what looked like super soft and washed-a-hundred-times black 501s and, grounding it all, freshly polished work boots and a day's dark stubble.

Mutt was too busy paying for his drink and returning Kitty's compliment to notice Nina arriving from her room and coming to a stop at the edge of the crowded bar with some papers under her arm as though she wasn't finished work for the day, but wearing a shimmering dress and heels that said she knew it was New Year's Eve and, dammit, she wasn't going to let the side down, even if she was a million miles away from her romantic celebrations in New York where Luke was probably planning on wearing his tux and taking Himari out on the town. There'd be so many client parties for them to choose from.

She'd fought against the urge to room service a bottle of wine and take it to bed at six p.m. and she'd determined to put on a good show of being absolutely fine, if only for the sake of her own battered pride.

Seeing there was only one space at the bar – and it was beside Mutt – she took a breath, preparing to ignore him in order to get a drink, and quick.

'Champagne, please,' she asked Kitty, knowing the Princess didn't serve cocktails. Beatrice had put her straight about that during the week, when she'd ventured downstairs wanting to drown her sorrows at having found most of the Highland businesses she'd tried to make contact with were closed for the holidays. Even the art and fashion colleges hadn't replied to her requests for an exclusive preview of the upcoming student exhibitions and runway preparations.

'Pull up a barstool, Nina. I'll need to go to the cellar for a fresh bottle. Won't be long,' Kitty told her as she left the busy bar.

Nina tried spreading her papers on the bar, tutting to find them getting damp from the condensation rings.

'You're working on Old Year's Night?' Mutt couldn't help asking.

'On *what*?' She dabbed at the bar with a fist full of napkins.

'Old Year's Night?'

'You mean New Year's Eve?'

'Same difference.'

'Not really. One sounds optimistic for the future; the other one is all maudlin and backwards looking.'

Mutt sniffed a laugh. 'Maybe so. The end of the year's for saying goodbye to the past as well as partying. It *can* be a bit maudlin for people. You know in Scotland, just after the midnight bells, we all take a minute to think about the people not coming with us into the next year?'

Like Luke, thought Nina, and her emotions churned once more. She couldn't let this smirking bloke see it though, so she said, 'I thought you were supposed to love New Year, you Scots? I thought you were supposed to celebrate it bigger and better than anywhere else?' Mutt was smiling back at her, quizzically. 'Except maybe New York,' she added, thinking of the way the whole city comes alive with celebration and glamour. She held in the sigh.

'We're nothing if not sentimental,' Mutt told her. 'If you're not weeping by ten past twelve, are you really Scottish?'

'*Hmm*, well, I'll be asleep by twelve, thanks very much. I don't fancy seeing a room full of drunk Scots crying and singing Old Lang Zine.'

'Syne.'

'You like correcting people,' she observed with an exasperated slow blink.

Mutt held his hands up and turned to lean the small of his back on the bar, looking out at the room. Nina faced her papers once more just as Kitty reappeared twisting at a champagne bottle. When the cork popped, a small cheer went up around the bar.

'Champagne, Mutt?' Kitty asked, after she'd poured Nina's tall glassful and passed it to her, saying she'd put it on her room tab.

'I'd rather have a malt than that stuff,' he told her.

'I've a fifteen-year-old Dalmore new in from our supplier. Let me know when you fancy one and I'll open it,' said Kitty, before drifting off to serve the long line of customers that had accumulated while she'd been gone, one of whom was Seth waiting patiently for a top-up.

Nina downed her champagne like she'd been wandering in a parched desert for a week. Mutt noticed but seemed to reconsider saying anything. Instead he greeted Seth at the other end of the bar by raising his glass before surveying the room in silence.

Atholl was busy bringing stacks of chairs into the centre of the room, setting them out in two long rows facing one another across a line of trestle tables. He turned down Mutt's offer of help with a wave of his hand.

Sullen, and with her head down over her papers, Nina said to herself, 'I wouldn't care if I never heard the word whisky again.'

'*Uh*, did you say something?' asked Mutt.

'Whisky.' She ran the point of her pen down a printed spreadsheet with slumping shoulders. 'Not one of these local distilleries wanted to meet with me.'

'Hardly surprising,' Mutt told her, 'they're all closed for Christmas. Nobody's malting this week.'

'How was I supposed to know that?' Nina looked defeated and held her empty glass up for a refill. Kitty was still busy, so Mutt reached behind the bar for the bottle, doing some kind of sheepdog whistle to make sure Kitty saw him doing it – this made Nina shrink in disbelief and annoyance – and he poured Nina another drink.

She lifted her glass once more and took a sip. 'And none of them would open up for me,' she said, addressing her papers again.

'Like whisky that much, do you?'

'Not especially. I needed to connect with them, for work.' She drank again, this time slower but still giving the impression of being very much on the edge of a full-blown champagne mini-bender.

'Speed dating will start in five minutes,' Atholl shouted. 'If you've a ticket, take a chair. There's still time to buy one, if you like. Five pounds at the bar.'

A chorus of *woos* and laughter rang out, and some of the fishermen and farming lads slapped shoulders and jostled one another in mock encouragement, but no more tickets were sold. Only old Seth took his seat in the centre of the room, looking around expectantly at the crowds and making good-humoured comments about 'nothing ventured, nothing gained'.

Mutt, however, was still observing Nina quizzically. 'Gene said you were a… what did he say? A trend predictor?'

'Forecaster,' she corrected. Nina didn't remember which one Gene was, but she guessed it was one of the barflies or busybodies she'd dodged all week as they tried to make conversation about the weather or to tell her about their daughters who were her age and sensibly living down south. She hadn't taken much interest.

'And what trends are you forecasting here in Port Willow?' He was doing that smile again. Nina's last nerve prickled.

'I'm here to scout for product to pass on to my colleagues in New York. They'll make it into the next big luxury brand,' she replied flatly.

'And?'

'And… nothing. I've been here for a week and the distilleries, crystal factories and tartan mills are either closed for Christmas or they've got their branding established and relationships with distributors already and they won't see me.'

By now there were a few more brave local men, most of them in their fifties and sixties, taking their seats while Beatrice collected their tickets and marked their names on the clipboard she'd bought especially for the occasion.

Mutt nodded his head towards them. 'Well, lucky for you there's at least ten local makers in tonight, some of them are sitting in those chairs. I'd say this is a perfect networking opportunity.'

Nina took another drink that emptied her glass. 'There's nothing here I'd pitch to my bosses.'

Mutt reacted just how she knew he would, drawing his neck back, offended. She'd read Gene's crafting classes brochure from cover to cover on Christmas Day and, as she'd already suspected, it had been a waste of time.

'I need something with international appeal. I can't sell trinkets. I need stand-out, luxury products, heritage brands, the next big thing. Not amateur handicrafts.'

Mutt definitely wasn't smiling now. 'Have you spoken to *any* of the locals? I think you'd be surprised. There's Murdina over there, for instance.'

Nina looked over at the elderly woman standing in a huddle with some of the crafters. She had long grey hair and, Nina couldn't help thinking, the air of something witchy about her. She wasn't yet aware that women like her were almost always the most interesting in the room.

Mutt raised his glass at Murdina across the filling floor and the woman smiled back. 'You know she makes her own yarns? Cards it, dyes it, spins it,' he told Nina in a low voice.

'She looks like she does.'

'She knitted this, you know?' Mutt angled his broad chest towards Nina, his hand touching the two dark brassy buttons at the side of the jumper's high neck.

Nina only internally admitted it was one of the nicest sweaters she'd seen and Mutt definitely wore it well. 'We have those in New York. Everyone's seen a fisherman jumper. I can't sell those to my bosses.'

'This isn't *a* fisherman jumper; it's *my* fisherman's jumper. Hand knitted just for me. You know this is my family design?'

'Huh?' Nina looked at it again. The jumper was plain apart from intricate stitches all across its deep yoke which brought out the breadth of his shoulders. 'What do you mean it's your family design?'

'Well, it's an old tradition in Scotland, and Ireland too, for the women to knit their family's or their village's pattern into their men's jumpers. They're called ganseys. Their pattern would give details about the fisherman's life. Some had diamonds to show they were married, others had zigzags called marriage lines to show the ups and downs of married life.'

Mutt ran his fingertips along one of the woollen cables down over his shoulder. The sight of this somehow made Nina want to look away. She concentrated on Bear instead who was now trying to clamber onto Mutt's lap and Mutt bent to the panting creature while he explained further.

'If a fishing boat overturned in the sea and a man was lost, the pattern could tell who he was and where he was from.'

He let Nina think that over for a second while he picked up the dog.

When he'd straightened once more he met Nina's eyes. 'Can you imagine being a sweetheart or a mother and knitting something like this for your lover or your son, thinking how it could be the thing that identifies him and brings him home from the bottom of the ocean? What a story every stitch tells. And this is my family's pattern. Murdina based it on my great-grandfather's own jumper. We were fisher folk going way back. In fact this pattern here, Murdina told me, is called a ridge and furrow; it represents my great-grandfather's kitchen garden at Pennan.'

'Wow.' Nina couldn't help but be impressed. 'But Murdina adapted his pattern for you?'

'Yes, she did away with the signs of marriage.'

'No diamonds or ups and downs in your pattern?'

Mutt's enthusiasm for schooling Nina seemed to fade and he looked down at Bear on his lap. 'No ups and downs for me.'

Nina's eyes were fixed to Mutt's face, but he wouldn't look at her now. He was so serious it was disconcerting. She'd written him off as the smirking Scot who thought she was ridiculous, but now some irrational, tipsy part of her brain was daring her to reach out and touch his cuff for some reason. She told her hands to stay put, clasping her empty glass, when he suddenly turned to her once more.

A different reflex seemed to be firing in Mutt now: a not entirely kind one. 'Mind you, you could take this pattern and have a machine turn out ten thousand of them for a fancy shop in America and it would lose all its meaning instantly. You're looking to mass produce something that can't be replicated without losing its magic.'

Nina's brows shot up. 'I don't want to mass produce anything. I'm not a Walmart buyer.'

'But you're here to turn something small and local into some over-priced stuff for toffs, am I right?'

His words lit an angry fire within her. 'Listen, Mutt, I know exclusivity. I know design. The people who buy our brands want the story *and* the authenticity, just the same as any other discerning shopper.'

He huffed a laugh. 'Well then, this room's bursting with authenticity. Why don't you dive in?' Mutt challenged, gesturing to the rows of locals now ready for the speed-dating event. 'I've only been here a few months and didn't know any of the villagers when I arrived. They welcomed me, offered me extra work, kept me company. You'd find they were good people too if you'd only talk to some of them.'

Nina wanted to answer him, she hated the feeling of being lectured, but she couldn't think of anything to offer in her defence. She hadn't spoken to anyone. She hadn't wanted to. Mutt was right. Now he was pointing out people in the bar room and singing their praises.

'That fellow there with the silver hair, that's Mr Garstang, the watercolourist. He's a *real* painter, unlike me.' He raised a wicked brow at Nina, confounding her even more. 'And that's Donald there in the red tartan, the silver smith. Can't get better than Scottish silver, you know? See the guy in the arty specs and the sticky-up hair? That's Munro the glass smith. Lungs like a bagpiper. You should see him blowing his molten-glass pipe, man's the very dab.'

Nina didn't know what that meant and wasn't prepared to ask. Mutt had laughter in his eyes once more as he provoked her while Bear snuffled at his owner's ear, putting his big paws all over the lovely jumper he'd been so proud of. 'To be fair, that one there's Patrick the fishmonger, and that's Jeemie the window cleaner. You'll not get any luxury trends out of them, I shouldn't think.'

'You're making fun of me,' she replied.

'No. I'm wanting you to see what we've got to offer here. Forget the distilleries and the factories. Even if they did want to see you, they'll not be open 'til the fourth at the earliest. Maybe not even then. You need to understand how the highlands work. This isn't some sweatshop churning out luxury items that'll sell for hundreds of dollars overseas when the women and children making them get paid barely enough to survive. This is folk in their homes or workshops doing what they love and honouring tradition.'

'And making zero money?' Nina had said it before she realised how brattish she sounded. Mutt didn't know she was shrinking with shame so he turned to her with heat in his eyes.

'Who do you think sewed that bonny dress you're wearing? Did they make money, or did their bosses make it? They'll have been ripped off, tied to some piece of paper where they signed their life away...'

'What have you got against making money?'

'Nothing, when nobody's exploited... or left behind.'

Nina glared at him, her heart thumping hard, she was so cross. Exploited? Wasn't *she* the one who had been exploited by Microtrends? By Luke and all the rest of them? She'd worked so hard, and for what? Not one of her clients had been taken advantage of in the process of making them and Seamus Gates richer, and she'd tell Mutt that if only she could get the words out, if only he wasn't unflinchingly returning her look with his chest expanding and falling heavily, no doubt with the effort and restraint required to hold back a further tirade about her exploitative ladyboss ways. If only he knew. Yet she found she couldn't speak.

Something electric buzzed in the atmosphere between them, something underlying their annoyance. Nina felt it keenly and it made her want to run away and hide under her duvet, it was so bewildering, and at the same time it made her want to dig her heels in and face down this relentlessly self-righteous man who made her feel spoiled and stupid.

'Here's your tickets!' Beatrice interrupted cheerily, appearing before them.

Nina looked at the paper stubs she was holding out. 'I already told... that tall guy, I'm not interested in doing the dating thing.'

'Gene?' Beatrice said, her smile fixed in place.

'You should do it,' Mutt urged, the tension seeming to leave his shoulders as the atmosphere shifted once again. 'We're trying to give you a leg-up.'

Nina turned on him. 'I don't need a leg-up! I can make it on my own. I got to where I was all by myself, you know?'

Mutt blinked. 'I didn't mean it like that. Are you always this touchy?'

Nina gulped back the feeling of having over-reacted, faltering. She *was* touchy about it. Of course she was. Having had over a week to think about Seamus's words, she'd come to wonder if maybe she *had* fast-tracked herself to success solely because of her connection to Luke. She hadn't proven what a good worker she was entirely by herself, and she hadn't shown her boss her worth; instead, she'd dated an exec and felt the benefits of that for her career, even if it was only momentary.

Now she was back at the start and with nothing to show for all her work. She couldn't even arrange a meeting with an established Highland brand. Nobody had a clue who she was here. There was nobody to introduce her at parties, no guest lists and no goodie bags. Without them she was floundering, and it hurt.

Beatrice looked between the pair a little desperately, but she wouldn't be put off. 'Right, well, remember it's New Year, Mutt. This is supposed to be a party,' she said, trying her best to bring him round. 'Here, this is your ticket.'

'Eh, no. I don't think so.' Now it was Mutt's turn to protest.

'Oh, go on, it'll be a good opportunity to network,' Nina threw in, enjoying the pinkness in Mutt's cheeks.

He snatched both of the tickets with a nod at Beatrice and, as soon as she turned away, shoved his into his pocket before casting Nina's onto the bar beside her spreadsheets.

'Not speed dating, then?' Nina heard herself ask. Her voice sounded brittle and unkind and she wasn't quite angry enough to avoid the cringing shame of hearing herself.

'No, I'm not.' Mutt drained his pint and turned to the bar. 'I'll take that malt now, please, Kitty.' He threw a glance back at the chairs, now all full. Beatrice was handing out pens and notepads to all the participants. 'Call me mad, but I don't want a date with Seth, or the fishmonger for that matter, and although those three women seem perfectly nice, they're probably my mum's age. One of them was Atholl's primary school teacher.'

He had a point. There were rather a lot of old men in the dating pool, a symptom of the population imbalance in the village and its surroundings – and something Beatrice hadn't quite factored in during her planning process.

'Well, neither do I,' Nina retorted. 'I'm here to rely on myself, OK? I don't need a speed date to find crafters, or a *leg-up* from you. The brochure's told me everything I need to know about them already. And despite this village's obsession with matchmaking, I definitely *don't* need a man.'

Mutt took his whisky glass from Kitty, who was eyeing him with a cautioning glance. He nodded to her, bit his lip and turned his attention fully to nursing his drink, leaving Nina to sink back into her thoughts.

She'd had more than enough of men these last three years. She was struck by vivid images of Seamus, Luke and Fournival, not to mention Mitch – and Mitch was one of the *nice* ones – picturing how they must have worked together to secretly stitch her up. Then, diving deeper into her humiliation, she found herself thinking about how

Luke and Seamus had gone about proving *their* worth in the business.

Hadn't *they* had a leg-up from their college networks, or in Luke's case, his parents' networks? Hadn't they benefitted from being part of the in-crowd? Why did she alone have to feel ashamed and embarrassed just because she'd been 'the girlfriend' and not the Old Boy and fellow business buddy? What difference should her failed relationship make to how she was treated now that Luke had got bored with her? She was still good at her job. Wasn't she? Her heart hurt as the truth hit home. Her utter failure to make progress this week suggested otherwise.

'I rely only on myself from now on,' she said, quietly, but still loud enough for Mutt to pick up her words. 'They're all the bloody same.'

'Who are?' he said, turning to study her again now that she'd swung round on her seat to survey the daters.

'Men. A pack of liars and cheats, manoeuvring themselves and everyone around them to get what they want, then *baam*! As soon as they're through with you, you're out.'

Mutt blinked, his jaw tensing. Something at the centre of his chest seemed to shift. He set Bear down on the floor once more.

'Right, well, Nina Miller from New York who relies only on herself, good luck to you in your search. There's umpteen makers in this very room, but you'll not see it because they're not dressed in… I don't know, Coco Chanel.'

Nina rolled her eyes. Mutt seemed to consider saying more, before he took a deep breath and held it.

He stalked away. 'Come on, Bear,' he called as he left, and the tumbling, fluffy pup followed his best friend out the bar room door just as Beatrice was holding a whistle to her lips and declaring the speed-dating event open.

Beatrice watched Mutt leaving and turned her head just in time to see Nina puffing her cheeks in exasperation and turning back to the bar and ordering another top-up.

Beatrice narrowed her eyes. Port Willow's resident matchmaker already knew she had to help these two and it wouldn't be easy. Nina was headstrong and hurting, that much was clear, but hadn't she been in a similar position once herself? It had taken her a while to see the beauty of this place and its people too, but she'd come around with a bit of help from the locals. Nobody was allowed to feel unhappy and alone at the inn, not if Beatrice had anything to do with it. Before Nina checked out she'd see her smiling, and if that just so happened to involve bringing some much-needed happiness to the wayward, fiery Mutt, well… that's the way it would have to be.

Chapter Sixteen

Ruth Firth's Hogmanay

The speed dating hadn't quite gone according to plan. Beatrice had watched on as the conversations took place, blowing her whistle every five minutes to switch up the pairings.

She'd collected the notebooks back from the daters and found not one of them had requested a follow-up meeting with any of the others. All in all, the event had been rather flat and awkward, and not exactly inclusive with its men-seeking-women vibe. Why wasn't her social engineering working? Where were all the lovers falling head over heels like she had with Atholl? She'd become so happy since she came to the village all she wanted to do was share that joy and bring a little more love to Port Willow. Why was everyone proving to be so reluctant?

'It was a failure,' she told Atholl in the kitchens while Gene glided about behind them, plating up Mrs Mair's freshly baked shortbread.

'It just wasn't the right mix tonight,' Atholl consoled her. 'I think we might hae to let love in Port Willow take its natural course, you ken? It's no' something you can force.'

'Nonsense,' she told him, and she'd returned to the bar room to clear tables and carry on making introductions between the crafters and locals, making sure nobody was left out.

It hadn't escaped her notice that Nina had slipped off to bed, taking her paperwork with her, and she hadn't been the only one not enjoying the party atmosphere.

Even with the locals demonstrating Scottish country dances and a fair few of the visitors mastering the Gay Gordons and the St Bernard's Waltz, one couple hadn't danced all evening.

The Firths, Beatrice's competition winners, had arrived that afternoon and so far they hadn't quite lived up to her loved-up expectations.

The Firths' application form had sung out amongst all the rest. The couple had been together for over thirty years, married for almost twenty-five, and had adult twin sons, one of whom, Stuart, had only weeks ago moved into a residential home for adults with complex needs. Beatrice had been able to feel the emotion coming off the screen as she'd read the words in answer to her question, 'Why does our month-long Highland getaway appeal to you?'

The Firths hadn't held back, explaining how winning the holiday would mean having their first break alone in thirty-four years and that they hadn't had so much as a babysitter or a night away since the boys were born. They'd even taken the twins on honeymoon with them. Beatrice got the distinct impression that these were parents who had never put themselves first but were intensely emotionally bonded from decades of united caring.

Yet, at check-in earlier that day, Beatrice had been surprised to find that what she'd imagined as 'Team Firth', a pair of joined-at-the-hip sweethearts, weren't quite the cosy couple she'd conjured up. Yet again her romanticising had got the better of her, it seemed.

Kitty and Beatrice had greeted the couple in the reception just after lunchtime. Kitty poured the champagne while Beatrice handled the check-in.

'Welcome to the Princess and the Pea Inn,' Kitty cried as the shivering couple, pale-faced from the shock of arriving in the Highlands in a minus-one rain shower that was clearing away the last of the snow, stepped inside. Mrs Firth was the first to accept a glass with a hot and bothered, rabbit-in-the-headlights expression.

The man, wearing a navy waterproof jacket that looked fresh off the peg at Millets, stayed one step behind his wife, his phone in his hand.

'Good journey?' Beatrice prompted, while scrolling for their details on the screen.

'Fine, yes...' Mrs Firth replied, glancing behind at her husband as though hoping he'd say something, but he didn't. 'Lovely,' she added. 'Beautiful scenery. We've never been to Scotland before.'

Kitty had pressed the glass into Mr Firth's hand and the little party stood looking at one another in a brief moment of silence which Beatrice immediately filled, chattering about a storm being forecast late tomorrow evening but the forecasts could be unreliable in this little corner of the Highlands so they shouldn't let it worry them. All the while, the pale, bedraggled woman with purple-rimmed specs and spiked white hair that gave her a vague rock-chick-in-their-late-fifties vibe glanced around at the wood-panelled walls (recently beeswaxed and shining now, thanks to Beatrice) and the great set of antlers above the reception desk.

'So, you're taking seafood cooking lessons with our head chef, Eugene Fergusson, Mrs Firth?' trilled Kitty, her soothing Highland accent reaching the woman through her daze.

'Supposed to be, yes,' the woman replied. 'And it's just Ruth. Mrs Firth still makes me feel a hundred, even after nearly twenty-five years married.'

'Ah, yes, it's your anniversary later this year, isn't it?' Kitty smiled. 'Congratulations. We're glad you wanted to celebrate with us.'

Ruth smiled politely, but her husband didn't seem to be listening.

'And, Mr Firth, you've nothing booked at the moment?' Beatrice asked.

'*Hmm?*' He raised his eyes from his phone. 'No, *um*, no classes for me. I'll most likely be working,' the man confirmed with an admittedly apologetic smile which Beatrice recognised as a plea not to inveigle him in anything crafty.

He didn't seem all that delighted to find himself holidaying in Port Willow. Being forced to do craft lessons might be enough to send him running home to Yorkshire.

'Is there anywhere I can get a signal here?' he said. He'd been searching for bars since he arrived.

'Och, one'll came along soon enough,' Kitty shrugged in her usual happy-go-lucky way. 'There's the payphone in the bar corridor if you're stuck.'

The man's face fell even further, prompting his wife to pipe up. 'Oh well, it's not a problem, is it, Mark? We're on a rather special holiday after all.'

Mark Firth didn't reply or mirror his wife's simpering smile. 'There's Wi-Fi?' he asked Kitty. 'A month is a very long time without Wi-Fi…'

Kitty interrupted what looked like could easily become an argument. 'The password's coral beach, no space, lower case.' She quickly handed Ruth Firth the key. 'Room one, double bed, full board. Evening meals start at seven usually. Hogmanay dinner's at four today, mind. Then there's haggis, neeps and tatties at midnight. Cookery lessons are daily at ten, starting on the second. Gene will come find you when it's time for class, Mrs Firth, I mean Ruth, sorry. It'll just be you and him for the time being. Hope that's OK?'

'That's fine, thank you,' she said politely, if a little nervously, clearly trying to make up for her husband's abruptness.

Kitty had directed the couple to their room, the only guest room on the ground floor, directly opposite Atholl and Beatrice's bedroom and the door to the managers' little private sun room at the back of the building.

'Ah,' Beatrice had sighed once their new guests were in their room and Kitty returned. 'I reckon we've got our work cut out with those two. I'd imagined a month with a sea-view, a few classes taken together here and there, and a little bit of winter Highland magic would be a dreamy second honeymoon for them, but now I see them together I wonder!' She inhaled through gritted teeth.

'They've had a long journey, poor things,' Kitty replied. 'Let them settle in a bit before you do your Cinderella's fairy godmother thing, OK?'

Beatrice had been keeping an eye on them all through dinner and the speed dating. After sharing a meal together and barely saying anything to one another, Mrs Firth looked a little stricken again, like she had after her train journey, and Beatrice was sure she could detect a tense, regretful appearance in Mark Firth too.

Ruth had however been happy enough making small talk with the staff throughout the afternoon and had already been introduced to Gene, had a tour of his kitchen and covered a range of foody topics, telling him she wasn't a cook, far from it, but she was excited to learn some new recipes.

At a little after ten, as Beatrice passed their table, she heard Mark announcing to his wife that he was heading to bed. She couldn't help but say something.

'You're not leaving, are you? You have to stay up for the bells, otherwise it's not a proper Scottish Hogmanay experience,' Beatrice implored, but he mumbled about not being one for parties these days.

'Well then, will you let me keep Ruth for a while?'

By then, she had her arm looped through Ruth's and the pair were exchanging glances – Beatrice triumphant and Mrs Firth, a little alarmed. 'I'll take good care of her for you, see she's back in the room by one.' Mark hadn't seemed to mind at all and bid them both good night and shuffled off without so much as a peck on his wife's cheek.

'Shall we have a drink? It's about time I took a break,' Beatrice asked Ruth when he'd gone, ineffectually kneading the small of her own back with both hands.

'I think that's a good idea,' the older woman replied, eyeing Beatrice with concern. 'You've been on your feet all night. Come on, sit down. I'll get the drinks. A soft drink for you, yes?'

When Ruth returned from the bar with a cranberry juice for Beatrice and another fizzy wine for herself, Beatrice asked her how she'd known.

'That you're pregnant? I trained as a midwife once, and to be honest if your posture or pink cheeks didn't give the game away, your bloke fussing all around you does – and that's not to mention the fluffy slippers.'

Beatrice laughed. Ruth seemed brighter now than at check-in. She thought she'd be shy or awkward, but she wasn't a bit, and Beatrice knew it couldn't all be down to the fizzy wine she'd been sipping all evening. In fact, there was something quietly assured about the woman, something mature and grounded that reminded her of her own mum.

'Your husband isn't one for parties then?'

'Parties?' Ruth laughed. 'I can't remember the last time we were out together on a night like this.' She looked as though she were searching her memory. 'Children's parties, yes. I've hosted plenty of those, but even those stopped about eighteen years ago.'

'Oh yes, you've got grown-up twins,' Beatrice said.

'Twin boys. My Stuart only moved away from home last month.'

'That's right, I remember from the form,' Beatrice said, and Ruth nodded with a smile. 'I'm so glad you won our couple's getaway. Shame Mr Firth isn't joining you for lessons. He doesn't like cooking?'

'He's made one or two nice curries over the years, but entering the competition was all my doing, really. I'm just glad he's here. It wasn't easy dragging him away from his office.'

'Busy, is he?'

'He keeps himself busy. He could retire if he put his mind to it, but he won't.'

'That's a shame; if you've got an empty nest, you could be enjoying yourselves.' Ruth seemed to flinch. 'Did I say something wrong?'

'That phrase, empty nest, it's…' Ruth gave up trying to explain with a sigh and a shrug.

'I'm sorry, I didn't mean anything.' Beatrice winced. She knew how hurtful people could be with their glib comments. She'd heard her fair share when she lost her baby. People couldn't find the right words and then they'd stumble into reliable old clichés without thinking and that's where the hurt lay. 'Sorry,' Beatrice said again.

'Don't be sorry. It's accurate. We're footloose and fancy-free.' Ruth's tone was wry. 'Empty-nesters. It's supposed to be a good thing, I think, but it also means my little brood's gone too. What does that make me?' Ruth took a drink, letting the question go unanswered and Beatrice only tipped her head to show she was still listening. 'Stuart wasn't exactly thriving at home with us, and one day he said he wanted his own place, and, well, who are we to stop him?' Ruth had told Beatrice as much in her competition entry form. There was a pride in her eyes, Beatrice recognised it, but there was something else too, something sad and a little guilty.

Ruth looked out at the bustling bar room as she spoke, matter-of-factly, if a little distant. 'I've spent my life mopping up, remembering to take something out to defrost for tomorrow's tea, shuffling paperwork and shopping lists, making sure everyone's got everything they need – school shoes, medicine, haircuts – all those laces tied and doses measured out, all those meals put on the table, and now both of the boys have moved on I'm feeling myself kind of… irrelevant. Invisible, you might say. It's a relief not to be needed all the time, but at the same time it's awful.'

'They're still your sons, they still need you.' Beatrice thought of her mother and the times when she missed her most. 'They'll want you when they've done something they're proud of. You'll be the first person they want to phone. And they'll want you when they've fallen in love and they're giddy with excitement and wanting to tell the world and show their partner off. And they'll want you when they're sad and they'll want you when they've heard something funny...'

'I hope that's true.'

'I know it is. You must remember it when you moved away from home yourself for the first time? What it feels like to want them, even when you're grown.'

'*Hmm*, well, that's what people always expect, isn't it? That you've had an upbringing like them. I was never the apple of anyone's eye. That's why I promised myself I'd do things differently, promised myself my boys would always know they're loved, so I told them every day. They'd groan, but I'd never let them forget it. I remember the midwife saying I'd kiss the pink off their cheeks the way I was carrying on, but I ignored her, miserable old bat. She was one of them, like my parents. A cold fish.'

Beatrice smiled in sympathy but feeling useless. 'It must be hard to adjust,' Beatrice said.

'Mark's taken Stuart moving away better than me, far better, though I think he must feel it too. Oh dear, look at me. Getting steamy again. I seem always to be crying these days, when I'm not dozing off, or having another bloody hot flush.' Ruth laughed at this, but Beatrice could see she was tormented.

'That's why I picked you both. You sounded like you needed to relax, have a bit of fun together.' An idea struck her. 'Was it you that filled in the form?'

'It was. Just me. I saw your competition in the magazine and the picture of the inn and the bay and the next thing you know I'd filled the form in and clicked send. Didn't even think to tell Mark, I just did it. Then I forgot all about it, didn't think in a million years we would win.'

Ruth looked at Beatrice as though trying to decide whether she should say what she was thinking. Beatrice smiled kindly and that was enough to make Ruth speak.

'It… it hadn't occurred to me we'd have to actually fill the silences on this holiday, not until we got on the train and had eight hours sat staring at each other.' Ruth looked at her glass before placing it down on the table as though it was to blame for loosening her tongue.

'I think I know how that feels.' Beatrice recalled the last few years of her marriage when Rich seemed so far away even when he was sitting across the dinner table from her. She remembered thinking it was like talking to someone beneath a layer of frozen water, everything indistinct, nothing communicated properly, never really seeing each other. Then the pregnancy had happened and for a few months they had something wonderful to talk about and so many plans to make. When their baby had disappeared through that wall of ice too, their marriage had been too fragile to survive.

Beatrice looked at Ruth who was watching Gene spinning Kitty on the dance floor.

'I hope your holiday is the break you need,' Beatrice ventured. 'A second honeymoon.'

Ruth smiled, determined to make light of her situation. 'I'm sure it'll be just what the doctor ordered.'

Beatrice's heart hurt for her. As Ruth watched the dancing couples she had the look of a woman wondering whether this was it, the way things were going to be for the rest of her life, wondering if she'd just have to potter on, getting by.

Lots of people do, thought Beatrice. They shouldn't. Not if it made them sad, as she suspected Ruth was. Beatrice couldn't shake the feeling that she had narrowly missed out on taking a similar path had she continued as Rich's wife. It could so easily have been her sitting here like Mrs Firth, aching for a little bit of love and sunshine, craving attention and comfort and never getting them.

Yet Beatrice wasn't convinced Ruth and Mark Firth were quite in the same space she'd been in. She'd fancied she'd seen something companionable and comfortable in the couple as they'd sat together silently. It was the same thing she'd seen in Gene and Kitty back in the summer. Something about the pair just fit, snug like two jigsaw pieces cut out only for each other. Awkwardly shaped and difficult to bring together, yes, but once they'd clicked they were irrefutably in the right place. Maybe it wasn't so clear in the Firths' case, but Beatrice could already feel the familiar buzz of interest in them and she could hear Atholl's voice telling her not to meddle. But it was too late.

'Ruth, have the pair of you made any plans for the morning?'

Mrs Firth tipped her head, intrigued.

-

Hogmanay at the inn ended with Beatrice and Ruth talking together right up until the bells rang out and the whole room had hollered a mighty 'Happy New Year'. Beatrice shared the story of how she'd run away to the inn and fallen for Atholl, and she'd told the tale of her lost baby too. Everything about Ruth's warm demeanour and openness encouraged her to share and they'd passed a happy evening in the bar.

She'd hugged Ruth goodnight just before Atholl came to find her and swept her up onto the dancefloor where he'd slowly spun her as everyone broke into song about old acquaintances being forgotten and never brought to mind.

Kitty and Gene joined them on the dance floor, while Seth staggered out the door, accompanied by his son, having discovered that the chief perk of being a local celebrity was having many free drinks foisted upon him. He'd been gracious enough to accept every one.

The revellers were so absorbed in their celebrations and their memories of the old year nobody noticed Ruth leaving the bar, her mouth fixed in a thin smile, and not one person spotted Mutt coming back from pacing the sea front with Bear fast asleep inside his black biker jacket. He scanned the room as though looking for someone but not spotting them before passing through the bar, into reception and up the stairs clutching a piece of paper, heading straight for the guest room at the very top of the inn.

Chapter Seventeen

A January Outing to the Coral Beach

Echo and Bear ran ahead, skipping over the ancient white algae beach, not seeming to mind the sharp shards that had made generations of unsuspecting tourists tempted by the glistening white shore instantly regret slipping their shoes off.

Beatrice and Atholl led the inn guests on their New Year's Day walk, Atholl's arm around her shoulder and her mittened hand around his waist.

Beatrice was tired this morning but unable to resist the temptation of bringing her guests together and showing them the beach she loved more than any other in the world. This was their chance to blow away the cobwebs from a Hogmanay indoors. If it just so happened that the beach was unusually romantic and windswept today, and the view out over the rippling blue water was captivating enough to get them exclaiming in wonder and chatting to each other, well, that wouldn't be her fault. And if they broke off into pairs to walk and talk? Well, blame the beach.

There was still the threat of snow in the white sky – all one mass of thick cloud – but there was also the fresh, chilly glare of Januarys in the north of Scotland where, when the winter sun manages to get up over the horizon, it does wonderful things with light and colour and texture, things Beatrice had never seen back home in Warwickshire.

Ruth, Beatrice could see, was already taken by the gorgeous scenery and she had walked all the way across the little half-moon curve of coral with her husband and was sitting on a black rock right on the edge of the cold, clear water, which even in the wintertime still had the look of shallow tropical shores about it.

Beatrice pulled Atholl into the shelter of the low, rocky cliff at the back of the bay where they could spread their waterproof blanket and watch on as the guests mingled and stared at the landscape.

Ruth had very sensibly kept her wellies on and was trying to shove her hair back under the hood of her yellow raincoat to stop it getting messed up with the damp air. She was cheerful, though, as she looked all around at the tall mountains far in the distance, enclosing them in a circle as though at the centre of a snow globe. Hazy, snowy hills, fresh air, watery winter sunshine, and time alone with her husband. This is why she'd come here, and she was determined to be happy.

'Have you not made any resolutions this year?' she asked Mark, who was perching, less comfortably than she was, on his own black rock, an arm's length away.

He looked out across the water, pulling a face that said he hadn't given the topic any thought.

Ruth gave him time to answer. Something she'd grown used to lately. When he didn't reply, she'd summoned all the positivity she could from the crisp newness of the January morning and told him she'd made a few of her own and did he want to hear them.

'*Hmm?*' Mark still didn't look at his wife.

'I thought we could resolve to go out more, now the boys have left home. See a bit more of each other?'

'We're out now, aren't we?'

'True. Here we are, together.' Ruth craned round to let Mark see she was looking straight at him, hoping he'd look up and smile.

He kept his eyes on the horizon. 'Well then.'

He said this a lot. Well then. Ruth knew it meant, 'well, there's an end to it'. She wondered if he'd found it worked well as a conversation stopper some time ago and he'd clung on to it, letting it round off awkward or stilted discussions, deploying it when he needed silence to work or when he didn't want to hear chatter about the neighbours' building work or what Ruth's sister had got up to on holiday with her new boyfriend, and Ruth would let their conversations peter out, not seeming to mind.

It was all too easy to stop talking, back in their home, in their Yorkshire town, where Mark always had calls to make and a laptop screen to monitor, even in the evenings – except when he was asleep in front of the telly by eight – or Ruth might have a hair appointment or yet another supermarket shop to do, or important letters to shuttle to the post office for her husband.

Somehow they were never in the same room at the same time and really getting into a topic, and if they ever did it was about that dodgy guttering in their converted garage bedroom or trying to remember when the car needed its next service or Mark was asking whether Ruth would be a doll and book it in. She thought she might die for the want of a proper talk. She tried to imagine what it might feel like if Mark actually asked her a question, and not about what was for tea or where the remote had got to, either.

She took a deep breath. Ruth wasn't going to let a 'well then' stop her this time. They were on a beautiful beach miles from their life back home. This place couldn't be more different to their familiar routines and here was her chance to explore ways she might be different from Ruth Firth, wife, carer and mother.

'I thought I might resolve to try a few more new things,' she said.

'Like what?' Mark said, turning his head to look at her, just for a second.

'I don't know, something fun. Something we could both enjoy? The cooking lessons will be fun. Gene's pub kitchen's the real deal! I never really got much beyond sausage and mash or trifle with canned fruit and jelly with the kids. Now your wife's going to be rustling up lobster bisque in a real kitchen! Who knew, eh?'

She smiled, her eyes falling on the side of Mark's unshaven face. He didn't bother shaving on days when he wasn't likely to see clients. Ruth supposed that now went for holidays away with her too.

Mark nodded, eyebrows raised, seeming to say she was right, that *is* impressive.

'So, you know, if cooking's fun, who knows what else I might be good at? I did always fancy making my own clothes.'

'You what?' Mark stifled a laugh. It wasn't unkind, just amused and, Ruth felt, a tiny bit dismissive.

'I wasn't always an M&S addict. Remember when we met and I had all those lovely eighties blouses… and those boots! Do you remember that PVC skirt? God, Mum hated that!'

Mark's eyes seemed to glaze a little. 'I remember.'

'Not to mention the massive perm,' she added. 'I was forever one spritz of Elnett and an open flame away from a towering inferno.'

Mark laughed once more, looking down at the coral now, reaching a hand down to scoop some up and roll the thick grains between his fingers. Ruth watched him, wondering what he was thinking. She talked on.

'I thought back then, before we met that night at Alley Catz, that I was going to marry Adam Ant, and learn French and live in Paris. I'd live off nothing but fags and baguettes and...'

'Mark Firth?' her husband said.

Ruth fell silent. She watched her husband press the phone to his ear and jump up, turning his back on their little perch by the water's edge, and wander up the beach to take the call.

She never heard that phone ring. The damn thing was always on silent in his pocket and when it buzzed it wouldn't matter where he was – if he was in the middle of a meal at home, or on another Saturday afternoon trudge around the garden centre – he'd answer in seconds. Every day, over and over again. He was, however, far trickier to reach when he was at the golf course on Sundays with his friends.

She could hear him laughing now, his voice loud and confident, carrying over the beach.

Beatrice hadn't missed the slump of Ruth's shoulders and she picked her way across the coral to perch on the rock beside her.

'Lovely day,' Beatrice said, as the wind picked up, buffeting her face and whipping the hood off her head. 'For January.'

Ruth smiled and turned her back from the water so as to avoid the chill wind. 'How are you feeling?'

'OK, yeah. Bit of morning sickness, and evening sickness, but it's a sign things are going as they should, right?'

'I'd say so,' Ruth said, forcing certainty into her voice to help quell the worries Beatrice's eyes belied. She couldn't help glancing at Mark tramping along the foot of the low cliff, shouting over the whipping winds to make himself heard. A little pinch formed on Ruth's brow.

'He's a busy man, your husband,' Beatrice remarked.

Ruth nodded, watching him. Mark was always transformed by the call to work. 'It really matters to him; his associates' good opinion of him.' Both women were watching him now. Ruth sank a little more. 'He's worked so hard all these years to keep his father's business going.'

'What does he do?'

'Independent financial planning, property investments and pension advice.'

Beatrice inhaled through her teeth, impressed.

'I know. He's got a head for figures and loves picking over legal papers. Not my kind of thing at all.'

Beatrice was nodding, watching him, and Ruth found herself spurred on to explain him, and she wasn't sure why. She was a tiny bit ashamed at the impulse. Was she comparing him to the sentimental, attentive Fergusson brothers? She didn't want to.

'He was voted Businessman of the Year by the town Rotary Club last year. Got a brass plaque and everything.'

Beatrice rounded her eyes and smiled at this.

If there was ever a raffle that wanted drawing, a school prize-giving requiring an inspirational speaker, or a cake competition needing judging at the summer fete, there he'd be, smiling and shaking hands. Mr Personality, Ruth called him on her grumpier days, but she wasn't going to tell Beatrice that. It felt disloyal. It was all part and parcel of his being a great big fish in a lucrative small-town pond. She knew she shouldn't begrudge him his work and his success, and she hadn't, not all that much, and not until recently anyway.

Since Stuart moved out she'd had time to think about it more. Sometimes, late at night, when the hideous hot flushes were scaring her and keeping her awake and making her wonder what Mark would do if she suddenly ripped off her nightie and stood by the open window to cool down, she'd entertain the notion he might secretly be having an affair. He'd always been busy, but since their son had moved away he seemed even more distracted and distant. She just couldn't get through to him at all.

'January in the Highlands, he'll soon come round to the art of relaxation,' Beatrice told her. 'I had to. It's a completely different pace of life here.'

'I hope so,' Ruth replied. It had been hard enough getting him to agree to the break. He'd made sure all his clients knew where he'd be and he'd insisted on bringing his laptop to keep up with emails. As far as Mark was concerned, he was on a working holiday. The only thing that had changed was the scenery.

Ruth was lost in her thoughts now. A month in the Highlands had seemed like the answer to their problems back in Yorkshire. He couldn't avoid talking to her for four whole weeks, could he? If there *was* another woman – and the thought made her want to smash things one minute and curl up into a ball and howl the next – she'd know for sure by the end of this holiday. You can't hide something like that on a long Highland break, surely?

She wasn't sure how seriously she'd been entertaining the idea of him having a lover, but their awkward train journey and Hogmanay had heightened her fears about it, or maybe it was all down to her crashing hormones and missing Stuart. She didn't fully trust her own judgement anymore. Maybe Mark was just a bit… hopeless, and their relationship had gone from a teensy bit stale to well and truly past its sell by date? Maybe those were the cold, hard facts she would have to wrap her head around on this trip if things didn't drastically improve between them.

'It's good to have an occupation you love, isn't it?' Beatrice put in, scrabbling for something else to say that might draw Ruth out of her introspection a little more. The Hogmanay bubbly had loosened her tongue last night. Conversation was harder going today.

'He certainly seems to love it still.' Ruth wouldn't sigh in front of Beatrice, but she felt her body wanting to gasp for air and slump further into the rock.

Mark had made his way up onto the meadow path now and was pacing there, the phone clamped to his ear, his voice lost in the winds.

Ruth's eyes followed him. He had never promised her Paris, or pop star good looks and impeccable grooming, she had to remind herself. There'd never been much talk of romance and adventure, not after the twins came along anyway.

'You said you were a midwife?' Beatrice prompted, refusing to let Ruth sink into herself.

'Yes, I was once, and I'd meant to carry on when my maternity leave ended, but once I'd been at home with the babies I didn't want to go back. Then, by the time I was ready, my qualifications needed renewing and then we'd realised Stuart needed a bit of extra care, more than little Adam did, and I was the one that was going to give it. Not that Mark wasn't good on that front. He adored the boys.'

Beatrice listened in silence while Ruth absentmindedly twirled her ring on her finger thinking how she hadn't grudged either of the boys the years she had devoted to them; on the contrary, she'd felt fortunate to be there with them. Still, she hadn't forgotten the mornings when she was tired and lonely as she'd stood at the window watching some of the other mums walking to the bus stop in their suits and heels with their travel coffee cups ready for a day at work and she'd found she was holding back tears while something that felt a lot like envy had constricted her chest, and she missed the fun she and Mark had had right at the start of things when they were mad about each other and didn't care who saw them acting daft and starry eyed.

Ruth realised Beatrice was waiting to hear more. 'And I had friends around me too, some of the other mums and the neighbours. We're still friends now, some of us.' The last thing Ruth wanted was Beatrice feeling sorry for her. 'We still go out for coffee every Friday.'

Fridays were when the respite support worker would come in to practise some life skills or do whatever Stuart fancied doing that week; playing video games, making pizzas, doing a bit of laundry, that kind of thing. Meanwhile Ruth would be drinking frothy cappuccinos and eating red velvet cake while the gang caught up on the news about their adult kids' jobs and relationship disasters and all the attendant worries and unhurried duties of being an empty nester without the demands of the workplace to rigidly structure their lives.

Even now Stuart had moved out, Ruth never let herself stop. She was always busy, what with those new curtains that needed hemming, and that eye test to get to, and all those conifers that always wanted pruning, and scrolling her friends' Facebook posts from their holidays and family barbeques signed off with hashtag blessed.

She knew she'd been lucky in so many ways, with two grown-up boys living independently like she'd always hoped they would, and a nice home, and a straightforward, universally respected husband with a Jag in the drive and carefully planned life insurance policies maturing all the time.

Yet, none of that could stop her wondering what on earth happened to the woman in the PVC skirt and electric-blue mascara who'd danced the night away at Alley Catz and had so many huge, unbearably exciting dreams and a great big life ahead of her.

Ruth's gaze wandered from her husband to the little cottage on the hill above the beach, not wanting to cry but thinking she might well do. Instead she took a breath and quizzed Beatrice about the baby and whether she'd met her midwife yet.

Mark was busy so she'd happily pass the time waiting for him to come back, something she'd been doing for years.

-

A little while later and Nina was struggling to see the funny side of things. Her foot had sunk right into the icy-cold rockpool and her Jimmy Choo suede hiker boots with the shearling trim were now, most likely, ruined. They'd suited her just fine on frosty New York mornings on her short walk to work, but, here, they just weren't right. She'd turned down Beatrice's offer of a pair of the inn's welly boots this morning and was coming to regret it now.

'Here, take this,' the voice called as it approached. She knew instantly who it was without turning to see Mutt striding across the little bay holding out his jacket. 'You can sit down and get yourself sorted out.' He was beside her in a second.

She reached for the coat and spread it across a large dryish rock. 'Thank you. Aren't you cold?' She pointed at his open denim shirt over a t-shirt, with a thick black wool padded cardigan half-zipped up over the top. He'd worn his work boots again. Very sensible.

'I'm good. I don't mind the cold all that much anyway,' he replied, watching her hobble up onto the rock.

'*Hmm*.' Pulling at the laces, she freed her foot from the boot, pouring a chilly stream of water from it with an unconcealed wail. 'Aww, no! That's just great!'

'Here, Beatrice told me to give you this.' He handed her the towel branded with the inn's new logo of the fairy-tale bed in green machine embroidery.

Nina instantly wrapped the towel around her cold foot and cowered further down inside her Burberry cape from three seasons ago that had seen her through the harsh New York winters. Somehow it wasn't keeping her warm enough today. 'Thanks,' she said.

'No bother.'

'I mean, thank you for the note. It was you, wasn't it?'

Mutt only nodded, shoving his hands in his pockets.

'Why did you help me?' she asked, genuinely perplexed.

'Because of what you said. Because we're *not* all the same. I know I can be... hard work; Atholl's told me as much lately. But you said we were all alike. Men, I mean. I don't agree. I wanted to help you, even though you're... *um*...'

'Also hard work?' Nina conceded.

Mutt smiled out at the horizon. 'You said it, not me.'

Nina smiled too, but it was curtailed by a sudden shiver and a great gust of ice-cold wind off the water.

'You can go join Bea and Atholl by their fire, if you're that cold? They've nearly got it blazing,' Mutt said.

She looked behind her at the couple with their shared blanket over their shoulders and Atholl feeding kindling into a smoking pit made out of beach pebbles and driftwood. She shook her head, not wanting to interrupt their cosy date, not now Beatrice was done talking with that other woman by the shore. The inn managers looked like they were in the first flush of love to Nina. She didn't want to be a gooseberry.

'You're allowed to light fires on the beach?' she said, changing the subject.

'It has been known. There's nobody to stop you doing anything you like at this beach. Here, at least let me take your wet boot over to the fire.'

Mutt looked all around his feet before finding a long stick and proffering it for Nina to slip her dripping boot onto the end, which she did.

She watched him turn away without either of them saying another word, his floppy dark hair blowing wildly in the breeze as he went. When he reached the fire he spoke unheard words with Beatrice and stuck the stick into the coral, leaving the boot dangling above the building flames where, no doubt, the suede would absorb all that black smoke and end up smelling like a barbequed dog's bed.

She was surprised to see Mutt sit down by the fire too, and extremely surprised to find that she minded. Why had she assumed he'd come back to talk with her on her little rock? Why had she wanted him to? She'd given him no reason to like talking with her, that's for sure. And, likewise, he hadn't exactly made it his mission to charm her, apart from his kindness in leaving her that note. But still. Feelings are funny things. Nina quickly turned to look out to sea in case he saw her looking his way.

She'd found the note taped to her room door when she'd reached for her breakfast tray this morning.

No signature, no Dear Ninas, nothing but the words 'All these folk will meet with you'.

She unfolded the paper now, shielding it from the others' sight. Each name on the list was accompanied by a mobile number, a direct contact at a woollen mill, a distillery she hadn't even heard of in her searches, a crystal works, a tartan designer, the leather worker – all locals, and all closed for the holidays but willing to talk with her because of a kind word put in from Mutt, on account of his being related to the Fergussons and living at the inn.

It couldn't have been easy gathering all those numbers, not on Hogmanay. Had he rung around asking if they didn't mind passing on their numbers to a green young woman who'd waltzed into town and completely failed to understand how Highland businesses conducted themselves? Whatever it had taken, he'd done it, and she couldn't understand why.

In fact everyone around here seemed to want to help her. Gene was set upon finding things she'd like to eat, Beatrice had tried to give her a dating ticket – however misguided that was – and Atholl had come to find her this morning to invite her on this walk to the beach. She had a feeling that was also Beatrice's idea. Yet, none of them expected anything in return. She'd only been in Luke's company for three years, but that short time had been long enough to make her forget the kindness of a selfless favour.

If only these thoughts had made it through the sullen, grumpy clouds that had gathered around Nina in the last week, but she wasn't perceiving things clearly at all.

She folded the paper again, slipping it into her pocket and she watched the dogs splashing and yipping, racing in and out of the water, feeling herself just a tiny bit warmer than she had been before.

Chapter Eighteen

Lessons at the Willow School

'I'll get the fire going. Beattie, you sit down there. Mutt, do you mind making the coffees? The new espresso machine's easy enough to use.'

Atholl had made sure everyone was seated and comfortable inside the But and Ben, up above the coral beach.

Its low thatched roof was being buffeted by the increasingly chilly onshore wind that had chased them all indoors after an hour or so of beach combing, boot drying and sea staring.

Mark Firth had watched the party retreating, but had been too afraid of losing his phone signal to follow them. He was still down on the beach now, talking to his clients back home.

Mutt handed Ruth her coffee first, and she accepted it with an almost ethereal calmness. She was red-cheeked but pale everywhere else, and the red lipstick she'd applied this morning (it had been years since she'd worn her statement red lip and Mark had only looked at her, a little taken aback, and said nothing) made her appear paler still now that she was enclosed inside the gleaming whiteness of the cottage's lime-washed walls and the white overhead beams that drew the eye up to the thatch's exposed underside.

Ruth had left a space on the bench beside her for Mark and would glance at the closed cottage door every time the wind made it rattle. Did he really have clients desperate for financial advice on New Year's Day? Her worst fears blanched her complexion even more.

Next, Mutt made sure Nina had a cup. She'd hopped her way up from the beach, rather huffily refusing his offer of a supporting arm. Mind you, he had found it hard not to smirk at the sight of her cursing the sharp coral and jagged sea hollies as she scrambled up the beach path to the cottage wearing only one boot.

Beatrice had whispered, 'Be nice,' to him as he'd followed in Nina's furious, stumbling wake.

With everyone clasping steaming mugs to their chests, and the dogs settling down to sleep in front of the fire, Atholl took the opportunity to tell the little party about his craft. Even Nina, who was shivering beneath her cape – she'd returned Mutt's coat – smiled to see Atholl's enthusiasm as he demonstrated a simple basket weave and passed around hoops of willow so everyone could try working the supple rods, gleaming in shades of copper and red, yellow, orange and deep sappy green.

'We're no' just making a basket, we're practising an ancient art, the origins of which are lost to time. I may not know when it began, but I know willow growing has taken place here in Port Willow for generations. Many years ago our baskets sold all over the world, before the industry was crushed by mass production overseas, of course.'

'Who buys your work?' Ruth asked, concentrating on interlacing her willow whips across the framework that Atholl had started off for her and finding it far harder than the craftsman had made it look.

'Well, it's a fledgling business but now that I have the online shop, thanks to Beattie's encouragement,' he smiled at his girlfriend as he spoke, 'we're sending parcels off across the world every week now. No' many, mind, but enough to show that folk still want something handmade and honest. They want one-of-a-kind creations, and there are plenty willing to pay handsomely for them too.'

Now Nina's curiosity was sparked. 'How much would you sell something like that for?' She nodded to the corner of the room where Atholl's unfinished stag sculpture stood, supported by wires and wooden blocks to keep it upright while he worked.

Everyone admired Atholl's creation. The antlers and head were already complete, as was much of its neck and shoulders. When it was finished it would stand six feet tall.

Even though it was a hollow and airy thing, the dense, seemingly random weave that made up its willow musculature and flesh somehow spoke of movement and personality. The very lift of the beast's antlers – tall, jaunty and slender – and the angle of its throat and the direction of the creature's gaze conveyed a sense of grandeur, pride and stoicism. It was a fine thing indeed. Atholl had expertly graded the willow shades so the beast's neck was a paler gold than its pricked ears and tufted crown between the dark-red antlers.

'Och, let me see,' Atholl said, thinking. 'A wee bit under a thousand pounds, maybe.'

'But how long will it take you to make?' Nina said, genuinely interested.

'Many weeks, especially with the inn to run and the weaving classes taking off.'

'You need to put your prices up,' Nina told him, matter-of-factly, and she heard Mutt tut.

'Not everything has to be out of the reach of us mere mortals,' Mutt grumbled. All eyes turned to him and Nina glared. 'Are you thinking of buying up Atholl's entire stock then?' he put in.

'No,' Nina said calmly. 'I've already told you. There's nothing here I can sell.'

Mutt huffed a sigh.

'You can't complain that I'm here to exploit people, then get cross when I say I'm not buying anything,' Nina added in a lower pitch, only for Mutt's ears. 'Anyway, you gave me that list of makers. Why help me at all if you're so suspicious of me?'

Mutt's eyes widened and his mouth worked, but no answer came. She'd really got him this time. Hopefully now he'd stop needling her. She turned back to her basket, smiling, but after a moment her face fell.

Why had he helped her when all his instincts seemed to say she was out only for herself and didn't care about craft or tradition? Why had he come all the way back to the inn after midnight to leave the note, and after they'd argued too? She didn't dare acknowledge the little glow of hope that was mixed in with her indignation and annoyance.

Atholl put down his basket and made his way over to the pair. He had the look of a teacher coming to sort out two squabbling pupils. He checked their basketwork as he spoke and made a few corrections here and there before handing them back.

'Nina's right enough,' Atholl told them both. 'There's nothing here she could sell. My business model works fine for us here in Port Willow. Anywhere else, it wouldn't make sense at all. Besides, I dinnae ken what America would make o' me, turning up at customs with forty thousand willow rods. I'm the maker. And I work right here. I cannae be exported.'

Nina smiled, grateful that at least Atholl understood.

'But you're right too, Mutt,' Atholl continued. 'I'll let that stag go to the owner of some country house or other, and I won't be sorry to sell it. It's a braw piece and I think a thousand is handsome payment, but it's a price tag still way out of the reach of most ordinary folk.' Atholl bent his head a little between the two pupils. 'Between us, I've only just started work on a new project that's far more precious.' Atholl glanced across at the large pad of paper on the bench by the fire in which he'd often lose hours at a time sketching ideas in charcoal. 'It's only a notion at the moment, but when it's finished I shan't part with it, not even for a *million* pounds. I ken the difference between something's price and its value, same as any traditional maker.'

Nina wasn't sure if she'd been politely put in her place, or if Mutt had, or if this was Atholl's kindly way of helping them see eye to eye. Either way, Beatrice was grinning proudly at him across the room and, feeling chastened, the young pair didn't say anything else to one another after that.

Nina had a lot to think about as she worked on. Not least the fact that she wished Mutt had a better opinion of her, not that she'd done much to encourage him. As she worked on the basket, struggling to draw the weave tightly enough to make a truly useful object, she had to sit silently with the little feeling of shame within her, prodding at her and wanting to know why on earth she must insist on aggravating Mutt when he'd helped her.

She wasn't used to people questioning her. Everyone at Microtrends and all her old friends had shared the same goal – to develop, brand and sell special things, and yes, that involved elevating those products out of the reach of most ordinary consumers. Was she expected to feel bad about that too, alongside everything else she had experienced lately to make her feel awful?

Just maybe, she was finding that she did feel uneasy about it all, and that she had all along, but it had taken this eagle eyed, smirking Scot to point it out, and here he was, still helping her in spite of his reservations about her.

Nina kept her head down, not wanting to meet Mutt's eye again.

As Atholl made his way back to Beatrice he found he hadn't addressed the bickering crafters quite so quietly as he'd hoped.

'What is it?' Beatrice asked. 'What's this secret project?'

'You'll see in good time,' Atholl told her. His smile made the corners of his eyes crinkle delightfully, and he reached a hand to her jaw, briefly rubbing her cheek with his thumb.

'I'll look forward to seeing it then,' she told him, and the pair seemed to get rather lost in each other's smiles for a moment, until the door of the cottage banged open and Mark stepped inside.

'Good God, I thought the weather turned quickly in Yorkshire, but that storm came in off the sea like I don't know what!' He shook the raindrops from his waterproof jacket.

Ruth couldn't help herself. 'Maybe if you hadn't been so busy on your phone, you'd have noticed it sooner,' she quipped dryly.

Mutt immediately made for the coffee machine and filled a mug for Mark, hastening him over to the fireplace where he sat cradling his drink and looking into the flames with glazed eyes. His phone call seemed to have exhausted him.

Ruth watched his back, her eyes boring into him, but she didn't move over to the fire to join her husband.

If the weaving party hadn't fallen to focusing on their baskets in silence they might have noticed how Ruth seemed to get lost in her own panicked, anxious thoughts, her flushed cheeks paling, unable to tear her eyes from the man who had chosen to spend the last hour pacing in the pelting Scottish rain talking intently with God knows who, rather than drinking coffee by the fireside with his wife and learning how to do something new.

Even with the wind and rain picking up outside, the school grew warmer, and slowly the general mood lifted as the baskets neared completion. Mark kept his eyes on the fire until Atholl produced a fat brown paper parcel of sliced black bun; Gene's recipe, of course.

Only Beatrice didn't eat, and while the crafters took a break, Atholl set his demonstration basket aside and sat down with an arm around his girlfriend by the crackling fire. He didn't say anything, only holding her wordlessly. They leaned their heads together. From the outside they looked a picture of contentment. Nobody knew the struggle waged within Beatrice between her hopes and her fears.

Nina's black bun and coffee didn't last long.

Never before had she enjoyed food like this, not even back home when she was younger. She wasn't even sure what black bun was; some kind of spicy fruit cake, black as treacle and weirdly somehow baked inside pastry like a pie. Whatever it was, it was heavy and boozy and tasted of wintertime. Gene's food was proving to be a sensation, and she found she couldn't get enough of it, even if eating alone in her room in the evenings while she researched Highland designers and makers wasn't exactly festive.

She turned back to her basket, almost finished, and not at all as accomplished as Ruth or Mutt's. She didn't look around but she could hear Mutt at the kitchen nook behind her washing up the mugs. Every so often she felt a prickle of awareness, like goosebumps at the back of her neck, and she could have sworn it was Mutt's glance passing over her.

She didn't want to give that any more thought whatsoever, so instead she did what the Buddhist meditation master had told her on that retreat in the Catskills that she'd tried to get Luke to go on with her way back when they'd first met. He'd found he couldn't get away from the city that weekend so she'd gone alone.

She focused on being mindful now. All that matters, she told herself, is the intake of breath, the body centring, the slow exhalation and the sense of calm. For the first time, she really thought it might be working.

As she breathed, Nina slowly became aware of the sweet aromas around her. Warm and natural, green and dry. It must be the thatch, the peat and the fire, she told herself, but then came a scent that was bitter and bright – the sharp goodness of the willow whips the little group had warmed with their touch, no doubt. Earlier, Atholl had cut out strips of supple brown leather that he intended to wrap around the baskets' handles and now she could detect the deep buttery scent of the hide too. There was something else in the air, woody and floral. Something she'd picked up in the air a few times since her arrival in Port Willow; that heathery honey smell, that soapy lavender, but she had no idea where it was coming from.

The sound of someone shifting on the bench behind her brought her out of her thoughts and she found herself blinking as though she had slept. She peered behind her only to see Mutt, his attention drawn from his attempts at finishing his basket by the sight of her stirring.

His eyes were no longer mocking; in fact, she thought they looked heavy-lidded, as though he were weary. She jolted her eyes away from his and was glad to have her attention drawn to the great copper contraption in the far corner behind him. 'What's that thing?' she asked, nodding her head towards it.

'That's Gene's lavender still. He has a field of lavender at the back of this cottage,' Mutt told her. He looked down at his hands, winding a long leather strip around the handle of his basket.

'I knew I could smell lavender all over Port Willow!' Nina said turning back to her work.

Atholl heard her and spoke across the room.

'Aye, in the autumn we pressed the entire lavender field's harvest. Produced two braw quart bottles of lavender oil. We're hoping for even more next summer. All thanks to Beattie.'

Beatrice was by now thoroughly warmed by the fire and making small talk with Mark about his work and trying to draw Ruth into the conversation too, but Mrs Firth seemed intent on finishing her basket and was short on words. Beatrice broke off and smiled back at Atholl.

It had been her who, back in the summer, had the idea of replanting all of the leggy dry-stemmed lavender plants that had been left to overgrow in the field next to Atholl's willows. She'd saved the field and added a nice new side line to the willow workshop business. Gene used the lavender oil in his baking, but other than that they hadn't quite decided what to do with their harvest yet.

'We should probably get back to the inn,' Beatrice said, glancing out the low window to the sea. 'The sky's not clearing at all. I think that storm's arrived earlier than forecast.'

Soon, Mutt was helping Atholl tidy the workshop, and Nina slipping on her cold, wet boot with a revolted grimace. Mark pulled the zip on his jacket and looked around for his wife and found she was nowhere to be seen.

'Ruth?' he called.

Her shock of white spiky hair appeared from beneath one of the benches. She was on all fours, sweeping a hand over the workshop floor.

'Something wrong?' Mark asked her.

'My ring! My wedding ring. It must have slipped off my finger.'

'Right!' Beatrice announced, stepping forward, very much feeling this kind of thing was her forte. 'Don't panic. When do you last remember having it?'

'Are you sure you were wearing it?' Mark said, looking all around by his feet.

'I haven't taken it off in nearly twenty-five years,' she told him dryly before saying to Beatrice, 'I'm sure I had it on the walk over to the beach. It must be down there somewhere, on the coral. I think I was still wearing it when I sat on the rock.'

–

The whole party had run down to the beach in the wind and rain and searched for as long as they could withstand the weather, now a howling gale.

Mark seemed to search the hardest, soaking his shirt and jumper well past the elbows, disturbing the rockpools and turning over pebbles, sifting through sand with his cupped hands. Nina and Mutt split up to search separate spots on the shore. Even Echo and Bear, refreshed after a long sleep at the But and Ben, played at digging and scraping at the water's edge, mirroring their humans.

After a while, Atholl said he wanted to take Beatrice back to the inn as it was growing dark and she hadn't eaten and Beatrice had protested and said she wasn't a child, but then Ruth had insisted she couldn't let her blood sugar get too low so eventually Beatrice gave up and bent to the ex-midwife's instructions to go back and have dinner.

Neither Mutt nor Nina gave up and renewed their efforts until Nina's hair was completely flat and water ran down her neck and made her shiver again.

At first Ruth cursed the storm, but, after a while, as they realised the ring really was gone, she was glad the rain hid her tears.

'I'm sorry, Ruthy. I think you might have to accept that it's lost,' Mark had said, and he'd beckoned for her to give up too.

They all trudged back to the inn in the dark, dejected after a fretful first day of the year.

Nina was so damp and distracted she even scooped up the sleepy Bear in her arms and carried the sodden bundle all the way across the muddy meadow towards the lights of Port Willow Bay. Mutt walked a little further behind, making a show of calling for Echo who wanted to walk clamped to Ruth's right leg, gazing up at her, nudging her hand, now ringless, with his soft wet muzzle.

Ruth took the comfort the collie was offering and patted his head often. She thought of the day in the registry office when Mark had put the ring on her finger and she'd been so thrilled at the words, 'I pronounce you husband and wife' that she'd closed her eyes and tipped her head back, elated and full of excitement.

Mark was matching her strides, but further than an arm's reach away, head down, his brows knitted. Every now and then he'd say, 'I really am sorry, Ruthy. What a pity.' And each time she'd wonder if he was talking about her lost ring or their lost spark.

She kept her face turned from him and let Echo lead her away from the Coral Beach that had claimed the delicate, glistening band that had once bound her man to her. She'd never have her ring back and the tide would slowly erode it, but what of the promises the ring represented? Ruth feared they too had been worn down and washed away.

Chapter Nineteen

A Glimpse

'Just a little jelly, it's going to feel cold,' the sonographer said, already squeezing clear gloop from a bottle onto Beatrice's stomach and brandishing the scanner wand. He looked young and surprisingly nervy. Ever since they'd arrived he'd been trying to drum up some sense of excitement in the worried-looking prospective parents.

Maybe he hadn't been doing this for long? Maybe he hadn't met a bereaved parent before? Faced with Beatrice's stony focus on just getting this over with, he'd soon given up and turned business-like, thank goodness.

'Ready?' he asked her.

Beatrice couldn't answer, even with Atholl squeezing her hand and leaning close to her like she'd told him to, she couldn't. Not even after the midwife's visit to the inn to 'book her in' on the second of January and all her bloodwork coming back fine. Nothing could reassure Beatrice that this wasn't all about to end the same way it had last time.

She definitely wasn't ready. She'd tried to explain it all to Atholl, telling him she felt so battered about by life she was having trouble adjusting to whatever normal levels of optimism feel like. She hadn't told him that she considered herself so incredibly lucky to have even met Atholl who was, it turns out, exactly the right person for her out of all the billions of people on the planet, and she was lucky to have found a welcoming new home and a job that she loved, all in one fell swoop. She really couldn't expect even more good fortune from the universe. That would be greedy.

Her knees had been weak and shaking all morning and she'd found she couldn't eat breakfast. Sipping on the water she'd been directed to drink ahead of the scan was hard enough.

The sonographer flipped a switch that dimmed the lights in the room, and the monitor glowed blue amongst all the clinical white. Beatrice shifted on the layer of paper laid out underneath her as though trying to get into the smallest, most protected shape possible while still letting this stranger have access to her exposed belly.

Atholl met her panicked stare. 'Dinnae be afraid. I'm here. I told you, we'll do this together. No matter what.' He nodded, holding her gaze until she nodded back.

'I can't look.' Her words were barely a whisper.

Atholl indicated to the sonographer to go ahead and Beatrice turned her face to Atholl's chest, screwing up her eyes and trying not to conjure up the image of the black screen that had haunted her memory since the day she'd seen it back in the spring of last year. She tried to brace herself for the words there's simply no preparing for or protecting yourself from: 'no heartbeat'.

But the man wasn't saying anything and she took this as a terrible sign. As he worked the wand over her stomach, she anticipated the things he was about to utter; the feeble apology, the calm, carefully picked words they're trained to say to make sure there's no equivocation, no confusion whatsoever, that you're not taking this baby home.

Atholl's shirt was tear-stained and her grip on his collar fearsomely tight when Beatrice heard the gasp and Atholl's chest heaved, rolling her like a ship on a great wave. He was sobbing.

'Beattie, look,' he said, his voice vibrating with emotion.

She lifted her head just as the sonographer turned a dial and a great, swooshing, thumping heartbeat resounded inside the darkened room as though it were Beatrice and Atholl curled snug inside the womb, clinging together like twins hearing strange, muffled sounds of blood rushing and a new world to come.

'There's your baby,' the sonographer said.

Beatrice didn't smile, even though she was aware she was expected to. All her concentration was fixed upon the shadowy image, a skinny thing with a big rounded head and spindly limbs, bucking and moving in tiny jolts she could not feel.

'Baby's measuring just under fourteen weeks. Does that match your calculations?'

Beatrice didn't answer. The midwife had estimated much the same thing. It meant she'd fallen pregnant only a few weeks after she'd met Atholl. She'd asked her midwife about the bleeding she'd had over the autumn, having simply assumed they were unusually light periods and she'd put it down to turning forty and the first signs of perimenopause. The midwife had noted it all down with unworried composure. Fourteen weeks meant she'd passed the awful milestone of her last baby's loss and this realisation afforded her the slimmest degree of relief.

Atholl pressed his face against hers and the pair watched their child in silent wonder, before the sonographer lifted the wand from her stomach and their direct line to the tiny person's world was cut off. Beatrice felt it keenly, like night-warmed covers being suddenly yanked from her sleeping body on a cold winter morning. She awoke from the screen's spell, blinking at Atholl.

The sonographer bustled out the room saying he'd taken some images and would get them from the printer next door.

Alone by the monitor the parents held their heads together, eyes wide and lips parted. Beatrice was still shaking.

'Dinnae be afraid,' Atholl said again, but this time there was an assured tone in his voice that told her he already believed this miraculous thing was actually going to happen, that the tiny shadow they'd just seen was going to perform its magic and bring itself into full being.

Beatrice gripped his shirt again, feeling suddenly tired and limp.

He pressed a kiss to her head. 'I ken you're afraid, but I have enough belief in that wee soul for the both of us. All you have to do is hold on, OK? Hold on, and our baby will come to us.'

Burying her head into his chest once more, she let him enfold her in his arms. Her mind turned as blank as the screen was now. That's what fear of hoping for too much can do to a woman who has already seen her deepest dream dissolve away. So she let herself not feel or think anything and held on to Atholl with what little strength she had left and he drove her home through the last of the thawing snow to the inn.

Chapter Twenty

Lost in the Highlands

Nina had turned down the offer of Echo's company that morning, asking exasperatedly why on earth she would take a mangy old sheepdog to a business meeting. Gene had protested that the inn dog 'wasnae the least bit mangy' and that John Cor, the distillery owner, would be glad to see the pair of them.

'Besides,' Gene had added, as he handed her the packed lunch he'd taken it upon himself to prepare, 'Echo's handy in the countryside. Scares off a' manner o' predators.' He'd proceeded to tell her about adders and wolves, adding that she'd most likely be all right seeing as it was January and she'd be sticking to the main roads.

Nina had reminded him she was taking the bus and not frolicking through the heather. She thanked him for the package and made her way out of the inn in her cape and heels. She'd relented and borrowed one of Kitty's Fair Isle berets (she'd referred to it as her Tam o' Shanter) and both women had agreed that Nina really suited its pale hues.

She'd felt she looked the part; somewhere between business-like and authentically Scotch (as Luke might have said, and Gene would have tutted and corrected him with a grumpy, 'it's *Scottish*').

Nina hadn't known she was causing the villagers to raise their eyebrows as she'd waited alone at the bus stop for the Highland shuttle service that morning, and everyone who'd seen her thought she looked chilly as opposed to chic.

She'd turned down Seth's offer of a lift on his handlebars and he'd cycled merrily away, over to Skye to take Mrs Fergusson her beef and pearl barley stew and clootie dumpling dinner. Atholl had sneaked a bottle of stout into the basket too, knowing it was his mother's favourite.

Nina cursed the self-confidence of this morning now that she was standing face to face with a bedraggled, cud-chewing Highland cow in some unknown location in the hills high above Port Willow. She'd have been glad of some of Echo's protective sheepdog skills round about now.

She'd been so pleased when the little shuttle bus collected her from the village at eight o'clock and she'd paid her fare with the strange Scottish note she'd withdrawn from the machine at the airport almost two weeks ago. She'd taken her seat right at the back and been bumped and jostled out of the village and up along the single lane A-road. She'd even enjoyed the scenery, which had grown increasingly frosted and hilly as the bus took her away from Port Willow and onto the higher, exposed ground.

Cosy in her seat, she'd snapped a few selfies – her complexion was surprisingly clear in the Highland light and her cheeks were so naturally pink she hadn't needed to apply her cheek stain that morning. There was definitely something healthful and glowing in her eyes too, something she hadn't seen for a long time, something all those one-hundred-dollar, celebrity-endorsed 'wellness shots' of apple cider vinegar, turmeric, and tart wild cherry hadn't been able to give her – even though she'd believed in their powers wholeheartedly when she'd helped bring those products to market. That had been quite the launch party. Gwyneth Paltrow and her nutritionist had flown in specially and spoken at the influencers' presser. What a triumph.

But Gwyneth wasn't here to help now that Nina was stranded up on the hills in the back of beyond. In fact there didn't seem to be a soul for miles around, not that Nina could actually *see* for miles.

Mr Cor had warned her about something called the Haar coming in and she'd nodded and thanked him for their meeting, not thinking to ask what a Haar might be – she blamed this now on the fact she'd sampled eight types of Mr Cor's whisky and felt extremely warm, light-headed and relaxed of limb as she'd stepped out of the distillery.

She'd found her way to the bus stop all right, no problems there; the driver had pointed it out as they'd sailed past it earlier that day. It had been a ten-minute walk downhill in her heels but she'd made it, only dimly aware that what had this morning been a breath-taking view of open sky and a hint of sea loch between rolling hills was by that point swallowed up in the rising white-grey cloud of thick fog.

'Ah, so that's haar!' she'd concluded, pleased she'd worked it out, opening Gene's lunch bag and settling down to wait for her bus back to Port Willow. One every hour, the timetable had told her.

Gene had done her proud with his packed lunch today; some kind of cream cheese rolled in toasted oats on rough wheaten bread. Simple, savoury and creamy. She'd devoured every bite and sucked her thumbs clean within minutes.

She'd been happy, even though she hadn't made any great leaps of progress with Mr Cor. He had been hospitable and listened to her pitch about developing a brand partnership with Remy's, one of Microtrend's client's exclusive east coast bar chains. He hadn't said anything to shut down her ideas of exporting a small batch of his most exclusive whisky in a newly designed bottle for a high-end market in New York. He'd even let her snap pictures of the surprisingly picturesque peat bogs beyond the distillery walls and shown her all the secret nooks and crannies of the old building. He hadn't flinched or smirked when she'd told him this was the perfect spot for the brand shoot and she could see their ads between the covers of *Vogue* and *GQ*. Condé Nast would lap these up. However, he also hadn't yet agreed to schedule an appointment for another meeting, this time with one of her associates from New York. He'd smiled and said, 'we'll see' and poured her another glass of his finest, but he hadn't actually shaken hands on anything.

Nina wasn't all that worried. This had all been part of her old job. Make contact, show them the possibilities, share your ideas, and let the relationship develop from there. These things take time, like all relationships. Nobody would be talking money for at least six months, but she'd made contact and that's what mattered. She'd let Seamus know later today and then she'd plan the follow-up discussions and get the creative team on board. There! Not bad for a day's work. Though it wasn't great for two weeks' work, she knew.

The other meetings had all gone the same way. Everyone was polite and welcoming, not as flattered by her interest in developing their products and taking them to new markets as she'd thought they'd be, but, still, she'd started talks with everyone on Mutt's list. She might even be able to fly home in the morning; it was after all the seventh and she had an eTicket on her phone. She'd need Seamus's go-ahead first though. Had she done enough to buy her passage out of this place and back to New York? She had no idea.

By the time the sun had started to set, barely visible through the thick white fog, and the bus *still* hadn't arrived, Seamus was becoming the least of her worries.

'Oh come on! I've waited over an hour now!'

Gene had mentioned snakes and wolves. Had he been joking? You couldn't tell with these smirking Scottish types.

The thing about a Highland haar is, it billows in from off the water, creeping silently up over the land, engulfing everything in damp white nothingness, and everything grinds to a halt, especially Highland hopper bus services. It sneaks in at open windows, makes its way down rabbit holes, steals away all visibility and leaves its chilly dew on everything it touches. The cow's eyelashes and pulsing nostrils were dark and spiked with the stuff as it barged inside the bus shelter, coming to a stop and staring impolitely at Nina.

She'd heard it approach through the whiteness around about the time she was scrunching up Gene's sandwich bag and resolving to march back up the hill towards the distillery, hoping Mr Cor would have the fire on. The velvety snout had appeared first, followed by the horns and its orange nest of hair, making Nina squeal in fright and flatten herself against the Perspex shelter.

She stared back at it now, trying to work out what to do. She had little to no experience of any cattle, let alone the Highland type. Those horns looked deadly, even with the big tufts of grass and moss dangling from them like streamers on a kid's bicycle.

What if she did a runner? Would it follow her? She'd definitely heard about cattle stampeding in fright and angry bulls goring innocent hill walkers who stumbled across their path.

'You don't look all that angry,' she told the beast.

It blinked through its matted red fringe, still lazily chewing and showing flashes of stubby round teeth and a pink tongue.

'If you're waiting for the bus to Port Willow, I think it's been cancelled.'

Neither of them moved.

'Well, I'll be going then,' she said, aware there wasn't much room to pass the great lump so she'd have to step onto the road.

Listening carefully for engine sounds and hearing only the dampened noises of stilling winds and the cow's jaw working away, she stepped gingerly around her companion, but it moved to watch her, a big black eye revealing itself through its shifting hair-do.

'Good cow,' she told it, reaching out a tentative hand to pat the side of its neck below its pricked ears. This was her first mistake.

Feeling her touch, the beast leaned into her hand, tipping its head with a grumpy lowing.

'You want scratches?' She'd seen the inn dogs doing exactly the same thing with any passer-by who'd stoop to touch them. 'Well, OK then.' Grimacing at the thought of what might get trapped beneath her beautifully gel-polished nails, she clawed gently at the creature's neck. It leaned heavily towards her, shifting its feet to get closer to the friendly human.

'Woah, careful!' Nina stepped back onto the black tarmac, scratching at the animal the whole time and finding she was actually smiling at the big monster, idly thinking through her whisky haze that she might christen her Gwyneth. It turned its great horns and snorted and snuffled as Nina scratched harder. 'Well, it's been nice meeting you, but I've got to find a way down off these hills...'

Gwyneth wasn't interested in hearing this and turned her body fully to encourage more scratches, her hooves clopping heavily, and before Nina could do anything to prevent it, she felt herself winded and knocked flying by the beast's great heavy haunches.

Nina's ankle twisted with a sickening rip as her shoe slipped sideways.

'*Oww!*' She hit the road heavily. The cow stomped and jolted as Nina screamed in alarm.

Only then did she feel the vibrations through the tarmac, hear the thunder of an engine, and see the head-lights penetrating the white cloud as her entire world reduced to the horrible realisation that she was lying in the path of a moving vehicle. The screeching of brakes silenced all other thoughts. She instinctively braced her body, it was too late to move out of its path.

This was it. She was going to die on a foggy Scottish roadside and the only witness would be a filthy touch-starved cow called Gwyneth. And why not? After everything else this winter, why the hell not?

But the impact never came. Instead there was a great crunch of rubber on gravel, a ratcheting handbrake, hooves clopping away into the mists, a door creaking open and a deep voice crying out, 'Jesus Christ!'

'I didn't even get to say goodbye,' Nina murmured, dazed and in shock. 'Come back, Gwynnie!'

'Oh my God, look at you! Your ankle! Is your back or neck hurt? I'll have to lift you,' the voice said through white fog, and Nina felt no pain – probably something to do with the whisky – as she was hoisted into the air and held against Mutt's broad chest.

Chapter Twenty-one

Beatrice and the Research Vortex

'Now the haar's lifting, shall we take the train into Fort William? Go to the Pram Warehouse, maybe? Get a few wee things for the baby?'

Beatrice was at her command centre in the sun room, huddled in intense focus over her laptop. 'No thanks,' she replied, cheerily, but Atholl seemed to detect something false in it.

'No thank you? You must have a list of pregnancy and baby things you're needing? You, Beatrice Halliday, the queen of list-making?'

'I'm going to keep working on this, if you don't mind. Maybe another day, *hmm*?'

'Right-o,' he replied, as he watched her at her screen. He didn't give in though. He'd seen first-hand what happened when Beatrice bottled up her feelings. He'd held her through the panic attacks that immobilised her with sudden fear, he'd listened when she broke down and blurted the story of her loss and how she'd felt none of her friends and family wanted to talk about the miscarriage anymore. He'd cradled her hands, taken his time, and let her know she was safe confiding in him. Atholl was a practical man. He learned from life's lessons and kept them as close to his heart as he held Beatrice herself. He wasn't about to let this silence of hers slide.

'I was just, *eh*, thinking about how it wouldn't hurt to be prepared. We havenae really talked about the baby since the scan the other day.'

Beatrice's fingertips stilled on the keyboard.

'It might be nice, gettin' a few wee bits and pieces. Some clothes for you, maybe? You cannae keep wearing my shirts, I mean, you can if you want to, but you'd be comfier in real maternity clothes, would you no'?'

Beatrice touched a hand to the pocket of the orange and brown plaid shirt she'd buttoned over a t-shirt this morning. It was big and warm and smelled like Atholl. She couldn't think of anything that would bring her more comfort, least of all a walk around a brightly lit baby superstore full of waddling pregnant women and young mums cooing over expensive car seats and breast pumps. She shook her head.

Atholl changed tack. 'Is it organising the festival that's got you so absorbed?'

Beatrice turned to face him now, smiling, a little strangely maybe, something only Atholl would be able to detect.

'It is! I've got the ice cream van booked now, and all the local makers have been assigned an exhibition stand in the village hall. The church is opening specially to display Easter flower arrangements. Reverend Park from St Magnus' is going to judge them and Mr and Mrs Shirlaw are donating a free Highland cream tea at the Kailyard cafe at the back of the General Stores for the winner. The school choir have agreed to sing some Gaelic fisher songs as well. Kitty's along there now, handing in the song sheets. There's still so much to do, though.'

Atholl couldn't help letting his concern show.

'Don't frown. Easter weekend's ages away. I'll have this all in hand in a week or so,' she told him, knowing this was a lie. She hadn't even begun the search for a bouncy castle, and where would she find a coconut shy and other traditional fairground attractions in the dead of winter in the Scottish Highlands?

Atholl peered past her at the laptop screen. 'That doesnae look like festival organisin' to me. Should I be worried?'

'What? Oh! No,' Beatrice laughed.

'Top ten tips to reignite long-term relationship passion,' he read aloud. 'Can you still rock his socks at sixty?' Atholl was smiling by now too.

'Just a little side line I've got going,' Beatrice said, relaxing now she wasn't under the spotlight of Atholl's concern.

'A side line in what, exactly? I shudder to think.'

'In helping the Firths, of course.'

'Nope, none the wiser, yet again.'

'Well, you know how I've always had a... passing interest in dating shows, and body language, and how people meet and fall in love, all that kind of thing.'

'Aye, I do, you've made me watch that many programmes about celebrity dinner dates, getting married to a stranger, love islands and a' that.'

'Come on, you've enjoyed them too.'

Atholl had to admit he had, but more so because he loved lying on the sofa with Beatrice curled up close to him where he could watch her eyes gleaming at the sight of these hapless, hopeful people navigating their way towards love, if they were lucky. He told her as much now, and it made her smile again.

'Well then, you'll know how much I want to help Ruth Firth, and Mark too, of course, even though he is a pain in the arse.'

'That's no' very nice, Beattie. Even if it is true.'

Beatrice shrugged and showed him the handwritten research notes she'd been making in her jotter which he held closer, raising his eyebrows and pulling an amused, impressed face as he read. 'I reckon that ought to work,' he said, and Beatrice's smile grew even more.

'They're here for ages yet. We've got loads of time to get their love affair rekindled.'

Atholl inhaled. 'Beattie, I know you're a braw match-maker but that pair have been married twenty-five years and together far longer. You cannae meddle in something wi' as much history as that.'

'I'm not going to meddle. I'm just going to make a few helpful suggestions to get them on track again.'

Atholl looked again at Beatrice's notes. 'And if Ruth Firth tells you to mind your own business?'

Beatrice exhaled at the thought. 'She won't, will she? She's so open and chatty, with me at least. Gene and her are getting along well during her cookery lessons too, and she's not exactly shy. She's definitely not happy, though, and neither's her husband by the looks of things, not really.'

'If you ask me, he's got a piece on the side back home.'

'What?' Beatrice was aghast. 'An affair? He couldn't!'

'He's always on his phone, sneaking off with it, no matter the weather.'

Beatrice thought about it. It wasn't often Atholl made assumptions about people, and he had good instincts, but she dismissed his idea. 'Something in him looks more sad than sneaky. I just can't imagine he's getting his end away somewhere else.'

'Well, just remember you've got to look after yourself as well as all these other folk you take under your wing.'

Beatrice agreed, but his words had sparked another little reminder. 'Oh, and then there's Nina and Mutt!'

'What about them?'

'They're an interesting couple, don't you think?'

'They cannae stand one another.'

'There was a time you couldn't stand me.'

'You werenae all that keen on me either. But that lasted all of a few days. I seem to remember somebody throwing themselves at me behind the Gowk Heid Rock over on Skye when I was innocently taking them out on a friendly picnic.'

'Ah, is that how you remember it?' Beatrice laughed, knowing full well they had both been awkwardly leaning nearer and nearer and totally failing to close the distance between them with a kiss. 'You took me to meet your family that day. I'd say that was serious.'

'They gate-crashed our date!'

'So it *was* a date?'

Atholl held his hands up in defeat and stooped to kiss her lips. 'Just don't go overboard with your matchmaking, or the event planning,' he pleaded. 'This festival seems to have a life of its own now.'

Beatrice turned back to the screen with a sigh. He had a point. The event had become grander than she'd first anticipated but it was nothing she couldn't handle. In fact, she needed the festival to divert her.

'Atholl… it's only because I *know* that the festival will definitely happen, but with babies… nothing's guaranteed. So, I'll control what I can, for now. I can't bear to let myself think about the future. You understand, right?'

She didn't need to look up to see the sadness in Atholl's eyes. He kissed her once again on the top of her head. 'OK, well, you say the word when you want to think about gathering together a few baby things and I'll be here. I even know what a baby bumby is now, thanks to Vic and Angela. I'd add one to your list when you feel ready to start writing one.'

'I will,' Beatrice laughed lightly, and Atholl watched her continue to work for a moment or two before leaving her in peace.

However, only moments later, the flashing of headlights outside the reception and the tooting of a car horn, followed by the sounds of an argument taking place on the pavement shattered any calm at the inn. Beatrice and Atholl ran to the door to see what the noise was all about.

Chapter Twenty-two

The Upgrade

'*I said* I don't need to be carried. Why do you think they gave me crutches?' Nina was practically shouting, as Mutt, with Nina's Birkin cargo bag over his arm with her broken shoe sticking out of one of the pockets, gave in and held open the inn doors.

Mutt bit back. 'You're obviously feeling better; you've started snapping at me again. What were you doing up in the hills in that haar and mucking about on the road anyway?'

'I told you, there was a cow, and it pushed me.'

'I didn't see any cow. Are you sure you're not concussed?'

Nina slapped Mutt's hand away from her forehead.

'Seriously, let's go back to the hospital, get your head checked.' Mutt tried to stop her by walking in front of her.

'Out of my way. I've got crutches and I know how to use them.' Nina nodded her head towards Mutt's crotch and he quickly moved aside.

Twisted not broken, but very painful to walk on for a few days, total bed rest and no flying. That's what the doctor had told her after he'd thanked Mutt for his quick-thinking in driving her to the hospital.

It had taken over an hour to get there and Nina had slept most of the way with Mutt's navy fisherman jumper tucked around her for warmth. The whisky and the shock had made her sleep, in spite of Mutt's attempts to keep her awake with small talk and singing along to songs on the radio.

She couldn't have known, as he'd helped her into the wheelchair at the doors of A&E, quite how rattled he'd been to have nearly struck her with his truck, even if he had only been crawling through the haar at less than ten miles an hour, coming back from collecting his big ladders from Port Willow castle where he'd done some work just before Christmas.

'Stay with me, Nina. No sleeping now. We're almost there,' he'd begged over and over again as he'd suffered through every slow mile until they were at last free of the haar and on the dual carriageway where he'd put his boot down to get her the help she needed.

He'd told the doctor, 'I thought she'd been hit by a car before I found her! I thought she was hurt, and badly too. With no way to get the helicopter out, I knew I'd be quicker setting off in the fog than waiting for an ambulance to come.'

The doctor had shaken his hand and Nina had rolled her eyes, telling them both, 'I'm right here, you know? And I *was* hurt!'

Her ankle was now a horrid greenish-blue beneath its bandages and there was no way she'd fit her foot inside the now-broken Jimmy Choo which the doctor had firmly – and rather arrogantly, in Nina's opinion – blamed for her fall. Nobody had listened when she'd shouted, 'I told you, it was the cow!' and the doctor had told Mutt he'd administered some pretty strong painkillers and she was to avoid any more early morning whisky sampling sessions while completing the course. Nina hadn't reacted well to this and everyone had breathed a sigh of relief when she'd been discharged on the condition she rested at the inn for a few days and didn't put any weight on the ankle.

'What happened to you?' Beatrice cried, overtaking Atholl to reach the limping woman first.

'I fell, but it's nothing. I'm just going to lie down for a bit.' Nina stopped at the foot of the stairs. 'Oh.'

Mutt was already beside her, making gestures as though she only had to say the word and he'd lift her again, but she put him off with a sharp look. He dropped back, rubbing the back of his neck helplessly.

'You can't stay up on the top floor now,' Beatrice told her, moving to the reception desk and its computer. 'We could swap you with…' Her eyes lit up like light bulbs. 'Actually, leave it with me. You sit in the bar for ten minutes. I'll sort it all out in a jiffy.'

-

'An upgrade? Why?' Ruth asked, standing bemused at the door to her ground-floor room.

'Will it cost us extra?' Mark shouted from the bed where he had a laptop over his legs.

'No, it's on the house,' Beatrice assured him. 'You are our competition winners after all and what with your silver wedding anniversary coming up this year, we're moving you to our honeymoon suite. It's called the Princess room.'

Mark scoffed loudly, and Ruth flustered to cover his rudeness.

'That's nice of you. We'd love to move. Wouldn't we, Mark?'

'There's complimentary champagne and chocolate truffles all set out for you. Do you need a hand packing?' Beatrice rubbed her hands together.

'We can be ready in twenty minutes,' Ruth assured her, and so that afternoon Nina had hobbled into the Firths' freshly made up double with en suite and bay view, while Mark and Ruth stood aghast one floor above, contemplating in horror the six-foot-tall fairy-tale bed in all its refurbished, gauzy white glory.

'Well, *umm*, it's... it's...' Ruth looked to Mark, pleadingly.

'It's different,' he said, taking the key from Beatrice, who was still standing in the doorway looking oddly hopeful and excited.

'Enjoy the bubbly and the lovely view along to the jetty. Dinner service doesn't start for another hour and a half,' she'd said, before slipping away, closing the door ever so quietly.

'Is that woman all right?' Mark said when she was gone.

Ruth ignored him. 'You'd better open that bottle before the ice melts in the bucket.'

She walked around the room, taking it all in, not entirely sure how she felt about their new habitation. Beatrice had told them the Princess room was almost always booked up but it had just become free yesterday and it was theirs for the rest of their stay. Ruth wasn't sure why it was so popular. It definitely wasn't for everyone. You'd need to be an Olympic gymnast to get up that ladder and safely under the sheets for a start.

Mark did as he was told, and he soon presented his wife with a frothy glassful.

'Well... here's to us,' Ruth said. 'Happy anniversary.'

'Oh yes, happy anniversary.' They clinked glasses and Ruth perched tentatively on the vintage green velvet chaise by the window, which Beatrice had recently had reupholstered.

'Twenty-five years, eh?' Ruth said before she drank. 'It was a nice wedding, even if it wasn't quite the big white thing little girls dream of.'

'*Hmm*,' Mark only nodded in agreement, looking around for somewhere to sit and realising there was only the spot beside his wife, unless he wanted to crawl into the bathtub which, mortified, Ruth thought he might well prefer. She patted the spot beside her and in the ensuing silence he shuffled over to join her, hoiking his trousers up at the knees as he sat.

'Still, we got to have the twins as page boys, didn't we?'

This brightened Mark up. 'That we did. Have either of the boys phoned today?' he added, looking hopeful.

'No.' Ruth shook her head.

Silence again. Ruth topped up their glasses and the couple gulped their champagne in the looming shadow of the towering honeymooners' bed.

Chapter Twenty-three

After the Rescue

'Scotch broth,' Beatrice informed Nina as she set the bowl down before her. 'And that's salty Highland butter and freshly baked oat bread.'

She'd reserved her a seat by the fire in the bar room after insisting she couldn't possibly eat alone any longer, not now she'd had this terrible accident and she needed watching. Nina had relented because she had a point; she *was* getting sick of her own company, and after the twenty-four hours she'd just had, she couldn't face another lonely evening working in her room.

Seamus hadn't replied to her email about the possible leads she'd established while in Scotland. Not all that surprising. He was a very busy man. Eventually, after some fitful painkiller-induced naps, Mitch had called her back and made it clear Seamus wasn't interested in hearing from her until she had something more concrete, something they could sell. Something unique.

'I've put a hold on your flight, take another few weeks. OK?'

'But, I want to come home, I…' Every second away from the office felt like another tolling death knell for her career. She'd be forgotten about if she didn't get there soon. 'The whisky idea's *good*! Can't we get Creative working on some mock-ups for the brand collaboration? I can talk with Remy's about it today if Seamus would just let me. I know they'll like the idea of an exclusive guest distillery in their bars, especially if we get the look right…'

'Nina, Seamus doesn't want you approaching Remy's or anyone else right now. If anyone's doing that it'll be Luke or Himari. *They* talk to clients now. You're the scout, remember? You make first contact, that's all.'

'But…'

'Just be back here in a few weeks and make sure you have some solid ideas. Seamus needs to be wowed if you're going to get back in his good books, and… between you and me, you don't want to be here. Luke's refitting your old office for Himari. You don't need to see that.'

Nina digested that horrid morsel in silence.

'Listen, honey, if someone was paying me to make myself scarce on vacation for a while, I'd make the most of it. Do you hear what I'm saying? You're injured, you're not allowed to fly anyway, what's the hurry? Go see some sights, chase some wild haggises – or is it haggi? Toss a few cabers, or whatever it is they do there. Just don't hurry home yet.'

It had hurt to hear, but there was sense in it. Better to come back all guns blazing in another week or two when she had a stronger portfolio of Scottish products and new connections than limp back into Seamus's office now with a handful of half-baked plans. And it was better to let herself brood over Luke and Himari from a distance than have her nose rubbed in their whirlwind romance close up.

The thought of them living her old life, of being replaced so easily, gave her a physical pain in her chest that made her wonder if that's why people call it heartache.

Luke had been everything to her until so recently. Her friend, her lover, her home, and her business associate. Now, there was just nothing at all, apart from the shock and the loneliness and the sense of having hit rock bottom somewhere around about the time she was hitting the tarmac on the roadside in the haar. Her humiliation was complete.

She'd been sent away from New York where everyone she knew would be whispering about her and air-kissing Himari, and now she'd made a fool of herself amongst the people of Port Willow too. She'd been stubborn and sullen, demanding and unsatisfied, and her sneaking sense of shame combined with her sense of being unwanted and exiled. She didn't really belong anywhere, it seemed.

Except here there was a cosy bed, and a chance to prove herself, and good people like Ruth and Beatrice who never walked past her without saying hello and asking how she was. It was a small sense of belonging, she supposed, and so she'd resolved to stay put and let herself recover a little.

The bar room was growing busy as guests piled in for dinner and the locals ordered drinks at the bar. No sign of Mutt again tonight, she noticed. He'd made himself scarce last night after it was decided she'd take Ruth and Mark's room.

She hadn't actually thanked Mutt, she realised. Technically, he'd rescued her, though something inside her hated to admit it. The same thing that told her she was supposed to be standing on her own two feet, proving her worth and showing she could make it on her own, in spite of what her colleagues might think of her.

Yet she couldn't help questioning where she would be now if he hadn't picked her up. She could have passed out on the roadside and really been in danger. He'd been there right when she needed him.

That's another thing she had to be grateful to him for. He'd helped her out even though he thought she was some overpaid, overprivileged corporate oik. He'd made assumptions about her that had riled her. He'd teased her and aggravated her. He didn't like her business ethos, he didn't approve of her high heels, he thought her insistence on seeking out luxury and scarcity ridiculous and exploitative. Well, he was wrong about all of that.

As she toyed with her soup spoon in the steaming bowl, her curiosity about Mutt grew at the back of her mind, but she didn't want to think about it, not when she was tired and still a little hungover from the whisky and the fall. Not when there were painkillers numbing all her faculties. Not when she'd liked being held in his arms and carried across the country safe on his passenger seat. Not when she'd worn his fisherman jumper all night long and felt guilty doing so for reasons she also did not want to examine.

She shook her head to clear it and concentrated on feeding herself. She had to build herself back up, find strength from within, not from some brusque, stubbly white knight on his pick-up truck charger who didn't seem to like her all that much but seemed to keep saving her and made her weaken a little each time she felt him gaze at her through those dark lashes.

'*Uh-uh*, nope,' she said to herself, shaking thoughts of him away, wielding her spoon and looking at the thick golden broth – the kitchen's own homemade ham hock and celery stock – specked with parsley and bobbing with soft pearl barley and fat peas. It looked wholesome. Just what she needed right now. And it smelled wonderful, salty and savoury.

Her appetite, suppressed years ago, was back with a vengeance. Why did the Highlands do this to her, she wondered? Was it because the air was so fresh and unpolluted that every gorgeous foody aroma and sweet scent off the sea or the landscape went straight to her head in an olfactory assault that left her salivating? Everything here tasted better than anything Luke had ever tried to impress her with back home. All those clean, lean dishes, every healthful, ascetic mouthful, all the skipping meals and never, ever feeling full. It hadn't been fun, and it hadn't been worth it.

Beatrice chalked the words 'sticky toffee pudding with proper custard' onto the specials board and turned to throw a wink at Nina, making her feel seen and indulged in a way she hadn't been in years.

Tears wanted to prickle at the back of her eyes, but Nina wouldn't let them. She grabbed a hunk of buttery loaf and tucked in, the warmth from the fire and the warmth in her belly holding her self-pity at bay, the closest thing to the hug she so desperately needed, and almost as soothing.

As Nina was adjusting her crutches ready to turn in for the evening, now full of broth and sticky toffee pudding and feeling really very satisfied indeed, Beatrice joined her for the walk back to her room.

'I'll get the doors for you,' she told her.

Nina thanked her. It was nice having someone look after her a bit. Beatrice was probably only a few years younger than her mum, though she wouldn't dream of telling her that.

Beatrice had the look of someone havering to get something off her chest, so she kept quiet and let her find the right moment.

'Listen, Nina, love,' the older woman said, as she opened the doors into the reception area for her. 'Don't mind Mutt too much. He's... he's got his own stuff going on.'

'Stuff that makes him be rude to women he doesn't even know?' Nina knew how that sounded. Sullen. Hypocritical. She felt herself shrink when Beatrice laughed.

'Well, yes, there's a little of that in him.'

'He's probably never met anyone like me,' Nina suggested.

'Well...' Beatrice screwed up her eyes as though pondering this. 'It's just... some people don't come to the inn for a holiday, or to work in Mutt's case, or for the food or even for the scenery.'

Now Nina screwed up her face in confusion. 'They don't?'

'Ah, they *think* they do, but, speaking from personal experience, that's only the half of it. Something about Port Willow draws people who *need* this place. It's a runaway's paradise. I came here to escape and... other people have too. Mutt's no different. He's here licking his wounds. He might seem all rough and tough—'

'And sarcastic,' Nina put in, struggling with her room key before getting her door open.

'Well yes, but there's so much more to him. He's a puppy dog really.'

Nina had listened and nodded, not really knowing what Beatrice wanted her to say, and so she'd thanked her for dinner, feeling herself suddenly wanting to kiss her on the cheek like family would. She said goodnight and let Beatrice close the door on her.

That night Nina barely slept and when she did she dreamed she was by the roadside in a great white fog and instead of a big ginger Highland cow bowling her over, it was Bear, Mutt's tumbling grey-black puppy, and she'd fallen and fallen, never actually hitting the hard tarmac, and all the time hearing a man's pleading voice saying over and over again, 'Stay with me, Nina. No sleeping now. We're almost there.'

Chapter Twenty-four

The Absent Husband

The thing about not having sex with your husband when you've been married going on twenty-five years is it's all too easy to forget about having sex altogether, and nobody really notices because there's always something far more pressing to be doing like the weeding, or buying yet another birthday present for a family member, or there's the supermarket shop, or one of you slept all evening on the sofa and then didn't come to bed until three and by then you were fast asleep.

The thing about being thrown together overnight with your spouse of twenty-five years is the not-having-sex aspect of your relationship is all you can think about. Especially when you're in a suggestively flouncy honeymoon suite where generations of young bucks have without doubt done the deed and probably really rather enjoyed it.

It had been a long night for entirely the wrong reasons. For a start neither of them could get to sleep, then Ruth remembered she hadn't applied her HRT cream and had to climb down the ladder to get it, and then Mark had needed to go to the bathroom again, and then both of them were thirsty and had really fancied a cup of tea after all that champagne earlier but by then they were both pretending to be asleep with their backs turned on one another so they'd both gone thirsty until breakfast time. And in all the slow, wincing, awkward, strained seconds that passed neither Mark nor Ruth could bring themselves to wriggle a little closer under the covers and just get on with it.

Ruth had tried to fathom it. How are you supposed to skip straight to whispering sweet nothings with someone you've barely spoken to all month and even that was about your brother-in-law's septic tank problems?

How are you supposed to get naked with a person who hasn't so much as held your hand in, oh, at least five years?

Years ago, she would joke with her girlfriends – thank goodness for girlfriends – about the need for regular marriage maintenance sex. Maintenance sex was a bit like sending your car for a service to keep it roadworthy – but, these days, Ruth wasn't quite so mouthy about the topic over the Pinot on Sunday afternoons while the men were at the golf club. None of her friends were, she'd noticed, but she couldn't bring herself to ask if they were all in the same boat.

If Ruth's sex life *was* a car, its road tax had well and truly expired and it was up on bricks in the driveway.

She'd been relieved when her alarm sounded that morning and she could get up and dress for breakfast, though she was well aware it was only another eleven hours until they'd be back up that ladder again.

Tonight, she knew, wouldn't be as bad. They'd endured the first night and dodged the bullet, tonight they'd probably sleep easier. Only Ruth wasn't really relieved. Far from it. She was woefully unhappy. This relationship needed jump starting, and she knew that's just what Beatrice had, in her naivety, tried to encourage yesterday with her champagne and truffles and the sudden room upgrade.

Beatrice, still in the first flush of love with Atholl, couldn't know how difficult these things were, how stultifying it was to lie there habitually untouched in your M&S nighty, listening to your husband snoring night after night. Ruth had seen Beatrice and Atholl glancing at each other with fire in their eyes. Everybody had seen it. She hoped that lovely young woman would never know what it was like to be lonely in a relationship.

Little did Ruth know that Beatrice understood what it was like only too well, and her memories of being affection-starved and careering towards divorce were the very reason she was meddling now, and for the same reasons Beatrice was excitedly clutching her notebook to her chest when Ruth had made her way into the kitchens at ten o'clock that morning, ready for her cooking lesson with Gene, instantly igniting Ruth's suspicions that Beatrice wasn't done playing Cupid yet.

'Sleep well?' Beatrice enquired, all innocence.

'Like a log, thank you.'

'Oh, right. Good stuff.'

She looked thoroughly put out, Ruth thought.

'I was just saying to Gene I'd appreciate some avo toast before your lesson gets started for the day. Hope you don't mind?'

Gene was bustling by the stoves, whistling a jaunty tune. Ever since he'd found out about the baby – after he'd stopped dabbing at his happy tears over the scan photo, loudly blowing his nose and hugging his younger brother over and over – he'd taken a very particular interest in feeding the baby nice things. It was his avuncular way of showing his love, and now he understood why Beatrice had been complaining for weeks that she found almost all drinks nauseating and she'd been craving strawberries and watermelon, difficult things to acquire over Christmas in the remote Highlands. He'd determined to find her things to eat that she'd enjoy.

His first successes had been wonderful concoctions of superfoods; blueberry smoothies, salads with seeds and raw greens, strips of seared steak with broccoli and noodles, salmon in ginger and chilli sauce; all the good stuff.

Beatrice had eaten all of it, loving every bite, and felt the queasiness that never quite seemed to go away lessening because her stomach was full.

She hadn't *desperately* wanted Gene's avo toast that morning, but she'd needed an excuse to catch Ruth alone.

'Where's Mark off to today?' Beatrice asked, pulling up a stool by the kitchen service hatch and the little domed bell.

Ruth was tying her apron around her waist. 'I expect he's got phone calls to make and he's off signal hunting.'

'*Hmm*,' Beatrice was cautious, recalling Atholl's suspicions about Mark and all the while remembering his warning about meddling in their marriage, but it was too late now. Her dating board had been a total failure, she'd entirely given up on that as a means of making people happy, but here were two lost souls in need of some romance. It would be wrong not to help them, she reasoned. 'Have you heard about the Burns Supper at the castle?' The words spilled out. 'I picked up a load of tickets from the laird's office. I told them I'd see if anyone from the inn was interested. It's a dressy kind of thing. Black tie.'

'I didn't pack anything fancy, not that I have anything that would have done anyway. It's a while since we've dressed up.'

'That's OK, I could arrange a shopping trip for you both? Get a taxi to take you to the Highland outfitters in Lochalsh and Lochcarron. They sell kilts, as well as hiring them, and they've evening gowns too and Scottish country-dancing dresses.'

'With the tartan sashes?'

'That's the ones! I can arrange that for tomorrow, if you'd like? You could skip a lesson?'

'Well, all right then. I'll take two tickets for the party.'

Ruth's cheeks were flushed. Beatrice saw it, but pushed on. 'You'll have to learn some of the dances first. Kitty can show you the basics.'

'I thought a Burns Night was all poetry and sitting around eating haggis.' Ruth was uneasy. 'Mark and I haven't danced together since, well, I can't even remember.'

'It's a dinner dance, quite formal, nothing like the relaxed ceilidhs we have here at the inn, or so Atholl tells me.' Beatrice's eyes misted remembering Atholl at the Harvest Home ceilidh in August when he'd held her close and spun her, lifting her clean off the ground and moving her round the floor, helpless to the feeling of his strong arms and the wild music. 'It's very romantic,' she added. 'The way the men take your hand and lead you to the dance floor, and they bow to you at the end of every dance and kiss your hand. It's like some Regency romance book adapted for the telly, all the lovely manners and handsome men in their kilts.' Beatrice sighed, making Ruth laugh.

'Someone's lovestruck for their Scotsman.'

'Oh,' Beatrice shook herself awake. 'I suppose I am. But you and Mark could show us a thing or two, I reckon. Silver wedding anniversary coming up and everything. It'll be a lovely way to celebrate.'

'I've no idea how to even begin dancing like that.'

'It all starts with just taking someone's hand in yours,' Beatrice said. Ruth looked like she was thinking very hard. 'It's easier than you think,' she reassured her.

With that, Beatrice smiled, wished Ruth a good cooking lesson, and scarpered with her avocado on toast.

She took a big bite as she went, heading for her spot by the reception desk where she'd spend the morning. When she got there she opened her jotter and looked at the list she'd compiled after reading all those online articles about reigniting cooling romances.

She'd outlined six steps to intimacy that seemed to come up in most of the experts' advice.

- Holding hands again
- Making an effort to dress well and compliment each other
- Non-sexual intimacy (dancing, for instance)
- Kissing, and only kissing. (The experts are very firm on this point, advising kissing for kissing's sake and with no expectation of anything else.)
- Showing appreciation and making romantic gestures
- Talking through feelings

That was the magic formula, apparently. It looked so simple set down here on her list. She inhaled, hoping the wistfulness she'd seen in Ruth's eyes (and the regretfulness in Mark's) was enough to suggest their relationship was salvageable.

No amount of handholding and dancing could have saved her and Richard's marriage, she knew. Were the Firths that far gone as well? Her gut told her that was not the case, that there was still so much hidden love and hope there, so much shared experience.

Yet, looking at her list, even Beatrice worried this was way over the top, that she'd gone too far this time, but that didn't stop her getting online to book a taxi to take the Firths on their Burns Night outfit-buying trip tomorrow, and it hadn't stopped her suggesting to Atholl this morning that Mr Firth might *really* be keen to join in his willow-weaving classes, giving the men a chance to talk and for Atholl to gauge, ever so subtly, whether her hunch about the Firths was right – that they only needed a little encouragement to find their way back to each other. She'd also wanted to prove Atholl's hunch wrong; that Mark might be having an affair.

She didn't know if Atholl had done as she'd asked and she wasn't sure if he'd even be able to convince Mark to go with him to the But and Ben. Maybe Mr Firth was already skulking away somewhere around the village with his laptop or phone.

Beatrice almost squealed with joy when Atholl's text message arrived a few moments after making the taxi booking.

> Right, I've got Mark up here at the willow school. He has the look of a man taken hostage. What is it you want me to do with him again?

Beatrice clapped her hands gleefully, then typed out her instructions.

Chapter Twenty-five

Man's Work

Mark was watching Atholl hefting the bundles of willow whips from his workshop into the chilly wide open expanse of the willow beds behind the But and Ben.

'Cheers for saying you'd help. It's a two-man job this,' Atholl said, indicating that the pair of them had a further walk to make, all the way through the willows towards one of the tall trees that bounded the property, behind which there was nothing but gently rising fields stretching inland until the earth lifted dramatically into snow-capped rolling mountains in the far distance. 'You didnae have any plans for this morning, did yi?' he asked, and Mark, possibly a little awed by the towering Scot, simply shook his head and told him it was nothing that couldn't wait. The men's breath created swirling white clouds in the chilly morning air.

'Right, so this is the brake.' Atholl stopped under the bare branches of a tall birch and laid his hand over the metal device strapped to its trunk.

Mark peered closer at the thing. 'It looks like a duck's bill, only metal. What does it do?'

Atholl smiled at the description. 'It's for stripping the bark off willow whips, making them better for basketry.' Atholl was already preparing to demonstrate, pulling loose from a bundle one long whip with lots of spindly branches at the growing end. 'Pass the whip between the two bits of metal like this and… can you take the other end? You push and pull it, running it through the brake, the whole length of the whip, until all the bark is sliced off.'

Mark grabbed the end and the two men worked the willow back and forth, the duck's bill clamp taking off a thin outer layer and all of the branches, creating long green ribbons of the thinnest bark which fell to the ground.

'I could do with one of these at home for peeling carrots,' Mark said, impressed. 'That's my job after the golf on a Sunday while Ruth makes the Yorkshires.'

Atholl let Mark pull the willow free and examine the now supple, clean whip.

'It smells fresh,' Mark said running his thumbs over the sappy willow.

'It's braw, is it no?' Atholl loaded up another whip and the men worked on. 'I reckon we'll get through a decent bundle afore the others arrive for their lesson.'

Mark worked silently at the willow, concentrating hard, not wanting to mess up in front of the expert.

'You ken, long ago, there would be special willow stripping holidays for school bairns to help with their family's brake work? Hector, my mentor – the man that taught me all this as an apprentice and sold me the But 'n' Ben – he told me he remembered working every springtime when he was wee, helping his mother strip the willow.'

'Kids don't know they're born these days,' Mark said, removing another beautifully stripped branch and placing it with the others, then noticing his palms were already red and likely to callous. Mark was well and truly out of his comfort zone of spreadsheets, air conditioning, and the familiarity of legalese, the smell of the photocopier toner, and the kettle and biscuit tin always no more than three feet away at all times in his cosy office on the high street. His little kingdom.

Atholl watched him as they worked on in silence, wanting to draw him out. Eventually he asked, 'Reckon you could get used to this? It's therapeutic, I always think. Except when the straps fail and the brake falls off the tree.' He set another new whip inside the brake.

'I'll have to take my jacket off in a minute if we carry on like this,' Mark joked, stiffly, his cheeks puffing.

'Who needs a gym when you can do this out in the fresh air, and with views like this, eh?' Atholl added.

Mark looked around as though wondering at Atholl's outdoor lifestyle. 'I get all my exercise on the golf course. Trouble is, the fry-up in the clubhouse puts it all back on.' Mark chuckled, beginning to enjoy the novelty of working up a sweat.

'Is that your hobby, is it? The golf?'

Now this was Mark's safe place, talking about something he loved. 'Played all my life. I joined my father's club when I was eighteen, and my twins joined too when they were old enough.'

'Ah, aye, you've children.'

'They're grown now, and left home. Stuart and Adam. Beautiful lads they are. It's not the same without them out on the links with me on a Sunday morning.' Something in Mark's eyes shifted, and Atholl saw right to the core of the taciturn businessman. He was more than just his stoic work ethic, he could tell.

Atholl fed another whip into the brake and, now that Mark was getting into the rhythm of it, he let him take control of the action.

'Where are they now?' Atholl pressed, wanting him to open up more now he knew the man's weakness.

'Adam's gone off travelling around Asia with his friends now that he's finished his doctorate, and Stuart's only recently moved into a residential home. He was ready for some independence away from me and Ruth.' Mark nodded to himself, falling silent again, his eyes dulling.

Atholl took his time. He knew all this, of course. Beatrice had shown him the competition entries and he too had agreed it had to be the Firths. 'That must be strange, seeing them go off into the world.'

Mark stopped working and raised the back of his hand to his brow, which was beading with sweat. 'The house is certainly quiet without them both. Adam's been gone for years, but without our Stuart, I...' Mark checked his emotions. 'I know Ruth misses them both terribly.'

Atholl refused to fill the silence and he wouldn't work the brake either. Instead, he watched Mark with soft eyes and waited for him.

After a while, Mark spoke, directing his words to his busy hands working the willow alone. 'It's funny, you want your children to grow up and be able to look after themselves – that's the dream, isn't it?' He glanced at Atholl, who nodded. 'And for a long time we thought our Stuart wouldn't ever do the things he's doing now. It's wonderful really, as much as it's sad he had to move away. Yet when they're finally off on their own, it's... it's...' Mark didn't have the words to finish the thought, and Atholl nodded again.

'I can imagine. I've all this to come.'

'You're going to be a dad?' Mark's eyes shone softer than Atholl had seen yet.

'I am.' He inhaled deeply, the excitement gripping him again. 'I'm guessing you were a young father, though. I'll be forty-two when this baby's born.'

The two men exchanged looks, Atholl's slightly worried and as though he was voicing something he hadn't dared to before, and Mark's surprisingly understanding.

'I was twenty-five when the twins came, so not all that young. Ruth and me, we'd been happy just the two of us, going out, seeing our friends, living together for a couple of years. It was still a shock, though, I can tell you. We weren't even married.'

Atholl grunted a laugh.

'The boys were our pages when we eventually tied the knot, they were nine then, and it seemed nicer that way. Anyway, I had three other people to provide for at the age of twenty-five and there I was working for my father in his office, not making all that much money. I took over the company when he retired and grafted day and night for years to get food on the table before I felt that weight of responsibility lifting from my shoulders and things got more comfortable, and by then we were thinking Stuart might never live independently and I started squirrelling away for his future. My boys turn thirty-five next year.' He shook his head at the very idea.

Mark seemed to get lost in his thoughts and in the motion of the willow work. Again, Atholl only watched him until he spoke, the motion of rocking the willows seeming to somehow soothe the married father. 'I remember the shock of them being born like it was yesterday. I didn't even know how to hold them. Ruth was only twenty-one. She had it a lot worse.' His eyes glazed and something a little guilty and sorrowful sneaked across his face.

Atholl let him stay with his thoughts. He untied another bundle of willows.

'Ruth and I were young, but you've already lived a life,' Mark said eventually. 'You'll be better prepared for fatherhood, I reckon. And you have all this.' He gestured all around him with a sweep of his arm. 'Any child growing up here will have everything they need.'

Atholl accepted this thoughtfully. 'When this bairn leaves high school I'll be sixty. Will I still be stripping willow then?' The same worried look returned; the look he'd never let Beatrice see, not when it was his job to soothe her worries, not add to them.

'You'll have the inn. Take it from me, I see it all the time in my line of work; the things you *think* will be a problem somehow resolve themselves, or they turn out better than you'd feared. The things that will *really* overturn a person, well, you couldn't anticipate those.'

'You're in the money business, aye?'

'Financial planning.'

'It's your job to help people secure their futures?'

'When it comes to money and property, yes. Life has a way of surprising you though, no matter how secure you make yourself.'

Atholl didn't reply. He was thinking of Beatrice and the sudden changes her life had gone through only a few months ago. She'd been on a completely different life path and suddenly she was diverted into his lane. Had he been alone at the brake that morning he might have said a few words of thanks to the sky and the sea and the wild rolling hills for that blessing. Instead he worked quietly at the willows until Mark asked him how he came to have the cottage school business.

'You said you were apprenticed here? And now you own the place?'

'I do, thanks to Beattie. Oh, that's what I call her.' He smiled a little shyly, watching the willow sawing back and forth in the brake. 'She taught me not to live my life as though my dreams meant nothing to me. It was her that told me to buy this place if I loved it so much… if I was afraid of losing it. So I did. I started building my workshopping business in earnest after that.'

'Good for you,' Mark said, pulling the last stripped whip free and adding it to the pile.

Mark didn't notice the birds lifting from the long grass of the meadow beyond the lavender field, but Atholl spotted them. He raised his eyes to follow their flight. It meant the crafters were making their way to class and they'd be here in a minute or two.

Atholl's mind raced. Had he achieved what Beatrice had asked of him? He suspected he'd made a breakthrough here with Mark, as though they'd both said things they'd bottled up for a long time.

Thinking on his feet, he offered the invitation Beatrice had insisted upon. 'Now you've stripped these willows, you'll stay and make something with them?'

Mark considered this for a moment.

'I'll get the kettle on, and there's fresh bannocks too,' Atholl offered as encouragement.

This prospect seemed to have an impact on Mark, who looked over at the cottage door. His hand patted at his mobile in his pocket, making Atholl worry he was about to flee.

'I, *uh*, I hate to say this,' Atholl added. 'But next week you're booked in for silver crafts, so you may as well surrender to the fact you're on a crafting holiday now.'

Mark drew his neck back. 'Silver craft? Who booked me in for that?'

'It was either that or paper quilling with Mr Abercrombie, and I really fought for the silversmithing for you. I'll level with you, Mr Firth, it's Beattie putting me up to it, and I darenae tell her no. She wants you to get the full Port Willow experience.'

Mark laughed. 'Does your wife always tell you what to do?'

'She's not my wife actually, but I admit I find that, generally, it's easier to be guided by her when she has a strong feeling about something like this. For your own sake, and mine, I'll beg you to go along with it too. You'll no' hear the end of it otherwise.'

Mark nodded, amused. 'I always thought that was the key to a happy marriage. Your wife wants to go to the garden centre, you go with her; she wants a shelf putting up, you put it up. That's what my old man told me anyway, back when we first moved in together. Do what she wants and keep her happy. And that's what I've always tried to do.' Mark seemed to think and reach an unhappy kind of conclusion. 'I thought that's what I'd done anyway.'

The willow crafters had turned into the little cottage garden and made their way round to the back door of the school, waving gaily at their tutor, summoning him to them, so Atholl couldn't say any more. He wasn't sure he needed to anyway.

Mark obediently followed Atholl inside the school, each of them carrying a bundle of willow and both of them feeling they had stripped away a thin layer of themselves, feeling a little lighter, if a little tender and exposed, having made their confessions.

That night over dinner and, as far as Ruth was concerned, completely out of the blue, Mark presented his wife with the stripped willow loveheart he'd made in Atholl's workshop.

The thin whips were bent and bound to form the simple heart shape and then sprigs of dried lavender were bound around its frame with even thinner strips of willow bark tied in tight bows.

Even more out of the blue, he'd thanked her for looking after the boys all these years, for giving up so much of herself, and then he'd carried on eating the excellent corned beef stovies Ruth had made that day during her lesson.

His wife had blinked in surprise and, feeling she might cry, watched her husband stoop to his plate and eating hungrily as though he'd worked harder that day than he ever had before. She felt a tiny spark of warmth; a spark that her husband had woven into the willow heart he'd carried home for her that day, all the way from the bonny willow beds above the coral beach.

Chapter Twenty-six

A Shopping Excursion

Mutt watched the minibus pulling up at the inn door from his painter's platform where he was giving the inn's Victorian roof cornicing a coat of glossy black paint.

He'd overheard the driver saying they'd only had the minivan left at the rank today but at least they'd be comfy, and he'd listened to Beatrice making sure the driver knew the addresses of all today's shopping excursion stops.

By the time Mark and Ruth had emerged from the breakfast room and were standing on the pavement getting ready to leave, Mutt had shimmied down from his scaffold.

'You're going shopping?' he asked. 'To the tartan outlets and all the rental places? And you're going to Florence Sakura's? Hold the bus for a minute.'

He dashed inside the inn, hurrying all the way to Nina's room door.

'You want to meet some new makers? Small scale, high-end stuff? You'd better grab your coat,' he'd told her when she answered his knock.

Within minutes Nina was hustled out of her room where she'd been on the phone with her mum assuring her that her ankle was getting better and promising that she was indeed eating and getting plenty of sleep. In fact, that's all she'd been doing since the accident, and it had been really rather lovely, if a tiny bit lonely. She had a nice routine going involving long breakfasts, working interspersed with lunch and dinner in the bar restaurant, then a seriously long bath and magazine reading before bed. The painkillers were still making her woozy but at least the swelling seemed to have reached its peak now and she could feel a little flexibility returning to her ankle.

She hadn't told her mother, but one of the most surprising things about the recent turn of events that had shaken her entire world was that she found she wasn't actually missing all the noise and striving, all those parties and air kisses quite so much as she thought she would.

Sure, she'd have traded a big wodge of her newfound relaxation for an appointment with her hair colourist or her eyebrow technician, but generally, she was starting to see the positive aspects of the snail's pace, peaceful Port Willow lifestyle, and a tiny bit of her was dreading the bandages coming off in a few days' time when she'd have to focus entirely on resuming Seamus's mission.

Mutt had looked so breathless and wide-eyed at her door, Nina had immediately reached for her crutch – just the one now she was feeling more confident – and she'd followed him out to the taxi.

Nobody noticed Beatrice hissing to catch Mutt's attention or the throat-slitting gesture she was doing at him. '*Psst*, Mutt. No, don't. Let them go on their own, Mutt! Mutt… Ah, I give up!'

When Mutt was sure everyone was belted in, he slid the van door closed with a loud bang and waved off the three excited shoppers and Beatrice turned to him with a weary look.

'*What?*' he asked innocently, but she simply turned for the inn door, shaking her head, leaving him to shrug, bewildered, on the pavement. 'What did I do?'

~

'Are you looking forward to going shopping?' Nina asked to break the awkwardness. She hadn't forgotten the frantic search for Ruth's wedding ring in the storm or how upset everyone had been walking back to the inn. This couple really didn't seem to have much going for them, but she liked Ruth with her mixture of softness and boldness.

'I'm not a shopper, love, but Beatrice seemed so excited to pack us off on a day trip, it seemed a shame to say no.'

Even Mark laughed. He didn't have his phone in his hand today. Nina wondered if he even had it with him.

'Enjoying your holiday, are you?' Mark asked, and both of the women's eyes snapped to him in surprise. He'd drawn out the flask of coffee Gene had handed him and was unscrewing the lid.

'*Um*, yes,' Nina answered, truthfully.

'It's a working holiday, isn't it?' Ruth asked. She had gleaned as much from the amount of time Nina was to be found skulking off to her room with a cup of tea or wandering into the media centre after breakfast in her sweats, at least before the accident.

'That's right. In fact, this is kind of my thing. Shopping. I'm in Scotland looking for products that could be picked up and marketed overseas. Something… quintessentially Scottish.'

'Have you found anything special yet?' Ruth asked.

Nina shook her head. 'Nothing concrete. Maybe today's the day. Either way, it'll do me good to get out of Port Willow. No offence to the place, obviously, but it is rather—'

'Eccentric?' Mark asked, surprising everyone with the joviality in his voice.

'Characterful,' Ruth said, thinking of the sweethearts Gene and Kitty, rugged, devoted Atholl and the meddling Beatrice.

They all smiled now and Mark handed Nina a drink in the flask's second cup. He and Ruth shared the other one. He even whistled a tune to himself as they settled in for the long drive through the frosty, hilly landscape.

He was happy because that morning they'd managed to get Stuart on FaceTime and he'd wanted to talk, enthusing about the day trip he'd been on the day before with his new friends and keyworker from his new home. Their hearts had lightened considerably to see him and, as they'd ended the call, Mark had kissed his son by bringing the screen to his lips and Ruth had felt a kind of gladness she'd forgotten all about. However, as the bus wound its way along the coast, Ruth felt the panic setting in over their shopping excursion.

Sometime around about her fiftieth birthday and her first horrifying hot flush, Ruth had developed a deep aversion to shop changing rooms. This all coincided with her realisation that sweaty, hormonal reality was about to put the kibosh on her plans to sail through the menopause without inheriting any of the symptoms her mother had experienced, but since then she'd had just about all of them including the red cheeks, tea time sleepiness, and a surprisingly fervent love for the Lakeland catalogue.

Ruth had mothered her twins in the parenting equivalent of SAS uniform: comfy jeans, cardis with pockets and any number of nice cotton tops bought at the supermarket while doing the big shop, and she'd been happy enough with her practical choices. Recently however, she'd had to give up the beloved comfy Converse she'd always worn when she reached the disturbing conclusion that her arches had collapsed, presumably with exhaustion, much like the rest of her. She'd switched to the FitFlops that she'd found in the sales and which she'd seen Adam's girlfriend, Katie, raising a sartorial eyebrow at on more than one occasion.

Not that she minded Katie's opinion; she was in her late-twenties and had all of this to come. She wouldn't burst her bubble of youthful naivety by telling her so. Katie probably wouldn't believe the entire mortifying process could possibly happen to her anyway. Ruth certainly hadn't believed it, not until around about the time she started buying her jeans online because she'd concluded it was better to rage-cry and swear in frustration in front of the mirror in her own bedroom than in a high street store.

Ruth had already taken twice the suggested dose of nerve-calming remedy drops when the people carrier dropped the three shoppers off in front of a very intriguing shop standing alone by a main road in the middle of nowhere.

They were the only customers, they'd discovered, as Ruth pushed the door open and helped Nina hobble inside, followed by Mark who had already adopted his shopping-for-clothes-with-his-wife habit of whistling, hands in pockets, loitering by the door, and generally being unengaged. Yet even he was glancing around the rails and shelves at the unusual offering.

'Wow!' Nina cried, running her hand along the hanging kilts that stretched the entire length of one wall, a confection of thick pleats and folds in a rainbow of colours ranging from murky blacks and greens all the way to confectioners' candy pastels. She snatched a pink plaid kilt from the rail and held it out to show Mark. 'You'd look good in this.'

'Let's not get carried away,' he warned, still stationed by the door.

The shop owner was a tall, elegant man in his forties with a hipster beard and a twisty moustache to rival Seth's.

'We're going to a Burns Night ball, and we've nothing to wear,' Ruth told him. The man delightedly brought his hands together and steepled his fingers in front of his nose.

Mark had been dragged to the 'gentleman's outfitting suite' at the back of the shop where he'd stood in socks and boxers, being measured with clipped efficiency before being treated to a bewildering introduction to Highland outfit styles for men.

Through the curtain Ruth had insisted he try each one on and she and Nina had taken a seat, found the bowl of complimentary soor plooms, and settled themselves in for a catwalk show.

When he'd emerged, Nina had looked away and Ruth openly snorted at the sight of Mark wanting to shrink from view in the traditional 'Highlander outfit'; a slashed to the breastbone lace-up shirt and long, warrior-style kilt hanging low at the back with something that reminded Ruth of her parent's tartan travelling rug draped over his shoulders. The whole ensemble was belted around his waist with thick brown leather. 'This isn't it,' Mark told the tailor and they'd retreated behind the curtains again.

The traditional evening kilt, black tie, starchy shirt and waistcoat hadn't felt right either. 'It's too… formal, too like a wedding. I don't feel right wearing it, somehow,' Mark said, surprising everyone.

Nina watched him, wondering if, despite appearances, maybe he did take an interest in clothes after all. That certainly wasn't the impression his uniform of chinos, thinly checked shirts, ties and golfing pullovers gave. Back behind the curtain he'd slunk.

The entirely moss-green 'Gamekeeper's Argyle' kilt, tweed jacket and thick hunting socks hadn't gone down well with his audience either and he'd looked pleadingly at Ruth and asked if he couldn't just wear a suit. The tailor had other ideas though.

'Sir, was there ever a time you felt most attractive in your clothes? A time you had a special outfit you loved?'

The couple's eyes had instantly met and, after a moment's thought, Mark nodded in resignation. 'Go on then, you tell the man.'

Ruth grinned her way through the whole story, eyes shining, as she described the night she'd met her husband on the dance floor at Alley Catz when he'd sidled over to her during Adam Ant's 'Puss 'n Boots'.

'Well, he was in leather trousers, a sort of white blouse and black bolero type jacket, do you remember that? It had those military buttons down the front, and *um*, and *um*... a little bit of eyeliner.'

Nina's jaw dropped, scanning Mark in his tweedy get-up and white knees.

'You can't imagine it, can you? I was a lot fitter then.' Mark's shoulders bobbed with the laughter now. 'She didn't even mention my long hair, and how I had high-lights!' Unconsciously, he raised a hand to the thinning spot above his temple.

Now everyone was smiling, and Nina found herself up on her crutch and leading the tailor to one side, talking through ideas with him in hushed tones, their backs turned on the Firths.

-

'OK, this is definitely the one,' Nina said, peeking in through the curtains. 'You ready to see this?' she asked.

Before Ruth could answer, her husband stepped out into the watery late morning light spilling through the shop windows.

'This is the Bonnie Prince Charlie style, favoured in the nineteen eighties and making a strong comeback now,' the tailor announced.

This time nobody was laughing and it was Ruth up on her feet and walking around her husband, her eyes wide, taking him in.

Midway between a bride groom and a hussar, his darkest navy velvet jacket fit snugly around his shoulders and waist, tapered neatly in folds and cuts at the small of his back, and studded all the way down the lapels with silver diamond-shaped buttons. A royal-blue and navy kilt in a thick Harris fell to just the right point mid-knee where the fabric met with long thick white socks pulled up over his shins and revealing a flash of the silver dagger tucked inside. Its glinting drew the eye down to his shining black shoes and black leather laces criss-crossed around his ankles and up his calves.

'Do you like it?' Mark asked Ruth. Only her opinion mattered now.

She brought a hand up to the cluster of white lace falling in a cascade from his throat. He held his wrists up for her to inspect, showing her the same white lace at his cuffs.

'Very dandy highwayman,' she told him quietly, and they'd both smiled, a little abashed, but with the familiarity of thirty-seven years since that fateful night at Alley Catz between them.

'Shall I wrap them up?' the tailor asked, and Nina had to answer for them, the Firths were so absorbed in looking at Mark's reflection in the mirror, saying unheard things and chuckling.

'They'll take it,' Nina assured him.

The rest of the excursion had been just as revelatory. Their second stop was a designer dress rental shop behind a light industrial unit on the banks of a loch where Nina's attention was drawn to the sounds of sewing machines running and she'd left to explore the other buildings, leaving Ruth and Mark to step inside alone.

Again, there wasn't anyone else there other than the owner, a young woman dressed from head to foot in vintage red tartan Vivienne Westwood and long spike-heeled boots. Ruth told her she used to have a little number like that herself, long ago, only it had come from C&A. The owner picked up on Ruth's nerves and made her and Mark a cup of tea before pulling out a selection of gowns in blues and blacks to complement Mark's outfit and leaving her to try them on behind the curtain.

Mark had been called upon to help with the zips and after only five changes they struck upon the perfect thing. A deep midnight-blue dress, fitted at the waist, with an A-line asymmetrical hem falling in thick gathers and longer at the back, giving the whole thing a glamorous hint of Christian Dior's full-skirted forties New Look. Or at least that's what the owner told her when she swooped back in to the changing room exclaiming, 'That's the one! That's it.'

The scoop neck came into its own when the owner suggested a thick double rope of faceted crystal beads and long black gloves. When she'd taken Ruth aside to pay, she'd also suggested some sheer black stockings and Ruth had asked her to add them to the bag, looking round to see if that had pricked Mark's ears up. He hadn't heard a thing.

Later, when Ruth told Nina she'd got everything but shoes, Nina had asked her size and assured her she had just the pair of ankle boots for her, if she trusted her, which Ruth told her she did. They agreed to meet on the afternoon of the ball when Nina would share her make-up products and help her do her eyes since Ruth told her she couldn't see well enough without her specs to do her eyeliner anymore, another gift of the ageing process – thanks a bunch.

They'd remarked upon Nina's not having bought anything for herself and she'd told them with a shrug she hadn't needed anything, she wasn't going anywhere, and she did a good job of hiding how crestfallen she was about not having found any products to recommend to Seamus either.

The Firths had dozed off in the minivan surrounded by their bags, their heads tipped together and clasping hands for the first time in a very long time.

All the way back to the inn, Nina thought about the workshops she'd stumbled across as she made her way round the little industrial estate.

There'd been a glassworks that was part store, part workshop, where the shelves were lined with beautiful bottles, baubles and suncatchers in speckled glass. When she'd told the owner that she was on holiday and staying at the Princess and the Pea Inn, the arty-looking man, Munro, told her he ran the glass-making sessions there during the quiet autumn months and asked if she'd send his best to the Fergussons. That's when she remembered seeing him at the speed-dating event at Hogmanay, one of the few locals brave enough to take the hot seat. She didn't think it wise to mention it.

He'd opened up the glass kiln and demonstrated how he made the hand-blown rounded bottles in rich fluid amber with speckled metal flakes that were somehow captured and turned liquid inside the molten glass.

She'd been thrilled at the extremes of heat and the hissing steam as Munro plunged the glass into water to cool it. She had bought a small, squat bottle off the shelf to post to her mother, knowing she'd definitely like this gift.

She'd been in a hurry to get back to the taxi by the time she left Munro's glassworks but had discovered a designer making her own garments inside a little lock-up office. The sign on the door told her to 'please come in and browse', so she had, and she'd been awed by the frock coats the woman was making in every colour under the sun.

She'd handed the young maker at the sewing machine a business card, but the woman hadn't shown any interest in the idea of New York markets or expansion of any kind.

'Don't you want to sell to new markets overseas?' Nina had asked.

'No' really. I'm happy here. I have my loyal customers and my online sales. I've enough orders in my book to keep me going all year long.'

'But you could expand, make a fortune?'

The woman smiled and turned to her pattern cutting. 'Why change a thing when I'm contented now? Bigger and better, more and more, isn't always the answer to people's prayers they think it is.' Nina thought how much she sounded like Mutt. The woman nodded a handkerchiefed head to the little window. 'Look at my loch, and my lovely workshop. Why would I change a thing?'

Nina had to admit she had a point. She hadn't wanted to leave the complex of shops, but Ruth and Mark were waiting for her at the little cafe kiosk and they had enough time to grab a takeaway lunch before hitting the road again.

By the time they reached Port Willow it was already growing dark and Mutt was finishing up securing his ladders in the back of his truck after a dry day's painting.

Ruth and Mark had insisted on paying the taxi fare and hurried inside to get a coffee in the bar leaving Nina face to face with Mutt on the pavement. He seemed to have been waiting for her. Bear was snoring in his arms. She wondered if Bear had grown since the last time she'd seen the little fur ball.

'Good day?' Mutt asked.

'Interesting. It was nice getting to know those two.'

'Good, good.' Mutt seemed distracted. '*Um*, did you get anything to wear to the Burns Night ball?'

'Why would I? I'm not going.'

'No?'

'No.'

'We can't have that. You need to see the castle all lit up for a party.'

'I do?' Nina stifled her smile.

'Aye, definitely. Will you, maybe… come with me? I know there's a busload leaving from the inn, but I could take you, if you wanted me to?'

Nina watched him trying to appear nonchalant and almost managing it.

'OK,' she blurted.

'OK?'

'Where do I get a ticket?' Nina asked.

'I happen to have two right here.' He tapped his pocket. 'I did some work at the castle recently, Lochlainn gave me them.'

'Lochlainn?'

'The laird himself.'

'Is that like Scottish royalty?'

'If you mean, is he skint and begrudgingly tied to a crumbling old country pile by duty and blood, then yes. It's on Tuesday night. I'll pick you up at six-thirty so there's time to show you around the castle before the rest of the guests arrive?'

Nina hadn't said anything else, only smiling her acceptance and reaching out to scratch Bear's sleepy head.

'Any luck scouting for makers?' Mutt added.

She sighed before she spoke. 'I met Munro, the glass-maker, he showed me round his workshop, and Florence Sakura, the designer.'

'Ah, I don't suppose she was keen on letting you have her designs?'

Nina only quirked her lips in a wry smile that told him he was right.

'I thought as much. She's a Scottish star as it is. Never mind,' he shrugged in sympathy. 'Munro's a good person too,' Mutt added. 'I'll have to buy some of his glass before I head back home to Pennan. They make good presents.'

'You're leaving?' Nina said, unable to hold back her surprise.

'Soon as I'm finished here. There's, *uh*, some unfinished business I need to sort out back home. Can't hide out here any longer.' Mutt hitched his tool belt up and looked truly sorry he'd be going soon.

'Another runaway?' Nina said, making Mutt squint at her. 'That's what Beatrice calls the people who come here looking to find something.'

'Or to lose something,' Mutt said gruffly, his mind elsewhere. Shifting his weight to his back foot, he fell silent.

'So… it's getting dark and it's pretty cold. I'm going to head inside.' Nina gestured towards the door but didn't move, not until Mutt stepped away awkwardly.

'Right you are, see you Tuesday.'

'You know it's a formal thing, right?' she told him.

Mutt ran a hand down his paint-spattered t-shirt. 'It'll come as a surprise to you, no doubt, I do own clean clothes.'

They'd both held their ground smilingly, saying goodbye until it really was getting ridiculous and Nina had walked inside.

She'd smiled all the way to the media room, firing up the computer and logging in to her work inbox only to be met with an email flagged red for urgent that wiped the smile away.

> I understand you've been injured on this trip. Legal need you to fill in some forms. Mitch is sending them. Your whisky idea was interesting. Find me another like that. Mitch has you booked on a flight January

twenty-seventh. The execs will give you twenty minutes to pitch your findings on the twenty-eighth first thing. Be prepared.

Seamus.

Chapter Twenty-seven

Mother Nature

'Sunday, Monday, Tuesday...' Beatrice dropped a little lilac pill into each compartment of the plastic medication organiser she'd picked up at the general stores a couple of weeks ago.

One purple pregnancy vitamin and one folic acid tablet now nestled in each of the chambers and she snapped the clear lids shut. It gave her a quiet kind of satisfaction to be refilling it again. Each refill was a tiny celebration. Another week navigated with a baby still safely on board. Popping each morning's lid open and swallowing the tablet was a secret, comforting ritual and the only moment of the day where she focused on the fledgling feelings of hope and progress before shutting them down again.

'Knock knock.'

Atholl's appearance at the bathroom door startled her. 'A parcel's arrived for you, from Warwick.'

-

They sat together on the bed while Beatrice ripped at the wrapping paper. 'It's from Vic and Angela,' she said, unfolding a yellow waffle blanket in baby soft wool. 'Ah!' Beatrice's face froze in a smile.

'That's a braw blanket,' Atholl said, keeping an eye on Beatrice. 'Very nice of them to send it.'

'Right,' Beatrice nodded, folding it again. 'It's lovely.'

'But?' Atholl took the little package from her hands. 'Do you want me to put it away somewhere?'

A little breathless suddenly, Beatrice agreed. 'Please.'

Atholl placed the bundle inside the wardrobe right at the back on a high shelf, pulling a pile of jumpers in front of it.

'Sorry, that winded me a bit.' She lowered her head.

'I know, and you don't have to do anything or think anything right now.'

'I'll… I'll send them a thank-you card.'

Atholl sat back down beside her, his hands clasped on his lap, mirroring Beatrice's posture. 'Of course.'

'I don't want to seem ungrateful.'

'I know.' His voice was calm.

'I'm *nothing but* grateful; for the present, and to be pregnant again.'

'I know that.' He took one of her hands in his. 'I'm grateful too.'

'I'm just… feeling so many things and not one of them is excitement or actual happiness, you know? And I can't really explain that to anybody because they'll think I'm horrible. I can't bring myself to be hopeful this time around. It's worse when you're happy and full of hope, when things go wrong, I mean.'

Atholl listened, eyes fixed on Beatrice. The feeling of his tender gaze made her want to cry, but she talked on the way she had learned to share her burdens since coming here.

'I struggle with how unfair it all is, not just for me, but for lots of us, in lots of different situations. All those mums without their babies out there. All the parents going through pregnancy again and being terrified when everybody expects you to be glowing and just desperate to talk babies.'

Atholl gave a sympathetic smile, rubbing his thumb over the back of her hand, letting her voice her feelings.

'I find it hard to have any faith in the universe, or in my own body, even when I have proof of what a clever devil nature can be in Clara. Angela and Vic went through so much to get her and *she* came to them, but I can't really believe it's going to happen for us. I…'

'Go on,' Atholl urged softly.

'I don't want to hurt your feelings, not when you're so hopeful.'

'I feel what you feel, Beattie. Go on, tell me the rest.'

'Well… if you're sure?'

He blinked his assent.

'Well… after so long with things going wrong in my life, things suddenly going right – and not just right, but like… perfect – it just feels unsafe, impossible even.' Beatrice fell quiet, and Atholl held her. She didn't cry. That would be too much like really feeling, and she'd fought hard to keep all this at arm's length for so long. 'You don't know what to do with me, do you? I finally get what I've wanted for years and I'm not even happy.'

'You will be happy. When the baby comes and you hold them against your skin and you feel their breath, you'll be happy then.'

Beatrice closed her eyes tight and hid her face from him.

'You know, I found something strange today when I was helping Gene clear the back yard,' he said, his tone shifting.

Beatrice opened her eyes, surprised at this change in direction. 'You were clearing the garden? Nobody's been out there in years.'

'Aye, well, soon there'll be a wee one toddlin' in the sun out there and they cannae dae that through six feet o' brambles, so we've been cuttin' it all back to make you a wee garden of your own.'

Now Beatrice really did want to cry. This man, she thought. How can he possibly love her this much when she was such a mess? She took a deep breath before asking him, 'You say you found something?'

'I did. Here, come with me,' Atholl stood, keeping her hand in his and guiding her out to the messy jungle behind the inn that, once upon a time, had been the garden of Atholl's childhood, a place where Mrs Fergusson had sat in the sun seeking five minutes' peace from her brood and the inn customers, and where there had been goldfish and frogs in a little pond and a heron always on the lookout for her supper.

Atholl told Beatrice all this as she looked out at the tangle of ivy and blackberry boughs. He pointed to a patch by the trunk of a scrawny crab apple tree where the brothers had been hacking at the undergrowth. 'There.'

'What on earth is that?'

Beatrice dropped his hand to crouch by the peculiar clusters which at first she'd thought were oysters or maybe mussels on a rope like she'd seen on Port Willow's beach.

'They're snails. Gene was disappointed they're no' the culinary kind.'

'*Eww*, I draw the line at eating snails!' Beatrice gulped, her eyes fixed on the shining shells. 'Why are they all huddled together like that?'

'They're sleeping,' Atholl told her. 'It's called a hibernaculum. When the hard frosts of winter hit, they gather for safety, make a seal around themselves and they cling together until the spring thaw comes.'

'There must be about… fifty of them,' she replied, her eyes fixed upon them.

'They wouldn't survive the winter without doing this. Poor things have been sleeping here undisturbed for God knows how many winters now.' Atholl reached for a handful of bramble cuttings and placed them over the creatures' safe spot, concealing them again.

'Amazing!' Beatrice said, struggling to stand and saying '*oof*' when Atholl helped her to her feet.

'*I* think it's amazing. I suppose what I'm saying, Beattie, is it's all right for you to hibernate and keep yourself safe here at the inn. You dinnae need to fash yourself with anything outside. Those wee beasties there, they're no' worrying about the future, they're letting nature take control. They're resting and waiting for spring. You do that too. Nature will do her thing whether you worry yourself sick or whether you go baby shopping mad and make up some lavish nursery room piled to the ceilings wi' wee yellow blankets.

'Cells, they will divide; wee sleepy creatures will hide away in the dark, gathering their strength; the blackberry will root itself in every nook and cranny and run wild all across what was once a bonny wee garden, and no conscious thought will go into those processes at all. And we'll all keep turning round the sun until the longer days come in and its time again for everything to wake up and come to life. You, Beattie, do not have to do anything either. Nature will do it all. I have nothing but faith in her.'

Beatrice leaned into the cosy nook of Atholl's chest and let her eyes roam over the scrubby garden. A robin was flitting amongst the undergrowth looking for grubs turned up in the soil disturbed by the Fergusson brothers' digging. Below the grey stone window ledge of the sun room were tufts of green, the first signs of snowdrops preparing to flower, slender heralds of spring.

Beatrice gripped Atholl all the tighter. 'Thank you,' she whispered, and the pair stood still in the fading light and listened to the robin's winter song.

Chapter Twenty-eight

The Chief's Chamber

Late January brings a second kind of winter in the Highlands. The first was gentle, hearth-fire scented and candlelit, a quiet time for family and a lean time for making do all through midwinter. Once Hogmanay becomes a memory, winter takes on a harder aspect and Scots must face the slow trudge towards spring, knowing it will be a long time coming and that the days will remain short, dark and bitterly cold.

This is the time of digging deep, of taking scraps of comfort anywhere they can be found. Grannies crack open summer fruit preserves and the harvest chutneys, the log piles are quickly burned through, and there is a deep sense of being rationed, of surviving until the lighter days come in – the feeling of hardy, impatient waiting.

This is why by the third week of the first month something peculiar to the Scots begins to emerge: the aggravated awareness of having been cossetted indoors, stuck with one's own thoughts and the loneliness of Christmas being long gone, and the keen need for friends, and a thirst that can only be slaked by one long, wild night of poetry and song, hearty food and birling dances, and, of course, a great deal of whisky.

That is why tonight everyone fortunate enough to have a ticket is dressing up to the nines and venturing out across the countryside through sleet and cranreuch towards Castle Carron. The castle rises out of the heath above Port Willow and tonight its every window is aglow against the starry darkness, promising a warm reprieve from the relentless winter.

On the ruins of Castle Carron's medieval battlements and lit by a flaming torch, a piper in full Highland regalia braves the weather to draw in the laird's guests. His music is carried on the wind over hill and glen.

This is an evening for sentiment and solidarity, when folk far from home wear their clan colours and wish themselves back in Scotland. This is a night for incanting words written three hundred years ago, a time for telling stories of witches and ghosts, drunkards and traitors. This is a night for sweethearts and for the spurned, the beloved and the wronged. There is a verse for everyone. This is Robert Burns Night.

-

Mutt's motorbike engine purred to a stop on the crunching gravel. Nina had clung to his black leather jacket all the way from the inn, glad she'd chosen to wear her black tux, bought off the peg and in a panic when she'd first arrived in New York and realising she'd need something smart to wear to evening events, and fast, but she couldn't afford any of the luxurious designer suits she'd seen at Tom Ford or Alexander McQueen. So she'd picked up this outfit for a hundred dollars and paired it with the best heels she had, simply mixing up her shirts every time she wore it. She'd been amazed nobody seemed to know it was a high street outfit and it became one of her favourite things to wear until it was relegated to the neglected end of her wardrobe, pushed out by the pretty things Luke gave her.

'Regretting the kilt?' she asked Mutt, stepping, stiff-legged, off the bike and pulling her black helmet off, smoothing her hair back.

'It's certainly breezier than leathers,' Mutt told her from behind the dark visor. She could tell he was laughing.

He'd opted for a heavy black utility kilt with the traditional socks, also in black, and his trusty work boots, gleaming with polish, laced messily and loose around the shin. Nina had been a little lost for words when he'd pulled up at the inn on a black Royal Enfield Bullet and even more surprised at the sight of him in the high-necked black jumper and beaten-up leather jacket.

Mutt let her re-live the feeling again now as he pulled his helmet off and raked back his dark hair, those lashes still spiked like on the first day she'd met him when she'd thought they must be his only redeeming feature.

Instead of gawping, she turned to look up at the castle wall towering above her. 'We're early. You're sure they won't mind?'

'Doubt it, it's a hotel after all. I'll show you around and we can grab a drink before the entertainment kicks off.'

'And then they feed us all haggis?'

'Aye. I took the liberty of requesting the vegetarian haggis for you though.'

'How do you know I hardly ever eat meat?'

'I just knew.' He shrugged. Nina squinted at him, unconvinced. 'Oh, all right, I asked Beatrice. She said you almost always choose the veggie options.'

'Impressive sneaking.'

'Consideration, you mean?' Mutt smiled wickedly, locking their helmets away in the bike's top box.

'Shall we?' Nina said, and together they crossed the castle esplanade, which was already getting busy with cars. They walked over the drawbridge that hadn't been raised in decades and entered into the castle.

Castle Carron has lived through many incarnations: first, a thousand-year-old wood-and-thatch castle keep, every trace of it long since gone; then a fortified stone medieval clansman's home; now, after a great many Victorian gothic touches and sharp twenty-first-century architectural additions, it stands as a sprawling, smart hotel, part ruin, part modern tourist attraction.

Mutt led Nina straight into the contemporary part of the castle, all red carpets, dark drapes, shining wood staircases and everything grand and imposing. He'd waved to the woman at the reception desk who knew his name and she'd greeted him with a cheery hello.

'I'll show Nina the old castle, if you don't mind?'

'Go right ahead,' she called back, and Mutt, his black kilt swishing, led Nina through open glass doors and past a vast ballroom with a huge stone mantle where a fire roared. She glimpsed white linen cloths on round tables all around the dance floor and a stage set for musicians.

'That's where the party'll be. We'll grab our seats in a while. I want to show you something first,' he told her.

Nina couldn't help gaping in at each room as they passed: an ultra-chic modern restaurant, a cosy snug coffee bar, all high ceilings and tartan everywhere, then a glimpse of industrial chrome in the busy kitchens. 'Something smells amazing in there,' she said as they passed by, hoping it was the veggie haggis.

They turned away from the stairs that led to the guest rooms on the upper floors, instead taking a corridor that seemed to be growing narrower and lower as they walked. White-shirted serving staff passed them going in the opposite direction and Mutt greeted each one.

'You know everyone because you worked here?' Nina asked.

'That's right. First I came to work at the inn but after I arrived in Port Willow I heard about the laird needing a painter and Atholl said he didn't mind me taking the job. He knew I needed…' Mutt drew himself up, not finishing his line of thought. 'Anyway, I was here for four weeks before I got stuck in to renovating the Princess. That was back at the end of October.'

'That's a long time to be away. You don't have family missing you at home?'

Now the ceilings were only a little higher than their heads and the carpeted floor seemed to be uneven and sloping downwards. With each step the temperature fell a little more. There were no windows in this part of the castle, only thick, rough stone walls painted white.

Mutt didn't say another word, and Nina didn't repeat her question, and soon they stopped at the very end of the corridor before an arched door of grey wood studded with beaten iron buttons.

'In there?' Nina wasn't so sure she wanted to go any further. 'It's not a dungeon, is it? Because I'm telling you, I went to the London dungeons once and nearly had a coronary.'

'Nothing scary, I promise. Place isn't even all that haunted. Just say a wee prayer we steer clear of Bogle McTavish, the Jacobite who drowned when thrown from the ramparts by a British army officer. Legend has it he wanders the ramparts with a cannon ball in one hand and his bloodied axe in the other. You can go first.' He nodded at the door.

'Right, thanks for that.' Nina rolled her eyes, but she still clenched her teeth when reaching for the cold metal handle. 'Aww, I was expecting the door to creak like in some creepy movie,' she joked as she opened it.

Mutt only smiled and waited for her reaction.

Mutt was right, there was nothing scary in here, far from it. 'Oh my...' Nina gaped, turning all around to take in the sight.

They'd passed right through the thick grey stone wall. In front of them was a wide bed swathed in heavy covers in a rich golden silk. Above an elaborate carved headboard hung a tapestry depicting the castle as it once may have looked rising out of the purple heath. The landscape was stitched in jewel colours with various Gaelic mottos and clan insignia in each corner.

There was no stone ceiling and no other old walls at all, only a curious construction, like a great glass box enclosing the warm and luxurious room. Nina walked over plush carpet and to the far corner, peering out through the glass into the darkness. The whole place was softly lit somehow from inside the thick layers of glass, Nina couldn't fathom it, but the effect was dreamlike.

Outside, she could just make out the lights of Port Willow in the distance and nothing else but a sense of the far black mountains.

'This was the clan chief's chamber, long ago,' Mutt told her. 'It fell into ruin like the rest of the medieval castle. I worked on this bit, through here...'

He pressed a finger to a panel to the right of the stone archway they'd entered through and a glass door opened, leading to a private dining room with a bar and then on further to a lounge and a grand bathroom. Each room had one wall of glass overlooking the wild countryside, the rest was immaculately plastered and painted, corniced and finished.

'You did all this stuff?' Nina guessed.

'Aye, chalk paint, you'll be glad to know.'

She was generous enough to laugh. 'Ugh! Sorry about that.'

'Ach, don't be. I wasn't very welcoming that day, if I remember right. Not to mention your ruined shoes.'

Nina let that slide and changed the subject. 'Why is nobody staying here?'

'It'll open to its first guests in the spring.'

'Well, it's beautiful. You should be proud of it.'

'Och, I only contributed a tiny part of this. The architects, the planners, the engineers, the laird himself, they all made it happen.'

Mutt led her back through the rooms to the bedchamber.

'You're happy being a decorator?' Nina asked his back, watching the way he moved in his leather and heavy black kilt, liking the way his hair shone under the discreet lights.

Back by the studded door, Mutt turned and observed her for a moment, his arms folded. He seemed to be thinking.

'I'm not sure that was a question,' she threw in, panicked. 'Just an observation really.'

'I am happy. I work hard and I like what I do. It might not be fancy enough for some people… but it makes me happy. I can work in great places like this. I get to work with Atholl at the inn. Who knows where my next job will take me.' He shrugged and assured her again. 'I'm happy.'

'I'm glad. You're good at what you do.'

'But?' he prompted.

'But what?' Nina said.

Mutt seemed to be about to say something, a hint of tension in his jaw, but it melted.

'I suppose… I thought you'd think I wasn't fulfilling my potential as well.'

'As well? Who else thinks that?'

'Nobody, it's… it's all right.' Mutt swept the topic away with his hand and was reaching for the door handle to leave when Nina came up close and stopped him with a hand on his arm.

'My dad's a decorator. In Brighton.'

Mutt looked at her. 'The New York trend forecaster's a tradesman's daughter?'

'You needn't look so surprised. I never claimed to be anything else, did I? You just assumed I was a spoiled brat.'

'Well, I mean… there were moments when you acted like one…'

Nina laughed and thumped his arm and the leather dulled the impact. 'I grafted to get where I was, OK? I worked really hard. Dad taught me how, I suppose.'

Mutt observed her once more, chewing his bottom lip a little. He seemed to make a decision on the spot. 'Wait here.'

He headed in the direction of the suite's private dining room once more, leaving Nina to watch after him. He returned after a moment, grinning wickedly and holding two glasses of whisky over ice, the bottle under his arm.

'Private bar, fully stocked. Yours for only nine hundred a night.'

Nina took a glass. 'Worth it, I'd say.'

'Who wants to waste that kind of money?' Mutt strode to another panel on the wall and hit a few buttons. The lights beyond the window suddenly came on, illuminating the low ruined walls amongst the scrubby heather and gorse immediately outside. 'Not when you can have it all for free.' He raised his glass to her. 'For a wee while, anyway. *Slàinte*.'

Nina lifted her own glass and repeated his toast, before pausing to inhale the whisky vapours. 'What is this? It's so rich, like cigar smoke, and there's something sweet too, caramel? And that same smell from Atholl's workshop, heather and wood.'

Mutt looked at the label on the bottle. 'You're getting all that?'

'*Mmm*.' Nina drank, savouring the creamy burn.

'You've got a really talented nose.'

'*Hah*,' Nina laughed. 'Nobody's ever said that about me. I guess I'm sensitive to these things.'

Mutt narrowed his eyes. 'You said you could smell the lavender when we were at the willow school.'

'I can, the whole village smells of it. Haven't you ever noticed?'

'Can't say I have.'

'Port Willow is lavender, sea salt and wet sand, and, thanks to you, paint. And the coral beach is something clean and chalky white, and the damp earth from the meadow, and there's a horsey, hay sort of smell from the wet thatched roof at Atholl's school. New York's exhaust fumes, fresh bagels, coffee beans and… this sickly-sweet, appetising smell from the candied nuts stands. *Ah*, I can smell it now!'

Mutt only looked at her, smiling curiously.

She carried on. 'And this room smells of cedar wood.'

'The bedframe,' he said. 'Handcrafted from cedar.'

'There you are!' Nina raised her glass to Mutt's once more and they let them chink brightly in the quiet room.

'I've never met anyone quite like you, Nina from New York.'

'Same, Murray from...'

'Pennan.'

'Where's that exactly?'

'Aberdeenshire. Nowhere near here, thank God.'

Nina saw the same pinch between his brows she'd witnessed earlier when he'd talked about his career choice not being enough for an unspecified someone. She didn't push him.

'Do you like being called Mutt?' she asked instead.

'I never minded before, but I liked it better when you called me by my name.'

The gruffness in his voice drew her eyes back to his. Alarmed, Nina felt sure he was going to kiss her, she even found herself leaning a little closer, but Mutt had already looked away, awkwardly. 'Let's sit,' he said, walking towards the bed, leaving Nina to press her cold glass to her forehead, exhaling and wide-eyed, wondering why she wasn't relieved that at least somebody had their head on straight tonight.

A short while later they'd stationed themselves on the floor, leaning against the soft fabric of the bedside, looking out at the world beyond the glass walls, their legs stretched out before them, crossed at the ankles, letting the whisky work its relaxing magic. They were talking about family.

'So your folks are divorced?' Mutt was asking.

'Since I was tiny. Dad remarried and now he has other kids. It was messy at the time; he was having an affair and mum was pregnant with my little brother while Christina was pregnant with William. That's my eldest step-brother,' she clarified.

Mutt gritted his teeth.

'I know, right?' Nina continued. 'Dad taught me a lot about working hard but I wouldn't exactly take relationship advice from him. Not that I've done all that well by myself.'

Mutt didn't pry, but he nodded like he understood. 'And your mum? Where's she?'

'In Hove, in the same local authority house where we were living when Dad walked out on us. She's a dinner lady at my old school, has been forever, since my brother was tiny. Bet you thought Hove was posh?'

Mutt was genuinely perplexed. 'Can't say I've ever thought about it. My dad's a decorator too, you know,' Mutt told her. 'When the fishing dried up in my granddad's lifetime the men adapted from scraping and painting hulls to painting houses. My mum's a housewife, though I'm no' sure she'd like to be called that. We're just ordinary folk too. If you don't mind me saying, Nina… you give the impression you're, *um*…'

'Rich? Privileged?' Nina said wryly. 'Of course I do, because that's the impression I've been trying to give since I arrived in New York on my internship. I was ambitious and everyone was so smart and flashy and they just assumed I had money because of my British accent, and I went along with it.'

Nina told Mutt all about those first days living in the interns' apartment, back when she was still dressing in the office where her mum had bought her at the Brighton branch of H&M before her big break in the Big Apple: the pittance-paying intern opportunity of a lifetime.

Her A-levels in Art and Design, Fashion and Business Studies had earned her three A grades and a glowing reference from her teachers which got her accepted on her college degree in marketing.

Her intern application had been picked out by Seamus Ryan during one of his drives to acquire staff through non-traditional routes, fed by his fits of working-class fervour when he'd remember he was a kid from Belfast who'd somehow ended up with a prestigious school scholarship in Dublin, then Harrow, and so on – that had seen him rise right to the top. Nina wasn't the same as him though. He'd acquired something during his education that she'd never have. He had a network, a safety net. Hundreds of rich, loud male friends all calling in favours and backing each other up.

Her own adaptability and Luke's advice had been enough to orientate her in her new world. She'd learned quickly how to avoid the condescending or downright disgusted looks of those who could see the chinks in her pose. She'd become a chameleon, the way so many working-class girls do.

Luke had selected her, Nina Miller, from the bottom of the ladder and fast-tracked her into the jet set (well, into their jet stream, maybe). Her ascent had been dizzyingly exciting, and she'd fallen hard for handsome, slick Luke and the world he opened up to her, even if, at first, some of the women in his set had raised their laminated brows at the red-bottomed Louboutins she'd saved up for from her first proper pay cheques – and which she'd been so proud of – directing her towards something, 'a little less… obvious, *hmm*?'

It was hard to slide back down into obscurity after the things she'd seen and done. She'd come to love the good life and the easy interactions, the way she could, until recently, get on any guest list she wanted. All she'd had to do was tag along with Luke or, if he was busy elsewhere, she'd ask Fournival to pull some strings. She'd loved it. At least she'd thought she loved it, until she'd come to Port Willow and slowly come to see how exhausting the pretence had been. She'd been on a treadmill for three years, always running, trying to hide her background, trying to keep up with her new peers and finding herself always in danger of slipping.

She told Mutt how once she'd had her bubble burst at a secret Brooklyn loft launch where everyone wordlessly read an exhibition catalogue and examined onyx sculptures while wearing white gloves. She'd been on the guest list as 'Luke Casson's Nina Miller.' At the time she'd told herself it was amusing, but it had led her to wonder more recently just how Luke's friends must have viewed her all these years. She'd never taken the chance to shine on her own; she'd always been Luke's.

'That was never my intention when I flew out to New York, determined to show the bosses what I was made of.' Nina's cheeks were burning with the realisation she'd let down that ambitious young woman. 'Seamus was right. I've no connections of my own. I'd be nowhere without Luke. I should never have got involved with him. But I liked all the blingy stuff, all the glamour.'

Mutt stopped her. 'I think you're being hard on yourself there. You said yourself you worked all hours, you were always available, always *on*.'

Nina nodded. That was true too, but her battered self-esteem meant she couldn't agree with him.

'And now?' Mutt said. 'Do you still want all that? The blingy stuff?'

'If I could have it on my own terms, then... maybe. If I could show Seamus I'm not the gold-digging girlfriend he thinks I am, then yes.'

'Right, then, well we need to find you something special to show him. I'm sure if we keep looking we'll find it. How long have we got?'

'I fly back on the twenty-seventh, that's two days.'

Mutt, who'd topped their whiskies up twice by now, looked suddenly sober. 'Two days? That's a shame.'

For a moment they froze, holding each other's gaze, suddenly aware of their breathing, and then increasingly aware of something else reaching them from somewhere inside the castle.

'Pipe music!' Mutt said, as if waking himself. 'We'll miss the laird's speech, come on.'

He pulled Nina to her feet while she fussed over the empty glasses. Mutt grabbed the bottle. 'We'll bring them with us. Let's go.'

He held her hand all the way through the snaking corridors, both of them running along, laughing and not knowing why, until they reached the ballroom door. They opened the door to a room now packed with people; every seat taken, apart from their two.

They drew up short because the piper was leading the head chef in his tall hat and whites into the ballroom in a stately march. The chef carried a silver salver and on it a great fat pudding. Eight waiters paraded behind, the first of whom carried a long knife wrapped in white linen.

They let the procession pass into the room before sneaking in and joining Mark and Ruth at their table, along with some other inn guests Nina recognised but didn't know.

After much applause, the chef set the haggis before the laird. He was surprisingly young and so smart in his family's tartan. Nina had imagined he'd be ancient like the castle somehow.

Laird Lachlainn took the knife from the waiter and leaned towards a microphone, surveying the room. He raised the knife dramatically and recited a poem that neither Nina, Ruth nor Mark understood much of, something along the lines of all other food suffering in comparison to the great Scottish haggis.

As he spoke, the laird thrust the knife into the haggis, slicing it across its great belly reciting the words, 'O what a glorious sight, Warm-reekin, rich!'

Nina felt glad she was getting the veggie option, but Mark and Ruth had their eyes fixed on its steaming insides spilling out and bit their lips hungrily.

At the end of the laird's address, he'd made a toast to 'the immortal memory of Robert Burns' and then recited a prayer about thinking yourself lucky you have meat and an appetite to eat it. Everyone had shouted 'Amen' like they were saying 'cheers' and the waiters hurried out with plates of the national dish, delicately presented with tender sprigs of green and purple on top of fat little rounds of haggis, swede and creamed potato turned out of their cooking rings and drizzled with a whisky sauce – a far cry from Gene Fergusson's rustic pub food of Hogmanay, but just as delicious.

'I didn't understand a word of that,' Mark told Ruth, and she agreed she hadn't either, but she'd certainly felt hungry and she gathered that was the desired effect.

The whole room fell upon their meals with gusto and in a loud wave of chatter while the waiters topped up wine glasses. There'd be more poetry later, but now it was time to feast.

Had Beatrice been there she'd have had to fight the urge to clap and squeal at the sight of Mark and Ruth so beautifully turned out, looking far more relaxed than usual, reaching for one another's hands every now and then when they weren't eating or drinking.

She'd have been delighted too to see Mutt sneaking looks at Nina, who was telling funny stories about the celebrities she'd met in New York, and every now and then Nina would glace back at him and hold his gaze for a second, her neck flushing pink, and not just because of the whisky.

But Beatrice wasn't at Castle Carron to see them. She was on a plastic hospital chair in the assessment ward at A&E, and Atholl was by her side, his face ashen.

Chapter Twenty-nine

Hold on

Two pink spots, faint, barely visible, but there all the same. Blood. Beatrice was sure of it. That's how it had started, and she hadn't said a word that morning, emerging from the bathroom already dressed for serving up the breakfasts.

She'd worked like an automaton, not hearing, barely seeing, and when she'd cleared the last table and waved off the last guest, she'd rushed to the bathroom and checked again.

This time it wasn't pink but red. Only tiny spots, but enough to send her screaming for the phone.

At the But and Ben, Atholl had thrown the keys to one of the students assembled in his workshop, he wouldn't ever remember who, and he'd run across the meadow, over the stile and alongside the train station and the primary school where the children were jumping hopscotch in the playground, his mind racing and beating his usual calm rationality to the same terrifying conclusion no matter how hard he tried to remember his faith in nature.

Beatrice was outside the inn, waiting in the passenger seat of Kitty's car, the engine running, a badly packed hospital bag on her lap, cursing her caution for not letting herself pack a proper bag like some other expectant mothers had as their fifth month approached, and at the same time glad she hadn't planned a thing, hadn't really let herself feel.

Kitty was talking through the open car window at her but Beatrice had no idea what she was saying when Atholl came hurtling down the waterfront.

Beatrice couldn't look at him. She didn't want to remember the look on his face. She'd learned it was the little details like that that popped up in her memory time and again, and they had the ability to wind her like she'd been socked in the stomach.

Atholl swung himself into the driver's seat and they'd driven the many miles to A&E through Tuesday lunch-time traffic, all tractors on the B roads and lorries along the motorway.

After the hurry of the journey and the obligatory form-filling-in, Beatrice found it hard to adjust to the slow pace everything seemed to take from then on and she wanted to scream in the strange silence in the triage waiting room. Instead she sat rigidly, staring at her hands on her lap.

Atholl had paced the corridors, asking any passing doctor, nurse or porter how much longer it would be, and he'd been told to sit down umpteen times until he had to give up and wait with Beatrice. He'd ground his jaw and agitatedly rubbed her hand with his thumb until at last the nurse came with a wheelchair and took her away.

-

'Nothing?' Atholl blinked when Beatrice told him.

'Yep, nothing's happening. They think I might have overdone it a bit and I'm to go home, get into bed and stay there. Total bed rest. The nurse is going to visit once a week.'

'But, the blood?'

'It happens, apparently. They said I was right to come straight in but the baby's fine. They did a scan. I saw her.'

Atholl staggered a little and gripped Beatrice's shoulders. His voice cracked as he repeated the word. '*Her?*'

The patients arriving and the doctors knocking off work had to squeeze past the pair of them as Atholl held Beatrice tight by the hospital doors and they'd cried, not caring who heard them.

Beatrice knew now the stakes were higher. Atholl's faith that this baby would arrive into the world safely and without complication had been shaken. Now there would be two of them trying hard to hold on for the spring time – only now Beatrice Halliday had the indelible image of a delicate girl, almost five months old and curled up like a fern frond, etched upon her heart, and she had never loved anyone as much or wanted anything quite so fiercely in her entire life.

Chapter Thirty

The Best-laid Plans

'May I have this dance?'

Mark presented his hand to Ruth with a slight bow, the way he'd seen the laird do with one of his guests a few moments ago.

'You may,' Ruth said, her voice crackling with delight, and she let her husband lead her into a waltz she'd seen the locals doing on Hogmanay at the inn.

Even with its easy steps, it was still nothing like the slow dance they'd done at their wedding reception at the pub with their family and a few friends almost twenty-five years ago. This was surprisingly energetic and rather a lot of fun, what with the ceilidh band making the most amazing, raucous sounds.

As Mark spun his wife under his arm then pulled her, not all that confidently, into a speedy waltz step, he told her she looked beautiful, and they'd danced on throughout the evening, not wanting to be out of each other's arms now they'd found their way back there, and Ruth remembered what it felt like to have her husband's palm on the small of her back, his mouth at her ear, and her hand on his shoulder.

They promenaded and pah-d' bah-ed, changed partners, found themselves being spun overenthusiastically by one of the many deranged, kilted Scots who seemed to have no respect for social niceties and people's personal safety now there was a wild reel being played, and then the couple had found each other again, dizzy and smiling, telling themselves they'd dance one more song then have a sit down but never actually leaving the floor. Ruth curtseyed to her husband – something she never in her life imagined herself doing – and he would make a low bow and kiss the back of her hand like Prince Charming in a fairy tale.

'Take your partners for Strip the Willow,' the caller announced from his spot by the stage, and people who had learned Scottish country dances at primary school and had a lifetime of practising at weddings under their belts got a bit cocky and remarked how this was a *really* tricky one, merrily patting Mark on the shoulder and wishing him luck.

Mark only smiled and told his wife it was all right; he knew what he was doing, he'd stripped willows with Atholl Fergusson and it was a piece of cake.

By the time Ruth and Mark were thoroughly confused and roaring with laughter at the mess they were making of this one, Mutt had reached the end of his endurance shouting over the music with Nina who couldn't dance because her ankle was smarting a little and he asked if she'd join him in the coffee lounge for a night cap where it would be quieter.

'Good idea!' she'd shouted back.

Once out of the hot ballroom, Nina wondered if her cheeks were as red as they felt.

'That was some pretty energetic dancing going on in there,' she laughed, shuddering as the chill in the corridor hit her.

'You'll feel the cold now. Here.' Mutt slipped his leather jacket over her tuxedoed shoulders.

'Do you want to...?' he started, holding his arm out for her to slide in close to him.

If she hesitated, it was only for a beat, then she let him wrap his arm around her shoulder and walk her to the bar, her head tipping automatically towards his.

'Oh, there's Mr Cor!' Nina cried.

They'd turned into the cosy snug bar to find the distillery owner sitting by the fire with a young woman. He was lifting two glasses of his own whisky from a waiter's tray and waxing lyrical about the malting process as he had done with Nina not so long ago before the incident with the cow and the dash to hospital, and long before the warm, tender hour spent conspiring with Mutt in the clan chief's glass bedchamber.

She instantly extricated herself from Mutt, but kept his jacket over her shoulders, telling him she had to go over and talk with Mr Cor.

'I don't know if you should, that's definitely not Mr Cor's wife he's with,' Mutt was telling her, but it was too late. Nina was already between their two chairs, making her presence known and wishing she hadn't had quite so much whisky.

'Mr Cor? It's good to see you again.'

He greeted her like an old friend, standing up and shaking her hand. 'Ah, Nina, it's you, is it? Glad you're here. Enjoying the party?'

The woman stood too, which Nina wasn't expecting. Nina recognised the dress she was wearing instantly; a smock style with cute dropped balloon sleeves. It was by a Colombian designer Microtrends had helped break in Europe.

'I have that same dress. What a coincidence,' Nina told her.

The woman looked down at herself, smoothing her hands over the thick fabric as if pleased with it.

'Are you having a nice time?' Nina asked Mr Cor.

Perhaps if Nina's mind had been fully focused on conducting herself in a more business-like manner and not quite so distracted by the electric buzz she'd been feeling every time she looked at Mutt that evening she'd have worked it out sooner. Instead she had to grasp for understanding as, to her horror, the penny slowly dropped.

'I am, thank you,' the old man said. 'I'd say we've had a very productive day and I'm glad to be signing the paperwork.'

'Paperwork?' Nina looked between the two, blinking and smiling, still failing to understand.

'Himari flew out with it herself. She's put forward a very impressive case for collaboration.' At this Mr Cor smiled at the woman, and Nina's face fell.

'Himari?' Nina looked again at the woman's dress. 'Of course, Himari.'

She felt Mutt shifting his boots on the floor just a little behind her. Slipping the leather jacket off her shoulders, Nina handed it to him, giving herself a moment to fix a smile.

'We haven't met,' Nina told the woman who stood cool and impassive, not at all ruffled. 'I'm Nina Miller.'

'Pleased to meet you,' Himari replied, taking the hand Nina had automatically extended. 'I'm Himari Nakamura.'

'Microtrends flew you out?' Nina said, unthinkingly. Wasn't that obvious?

'To seal the deal,' Himari replied. 'We had a lot to talk about but I'm glad to say Mr Cor's whisky will be in Remy's bars and restaurants by Christmas and in an exclusively designed bottle.'

'That's… that's fantastic,' Nina faltered, finding it almost impossible to smile now.

Nina couldn't help staring at Himari's dress. She knew now it must be hers, taken from her wardrobe. Come to think of it, Fournival had kept a few of Luke's gifts back, some of the more expensive items.

Himari smiled. 'Have you enjoyed your scouting trip?' she asked.

'I have. It's been… very interesting. *Um*, Mr Cor, do you mind if I borrow… my colleague for a moment?' Nina said, trying to sound as sober as possible.

Mr Cor was nothing but cordial and calm. He obviously only saw normal business practice at work. Nina had scouted him out, made first contact, pitched the idea of a relationship to her bosses and then they'd sent a real representative over to talk money.

Nina knew she couldn't be seen to be having a full-blown tantrum and she fought her thumping pulse and shaky legs to function normally. If only she didn't feel so unbearably sorry for herself and as though she was going to burst into tears right there in front of the unflappable Himari, who followed her over to the bar.

Mutt was left to make small talk with Mr Cor, but kept a close eye on Nina's turned back.

'Are you all right?' Himari asked expectantly and, Nina had to concede, kindly. She was making it very hard to hate her so far.

'I'm fine. *Umm*, so… the deal's done?'

'Yes, I'm flying back first thing.'

'Right,' Nina gulped. 'And I'm to stay here for a couple more days looking for more relationships like the one with Mr Cor?'

'I don't know.' Himari shrugged. 'Nobody discussed your schedule with me.'

'Right. Right. *Umm*, that really is a nice dress.' Nina had to risk it. She needed to know what Himari knew about her.

'Thanks, it's a Colombian designer...'

'I know.' Nina couldn't help interrupting. 'Did, *umm*, did Luke ever talk about me?'

Himari blinked at her, probably thinking she was a bit odd, maybe even detecting the smell of whisky on her breath – not something she wanted to get back to Seamus and Luke.

'If he did, I don't remember.'

Nina let this sink in. Himari was definitely telling the truth. She'd been flown in to New York, settled in to life at the office and West End Avenue, and now she was here, just doing her job.

Nina couldn't help asking, even though it made her wince and her pride begged her not to say it. 'Did you, *um*, did you have a nice Christmas?'

'I did, thanks. It was my first in New York.'

The picture of professionalism, Nina clearly wasn't going to get any painful, horrible details from this woman. She resolved to leave her in peace. Would Himari end up being passed over eventually too? Nina found herself hoping that wouldn't be the case.

'You seem nice,' Nina gulped, 'and good at your job.'

'Okay... thanks,' Himari replied, accepting Nina's words the way a senior colleague accepts the gushing adoration of a young intern with stars in her eyes hoping one day she'll be in her position. Himari didn't know anything about Nina's demotion, that much was clear.

Himari looked over her shoulder at Mr Cor. 'I've called a taxi for him. I'd better make sure he gets in it.'

'Of course.' Nina said, feeling her shoulders fall after the effort of maintaining her dignity. Crestfallen, she told her it had been nice to meet her and she congratulated her on making the deal.

'Thanks,' Himari replied, stepping away. 'Shall I give Mr Casson your best when I see him tomorrow?'

Nina wanted to cry there and then in the wake of Himari's elegant, retreating form, but she held it together until Mutt approached her. Only he heard her say, 'No, don't do that. I already gave Luke my best. He's not getting anything else.'

Chapter Thirty-one

The End of the Night

She'd only cried for a few minutes, but it had been a howling torrent, enough to thoroughly surprise Mutt and to wreck what was left of Nina's end-of-the-evening make-up. Mutt had pulled her all the way back to the clan chief's chamber to be sure Himari wouldn't witness the scene and he'd held onto her the whole time.

They'd slumped by the bedside once more. After she'd blown her nose and got her breathing back under control she'd let the words spill out, and they were angry ones. 'They liked my idea, really liked it, enough to fly her out and get it all wrapped up as soon as possible. And now it's Himari's account. I won't get any credit for that whatsoever.'

'How do you know?' Mutt had consoled. 'Your boss knows you scouted out that distillery, you came up with the idea, and you started the negotiations.'

'I *used* to get the credit. I had some accounts of my own and I was going to be given my own brand to manage this year. Seeing Himari here just shows how far I've fallen. If they won't let me have the whisky account, they won't let me have *any* of the accounts I uncover here.'

'Maybe if you work your way back up, they will? It won't take that long, surely?'

With a wry smile Nina told him there was only one way for young women to get to the top at Microtrends. She could see that now. 'I've burned my bridges there. I'll be down in Creative for ever, if they let me stay on.'

Mutt had a bright flash in his eyes. 'You told them about the whisky idea and they didn't waste any time flying someone out here to grab that deal, right?'

'Right.'

'Then you need to keep your *next* big discovery under your hat until you're face to face with your bosses. Tell them straight that *you* discovered it, and you want in on the account. It might be easy to take your ideas from you when you're on the other side of the world but if you're pitching in front of the entire executive board, there'll be a whole pack of them to impress and someone amongst them will recognise your hard work and make sure it's rewarded.'

Nina listened. 'That's not a bad idea, but what new discovery is this? I've nothing to take home, just a list of factories and workshops who already have all the business links they need, thank you very much. I can't make headway with any of them. They're already branded and networked to the hilt. And I'm realising that the smaller makers want to make and sell their products on their own terms, and honestly, who can blame them?'

'You just need one good thing of your own to take back to New York. Just one really good thing,' Mutt said. 'I'll help you find it. It must be right here under our noses.'

'Who haven't I spoken to yet?' Nina shrugged.

'Well, we've a whole village full of talent and crafting skills. Sure they may be small, and a wee bit eccentric on their own, but look what they've achieved by coming together: a whole crafting holiday collective.'

'A collective?' Nina nodded, thinking hard, looking around the glass room and remembering what Mutt had told her earlier about how this amazing restoration extension was the result of a network of people working together: engineers, designers, the visionaries, the laird with his money, and Mutt with his skills and precision. 'OK. I'll try to talk with them all. But if I can't turn something up, I'll have to admit defeat and head back home.'

'Right then. Well now we've got a plan, I'll go call us a taxi, shall I?'

'No,' Nina said flatly.

'No? I can't ride my bike after those whiskies.'

'Let's just lie down here. My head's spinning.'

'Here?' Mutt echoed.

'You said nobody was staying here 'til the spring, right?'

'That's right, there's furniture still to arrive… not to mention the curtains.'

Nina nodded sleepily and made to lie down on the floor where they were sitting, but Mutt jumped to his feet. 'Wait a minute.'

He was only gone for a few minutes and returned with two pillows. 'Here.' He slipped one under her head as she lay by the bedside.

Nina watched drowsily as he unlaced his boots, threw his jacket on the floor and came to lay beside her.

'Do you want me to lie further away?'

'No, Murray,' Nina told him, her eyes already shut. 'Stay close. You never know when your friend Bogle MacTavish might make an appearance with his axe.'

Laughing, Mutt stretched out beside her, watching her with soft eyes as she drifted off, shifting the strand of hair that had fallen down over her forehead, making her smile in her sleep, and reverently leaving a little distance between them.

Mutt eventually fell asleep while the laird's guests spilled out of the castle and piled into taxis and minibuses to be whisked away into the night. The sounds of the piper's midnight lament played from up on the ruined battlements and snatches of old Scottish poetry resounded in their woozy minds all the way home to their beds.

-

The Firths had giggled and shushed at each other as they stumbled through the door of the Princess room. Mark let the keys fall to the floor once they were sealed inside, alone.

Ruth clambered precariously up the ladder, still wearing her pretty dress and the black boots with the cut-out heel and toes Nina had loaned her earlier that evening. Mark watched her climb from the foot of the ladder, untying his shoes and reaching for the cascade of lace at his neck, ready to unclasp his collar and get dressed for bed.

'What are you doing down there?' Ruth called, poking her head out over the edge of the towering bed, making Mark laugh at the sight of her so high up and grinning madly. 'Keep it all on and get up here.'

Mark Firth did not need to be told twice. He followed the sound of his wife's laughter up the ladder and under the canopy.

'We're going to kiss,' Ruth informed him, watching the familiar, slightly dazed, desirous look burn in her husband's eyes. 'Like we used to when we first met. OK?'

He let this sink in. 'Well then,' he said, crawling closer, laying his wife back onto the mattresses and gazing down at her. 'Let's do that.'

After so long without the deep comfort of each other's lips, Mark and Ruth sank instantly into the slow, intense magic of kissing for kissing's sake, wordlessly turning back the clock to the days when they'd lose themselves in each other's embrace in nightclub doorways and at the bus stop heading home from yet another night out, long before there was always something more important to do than kissing.

As Ruth tipped her head back allowing Mark to bring his mouth to the soft spot on her neck that he hadn't thought to touch in so long and she sighed at the sensations turning her nerves to crackling, bursting fireworks, neither of them could understand in that moment how anything could ever have been more important than this.

Chapter Thirty-two

Home Truths in the Sun Room

Mutt and Nina had sneaked out of the castle at first light, having woken up only to find a wide-eyed roe buck peering in at them through the glass.

At some point during the night Mutt had pulled the gold cover from the bed and thrown it over them and in the dead sleep of the hours that followed they'd ended up wrapped in each other's arms, Nina's head against Mutt's chest.

When they woke, they'd jumped apart at the realisation and rubbed at their aching heads, smiling sheepishly at sleeping on the floor like stowaways and regretting nothing.

'Come on, we've got work to do,' Nina had told him.

His motorbike carried them away to Port Willow to begin their mission of finding Nina the ultimate Highland product to pitch to Seamus and the board.

She'd awakened knowing exactly what it was she was going to do and this time she was going to keep it secret until she was pitching her idea in New York.

She had one chance to prove her worth and that thought spurred her on over the next two days as Mutt shuttled her between impromptu meetings and introduced her to the local makers she wanted to see, and all the time they worked together Nina had a fire in her belly to succeed that she hadn't felt since the day she got her internship.

She wasn't going to be slowed down or distracted by the inconvenient fact that she liked gripping Mutt's waist as she rode on the back of his motorcycle or that it had been her who had shifted closer to him during the night at the castle, pulling him near as he'd slept, breathing in the scent of him, leather, whisky and warmth.

-

'Where is everyone this morning?' Kitty asked Beatrice, popping her head around the door to the sun room. 'It's half ten and I haven't seen the Firths or Nina.'

Beatrice was lying under a blanket on the sofa where she'd been receiving concerned visitors since just after nine.

News of Beatrice's dash to hospital the day before had reached all the way to Skye, thanks to Seth, and Mrs Fergusson had called a taxi in an instant.

Seth and Mrs Fergusson were there now, by the fire, still fussing over Beatrice and recounting all the things she'd have to cut back on now the doctors had told her to rest.

'The Easter arts festival, that'll have to be cancelled,' Mrs Fergusson said, but Beatrice wouldn't hear of it and told her so, saying she could conduct the last bits of planning from right here in her command centre.

She only had a little more to finalise, she'd lied, including letting the owner of Glenda, the vintage cinema mobile, know what movie reels she was to bring with her. She'd known this would spark some debate between Seth and Mrs Fergusson and was glad when they turned their attentions on each other, bickering about Gene Kelly's best works just as Kitty popped in.

Beatrice was glad of the interruption, telling Kitty that, 'Nina went with Mutt to the ball last night, but I didn't hear them come back,' not knowing whether to be delighted or concerned. 'Have you tried Mutt's mobile?'

'Engaged, I'll try again in a bit,' Kitty said, raising her voice over Mrs Fergusson who was chiding, 'Seth McVie, I dinnae ken how you can say such a thing.'

'Whit? All I'm saying is *Singin' in the Rain* is far superior to *Brigadoon* and a' its phoney accents and squawking singers.'

Mrs Fergusson crossed herself dramatically before launching into a lecture Beatrice had heard before about how *Brigadoon* was Gene Kelly's finest work.

'I might come with you, help you look for them,' Beatrice shouted back to Kitty.

'No, you won't. You sit there. You're lookin' fair tired,' she added pointedly, causing the elderly film buffs to stop their bickering.

'Perhaps Kitty's right,' Mrs Fergusson said. 'Come on, Seth, we'll take a coffee in the bar together and settle the matter. Now mind you don't move a muscle, Beatrice. Do you know I wasn't allowed out of bed for six months when I was carrying Kelly? It's no' an easy task, but you'll need to set your mind to it.'

Beatrice nodded, feeling chastened but also very much as though her own mum would have said something similar.

Seth took Mrs Fergusson's arm and led her out saying, 'Can we at least agree Debbie Reynolds was his best dance partner?'

'Debbie Reynolds? Cyd Charisse, now there's a dancer!'

Their voices faded and Beatrice widened her eyes at Kitty. 'Can you tell people I'm sleeping if anybody else calls by?'

'Got it.' Kitty saluted.

'Except Ruth Firth. In fact, if you see her, will you ask her to pop in?'

Kitty raised an eyebrow.

'What? She's a trained midwife, I'll have you know. She told me herself.'

'Wantin' to see her's got nothing to do with you gaspin' to know how the pair of them are getting on now you've made your marriage on the rocks recovery list?'

'Who told you about that?' Beatrice cried.

'I saw it. It was on their dresser yesterday when Gene was changing their towels. He recognised your handiwork, and you know Gene and I have no secrets. You *gave* them that list?'

'I gave it to Ruth, yes.' Beatrice shrugged, as though that were a perfectly normal thing to do. 'What?'

Kitty only blinked.

'They needed a bit of expert advice.'

'And you were that expert?'

'No,' Beatrice shifted on the sofa, getting agitated. 'I found all that advice online from real relationship gurus. I'm just a matchmaker.'

'Right, well, let's hope they're busy ticking items off your list and not heading home to Yorkshire in a huff because the inn manager's a busybody meddler.' Kitty was smiling.

'Have you been talking to Atholl?'

Kitty threw her a wink and told her to get some rest before closing the door, leaving Beatrice to surreptitiously pull her laptop out from under the sofa and set to work again.

'Right, where was I? Oh yes, bouncy castles.'

-

The creak of floorboards woke Beatrice, and her eyes sprung open catching Ruth Firth tiptoeing out the sun room door.

'Don't go,' she said, finding her voice was croaky.

'I don't want to disturb you,' Ruth whispered. 'Kitty told me what happened yesterday at the hospital. Go back to sleep.'

'My laptop! Where is it?' Beatrice sat up straight. She'd only nodded off for a second surely? Where could it have gone? She still had the Punch and Judy arrangements to firm up.

Ruth tipped her head sagely. 'I took it off you, you were fast asleep.' She pointed to the shelf behind her where she'd safely stowed it.

'Oh.' Beatrice felt stiff from lying down all morning. 'Ruth? Will you report me to the elders if I sit up and have a decaff with you?'

Ruth laughed and nodded. 'Right you are, stay there.' She made for the door.

'Ruth? Can you get some of Gene's shortbread too?'

She replied with a thumbs-up as she left.

-

'So?' Beatrice was wide-eyed over the rim of her coffee cup.

'So?' Ruth echoed mischievously.

'You had a nice time last night? At the Burns Night Ball, I mean?'

'You're asking if we ticked anything off your list, aren't you, you little weirdo?'

Beatrice grinned. 'Oh my God, you definitely did! Look at your face!'

'We only kissed, like the experts said. I was very firm about that.'

Beatrice bit her shortbread contentedly and shook her head thinking how easy this matchmaking was.

'You needn't look so pleased,' Ruth said.

'What do you mean? It's working, isn't it?'

'Mark was gone this morning when I woke up. Off to do some more work, I imagine. Slipped out at seven. God knows who he needed to talk to that early.'

'Maybe he felt like walking?' Beatrice said, a little desperately.

Surely that didn't mean anything. There's no way Atholl's hunch could be right, not with Ruth and him getting on a little better. If Mark Firth *really was* having a sneaky affair there was no way this was salvageable with a simple list that basically boiled down to the advice be courteous and appreciate each other.

'I know what you're thinking,' Ruth said grimly. 'I don't even want to consider it... but it would make sense.'

'Would it?' Beatrice gulped her coffee, feeling very guilty indeed for getting Ruth's hopes up for a cosy, intimate future with her husband when he couldn't give up his habit of skulking off with a phone to his ear.

'Well... this is our first trip away together in forever. If he has been, you know, cheating back home he'd have had plenty of opportunities to get away to see her or to phone her any old time, only now we're stuck together on holiday maybe it's more obvious when he can't keep away from her.'

'But you kissed last night? And you danced?'

'And it was like a second honeymoon, just like you planned when you picked us in the giveaway. I hate to disappoint you, Beatrice, but the reality is, we're a mess.'

'You're sure he's not with Atholl at the workshop?' Beatrice asked, suddenly hopeful.

Ruth shook her head. 'He can't be with Atholl. Your fella's pacing about in the reception telling everyone to be quiet because you're in here trying to sleep.'

'He's not, is he?' Beatrice's mouth gaped. '*Atholl?*' she shouted. '*Go to work!*'

The women were silent for a moment watching each other's changing expressions. They heard a sharp whistle from behind the door, the *thump thump thump* of Echo running downstairs, responding to his master's call, followed by Atholl's heavy tread on the reception floorboards as he left reluctantly for a day at the willow workshop.

'He's going to fret all day, you know?' Ruth said.

'I know. He's going to fret until this baby comes.'

'When is she due?'

'You know it's a girl?' Beatrice asked.

The women looked at each other once more. 'Gene,' they both said at once.

'To give the man his due he was weeping a little when he told me. I think Atholl had only just broken the good news. Anyway, I told him I didn't feel up to cooking calamari this morning, not after all that red wine last night, and he let me off the hook.'

Beatrice smiled. 'Gene's very sentimental.'

'You've got an army of people here looking after you; good, kind-hearted people.'

Beatrice nodded. She knew it. 'She's due around about the middle of June, the midwife reckons.'

'Plenty of time to prepare.'

'Plenty of time to sit around gusset gazing.' Beatrice rolled her eyes comically.

'Knickerwatch,' Ruth added. 'Been there, carrying the twins.'

'Like *Springwatch* on the telly, only with knickers?'

'That's it!' They laughed, both of them feeling lighter just by being in each other's presence.

'I miss my girlfriends,' Ruth said, suddenly. 'They all got very busy when their husbands retired. I should definitely make a list of ways to get them back in my life, and not just for a quick brew or a glass of wine either. We need to get action planning for lives of our own after kids.'

Beatrice agreed. 'Is there anything you want me to do? Do you want to call one of your sons, or a girlfriend, or...?' She felt useless. 'I shouldn't have got myself involved. This is my fault. I'm sorry. I've freaked you both out, made things weird between you and Mark, started you off questioning everything.'

'No, no you didn't,' Ruth insisted. 'You encouraged me to try, and I did. But maybe this is it for us. We may have clawed back a bit of closeness but we haven't really talked.'

'That's the last thing on the list,' Beatrice said, and Ruth sighed.

'Trouble is, that's probably the hardest thing to do. You'd think after all these years we wouldn't have much left to talk about, but it's quite the opposite.'

'I understand. I was like that with Richard, my ex-husband.'

'You're divorced?'

'Ten years married, three months divorced.'

'Ah, well you *do* know then. When you're young and in love people ask you all the time how are things going with so-and-so? And you talk about your dates and meeting his mother and all that stuff, but when you get married nobody thinks to ask. I suppose it doesn't seem as relevant, or as romantic. What could possibly be going on in the marriage of two old farts that needs talking about? So you stop checking in with friends about your relationships, and then you stop checking in with your own husband about it, and, before you know it, you're living like strangers.'

'Strangers who know absolutely everything there is to know about each other,' Beatrice threw in.

'Exactly. I suppose you're thinking we should just get it all out in the open? That we're old enough to know better than to moulder and stew about things, but we're not, see? I feel exactly the same as I did when I was twenty. Nobody ever tells you that, when you're young. That you'll age and bits of you will start going wonky and decrepit and you'll pay off your mortgage and look to all the world like fully functioning adults but you'll feel just as insecure and confused as you did when you were a kid, and it hurts just as much when you're lonely in a relationship as it did when you were in your turbulent teens and wondering why that guy doesn't call you back. It hurts more, in fact, much more, because everybody just expects you to rub along together like two dry old sticks getting excited about their next Saga holiday and *Gardeners' World*.'

'Oh, I love a bit of *Gardeners' World*,' Beatrice confessed.

'Me too.' Ruth laughed again, but her eyes had lost their shine.

'You need to get all of this out,' Beatrice told her. 'You need to say it out loud.'

'Or write it all down?' Ruth said.

'Maybe,' Beatrice scrunched her nose. 'But face to face is probably better. When Mark gets back, have a nice dinner and just say it all.'

'What? That I love him better than anything? That I miss our little family and I wish I could go back thirty-seven years and do it all over again with him?' Tears welled in Ruth's eyes.

'Exactly that,' Beatrice reached for Ruth's hand and squeezed it until she'd sniffed away the tears.

'And you? Are you going to be all right?' Ruth said.

Beatrice thought for a moment. 'I think yesterday was helpful, in a way. I think it did me good to rehearse all those feelings. I'd been in a kind of daze since the pregnancy test at Christmas and I needed a bit of a reality check. You see, when I lost my baby last spring, I fell apart with the grief. I know you hear about women coping in different ways, but I was one of the ones who couldn't cope at all, not until I came here.' She shrugged wistfully and looked around the room. 'Yesterday I got to go through all the horrible emotions again, the ones I'd been so afraid of – the dread, and the panic, and the sheer terror – but then I got to come out the other side and feel this overwhelming sense of relief and gratitude. Now I feel as though I'm better prepared for whatever's going to happen, if that makes sense? Instead of holding all the scary feelings at arm's length, I got to process them a bit. Now I just feel glad this baby is on board, and I'm feeling tired, of course. I definitely feel very, very tired. I don't think I'll dwell too much on the awfulness that *could* happen quite so much now, but I still can't let myself feel one hundred percent happy yet either.'

Ruth squeezed her hand. 'I think that sounds perfectly reasonable, and very human.'

'Atholl's a bit confused by it all. Normally by now I'd be researching nursery wallpapers and fabrics, nappy rash creams, the lot! But I've been too afraid to, and I still don't want to do any of that stuff. I think he'd be reassured if I was planning those things, but...'

'Your self-preservation has kicked in?' Ruth interrupted.

'Yes.'

'Just like I don't want to ask my husband if he's having an affair. Who runs towards pain if they can avoid it?'

Beatrice nodded, stifling a sudden yawn.

'Come on, lie down again. You need to sleep,' Ruth told her.

'I'll only need to get up for a pee in five minutes.'

'Still, five minutes' sleep is better than none. I learned that with the twins, believe me.'

As Ruth was tucking her under the blanket, Beatrice suddenly flinched then froze, her eyes huge. '*Woah!*'

'Are you all right? Did that hurt?' Ruth reached for the mobile in her handbag.

'I felt something!'

'Like a kick?' Ruth asked.

'Like a salmon turning in a net!'

Ruth laughed delightedly. 'Was that the first time you've felt anything?'

Beatrice pulled Ruth's hand to her stomach. 'I thought I felt something like bubbles before, so I couldn't be sure if it was really the baby, but this was more like a washing machine.'

'It could be the first wiggles,' Ruth reassured her. 'I can ring the hospital if you like?'

Their question was answered by a restless baby pressing hard against Ruth and Beatrice's spread palms. '*Ha!*' Beatrice gasped again. Their eyes met in wonder and Beatrice instantly burst into sobs. 'And I sent Atholl away! He missed it.' Yet she was still laughing even as she cried. 'What's with all these emotions happening all at once?' she said, a huge, wobbly smile on her face.

'Oh, honey, welcome to parenting,' Ruth told her.

Chapter Thirty-three

Polly

Mutt and Nina rushed into the busy bar that evening, both of them carrying a cardboard box of something clanking and rattling, and Nina trying to read something on her phone screen.

'Can we have something quick to eat, please, Gene? We're celebrating before Nina flies out first thing,' Mutt asked.

'There you are!' Gene said, coming round the bar to talk to him. 'We've been hunting for the pair of you, high and low.'

'We've been product developing,' Nina told him triumphantly, almost breathless with the mad dash of the last two days. Her beautifully quiffed hair had been flattened by the bike helmet and her boots were scuffed and muddy, and she didn't care at all. Bear was dancing around Gene's feet, hoping to be offered something tasty from the kitchen.

'What's wrong, Gene?' Mutt asked, seeing his grave expression.

'We weren't the only ones looking for you. Mutt, you've a visitor.'

Nina and Mutt followed Gene's eyes to the woman sitting alone by the fire.

'Polly?' Mutt instantly placed his box on the bar and walked over to her, leaving Nina to watch. 'What are you doing here?' he said to the woman. 'Are you after the shirt off my back, as well as my money?' he asked in a growl.

'His money?' Nina mouthed the words, staying right by the bar.

Gene told her it might be for the best if she left them to talk and that he'd bring her something to eat if she'd wait there. She wasn't really listening to him though, she was straining her ears to hear what Mutt was saying to the woman he hadn't even thought to introduce her to, the woman he'd taken one glance at and entirely forgotten Nina even existed.

'Had you forgotten about our paperwork?' the woman was saying. 'There's still the details to iron out.'

'If you think you're here for Bear you've got another think coming, Polly. You were the one that wanted him, then, no sooner had we picked him up from the rescue place, you disappeared.'

'You never wanted him,' Polly bit back.

'You didn't take him with you. God knows, you took everything else,' Mutt replied, his voice shaky now.

Still at the bar, Nina picked Bear up, cradling him protectively in her arms, not minding her jumper getting mucky.

'Who's that?' the woman asked, lifting her chin in Nina's direction.

'Never you mind,' Mutt told her. 'You can pack up and get out of here.'

'Not until you sit down with me. We need to talk.'

'You disappear in October and I don't hear a word from you, and now here you are. You must be wanting something.'

'I want what's mine. We had an agreement. What's yours is mine and what's mine is yours.'

Nina had heard enough. She took a few steps closer to Mutt and set the pup down on the floor once more. 'Clearly you two have a lot to talk about. I'll leave you to it.'

'No, Nina, wait there,' Mutt pleaded. 'I won't be long.'

'I don't think so,' Nina said, backing away, seeing how dark and unfriendly Mutt's eyes were. He'd never looked like this before and it scared her.

Mutt clearly didn't like Nina seeing him like this, but he wasn't planning on walking away from Polly either.

Polly, eyes fixed on Mutt, patted the seat beside her, drawing Mutt's attention back to her. Mutt pulled out the chair across the table from her.

The last thing Nina saw as she retreated from the bar was Bear scrambling onto Polly's knee.

'Come to Mummy,' the woman said. 'You're so big! What's Daddy been feeding you?'

Back in her room, Nina tried to think rationally. Whoever this stranger was, Mutt hadn't responded warmly to her, but, then again, he hadn't made any effort to include Nina in their conversation. It was as though he'd taken one look at Polly and forgotten her. Not that they'd made any kind of promises to one another in the last two days since their night at the castle. They hadn't even kissed; even if she'd thought there were moments when they might, Mutt always seemed to pull away at the last minute. There wasn't anything going on between them, nothing spoken anyway.

Hadn't he gone out of his way to help her these last few weeks? Once they'd got over their initial needling and distrust of one another. Hadn't he stayed up half the night working with her and Mr Cor and Munro at the But and Ben, trying to get her pitch product right? Why would he do that? 'Unless…' she said to herself as the stark, painful thought struck her. Unless they were just friends. Unless affable, friendly Mutt was like this with everyone?

Hadn't he known everyone in Port Willow by name, and up at the castle too? And he'd only been here since the autumn. Maybe he's just that kind of guy, befriending everybody? Though she'd certainly never seen him react to anyone in the same agitated, gaping way he'd reacted to Polly tonight.

Her mind raced, trying to figure out what she'd just witnessed. 'What's mine is yours,' she'd said. 'They had an agreement,' she'd said. 'Did she want the shirt off his back,' he'd said.

If Nina and Mutt were anything more than fleeting friends, surely she'd know something about this woman and what kind of a hold she had over him? For God's sake, they'd even rehomed a dog together! She'd called herself Bear's Mummy.

'Oh no,' Nina said, slumping on her bed beside her open suitcase. 'Oh no. I've done it again. I've let someone else in, let them give me the leg-up I needed, relied upon them instead of showing my worth, instead of doing it on my own. Now he's off with someone else. Maybe he's been committed to her all along?'

This all felt very familiar. She packed her case, cursing her own stupidity.

When she heard Mrs Mair clearing the bar of punters after last orders, Nina sneaked through the reception and into the bar, peering around the door, not wanting to be seen looking for him.

There, in the same spot she'd left him, was Mutt, his head propped on one hand, his elbow on the table looking straight at the woman. Polly was talking animatedly, Bear fast asleep on her lap, only now she was on a chair beside Mutt. There were four empty glasses on the table in front of them.

'He *has* forgotten about me,' Nina told herself, carrying herself off to bed. Her taxi would arrive in four hours to whisk her away to Edinburgh airport and out of Mutt's life forever, just as Polly had swept in to reclaim him.

Nina told herself that come her seven a.m. take-off she'd have forced herself to forget the bubbling, excited feeling he gave her whenever he was near. She'd made a friend in the Highlands, he'd helped her, and now she was leaving. She could call him to say goodbye from New York. No need to make a soppy scene, not now she understood what she'd been to him.

She locked herself in her room, climbed under the covers and turned out the light. She was going home and she had a product to sell all by herself. She'd show Luke and Seamus that she could do it. They didn't have to know she'd had Mutt's help, and all his friends' too.

'Mr Ryan, Mr Casson, members of the board, I'm delighted to return from the beautiful Highlands of Scotland with a craveable new product prototype. And after the success of our, I mean, of Himari's whisky collaboration, I'm sure you'll be as excited as I am too...'

She gave up running lines for her pitch, her head aching, curled up on her side and hugged her pillow with a sad sigh.

Beatrice had told her Mutt was a runaway, she berated herself. She'd already known he was here licking his wounds. 'Well, now the runaway's been caught again.

Polly's come back for him, and he's not exactly trying to run now, is he?'

Nina had arrived at the inn crying and regretful, full of frustration and anger, and soon she would be leaving feeling exactly the same way. Well maybe not *exactly* the same, she told herself. Beatrice had told her Port Willow helped fix people who needed fixing; and sure enough, a tiny part of Nina had clicked into place this last few weeks.

She knew now that she really did have to go it alone. No more helpers. No more men. Nina Miller had to shine all by herself. It had taken seeing Mutt beguiled by Polly to finally drum the message into her. She was all alone from here on in.

Chapter Thirty-four

Messages on Water

Earlier that evening and as soon as Atholl got home from the willow school, Beatrice told him about the kick, and after he'd stopped holding his face to her belly where he'd been roundly socked in the cheek three times, she also told him about her letter idea.

'Write a letter to our unborn daughter?' he'd asked, repeating her words.

'Yep! I think if we just wrote out how we were feeling it would help me. It was Ruth who gave me the idea. So...' She held out a pen. 'Shall we?'

It had taken them a matter of minutes, sitting at Beatrice's command centre in the sun room. Beatrice wrote the lion's share, but Atholl said his piece too. They bundled themselves into coats and hats and left the inn with their letter.

'You're sure you want to send it by water?' Atholl asked as they crossed the road and stopped at the low sea wall where the high tide had covered the curving bay.

'Just like I did before.' Beatrice nodded, and they both thought of the wild flowers she'd collected on Skye last August, when Beatrice had finally broken down and told the story of her lost child. Atholl, heart breaking in his chest at the sight of her distress, had rushed to his workshop and returned carrying the tiny willow bassinet, a model he'd made for a talk Seth had given a while back on Highland traditions. She'd woven the flowers into the empty bassinet and floated them on the water. She'd watched them drift until out of sight on the horizon, at last beginning the slow process of saying goodbye to someone she'd never met but loved with her whole heart.

Yes, she wanted to send this letter in exactly the same way, and so, in the streetlight glow, Beatrice unfolded the letter and she and Atholl read it aloud huddled together above the dark water.

'To our darling daughter,' Beatrice read. 'You're more than four months away from us but we cannot wait to meet you.'

Atholl added the next line. 'It isn't easy waiting for you and your mum isn't a very patient person at the best of times.' They both smiled at this and Beatrice took over again.

'When you get here, there are so many lovely things we want to show you. You'll get to meet Echo, your sheepdog. He's getting old now but we know he'll always keep an eye open in case you get yourself into trouble and he'll enjoy sharing your snacks with you.'

Beatrice read on. 'You'll love the beaches and the meadows here in the Highlands. Your dad says you'll probably have learned to weave willow before you can talk but we'll see about that.'

Atholl placed an arm around her shoulder and he cleared his throat before he read the next part. 'There'll be days for paddling and picnics, painting trips too. You'll have a never-ending stream of new friends coming to the inn, just like your old dad had when he was growing up, and you've about a hundred redheaded cousins spread all over the Highlands and islands to play with, and there's your cousin Chloe in England who'll be a special friend, I know. You've also a granny who's longing to see you, and Seth's already called dibs on teaching you how to fish and to ride your first bike. God help you!'

They laughed and Beatrice read again even though her eyes were misting.

'I'm not quite ready to make you a nursery room, yet, but they say a baby comes into the world with everything they need. I hope that's true. There'll certainly be enough love to sustain you, and warmth too.

'Your Uncle Gene will keep making you any tasty thing you ask him for, and your Auntie Kitty – she knows the Gaelic word for everything there is, and the steps for every Scottish dance. She'll be a good teacher until you go to the little school.'

Atholl didn't even try to hide his tears as he took over, sniffing and smiling as he spoke.

'There's so many good things here waiting for you. The taste of chocolate, the sound of the sea, the smell of lavender and willow, the sunset over the coral beach, and the way your mummy looks when she's getting sleepy and fighting it. I hope you'll have that same look too.'

Beatrice's voice shook, but she wasn't sad. 'Life is full of surprises and comfort. And there's some unhappy things too, but they're all part of being alive, and you can't have happiness without some of the sad stuff as well.

'You have an older brother who none of us got to know. I'll miss him every day until I get to meet him. But grief is what is left of love when the person is gone, it's not always the dark, terrible thing you think it is, not all the time anyway.

'I'll tell you all about him one day, and he won't be kept a secret. Maybe if we talk as a family about him, if it ever happens to you one day or to someone you love it might not come as such a horrible shock as it did to me, and you'll know what to do, better than Richard and I did. If it hadn't been an off-limits subject we might have coped better, talked more, shared the pain, and our friends and families might have been better able to comfort us. Instead nobody said anything, and we bottled it up, keeping it inside. A terrible mistake.'

Beatrice let her tears fall, holding the letter closer to Atholl's eyes so he could take over while she caught her breath.

'So, here we are,' Atholl read. 'Your mum and dad, not keeping any secrets inside, telling the world we love you and we want you, and asking the universe to bring you to us when you're ready to come.

'We are so happy you chose us. We'll do our best to be good parents. We'll make mistakes, I'm sure, but we'll say sorry and try to carry on. As long as we keep sharing, we'll be all right.

'We love you. See you soon, Mum and Dad, kiss kiss.'

Atholl took the letter in his hands and folded the paper lengthways until it was as thin as a ribbon, then he tied it. 'It's a love knot,' he said, handing it back to Beatrice, who slowly bent over the sea wall and placed the twisted paper on the surface of the dark water.

Atholl held her as they watched their message of hope floating out to sea where somewhere there bobbed a willow bassinet full of Beatrice's love, all bound with Highland forget-me-nots.

When they returned to the inn, Atholl made hot cocoa and they went to bed, deeply tired but calm too. Atholl slept with a protective hand on Beatrice's stomach where, safe and warm, their baby swam and danced all night long.

-

That same evening, before the letter and before Polly turned up, Ruth had determined to talk with Mark, but because he'd spent most of the day away from the inn and come back exhausted having been who knows where, they had eaten together in the bar restaurant and the words Ruth had wanted to say wouldn't come.

Mark was still just as smiling and affable as he'd been at the ball the evening before, only perhaps a little soppier after their night under the canopy of the princess bed.

She'd determined to do it after dessert but when Ruth had come back from the bar with Gene's lavender ice cream and raspberry meringues and the cafetière, she'd found Mark poring over some documents, reading glasses on his nose, utterly absorbed.

'You go up, I won't be long,' he'd told her, but he hadn't climbed the ladder until after midnight and by then Ruth had exhausted herself with furious tears and fallen asleep.

He'd passed Nina in the reception area when he eventually headed upstairs to bed. She'd been sneaking towards the bar in her pyjamas to see if Mutt was still with Polly, but she'd been in her own world and hadn't said goodnight to him.

-

The Princess and the Pea Inn was utterly silent when Nina checked out at four o'clock, her taxi idling on the roadside, a great cloud of exhaust fumes illuminated in the dark of the winter's morning by the brake lights.

She'd pressed her ear to Mutt's door as she left, half wanting to hear nothing at all – which is exactly what she heard – and half dreading she'd hear him in there with Polly.

Nobody came out to say goodbye to her; it was, after all, the middle of the night, so she left her key on the reception desk beside the little willow tree that she wouldn't get through Customs. It had hurt her to leave it, the only gift she'd had that Christmas.

Chapter Thirty-five

The Pitch

It was colder walking through the streets of New York City than it had been back in Scotland. Everything she loved, everything she was familiar with, was all around her, but now it didn't feel like home at all. Nina couldn't comprehend it.

Maybe it was the jetlag and the fact she had barely slept? Maybe it was because she'd booked herself into the Holiday Inn and she wasn't looking forward to spending the night in a sparse room by the elevators where all her worldly possessions were contained in three suitcases now that she'd retrieved her baggage from the airport lockers.

She had no appetite for the bagel she'd bought herself for breakfast and the ten-dollar Vietnamese iced coffee did nothing to comfort her either.

Feeling flat and exhausted, she'd styled her hair and carefully applied her make-up, putting on a black cropped jumpsuit with the harness-style straps Luke had told her he loved. Her hands were numb, she noticed, as she rode the elevator up to the top floor.

Mitch had greeted her in amazement, saying she looked so 'healthy' and Nina really didn't know if it was a compliment. 'They're all waiting for you,' he told her. 'You got this.'

'I think I do too,' she told him, but instead of feeling triumphant and charged up ready to pitch like she used to, there was something missing and she didn't know what.

The elevator doors opened and she stepped out into the corridor leading to Seamus's office. She used to dream of walking this corridor, lined with minor works by modern artists, thinking that one day, with her instincts and dedication, it could be hers. That hunger had become nothing but a bitter taste in her mouth now.

As Seamus had promised, all of the executives were there. Himari was the only other woman in the room and the only person to greet her with a genuine smile. Luke was at the head of the table next to Seamus. He didn't react at all to her arrival.

Nina wished she was as unreadable as him but she knew everyone could see her nerves were frazzled. As soon as she opened her mouth they'd hear how much her confidence had been knocked lately.

Clearing her throat, she waited for Seamus to welcome her back.

'Nina, right on time. How was your trip?' he said, looking relaxed.

'Good morning.' She reached for the water bottle and poured herself a glass. 'Scotland was productive and… interesting, thank you.' She found she couldn't trust herself to lift the glass to her mouth without her hands shaking so she left the water she so badly wanted on the table. 'Shall we make a start?'

Nobody said a thing. Himari clasped her hands together and placed them on the table, very serious.

'Well, you've already heard my whisky idea and you've signed off on a deal for an exclusive relationship between the Cor distillery and Remy's bar and restaurant chain.

Congratulations, Himari, for taking the lead with that account.'

Unexpectedly, Himari interrupted. 'I think we can all agree that was an excellent find. Well done, Nina.'

'Yes, well done,' Seamus added, not at all grudgingly. Perhaps he was pleased with her after all?

She was surprised to see the ripple of admiration and agreement going around the table. Some of the execs took notes, others whispered between themselves. This was going better than she had feared. Maybe she was closer to getting her old position back than she realised?

'I *um*, I met a number of creatives and company directors while in the Highlands. I emailed the full list to you this morning.'

More nodding from the execs around the table and lots of consulting of tablets and scrolling through her document.

'I established a dialogue with each of them and even though they didn't, *um*...' she faltered, her neck flushing hot then cold. 'I didn't get as far as discussing potential collaborations or brand extension opportunities with them...avenues are open for you to explore if you wish to.'

Seamus steepled his fingers under his jutting chin. 'Do you have anything concrete to show us?' he asked. 'I don't think I need to stress the importance of bringing us another deal along the lines of the distillery connection.'

Nina opened her palm where she clasped the USB stick containing her presentation. She glanced at the tech stack on the desk. All she had to do was load it up and give the pitch she'd prepared with Mutt back in Port Willow.

He'd sat cross-legged on her bed while she rehearsed, scrolling through the flashy presentation on her laptop.

He'd been grinning and nodding encouragement, leaning forward intently, hanging on her words. She'd felt ready to take on the world then. Now, however...

'Nina?' Seamus called to her through the haze of memories and the sound of her accelerated breathing.

'I've made a presentation,' she said, still looking at the stick in her hand, 'but, *uh*, the product speaks for itself really.' The truth was, she didn't want to give them the perfect pitch she'd prepared. Deep down she already knew they'd want her product. 'I... *uh*...' Nina fought hard to focus on the expectant eyes staring back.

Someone looked at their wristwatch, another folded their arms, getting fed up waiting. Himari looked concerned. Luke didn't move a muscle.

She'd seen him in meetings just like this, watching other hopefuls presenting their ideas. He'd been just as cold and unmoved with those strangers as he was watching her now.

How had she spent three years sleeping beside him? What a horrible waste of her time and energy. In that time she'd courted so many investors and influencers, set up so many collaborations, and she'd brought in money for Microtrends Brand Development and Lifestyle Forecasting. It struck her that she'd proven her worth time and again.

Had she been proportionately rewarded? Surely if she had, she'd have her own apartment by now and she wouldn't be camping out at the Holiday Inn tonight. If she had, she'd have a bank account bursting with cash, like Luke's. 'If you're valued, you're rewarded,' Luke would say in meetings. She'd seen him argue for generous employee packages and lavish contracts for his friends and valued associates. Had he fought for her? Had she fought for herself?

'You asked me to prove my worth, Mr Ryan, and I think I've done that. You sent me away, having demoted me.' She looked at Luke now, 'Having dumped me, in the middle of the Scottish Highlands, and I found you a whisky collaboration deal. I knew that wouldn't be enough, so I gathered together some of the local creators and we workshopped a new product.'

Seamus leaned forward in his chair as Nina pulled the black bow on the gift box on the table.

'I made use of our contact, Mr Cor at the distillery, to source the right kind of cosmetic-grade denatured ethanol, that's pure alcohol to you, and I worked with Munro, a glassworker, who designed a special bottle, and Eugene Fergusson,' she couldn't help smiling as she said Gene's name, picturing him stooped over the great copper still at the But and Ben, demonstrating the lavender oil distillation process, 'provided the essential oil.'

Everyone was watching Nina's hands as she lifted the lid off the box and reached her hands inside. The scent hit her as she cradled the bottle she'd watched Munro make from scratch. Touching the cold, pale lilac glass she felt herself transported back to his workshop by the loch in that buzzing industrial estate full of makers. She could still smell the heat from the furnace and the sizzle of the metal filings as they were incorporated into the molten bauble on the end of the glass-blowing rod. She felt the hiss of the steam in her very blood as she remembered how he'd cooled the bottle having shaped it so carefully into the rustic rectangular apothecary-style bottle she was turning in her hands now. It was so slender and beautiful and inside the liquid glinted in the harsh white office light.

Looking at the product she'd worked so hard to produce, she was hit by the heady smell of the lavender oil diffused through pure, clear alcohol – green, soapy and fresh – and the magic ingredient, white willow, *Salix alba*, so clean and woody. Atholl had shown her how to extract and mix the tincture following the advice of his old tutor, imparted long ago.

'Nina?' Seamus was impatient now.

All she had to do was spray the fragrance in the air, let it diffuse its way through the penthouse office, insinuate itself into the air vents, seep into the execs' skin, and she'd have handed over another perfect deal.

All she had to do was tell them she'd bottled the scent of the Highlands, capturing its very essence. Craveable luxury and Scottish authenticity in a bottle.

She touched her fingers to the thin leather bow around the bottle's neck, just below its round glass stopper. Freshly cut leather, the scent of Murray's beaten-up biker jacket. The entirety of her Scottish experience refined into something she could hold in her hands, anoint her body with, sink into.

Hiding the bottle from the execs' prying eyes, she pulled the stopper out. The wave of scent hit her fully and the room spun around her. She heard the fires crackle and spark in the willow craft school, she tasted the whisky in the clan chief's chamber and felt it burn her throat, and she relived the sensation of tramping the wet, white shards on the coral beach where the air pockets inside the slippery seaweed popped beneath her feet as she trod upon them, and she missed – no, she craved – the whole place and everything about it, and, most of all, she craved Murray who she hadn't even said goodbye to. The man who'd tried so hard to save her career, who'd biked her all over the coast to gather materials and ingredients for their coral beach fragrance, the person who'd brought together their collective, their little gang of makers.

Even if he loved this Polly, even if he'd been running away from her and now they were reunited, she still wanted to save whatever was left of their collaboration, of their friendship. That would just have to be enough. If she couldn't have the whole of him, she'd take the essence.

She'd take his kindness and the way he saw her and not just the exhausting chameleon performance she'd perfected over the years. She'd take that and a great big dose of longing and heartache any day of the week if it meant she got to talk with him now and again, and if it meant they could keep working together. It wouldn't matter if it still hurt like it did now. She just wanted him close.

She stoppered the bottle. Her eyes snapped to the board members. 'I'm sorry… I can't. You asked me to prove my worth. I think I've done that, and not just on this trip, but over the last three years.' She replaced the bottle inside the box and covered it with the lid, gathering it protectively under her arm. 'I don't have anything here that you would value.'

'Where are you going?' Luke said, standing up, his eyes firmly on the box under her arm.

'I'm going home,' she said.

Chapter Thirty-six

Time to Talk

Ruth had been pacing the floor of the Princess room all afternoon. A second day had passed when Mark had disappeared before breakfast having told her he didn't have any specific plans for the day. He'd kissed her on the lips, told her to enjoy her cooking class, and wandered out of the inn.

Rain had fallen steadily all day and Ruth hadn't had any appetite for lunch. She'd tried phoning her husband's mobile and had been told her call couldn't be connected four times before she gave up.

So she paced and fretted, wondering if, when confronted, he'd tell her straight or whether he'd try to wheedle his way out of it. Would he lie? It would be worse if he lied. She tried to imagine him saying it; he didn't love her, he was sleeping with someone else, he was leaving.

The thought of being abandoned after everything she'd done for him and his children made her heart heavy with sorrow, and yet she was angry too. Angry that she'd given him everything she had to give and kept so little for herself for so long, and now that she was ready for the knacker's yard, he had found some other woman. He must have!

Who could it be? She tortured herself picturing the mysterious woman. There was that membership secretary from the golf club, the one with the lipstick on her teeth, Jean, or possibly June something or other? Ruth had thought she was pleasant to talk to at the Christmas dos, but you would be, wouldn't you, if you were barefaced shagging someone else's husband? You'd have to be nice when confronted with the wife.

There was always Mark's accountant, of course, Mrs Dorkins. Brown bobbed hair, Peter Pan collars. She didn't look the type for extra-marital nonsense in her neat little office over the chippy on the high street, but they never do, do they?

She'd read an article once that said men are more likely to cheat with women who are the polar opposite of their wife. Yes, it could be her.

She knew she was really reaching when she started imagining which of her own friends it might be. Maybe they were all at it, like some great sordid wife swap. Their little corner of rural Yorkshire might be rife with it.

Ruth was getting exercised now, and very, very hot. She threw the windows open, then drank two glasses of tap water one after the other.

Men who cheat give themselves away though, don't they? They suddenly get interested in buying their own underwear for the first time in their entire life, or they start swanning around like a *Top Gear* presenter in double denim and aviators at the age of fifty-nine. Mark hadn't done any of that. He plodded around wearing the clothes she always bought for him, having his hair cut at appointments she made for him, driving the same old Jag he'd had for eighteen years now, washing and waxing it every Saturday morning even when it was raining. He hadn't really changed at all.

Ruth looked in the bevelled mirror on its stand by the bath in the corner. She'd changed, that was for sure. Short-sighted, red-cheeked, elasticated waists, big knickers, night sweats, and the menopausal rage that sneaked up on her at stupid times and, now and again, sent her frothing with fury at the cold callers who'd bother her at home when she just wanted to get on with the ironing and watching *Midsomer Murders*.

Worse than the rage, her hormones would send her into awful patterns of sleepless nights where she'd grip the bedsheets and whip herself up into panting anguish at the thought of her son in danger overseas, or driving too fast, or vulnerable and too trusting in their own home. They needed her and she wasn't there to help them.

On nights like that she couldn't talk herself down so she'd get up and mope around in the dark, drinking tea at four a.m. and trying not to look at the frames on the walls where her baby boys grinned gummily, or waved at her on their first day of school with grey shorts and skinny white legs, beaming and holding hands because they were going on an adventure together like big boys, and she couldn't face the snaps taken in the garden by the flowerbeds or at Filey or Scarborough on summer holidays when they were small enough to clamber on her lap and squash their faces against hers as though they wouldn't be satisfied until they were under her skin, as though their hearts might burst they loved her so much.

She'd changed all right. She'd become a tired, cross, bored woman, irrational with creeping night-time fears and weepy with daytime hormone and sugar crashes.

She turned away from the mirror to stand by the window. Three years and six GPs it had taken to find one who'd take her seriously and prescribe her the right tablets and creams. Maybe the prescriptions had come too late when she could lose herself in panic like this? Maybe she'd lost the plot completely and no amount of long baths, Radio Four and HRT could bring her back from the brink? Was it any wonder Mark had gone AWOL on their first holiday alone together since before the twins?

She caught sight of him out of the window then. Mark, walking – no, *running* – through the rain under the street lamps towards the inn, and behind him followed that daft inn dog, Echo, barking and wagging his tail. He hadn't taken an umbrella and was, most likely, as drenched as that dog. She was glad she'd bought Mark that waterproof jacket. No, actually, she was furious she'd had to select a winter coat for a grown man who must be perfectly capable of deciding when his old coat's knackered and needs trading in, if he's capable of realising his wife is.

Her legs carried her of their own volition, a wave of pure anger and emotion whisking her out of the room and down the stairs. He wasn't setting foot in their bedroom. They'd talk downstairs in the bar, away from the fire preferably, and where there was a supply of Gordon's and tonic in easy reach.

She was going to confront him. She was going to get it all out tonight. All her cards on the table. All the unsaid stuff.

Holding hands, compliments and kissing – they could still do all that stuff just fine, it turned out, but they didn't mean a thing when she still felt like this.

She waited, breathless and shaking at the foot of the stairs, rubbing her hands over her face, shoving her damp hair back – even though it just spiked straight up with the body heat she was generating – and she went to meet him.

'There you are!' Mark said as soon as he bustled in through the bar room door, coat dripping and his glasses steaming up and rain spotted. 'I need to talk to you.'

His eagerness to get it off his chest, his willingness to hurt her was shocking. 'No, *I* need to talk to *you*,' she countered.

The inn dog had followed Mark inside and was shaking himself vigorously right in the middle of the bar. Now he'd got that over with, Echo sauntered over to the fire and, after making a few circles, dropped himself in a curled ball on the hearth rug. He didn't sleep though. Anybody watching him would see he had one eye open and fixed on the Firths.

'Come and sit over here.' Mark hastened Ruth into a corner seat in the bar by the door and Ruth followed him. There were a few crafters in, but the rain had kept the locals at home. 'I've been out all day today and yesterday, and it gives a man time to think...'

'No,' Ruth protested. 'I'm the one that's been thinking. I get to talk. I get to ask the questions on my terms.'

The thought of him coming out with it now, the sordid truth, was too much for her. She called over to Mrs Mair at the bar for a double G and T, and Mark shouted, 'Make that two', which made Ruth even more exasperated.

'I know what you've been up to,' she hissed, sitting down, holding one of the bar room cushions across her lap for comfort. Mark took the seat facing her.

'You do?' Mark's face fell instantly. 'Oh.'

'Yes, *oh*!' She took a moment to gulp for breath. She hadn't thought it would be this easy. It was all coming to a head so suddenly. Thirty-seven years, a whole life together poised on the edge of the plughole, about to be washed down the drain.

Mrs Mair arrived with a tray and set their drinks down without a word. She left a little dish of shortbread too, as if that was going to help in a crisis.

Mark reached for one of the crumbly squares instantly and Ruth had to stop herself from slapping his hand away. How could he eat at a time like this?

'I might as well just come out and say it, Mark. I know what's going on, and I'm so… *bloody disappointed*!'

'You are?'

'You've made a fool out of me and you've made a mockery of our life together, and the boys' lives too.' She held in a sob out of pure spite brought on by the sight of Mark with his mouth full of shortbread and with crumbs all down his front. He was wide-eyed and frozen.

'What?' he mumbled, trying to chew and swallow as quickly as possible, losing his colour like a bottle of strawberry milkshake being drained through a straw.

'Who is it, then?' she demanded.

'*Huh?*'

'The person you've been sneaking off to talk with? Who is she?'

'She? I've been with Gene.'

'Jean? From the golf club? I bloody knew it!'

'No, love. Gene, the cook.'

Ruth blinked. 'I'm not sure what you're trying to tell me.'

Mark laughed gently and reached for her hand. 'I've been trying to tell you for the last five minutes.' He reached a hand into the pocket of his navy-blue Millets jacket which Ruth Firth had picked out on sale, XL to make sure it was roomy enough for a jumper underneath, and he pulled out a gold band, placing it on the table.

'I've been out searching whenever I could get away, trying to find your wedding ring. I swear I've turned every rock and lifted every bit of seaweed on that coral beach these last few days.'

Ruth was hurting now. A great burning surge of feeling, all directed at that little scrap of gold that she'd worn for so long that her finger was now white and smooth where it had worn her.

Mark was smiling softly. 'That daft dog helped me too. You wouldn't believe what a good little digger he is. Worked all day in the rain, he did, until I was set to give up for the evening and – would you credit it? – he turned up some sand right by my feet and there it was, and in the last light of the day! I don't mind admitting, Ruth, I cried at the sight of it.'

'But... you...' Ruth felt herself dissolving.

'What, love?' Mark leaned closer.

'You're *not* seeing someone else?'

Mark let the silence speak for him, his lips parted, seemingly aghast she was asking him.

Ruth pulled a tissue from her sleeve. 'Well, aren't you? You're never around. You barely speak. You're not...'

'Not what?'

'Not interested in me.' Ruth unfolded the tissue and dabbed inside her glasses where tears were streaming now.

Mark was smiling, indulgently but soft too. 'Not interested? *Not interested?* I've cut my fingers to shreds turning over all that coral, hunting for the ring I gave you that day at the registry office because I promised then it was a sign of my bond to you, and there was you walking around without my ring on your finger. Well, it just doesn't make sense. Like me without you. Us without the boys. We're a family. We're joined forever, all four of us.'

Ruth let her tears fall and, seeing her, Mark followed too.

'Coming here has been the best thing we've ever done, apart from getting married in the first place and having our boys,' he told her, trying to keep his voice steady.

'But you're... so sick of me,' Ruth replied, somehow sadder than she'd ever felt.

Mark rubbed her hand, falling silent again. This was familiar territory. Him nervous and unspeaking; her upset about something or other. Ruth ran with it.

'We don't talk. I'm not sure we ever did much, but, now, I'm lucky if I get a "Good Morning" from you. And you work all the time, or you play golf, or you're asleep on the sofa. What kind of marriage is that? What kind of life is it?'

Mark swallowed but said nothing.

'I thought if we came here for a good long holiday it would be the start of a new chapter. We'd get back to being us again.'

Mark spoke up at this, adamant. 'We have, haven't we?'

'I thought we'd started to, but then you retreated again. You disappeared into yourself again. You were working all night last night on some paperwork or other. We'll go home and nothing will have changed. You'll get just as absorbed in work there too, just like you always do.'

'Of course things won't be the same,' he said, and Ruth froze this time, staring at him. 'How can it be the same as it was? When we're both so sad about our Stuart moving away.' At this, Mark's face contorted so horribly with grief, Ruth's heart cracked to see it. He sobbed. 'I miss him. I miss him every day. I go into his room and he's not there and I sit there on his bed and I… I miss him.'

Ruth's shoulders shook from crying.

Mark wouldn't be stopped now. 'All those years, Ruthie, all those years worrying for him, celebrating every little victory and milestone, rooting for him, wanting the best for him, and fighting for every little accommodation for him at school and every doctor's diagnosis, and listening to the opinions of all those bloody psychologists and physicians and clinicians and teachers and not one of them knew what was better for him than you or I did. And all the laughter and the silly times, all the things he loved doing. I want to do them all over again. I said I'd never want to see that bloody DVD about the steam trains one more time, but I'd give anything to have him here now to watch it with him.'

Ruth gripped his hand and hung her head.

Mark had found his voice and was going to use it. 'I miss him, and I think you miss him even more than me, if that's possible. And I know you feel guilty too, because God knows I do, but he loves having his own place, and his own friends, and he's learning things and doing things we couldn't give him at home.'

'I know. I know.' Ruth blew her nose. 'He made the right decision.'

'He did, and we must respect that and let him live his life. And we must live ours. That part of our life where we were raising children is over. Our boys are grown and living independently. That's all we ever wanted. That was our biggest dream and it came true.'

Ruth breathed deeply, nodding, her face blotched with crying.

'I'm sorry I never said all this before,' he told her. 'I was trying to be strong for you. I was trying to be the man.'

'I thought I'd lost you just when I needed you the most,' Ruth said shakily. 'I thought you were going to leave too.'

'Leave? I've only just found you again.'

They looked at one another through their tears.

'Come here.' Mark shifted until they were side by side and he pulled her close. 'I'm sorry I've been so… far away. I'll do better. I'll *be* better.'

'I don't want much. I just want you to see me, and talk with me. I want you to be interested in me, and interested in yourself.'

Mark exhaled, his shoulders sinking. 'All I'm interested in right now is putting that ring back on your finger. That's what I wanted to tell you. When I was out on the coral beach in the pissing rain all I could think about was how we never really had a proper wedding. The registry office and our boys with us on that honeymoon at Grange-over-Sands was all very well, but it's not much of a honeymoon, sharing a put-up bed in a guest house with your twin boys, is it?'

Ruth laughed and sniffed into his jacket collar. 'Not really.'

'Let's do it properly. Let's really go to town. Anything you want. A wedding cake, a horse and carriage, Bermuda or Barbados, anything. Just put that ring back on and remember I gave it to you for a reason.'

Ruth pulled back and looked into her husband's eyes, wanting him to go on.

'I gave it to you because you are the best person I ever met, and the most beautiful too. And I know I let you down. I wasn't the husband I could have been. I thought it was my job to graft and keep you all comfortable.'

'You did that,' Ruth insisted. 'You did.'

'But we got a bit lost along the way. I forgot that I was supposed to be happy as well as being successful, as well as earning more and impressing more. And I forgot you. I did. Dad told me to do everything you *told* me to and that was supposedly the secret of a happy marriage, but it's not. I should have done everything *I could think of* to make you happy, by myself, without being told, without being asked, and I should have done more of the things that made me happy too.'

'What sort of things?' Ruth sniffed.

'Well that's just it. I don't know. With the boys gone, I don't want to play golf on my own. I've listened to Roger Borthwick talk about his sciatica every Sunday for months now. It's not the same as when the boys would come to the club. I've liked doing new things here – I liked the beach and the willow stripping. I liked the ball. I even liked the shopping and the silversmithing class. I know, I'm as surprised as you are.' He smiled again, wiping his eyes. 'I even tried to make you a silver ring, in case I couldn't find your gold one, but it turned out to be such a sorry looking thing, I couldn't ever give it to you.' Mark laughed at this.

Ruth squeezed his hand. 'I think we've both neglected ourselves and that's made us neglect each other.'

'I think so.' Mark picked up the wedding band and held it between finger and thumb, shuffling out from his spot at the table, pulling Ruth to her feet too.

'What are you doing?' Ruth's eyes were shining under the bar lights.

Mark sank to one knee. 'I know I never asked you properly before, but I'm asking you now. Ruth Jennifer Firth, will you marry me? Can we do it all over again?'

Echo lifted his head at the commotion in the bar as everyone seemed to shriek and cheer at once, and Mrs Mair rushed over with a bottle of bubbly, and Ruth gripped her husband and let him rock her in a swaying hug, the gold wedding band safely back on her ring finger once more.

Chapter Thirty-seven

Comings and Goings

'Will ye no' stay, Mutt?' Atholl charged after him.

'The painting's finished.' Mutt loaded his bag onto his bike at the front of the inn. 'I've nothing to stay for.'

'At least try to get some sleep before you go, it's no' safe. Your mother wouldnae forgive me if anything happened to yi.'

It was true, Mutt had barely slept in the last twenty-four hours. First he'd listened to Polly until gone midnight, then he'd read and re-read the paperwork she'd left him with, cursing himself for promising Polly so much that he wasn't willing to give her, and then, when he'd sat up alone in the bar for the rest of the night, listening out for Nina setting off for the airport, he'd foolishly fallen asleep and awakened to the sound of her taxi pulling away. It had been too late. She was gone.

He'd spent his final day in Port Willow finishing the last coats of paint on the corridors upstairs, working like fury, wanting to be finished so he could get away from the inn for good. He thought he'd seen the little grey-black shape that was Bear flitting by his feet so many times as he worked, and he'd even reached down to offer him the crust from his sandwich at lunchtime, but he was gone too, with Polly, back to the house they'd all shared until not so long ago, until Mutt become another Port Willow runaway.

He was exhausted now and it showed on his face.

'At least wait 'til the morning, it's pouring,' Atholl shouted from beneath the stone lintel between the pillars at the reception door. 'And it's dark. Where will you even go? Are yi heading home?'

Mutt told him he hadn't thought that far ahead.

He'd stayed close to his phone all day, checking its signal, waiting for Nina's call. He owed her an apology for getting all bound up in Polly on Nina's last night here. Polly had a habit of tying him up in knots and he'd found her arguments so binding, he couldn't fight himself free.

If Nina wasn't interested in hearing an explanation, however weak, surely she'd want to let him know how her pitch had gone? Yet she hadn't called, and no matter how often he rang her, her phone was always off, or maybe she was just so far away he couldn't reach her. She'd be back where she belonged now, forgetting all about him, no doubt.

Even now, straddling his bike and clipping his helmet straps at his throat, he felt glad at the thought of her striding through Manhattan, reinstated in her job, living the life of glamour and excitement she'd missed while in the Highlands. She'd needed to make a triumphant return to New York and he was confident she'd done just that.

'At least take this week's pay, Mutt.' Atholl had tried to give him the roll of notes already, even though he'd not completed the week. Mutt waved the money away and pulled on his black gloves, strapping them across his wrists. 'You've become part of the family here at the inn. It's no' right to let you go like this.'

Mutt started the engine. 'I'm sorry, Atholl. I can't stay. Thank you for giving me somewhere to be.' He kicked the bike off its stand and pulled away into the dark night.

He didn't look out at the water in Port Willow Bay, or at the jetty with its white lightbulbs reflecting in the dark water. He didn't gaze out at the last train, its two short carriages lit up as it pulled out of the village, snaking its way around the bay. He *did* spot Echo on the street corner by the school, barking and turning in circles all by himself.

Mutt wondered if he should stop and take him back to the inn. He was an old dog for wandering the streets at night now. Mutt pulled in to let the Highland hopper bus go by, and looked in his wing mirror where Echo was framed, still barking and trotting his front paws off the pavement in an agitated dance. Daft dog.

The road cleared and he accelerated hard just as the figure fighting to control three suitcases and a flyaway umbrella stepped into the road in front of him. Mutt had a split second to avoid her.

The woman screamed and the bike's brakes screeched. Mutt veered out onto the road, ditching the out-of-control bike and sliding along wet tarmac, the side of his helmet bumping and juddering hard off the ground. He didn't feel the impact as his body met the road, but he was aware his hands were suddenly cold and wet. He wondered how his gloves could have come off. His jacket was split too, all down one arm, and the rain was seeping in as he came to a heavy stop against the kerb. He heard his bike hit a wall somewhere at a distance, and there was a dog barking, but it wasn't his Bear, he knew that for sure, and he knew there was a woman with clicking heels pounding the tarmac and screaming his name, his real name, before everything in Port Willow turned black and silent like sleep.

–

'Stay with me, Murray. No sleeping now. We're almost there.'

Someone gentle was holding his arm just above where it stung and someone else was doing something far less gentle to his other arm where his bones felt like fire. Everything else was numb and painless, and he was being rocked bodily from side to side. There was an ambulance siren somewhere in the far distance. Some poor sod's night ruined. He smiled and slept again.

–

'Murray? Murray. Ah, there you are!' The blurry woman was smiling at him. He blinked, bringing her into focus, making out a stethoscope around her neck and black hair tied up. His heart sank for a reason he couldn't quite isolate. He didn't know he'd been hoping to see someone else.

'You've just come out of theatre. Do you remember what happened?'

He tried to shake his stiff neck, but it sent a thunderbolt of pain shooting into his shoulder. It made listening to the woman difficult. There was a burning sensation all down his throat and an awful taste in his dry mouth. She was saying something about coming off his bike. Broken bones. Blood loss. An operation. He needed to sleep, she said, and his body obeyed.

-

There'd been so many people with their hands upon him. He'd been lifted from one bed to another, softer bed. Someone had sponged his hands and face with warm water and he hadn't been able to open his eyes to see who it was.

Atholl was there, definitely, cursing himself, talking on his phone. Then his mum was there and he'd opened his eyes for her and croaked that he was fine. She couldn't hear him for some reason. Then a man came, fiddled about with the back of his hand, injecting him with something cold he could somehow feel all the way up his arm and taste right in the back of his throat, and he'd slept again.

-

There were far too many voices when he woke up and looked around. An elderly man in pyjamas was shouting at him from the bed opposite. 'Who are you?' he was saying.

Mutt scrunched up his gritty eyes and tried to widen them, wanting to see more clearly. He needed to drink something. As if he'd conjured her up, a nurse appeared right away with a plastic cup. She helped him sit up a little, telling him his arm was badly broken and he might be faint from loss of blood. They were still deciding if he needed a transfusion.

He accepted this information passively, not minding at all somehow.

She said he was on a lot of pain medication so he might feel strange. The water was icy cold and gave him his voice back. He told her he did feel strange.

'Who's Nina?' she asked.

'What?'

'Who's Nina? You've been asking for her since they brought you down to the ward.'

'Nina's…' The effort of inhaling made his ribs burn, and he grabbed his chest.

'Don't try to talk, just rest.'

'Nina's everything,' he said in a whimper, but the nurse was gone.

-

The first thing that struck him was that it was broad daylight and there was a new pair of plaid pyjamas folded on the table over his bed. Someone had pulled a TV screen out from the wall on a big plastic arm and a quiz show was playing with subtitles and no sound. There was a clattering of plates and a stink of something stewed that told him he'd missed meal time and he was glad about it. He looked at his hand and shrunk at the sight of the cannula taped there. He wasn't good with needles. He needed to tell that nurse quickly, ask her to get it out.

The ward had been cleared out. The shouting man was gone. Someone in the corner had their curtain pulled around their bed. It was hot, far too hot. 'Nurse?'

A gasp from the space behind him startled him and he tried to turn his neck but it ached. '*Owww!*'

'Murray!'

Someone had been sleeping in the chair by the side of his bed, just out of sight. She sprang to her feet and moved in front of him. She was so pale and drawn it hurt to see her almost as much as it made his heart swell.

'Nina!'

She took his hand ever so gently and with it she brought the sweetest scent of lavender and willow all around her. 'Thank God you're all right. Murray, you came off your bike.'

'I know,' he blinked, his memories running like a black and white cinema reel. 'That was you on the road?'

'It was. I'm so sorry, I didn't see you until I'd walked out. I was watching Echo going berserk at the side of the road. He must have seen me getting off the train. I think he was trying to warn the whole village I was back to make even more trouble.'

It hurt to smile but he did anyway.

'They think you'll have to stay in hospital for three or four days. Then you'll have to go home and recover in your own bed for at least three weeks, maybe more if that pin in your shoulder doesn't hold and you need more surgery.'

Mutt felt queasy at the thought of bone, flesh and metal mashed up underneath the bandages. He was glad his arm was bound tightly to his side. He didn't want to see it and he couldn't bear the thought of moving it.

'Home,' Mutt said as if he didn't know what the word meant, and Nina nodded. 'You're... you're here though? The perfume...'

'You shouldn't try to talk.' She pressed her palm to his forehead and watched as he automatically closed his eyes in response.

'Murray? Murray!' She thought he had swooned away, but he opened his eyes a little and smiled back.

'Go on. Tell me about the pitch,' he whispered.

Drawing her hand back, she filled him in.

'I couldn't do it. I didn't want to hand the bottle over. Not when we'd made it ourselves. I was so proud of it. They didn't deserve it. And all I could think of was getting out of there and coming back here.'

'Really?' His voice crackled into a cough.

'I told them I quit, there and then. I wanted to get back to you. I think we're a good team.'

'I do too.' He breathed out the words.

'I think we have a good friendship and a good business idea and we can really make a go of building a perfume brand.'

Mutt watched her speaking, his eyes on her mouth as though he wasn't really hearing her.

'You're exhausted. You need to sleep,' she told him, putting her hand to his head again, but this time on his hairline where she stroked him with soft fingertips.

Even though he tried to fight the drowsiness he couldn't win against the gentleness of her touch and the warm scent of lavender and the way she shushed him like a baby, her breathing raspy and low, close to his ear.

'*Shh*, you can sleep now, it's OK. I'm here. *Shh*.'

'Home,' he whispered, as sleep took him once more.

Chapter Thirty-eight

The Agreement

This wasn't the sound of daytime TV, and it certainly wasn't the sound of Nina shushing him to sleep. It was two people from Yorkshire rabbiting on about how one of them really fancied going to see Adam Ant in concert, and another one saying he wanted to wake up in a hotel with a view of the Eiffel Tower, and there was a lot of giggling and… was that kissing sounds?

'You're awake. He's awake, Ruth, look.'

'Mr Firth?' Mutt whispered drowsily.

'Pour him some squash, quickly. Oh the poor lamb.'

Mutt tried to sit himself up and the whole ward seemed to break out in excitement at that. A burly nurse came over and hauled him gently up and adjusted his pillow at the same time. Then he gave him a shot of painkiller and told him with a smile that this was his last dose of the strong stuff so he should make the most of it.

Mutt felt the wonderful anaesthetising effect immediately, but he wasn't going to drift off again. 'Where's Nina?'

'She's gone to get you something to eat. You slept through dinner again,' Ruth told him.

'Oh.' Mutt licked his parched lips. 'Why… why are you here? Weren't you supposed to have left already?'

'We're going first thing tomorrow. We extended our stay by a few days,' Mark told him, pulling some papers from his coat pocket. 'I couldn't go without showing you this. *Ah*, here she is!'

Nina was back by the bedside, not as pale, but still not like herself, not how she'd been in the chieftain's chamber, all light and laughter.

'Here, I got you ham and cheese, there wasn't a lot of choice. They did have Um Bongo though.' She pierced the straw into the carton of kids' drink and held it to his lips.

She smiled as he sipped. 'The Firths arrived a second ago. Isn't that nice?'

'We wanted to say goodbye,' Ruth added. 'You know this one's been sleeping here at the hospital pretty much since the accident happened?' She hiked her thumb at Nina. 'Wouldn't come back to the inn even when Beatrice insisted, and you know how insistent she can be.'

Mutt stared at Nina with a look that made Mark and Ruth exchange starry-eyed glances.

'They wouldn't let me in at first,' said Nina. 'Not until your mum told them it was OK. She was nice, your mum. Don't worry, she's coming back tomorrow.'

Mark placed some documents on the table beside Mutt's sandwich pack. 'I wanted to return your paperwork to you, Murray.'

'What's that?' Nina asked.

'It's Polly's,' Mutt confirmed, grimly. 'And mine.'

'Oh.' Nina dropped into the chair by his side.

Mark took over. 'Murray here showed these to me the night before you set off for New York, on a round trip, apparently.' Ruth and Mark grinned at her but Nina was staring at the papers, uncomprehending. 'He wanted my opinion on them,' Mark added.

'What with him working in financial planning and property and pensions; he knows about these things, you see?' Ruth added.

Nina told them she didn't see.

'It's a cohabitation agreement. A bit like a pre-nup,' Mutt said, and the words stole Nina's breath. She tried to cover it.

Mutt exhaled in a huffing sigh before he carried on. 'Polly and her mum moved to Pennan a year or so ago. They were in some kind of financial straits, something to do with her mum getting divorced and the pair of them being left with nothing. We, *uh*, we ended up going out and,' Mutt shrugged, 'I'll admit it was serious, or I thought it was. She moved in with me and for a while things were... good.'

Nina nodded, casting her eyes down at her hands.

'She was the one that wanted me to get Bear – kept saying we weren't a family without a dog. I didn't want him at all. How could I look after a dog when I was out all day, and Polly was studying? She was doing a law degree and was often away at the uni in Glasgow through the week, or, at least, that's what she told me. Anyway, she had this shop job, apparently, bringing in a bit of money every now and then and she wanted to contribute to my mortgage. I told her I didn't mind paying but she insisted, so we set up a joint account, and things just ticked over and one day she showed me the picture of Bear in the rescue centre and I couldn't very well say no, she was determined to bring him into the family.'

Nina swallowed hard and Mutt talked on.

'I got to know her mum a bit, did some painting for them at her mum's place. She seemed nice enough, and one day Polly tells me her mum had been seeing some new bloke who'd moved in with her and ripped her off – taken her money, her jewellery, everything. A real sob story it was, and she said to me she wanted to get some kind of protection for herself and didn't I understand it was sensible to make a legal agreement to protect her share of the money she was bringing in. Polly told me about some papers she'd learned about at uni, something we could do ourselves that wouldn't cost any money but it would protect her if I ever left. It was a surprise. I had no intention of leaving her.'

Mutt's eyes flashed to Nina's for a moment, but he steeled himself to carry on, even though she was growing paler by the second.

'So she talked me into signing a cohabitation agreement. It seemed only fair and sensible, the way she explained it, saying women had to protect themselves since they were so financially vulnerable to dickheads like her father and this fellow her mum had been conned by. So, what was the harm in signing it?' Mutt shrugged, his voice wry and bitter. 'I'm no legal expert, I'm just a decorator, as she liked to remind me, and I just signed it there and then. To me it was all just to make her feel better about earning less and give her a sense of security, and she said it would come to an end when we got married.'

Nina wrapped her arms around herself. 'It's cold in here, isn't it?' she said suddenly. 'There must be a window open.' She flustered about, looking for the imaginary draught, giving herself time to think as Mark Firth started to talk.

'She was right there, of course. Cohabitation agreements are very common between anyone living together as friends or as, *ahem*,' he cleared his throat, receiving a warning glance from Ruth, 'or something more. If the two parties marry, the agreement becomes void.'

'You were going to get married?' Nina said, trying to sound casual, remembering how she and Mutt were friends, and hopefully future business partners. They'd had no time to discuss it and he needed to recover first. She wasn't planning on rushing him into anything he didn't want to do.

'I hadn't asked her, but she talked about it a lot as though it was inevitable, and we had Bear, our baby, as she called him.' Mutt was looking at the cuts and grazes on his hands. 'She was supposed to graduate with this law degree in September and we were all looking forward to the graduation. She was working in London by then – some fancy job to help prepare her for the bar. I didn't really understand it all, only that she was well on her way to being a top-flight lawyer, and I was so proud of her and… in awe, really.

'She'd tell me how she'd earn the money and I'd be able to do whatever I wanted. I couldn't be a decorator forever, she'd always say. Always with the little jibes. I was never smart enough, or quick enough for her. And it turns out she was absolutely right about that. I got home from a painting job one night and she wasn't there. A few days passed, she didn't ring, I couldn't reach her, and then the letters started to arrive from the bank. There was a massive overdraft on the joint account and all my money had been cleared out. I went straight round to her mum's place and it was empty. She'd shipped out too.'

Mark butted in. 'It's possible they were pros, preying on men, making them think they had a future, getting them to sign documents and then scarpering with the cash. Maybe they're travelling around the country ripping off blokes for a living.'

'But she was a lawyer?' Nina said, and Mutt gave her a level look. 'Oh, she wasn't.'

'Probably not,' Mark Firth said.

'I know what you're thinking.' Mutt cast his eyes down. 'I was a gullible fool. I fell for her and believed everything she told me. I still find myself stumbling over things she told me, realising they couldn't have been true, all these months later.'

Ruth piped up at this. 'It's not uncommon. My friend Wendy married a man she'd met online. Told her he was from the UAE, something big in oil. Well, he turned up, spent the honeymoon with her, cleared her bank accounts and was gone, in her car, no less, within three weeks. Read the women's magazines. You'd be surprised how often it happens.'

Mutt snapped his head up. 'But I'm a...'

'A man?' Ruth retorted. 'And that makes you immune to scammers, does it? If you must feel ashamed, feel ashamed for not listening to your family and friends warning you, trying to protect you, but don't feel ashamed for falling for something you think only happens to women.'

Mutt definitely looked ashamed. 'Polly was right. I'm not smart, not like her. And it's all legal too.' He pointed at the papers. 'Look, it's executed as a deed, and was signed in the presence of witnesses. That's what she turned up to tell me the other night. She told me I have to get the house on the market and give her what's rightfully hers.'

'I'm glad you had the idea of showing me the papers,' interjected Mark. 'Even if it did cause a bit of a misunderstanding between me and my missus. Ruth saw me reading them on the night Polly arrived and thought I was back to my old overworking ways.'

The Firths exchanged another meaningful glance, and Ruth patted his arm.

'I was instantly suspicious,' Mark continued. 'You see, when a cohabitation agreement can be proven to be unfair to one party, it may not be enforceable. I read those papers clause by clause and I can tell you now, Murray, she was no lawyer. It may *look* like she's stitched you up like a kipper, if you're not used to legalese, but the long and the short of it is, this agreement is void and couldn't be used against you to take half of your home, or indeed any of your money if you can prove you earned it.'

Mutt's eyes rounded. 'You're sure?'

'Absolutely. I think when she was browbeating you in the bar the other night, she thought you'd believe she had you over a barrel.'

'That she did!' said Mutt.

'But your home is your own and she's not entitled to it.'

'But Bear?' Mutt said, his mouth twisting. 'She's taken him, said he's hers. She paid the adoption fee. I had no choice but to hand him over.'

'Oh no,' Nina was on her feet. 'No, that can't be right.'

Mark spoke up, grave and cautioning. 'I'm afraid that might be one area where she really does have rights over Murray. She can prove she paid for the pup. He might never be recovered.'

'Well, where is Polly now?' Nina cried.

Mutt shook his head. 'No idea. I told her I'd speak with an estate agent, and she told me she'd be back when the house sold. I assume she's planning on keeping an eye on me from a distance, like she must have been all along, thinking that, like an idiot, I'd hand over my money whenever she showed up again waving her papers under my nose.'

Mark raised an eyebrow. 'My guess is she's run out of money again. She might have a few of you on the go, who knows, but she obviously thought it was worth the risk coming back for more.'

'Then we need to tell the police,' Nina said, reaching for her mobile.

'I'm not putting the house up for sale, that's for sure, now you've put me straight, Mr Firth. I'll let her keep the overdraft money, a reminder not to be taken in again.'

'No, that's not right, she stole that money,' Ruth protested.

Mutt shook his head. 'I was daft enough to let her have it in the first place, but I can't let her have Bear.'

'She may well already have sold him,' said Mark.

Nina dialled the number and handed Mutt the phone as it rang. Everyone watched him as he spoke down the line.

'Police, please. That's right. Yes. I want to report a fraud.'

–

That night, after Mark had met the police officers at the hospital, handed over the papers and given his description of the woman from the bar who'd called herself Polly, he'd sat in the back of the cab while Nina slept and Ruth held his hand proudly.

Once they'd made sure Nina was safely back in her old room on the ground floor of the inn, they had taken care to bathe and dress for their last dinner at the Princess and the Pea Inn where they'd talked and reminisced and made plans for visiting their sons as soon as they could to ask them if they'd be their best men at their second wedding.

There seemed to be so much to talk about that the evening had passed quickly and at bedtime, as they settled their bill, ready to leave early on the morning train, Mark had told Gene Fergusson to make sure Beatrice had a look at her dating board the next time she was up and about around the inn, and then he and Ruth climbed the ladder for one last night in the fairy-tale bed.

Downstairs in the empty bar that night, with the doors bolted and the optics lights off for the night, Beatrice and Atholl sipped their cocoa in their pyjamas, their arms around each other's backs, reading the handwritten lonely heart pinned beside Seth's on the board.

NAME: Mark Firth

AGE: 59

OCCUPATION: Financial planner. Recovering workaholic. Family man.

ADDRESS: Wherever Ruth and my boys are.

HOBBIES: Until now, not much, but trying my hand at willow-weaving has been eye-opening. I'll be saying yes to all kinds of new things from now on.

HOW WOULD YOU DESCRIBE YOURSELF: Too busy. Neglectful. Trying to do better.

LOOKING FOR: My wife. Kind, tolerant, beautiful and forgiving (I hope), for exotic travel, romantic nights by the fire, and a new beginning.

Chapter Thirty-nine

Arrested

'Careful, careful,' Nina fussed.

'I'm fine, honestly, *aah*!' Mutt didn't look fine but he'd made it into the armchair in his old room at the inn.

Beatrice pulled Atholl away from the doorway with a meaningful stare. 'We'll leave you to settle back in. Shout if you need anything,' she told them.

Mutt watched as Nina unpacked his bag and went to the kitchen to make him some tea. It seemed a long time before she finally came back and perched on the edge of his bed.

'So, there you are. Home,' she told him.

'Yup.'

'I mean, obviously you're not *home* home, but this should do for now, and it's near the hospital, and the garage. They said your bike will be fixed by the end of the month.'

'I'm in no hurry to go anywhere.' Mutt examined his arm, now in a lighter bandage, his skin impressively scarred and still tender.

'He'll be here any minute, I'm sure,' Nina said.

'I won't believe it 'til I see him.'

'I'm glad I'm not leaving 'til tomorrow,' Nina said, tentatively. 'Give us a chance to talk.'

'Are you looking forward to seeing your mum and your brother?'

Her wide grin told him she was. 'Listen, I wanted to talk to you before you took your night-time painkillers and you get all woozy.'

'Best part of my day,' he lied.

Nina pressed on. 'About the perfume. I think we really could make a go of it.'

'We?'

'It's our recipe, our little cooperative, isn't it?'

'I suppose so, but I helped you make that perfume for you, not for me.'

'I know. I just think if Mr Cor and Munro stick to their agreement to help us produce a small batch for our product launch, I can sort the industry tests and the licensing and maybe you could speak to your friend the laird about selling a few bottles in the castle gift shop? Atholl's already said he'd sell it up at the willow school and on his online shop. There'd be a display case in the reception here at the inn too, and at the distillery and Munro's workshop. That'd be a decent start, I reckon.'

'You've got it all planned, I see?'

'And we'd all get an equal share, every one of the collective. It has to be fair, or I'm not interested.' Nina was decided.

'Fair enough. I've had my share of dodgy deals; enough to last me a lifetime. So, what do we do now?' Mutt asked.

'We should probably shake on it, partner?'

He raised his good arm and they shook a little awkwardly.

'OK then,' she said.

'That was easy,' Mutt told her.

'Now the hard work starts, for me anyway. Once I've been home to see Mum, that is. I'll have to come back here to meet all the suppliers, get some costings going, write the business case, meet the bank...'

'I'll be there with you,' Mutt interrupted.

'Good.'

'I can't very well paint in this condition, but I can help you get our collaboration off the ground. Can't promise from my track record I'll be much good with the paper-work, mind.'

Nina gave him a level look. 'Stop that. She can't have your self-esteem like that, she's not getting to have it, Polly, or whatever her name is.'

'Eleanor James, the investigating officer said.' Mutt sniffed an ironic laugh.

'Well, Eleanor put you down and took advantage of your kind nature, because she was a crook, not because you're not smart or talented or a good businessman. You're all those things. I won't let her take those things, not when she's already had so much from me.'

'From you?'

'From you, I mean, obviously.'

Mutt watched her. 'So we're business partners?'

'Yep,' Nina nodded slowly. 'Good, right?'

'*Hmm*, not sure really.'

'What's that supposed to mean?' Nina was alarmed.

'It means, I hoped... maybe, when you flew all the way back across the ocean to, what did you used to call it, oh aye, the back of bloody beyond, the middle of nowhere... that maybe you were missing something?'

'I was,' Nina smiled shyly. 'I was missing the ingredients for the next big thing in fragrance.'

'*Ah*, is that all.' Mutt nodded sagely.

'One vital ingredient is still missing though,' Nina conceded.

Mutt quirked a scarred eyebrow, then winced. 'Oww, that hurts.'

'Well don't do it then!'

They both laughed and she stepped across the floor to him. 'When I was standing in front of all those execs all I could think about was how much fun I'd had with you, and how much I missed you, and if I was going to do anything with our Highland fragrance, I only wanted to do it with you involved at every stage. You helped me make it, you should help me sell it.'

Mutt reached his hand out to take hers and pulled her gently onto his lap.

'I can't, I'll hurt you,' she yelped.

'Everything hurts anyway, you can only make it better,' he said, his voice low.

She settled across his lap, face turned to his, her hand still in his grasp.

'Nina, when I realised you'd gone to the airport and I'd missed you that morning, I felt something I never felt with Polly, or anybody else for that matter. I was utterly lost. I was leaving on my bike, going anywhere, because I couldn't hang around here and not see you every day. The thought of not knowing what you were doing or if you were OK was too much for me, and I just got on my bike and… God knows where I'd have ended up, but I know one thing; I'd never have forgotten you. I'd always have wanted you.'

Nina couldn't quite believe what she was hearing. 'I came back thinking you'd want to be my friend at best. I was ready to accept that, just to have you in my life,' she told him.

'I *do* want to be your friend, and everything else I can be to you. You're the missing ingredient in my life. I can't be without you.'

First, Nina brought her lips down to the cut above his brow and pressed a soft kiss against it, making him inhale deeply. As her lips travelled across each little graze and scrape on his cheekbone and jaw, Mutt drew his hand up her arm until he cradled her face. He lifted himself a little in the chair to reach her lips, and she tipped her mouth to his.

If she could have kissed him better in that instant she would have, but Nina was satisfied to know they'd have the rest of their lives to recover and grow stronger, and that would take many, many kisses.

When they drew apart, smiling into each other's eyes, they heard the knock. Nina jumped up from his lap but Mutt wouldn't surrender her completely, keeping her hand clasped in his.

'Come in,' Mutt called.

There was a muffled sound of struggle behind the door, then a soft bump of something small and bouncing jumping from a height. As the door pushed ajar, in bound Bear, wriggling and drooling just like before. He had leaped into Mutt's lap before the inspector was even inside the room.

The policeman stood back and let them have their reunion and then, once everyone had exclaimed how much Bear had grown in a fortnight, the officer told them about the court date, and the other witnesses; men across the country taken in by the mother–daughter con artists.

Mutt had grown quieter then, holding Bear close and scratching his ears, and Nina was finally able to relax for the first time since she'd flown home from New York.

She watched Murray shake the officer's hand, hearing the embarrassment in his voice that told her there was a long road ahead of adjustment for all of them, and it wouldn't be easy for him to forget the way Polly had dragged down his self-belief, but at least now they could make a fresh start, now that the three of them were together, they had all the ingredients needed for a new family.

Chapter Forty

Easter Sunday

The day had dawned soft and mellow bringing in a baby-blue sky with cotton-wool clouds; the very weather Beatrice had ordered for her Port Willow Bay Arts and Crafting Festival.

'Got everything?' Atholl asked back in their bedroom after an early breakfast.

Beatrice sat on the bed and rummaged through her bag. 'Clipboard, mobile, exhibitors' information, the key to the village hall, yep, got it. Could you, *um*, help me get my sandals on?'

Atholl laughed, but not too much; he knew Beatrice wasn't exactly loving this stage of pregnancy, thirty-one weeks, and counting down the days until their daughter arrived in June.

'You can smirk, you're not the one going *oof* every time you roll over in bed or try to bend over. Do you know I had to pee four times last night? Four! Echo followed me to the loo each time. If I wasn't before, I am *definitely* feeling forty.'

Atholl strapped her shoes onto her feet, crouching on the floor in front of her.

'Did I mention the indigestion?' Beatrice added and Atholl told her that, yes, she'd mentioned it once or twice.

'You'd think I'd have learned some patience waiting for this baby – through all the grief and loss – but it's made me worse. If anything, I'm more impatient.'

Atholl looked like he was in full agreement but didn't like to say so.

'Thanks,' she told him, looking over her bump at her toes. 'I have no ability to console myself that she'll be here when she's ready, instead I'm just grumpy and fed up.'

'You'll get plenty of rest when the festival's over, I'll be seeing to that,' Atholl informed her.

'I don't mind the idea of having my own personal butler,' she told him as he pulled her to standing and she tried to hug him, feeling ridiculously far away. They both smiled down at the baby between them. Beatrice had a new maternity sun dress especially for the big day and she'd been careful to slather on the sun cream.

'Midgey repellent?' Atholl asked.

'I think I'll risk going without.'

'*Tsssh*,' Atholl inhaled through his teeth, tipping his head. 'I dinnae think that's too wise,' and he dowsed himself in the citronella spray.

'Come on, waddle with me round the village. Let's make sure everything's set up and ready for the grand opening at ten.'

Atholl took her hand and Echo jumped up from his spot by Beatrice's legs. He'd been stuck to her like glue for three days now and nobody could account for it. If his head wasn't pressed against her thigh he wasn't happy, and so everyone had accepted Beatrice had a sheepdog as an appendage as well as a taut, round baby bump.

–

Once out on the waterfront, Beatrice wielded her clipboard.

'Does Gene have the barbeque coals going down on the beach?'

The smoke rising from over the sea wall told her he was already at his station. Beatrice shuffled over the road to take a peep and, sure enough, there he was down on the sand in his full chef's whites, Kitty by his side pouring them each a coffee from a flask. Patrick the fishmonger had already dropped off the two big iced crates of seafood ready for cooking. They waved to one another and Beatrice happily put a tick on her clipboard.

'Next the village hall,' she said, just as the church bells of St Magnus' peeled for Easter Sunday service.

'Hold up, Atholl, can you go a bit slower?' Beatrice puffed, keeping a tight hold of Atholl's arm, Echo still trotting by her side, his obedient eyes fixed on her face.

All along the front the little gardens that interrupted the sea wall were in full spring colour. Tulips and daffodils, grape hyacinths and crocuses bobbed their heads cheerily.

'It's going to be a perfect day,' Atholl said, slowing his steps and looking out at the still waters of low tide.

Behind them the crunch of tyres told them they'd better get onto the pavement, and they stepped aside to let a big silver vehicle pass.

'Glenda!' Beatrice cried, waving to the driver, who waved back, beeping the vintage mobile cinema's horn as she rolled by.

'Right on time,' Beatrice said. 'I told her to park up on the green in front of the church.'

Sure enough, up ahead the silver bus pulled off the road and Beatrice amended her clipboard accordingly.

'Your mum'll be pleased. They're showing *An American in Paris* for the matinee and *Brigadoon* after lunch and then tonight it's *Singin' in the Rain*.'

'She'll be made up,' Atholl said, stopping Beatrice as they reached the village hall, all decked out with pastel bunting strung between the pink blossoming cherry trees.

'What is it?' she asked.

'Beattie, I never thanked you properly for organisin' this. It all came about because you wanted Mum to see her movies on the big screen. I don't say it enough, but you've a kind heart and since you came here you've made a' our lives better, mine especially.'

Beatrice smiled. 'You don't have to thank me, I've loved every second.'

'Still,' Atholl smiled down at her, lifting her face to his in a cupped hand, his fingertips soft behind her ear, his thumb stroking her cheek. Bringing his lips down to meet hers, they kissed, soft and slow in the airy warmth of the spring morning.

The people of Port Willow, never ones to be late for a gathering, were coming out of their doors now. Some set out deckchairs on the pavement by their steps, others dropped lengths of saltire flags from their upstairs windows to be taken up by neighbours so the whole street quickly became swagged with flapping bunting. The whole curving length of the sandy bay was busy, as was the playpark by the shore with children in their summer shorts and t-shirts.

The chimes of the ice cream van as it trundled along the waterfront and pulled up by the general store sent a stream of kids running home to ask for spending money.

The church doors were propped open and through them Beatrice could see the locals' floral displays on their stands ready for Mr Park, the minister, to judge the entries right after his sermon was done.

Beatrice had a hand on her back and was breathing a little too sharply for Atholl's liking by the time they stepped inside the cool village hall. As planned, each exhibitor was already at their stall, setting out their handicrafts.

Murdina was displaying her beautiful fisherman's gansey jumpers, with a spinning wheel set out for anyone that wanted to try their hand at making yarn.

Mr Garstang had a fine display of watercolours, both his and his students', on display, all marked up with price stickers for sale – thirty-five dreamy replicas of scenes from Port Willow. There was one of the coral beach and the willow school that Atholl had his eye on already.

The silversmith and the brewer, the paper quiller and Munro the glassmaker were all there too, busily setting out their wares. It was a wonderful sight, and Beatrice greeted everyone assembled as she passed through the hall.

The refreshments stand was all ready to keep the teas and cupcakes coming all day long, and there, beside it, was another stall.

In pride of place under its subtle tartan banner was the Highland Coral Beach Fragrance Company. On a heather-coloured cloth there were laid out many beautifully packaged boxes of their unique lavender and willow perfume. Beatrice and Atholl headed straight for the stall and drew its proprietors into a hug.

'Happy launch day,' Beatrice said, kissing Murray and Nina once each upon their cheeks.

Bear, in a matching branded bowtie, snuffled at everyone's feet and jumped up to be patted too.

The business partners grinned proudly. Murray (he'd told everyone he was done with being nicknamed Mutt, now, it didn't seem to suit him anymore) modelled his new apothecary's apron with the embroidered shape of Munro's unique glass bottles on the front pocket. Now that his arm was only in a cloth sling, he could move around a little easier than before.

'Very nice,' Atholl told him.

'It smells divine over here,' Beatrice said. 'You all set?'

'Uh-huh, almost,' Nina nodded, pressing the remote control and making a screen behind the stall burst into life where a film showing the craftsmanship that went into making each bottle of their perfume would run on a loop all day. She'd had it made to show at the World Perfumery Congress in Miami, where every industry insider would be showing or sampling new products. Nina had found she didn't need to draw upon her old contacts to secure a spot on an interview panel for exciting new fragrance brands that were already making waves across Europe; all she'd needed was a worthy product people would crave.

One person had been extremely interested in her new product: Luke Casson.

The calls had started a few weeks ago, once he'd got wind of her new business venture. There was a note of desperation in his voice, and it had reminded her of the look in his eyes while he'd stared intently at the box in her hands as she made her hasty exit from her pitch meeting. It had been a look of intrigue and a fear of missing out.

She'd been glad to tell him over the phone that he *had* missed out and, once he'd got the message that Nina really had discovered her true worth – and all without him and his exhausting culture of phoney friendships and overwork and the feeling of simultaneously being vital to Microtrends whilst always remaining precarious and disposable – the calls stopped.

Last month Mitch had WhatsApped Nina to let her know that Luke had been enraged not to have a stake in what she fully intended to be her and Murray's Highland perfume empire. Apparently Seamus had talked Luke out of pursuing a legal challenge.

The news had shaken Nina at first but upon consulting Mark Firth she'd been glad to have it confirmed Microtrends had no claim to her product development. She had, after all, been sent to Scotland with the brief of talent scouting. Nothing in her brief had precluded her from developing her own products in her own time while there. Mitch had overheard Seamus say as much to Himari who, incidentally, had stunned everyone recently with the sudden announcement that she'd been headhunted by a Japanese designer whisky company and had wasted no time in dumping Luke and setting out on her own for Tokyo.

Luke was, reportedly, stalking the corridors of Microtrends, sullen and bitter, presumably, Nina liked to think, none too pleased to have found himself slighted and replaced for the first time in his life.

'Take a leaflet,' Murray told Atholl, proudly handing over a sleek pamphlet boasting the unique qualities of their locally sourced, ethically produced and tested products.

'Will you put aside a box of the baby soaps for me?' Beatrice asked Nina, who told her she would.

Nina wasn't too busy to stop Murray from pulling her close to kiss her and wish her luck. She brushed her lips across his and told him she already counted herself very lucky indeed.

Beatrice was outside in the sunshine happily adding the last tick to her clipboard as Atholl cleared the hall and tied the red ribbon across the outer doors ready for the grand opening when it happened – and because he was right by her side, Echo was the first to know.

The dog howled as Beatrice cried out, wracked by the deep, throbbing pain radiating from her spine and all down her legs. She doubled over, trying to get onto her knees.

Atholl was on the move through the crowds already. 'Beattie!'

'No, no, no, no!' she cried, holding her stomach.

'Hospital!' Atholl said.

'What? The festival!' she said through gritted teeth, her breathing entirely getting away from her as though it were being controlled by some other thing.

Atholl was resolute. 'The festival's underway and happening now with or without you. We're going!'

She was crying now. 'But I'm only thirty-one weeks. This isn't right, Atholl!'

'Ambulance is on its way,' Murray shouted over the crowd and Atholl gathered Beatrice up and led her slowly across the church green where everyone in Port Willow stood watching, some with their hands over their mouths, some looking away so as not to distress her further. Beatrice, unable to prevent herself, screamed her heart out as she folded onto her knees on the grass, half in fear and half in agony.

Chapter Forty-one

Journey's End

There followed: one hour, six minutes and eleven seconds and thirty miles of frantic ambulance dash, one waiver signed, one anaesthetist and two surgeons prepped, a careful incision, so many tears cried, and two-and-a-half agonising minutes of utter silence while the nurses attended to the bundle.

Not even a beep from one of the many, many machines in the operating theatre sounded, and the whole time Beatrice's eyes were fixed on the nurses' backs and she didn't breathe once. Atholl rattled from head to toe, utterly undone with the panic of it all, until tiny Willow Fergusson took her first breath and proceeded to wail like a siren from the sea until she was placed onto her mother's skin and the pair of them were wrapped under blue hospital blankets and Beatrice's heaving, silent sobs rocked her daughter straight to sleep.

-

That had been six days ago and Atholl finally had his colour back.

Beatrice and Willow had spent many silent hours on the ward examining each other in wonder while she thanked her baby for coming to her and kissed her little fists and velvet head, utterly in love and in perfect peace.

There had been tests and watchfulness and all manner of charts and results coming back from labs, until finally Willow was declared by the registrar to be 'fit and well, only very wee', and they were allowed to leave.

Now they were in the back of a taxi with their daughter in a hastily obtained car seat.

'She looks tiny in this thing,' Beatrice remarked for the third time. Atholl sat in the front, staring down the cab driver, telling him to take it easy every time he dared to drive over thirty miles an hour, even on the dual carriageway.

'We'll have to get a pram that takes this car seat attachment,' Beatrice said, her eyes fixed on her sleeping baby.

'We havenae a car of our own to put it in,' Atholl told her from between the seat backs.

'Well then, we'll have to get a car as well.'

Atholl smiled, and told her he'd look into it.

'We don't have anything, Atholl. How can you be so calm? Who was it that said a baby comes into the world with everything it needs? Because they lied. I'd have been very surprised if Willow had popped out holding a tube of Bepanthen and a packet of Pampers.'

Atholl laughed, but Beatrice was serious and, ever so slightly, losing it. 'Ten nappies a day for twenty-four months is...' She tried counting in her head and, finding it fogged with hormones and spiralling panic, she gave up, blurting, 'I don't know how many, but a lot. I don't have a thing organised!'

'Don't worry,' Atholl told her again.

'Where will she sleep? Oh God, I should have gone to that baby superstore or at least had an online splurge. What was I thinking? I've heard of babies sleeping in drawers but that was in, like, the nineteen-fifties! And in some Scandi countries they sleep in cardboard boxes at first, don't they? Like a veg delivery from the greengrocer. Atholl, why are you laughing? I'm serious. I didn't even get her any clothes.'

By the time they pulled up at the kerbside by the inn door, Beatrice was deep inside a planning vortex. If she got online right away maybe she could have some clothes and baby gear delivered by the end of tomorrow? They'd need a baby bath too, but could probably use the washing up basin for a night or two...

'Beattie?' Atholl pulled her from her panic, holding the car door open for her and she carefully stepped out, looking around. It was nine o'clock and only just getting dark now the light spring nights had arrived.

Beatrice felt as though she'd been in hospital for weeks and the season had leaped into full bloom while she'd been away. How could it be only six days? There was a scent of cut grass in the air and warm sand too. It was all utterly disorientating.

She'd been told on the grapevine that the festival had been a huge success, even with all the locals being worried about her having somewhat taken the shine off the day.

The hospital reception had received over twenty calls asking after her by Easter Sunday lunchtime before they'd come to ask Atholl to *please* ring home and spread the message she was fine. She'd also heard from Atholl that the village grapevine reported Seth and Mrs Fergusson had been spotted holding hands and sharing a bag of cinder toffee in Glenda's front row during the late showing of *Singin' in the Rain*. Beatrice was looking forward to having the story confirmed, but first she had a million things to do, if only she wasn't so tired and in need of a long sleep.

'Nobody's about,' she said, watching Atholl carefully lifting the car seat out of the taxi.

Atholl brought their daughter to the doorstep of the inn where Beatrice stood.

'Beattie?' Atholl said softly over the sound of the taxi driver pulling away. 'See that step there?' He pointed to the stone threshold leading into the reception. 'My own father carried me across that step when I was born, Gene and my sisters too. Now it's our turn.'

Beatrice looked at him and then down to Willow, who'd managed to sleep the whole way home and was going to miss this momentous homecoming. His words had helped still Beatrice's brain and she tried to be present and take it all in as Atholl unstrapped the car seat and lifted Willow out into his arms, cosy in a pink sleepsuit and blanket and white woollen hat donated by the hospital.

He held his daughter close to him, breathing her in, his hands covering her entire curled body, before passing her to Beatrice, and lifting the car seat.

He opened the reception door. 'In you both go,' he said softly and his eyes misted again, like they seemed to do every few minutes since Willow had arrived.

Beatrice stepped inside to be greeted by a circle of grinning, weeping family. Mrs Fergusson, Seth, Mrs Mair, Gene, Kitty, Murray, Nina, Bear and Echo, each one of them holding their hands up – or waggling their furry bottoms – and the humanfolk all silently mouthing the words, 'Welcome Home!'

They crowded round to coo over Willow in her mother's arms and Mrs Fergusson was pressed to the very front where she kissed her granddaughter's head. 'I see you,' she told the sleeping baby. 'I see you, darlin'.'

Atholl shook hands with everyone and had to hold Gene for a long time as he bawled heartily on his little brother's shoulder and told him over and over again how he was now an uncle, a role he intended to take *very* seriously. Kitty eventually took Gene by the hand and said, 'Are you not going to show her?'

All eyes fell on Beatrice.

'Show me what?'

'Come on,' Atholl said, smiling. 'This way.'

He led Beatrice through the inn to the sun room and pushed open the door so she could step inside and see it all for herself.

'Mr Gastang, Kitty and Murray painted the mural,' Atholl said, as Beatrice gaped at the blue sky and white clouds, the green hills and purple mountains and the white coral beach with the little white cottage above it, all painted in soft colours on what had been white walls.

'Is that Echo and Bear?' Beatrice asked, blinking and amazed, pointing to the dogs immortalised in the mural, running along the painted waterfront.

Everyone smiled indulgently, watching her surprise.

'Oh my goodness, what's this?' Beatrice asked. Everywhere she turned there was some new thing to see.

'That's from the Shirlaws at the General Store,' Seth put in. 'Enough nappies and such like to see you through the first wee while.'

Beatrice gazed in amazement, touching her fingers to a crocheted mobile hanging over a changing table. 'Murdina?' she asked.

'Aye,' Atholl told her.

A suncatcher in the window drew her eye; delicate raindrops hanging from a cloud and all in translucent rainbow colours.

'Munro made that,' Nina told her.

'And those were Nina and me,' Kitty put in, pointing to the rail in the corner where there hung on tiny wooden hangers an assortment of sleepsuits and baby outfits.

'We couldn't resist a little trip to the shops in Inverness,' Nina added.

'And this?' Beatrice asked, inspecting a beautiful gift basket of creams and lotions, magazines and novels, chocolates and socks, lovely knickknacks of all kinds. She read the card aloud.

> *To Beatrice, upon bringing home your baby. These treats are only for you, a reminder to always look after yourself too because nobody can pour from an empty cup. Love from Ruth and Mark, x*

Beatrice shifted Willow in her arms, kissing her head and dancing her gently. She smiled weepily and turned to look at the little yellow blanket Angela and Vic had sent her weeks ago and she'd been too afraid to look at for fear it would make her hope for too much. She pressed another kiss to Willow's head.

That's when she saw the Moses basket by the window and she turned to Atholl ready to cry again. 'You?'

He nodded.

A strong basket weave of stripped white willow made up the lovely cradle, suspended on a wooden frame.

'This was your secret project that you were working on up at the school?' Beatrice gasped.

'It was. I started it the day you told me you were expecting.' Atholl reached for his daughter. 'Can I?'

Beatrice stepped closer to hand Willow over.

Atholl kissed his baby girl and laid her down in the bed that he had made for her, weaving all of his hopes for the future and his faith in nature into it.

Echo immediately took up his station at the foot of the little bed and rested his chin on its rim as though he intended to stay there watching over the tiny sleeping creature for the rest of his life.

'I can't believe you did all this,' Beatrice said, sniffing back tears.

'It took the whole village, but we did it,' Atholl told her, pulling her close.

Beatrice looked around at the faces of her friends all smiling back at her and in that moment she knew that even without their generous gifts, she had everything her little family could ever need right here in this room.

A letter from Kiley

You're here reading my sixth book and, honestly, that blows my mind. *Six!*

Thank you for picking up this sequel to *Summer at the Highland Coral Beach*, my sweet and sentimental story about love after loss. It's set in a village that looks a little like Plockton, a real – and stunningly beautiful – place in the Scottish Highlands where I was lucky enough to spend some holiday time with my family. I borrowed the look of the place and then made it my own eccentric, magical Port Willow, just for you.

I hope you enjoyed reading *Matchmaking at Port Willow*. It's a book about all the small things that bring us comfort: having a go at creating something, eating good things, making new friends, and meeting old friends. It's about love and endurance too, and kindness. All things we understand so much better and need so much more of at the end of 2021.

If Beatrice's story of pregnancy after miscarriage struck a tender chord with you, please know I was holding your hand throughout this book. I told it from my heart.

I did some research into the menopause this year too, at first for my sake as a forty-two-year-old woman feeling herself getting a 'little bit ragey', and then for the sake of Ruth Firth in this story for whom menopause is hard-going. I wanted to do her justice and bring the conversation about menopause into the mix here. Like so many things some women go through, peri-menopause and menopause are often hidden from the menfolk, ignored, downplayed or only whispered about. Well, Ruth Firth is here to be one more voice in keeping it real and challenging the stigma of menopause simply by representing one woman's experience of it while trying hard to keep her sense of humour. I sincerely hope I did good here, and not harm.

Port Willow is my kind of place. It's a community that pulls together and protects its most vulnerable members first and foremost. It's a place that knows how to party too, and you're never too far away from a fish supper or an absolute hottie in a kilt.

I hope you've found comfort in spending time at the Princess and the Pea Inn. If you have, please leave a review anywhere you like – spray paint your love for Atholl and Beatrice Banksy style on the side of your house if you feel the urge – or simply pop a few words up online, that would be really nice too. Reviews help new readers find my books and it could bring a wee bit of comfort into someone else's life too. Thank you for all of your support. I seriously appreciate it.

Oh, and if you want to talk cosy books any time of the year, come and meet me on Twitter @KileyDunbar or sign up for my quarterly newsletter on my website at www.kileydunbar.co.uk

Cheerio for now,

Kiley, x

Acknowledgements

For those of you with the fortitude to stick around for my acknowledgements pages, you'll know I have a tendency to name-check many, many people in the style of an overly emotional actor during their Academy Awards acceptance speech. This time it's no different because I really feel like I've received the Best Supported Author Award these last few years. So here it is, my weepy, mascara-smudged list of luvvies.

First of all, I'm grateful for my family near and far, thank you.

Nic, Robin and Iris, I can't say how much I love you. Thank you for loving me.

I love you, Michael Mouse. Thank goodness you are my friend. I'd be lost without you. Big wigglie hugs and love.

Thank you, Sara, for being lovely as well as for saving me from knitting know-how shame! You knew exactly what I needed to learn and I'm grateful.

Especial mention goes to Bryan and Stacey, Karyn and John, Jessica, Scarlett and Summer. I hope lockdown easing (crosses fingers, says a wee prayer) means we can all see each other more.

Thank you to the Romantic Novelists' Association. I was completely amazed and delighted to be shortlisted for the RNA's Romantic Comedy Novel Award earlier this year. It was fantastic to put on make-up and a sparkly frock for the online awards and celebrate with you all. Congratulations Carole Matthews for winning in our category, x

Thank you Vicky and Lisa for everything, x

@DMeachamDesign, you've made me so many beautiful book covers, thank you!

Thank you to all my friends met on Twitter and on my Facebook page.

Thank you to everyone who took part in *The Borrow a Bookshop Holiday* blog tour with Rachel's Random Resources. What an epic tour that was and I'm so grateful to you all! To everyone on this book's blog tour, I'm so grateful you signed up! Thank you!

I think they're about to play the 'get off the stage' music, so my last thank you is for Keshini Naidoo and Lindsey Mooney. Thank you isn't enough, really. What a massive privilege it has been working on these six smashing books with you. I'm so grateful for all your hard work and kindness.

Snotty sobs, big smile, wave to camera. Now I'm off to the after party.

Come join me at the Kiley Dunbar Author Facebook Page, or on Instagram @kileydunbarromance.

Love, Kiley, x